FOOL'S LAKE

by

Cynthia Moe

CYNTHIA MOE

FOOL'S LAKE

Paperback ISBN: 979-8-9884679-1-5
Ebook ISBN 979-8-9884679-0-8

February 5, 1924

Clinton rubbed his aching forehead and wondered why he'd answered the door. He leaned against the brass mule, staring at the closed gate in front of him, slowly curling and uncurling his toes inside his boots. The mine floor was always wet, and even the oiled leather and heavy wool socks couldn't keep his feet warm in the muck. He was bored and bone tired, and mentally assaulting himself for responding to the knock that had come before sunrise. He should have known it would be bad tidings. News delivered in darkness was always bad. Frank Limming stood on his doorstep, dressed for work and carrying a scrubbed tin lunch bucket, and told Clinton that the new tender was sick and they had no one to tend the skip. The captain called Frank's phone—the Harrises' had none—to tell him to roust Clinton on his way in and let him know that his rare weekday off was being cancelled due to another man's illness.

The mule's frame was cold against his hip. It stood squat and silent on the track, a train engine miniaturized to fit the low and narrow drifts of the mine's tending station. A straight length of track stretched from the tending station back to the ore chutes and three loaded trams waited before the empty shaft for the elevator to lift them up the mine's 200-foot shaft to the railroad cars waiting above. Clinton's bored mind slipped along the length of the drift though he didn't turn to look, identifying each of the small sounds that floated into the station from the darkness, sounds so low that most men would have dismissed them as imagination spurred by the cloying gloom of that place. A tumble of ore hit contact eight's chute. Eight was on the highest of the mine's three levels, and they were busy today, their chute more than half full. He would need to get down there and empty it soon, a job he could not do without empty trams. There was no grind of the hoist that signaled the cage's descent, and nothing that told him to expect it.

He shifted restlessly. The Layne and Bowler pump belching water from a shallow pit just behind him echoed with a strange looseness when the cage wasn't present. The shaft, an 8-by-15-foot square chiseled into a solid wall of earth was blocked by an iron scissor gate dully reflecting a blotch of yellow from the station's dangling bulbs. The light shone a few inches into the shaft, just enough to illuminate the hard edge where the floor of the tender station ended and the shadows hung suspended over it's black drop. The shaft was the sole artery that pumped men and equipment into the mine and iron ore out. The scissor gate guarded the shaft, ensuring a careless tender could not drop a tram into it while the cage was not there, clogging up the pit and making it impossible for the cage to land. If Clinton couldn't land the cage level with the floor of his station, he couldn't roll the full trams into it to send them up or receive them back empty after they were dumped on the surface. No ore going to the surface meant no empty trams, and no empty trams meant there was no way to empty the chutes the miners thirty and more feet above him were working so hard to fill. Soon those chutes would spill overfull onto the floors of the drifts above. That would shut the mine down and cost them all a day's pay.

He knew each miner on at the Foley. He knew their work, every detail of it; he knew the hardships of their lives underground and on the surface; who was injured and who was sick, who owed too much money to the company store or the saloon over in Crosby. He knew whether someone had lost a wife or a child, who was in danger of being fired or of dying in the mine due to carelessness or laziness. His work was monotonous, isolated and unvaried, but his service was not. His work as a skip tender meant he needed to know what was happening to the men on every level of the Foley. And one thing was universally true; no man working in the Foley mine could afford to lose a day's pay because Clinton hadn't emptied the chutes on time.

The young mechanic who had taken the lift to the surface was an irritable fellow. That state was not helped when he was called away from some important chore in the drifts and ordered to the surface to work on a rail loader that balked in the February cold. Such interruptions were common in the frigid months when the cold found every weakness in man and machine. The mechanic would spend the rest of his shift squinting in the wind, cursing broken sprockets and frost-covered belts. Why he hadn't sent the lift back down was the question.

The men in the drifts were having a slow day. There were long stretches of quiet between the rushes of ore tumbling into the chutes. Clinton yawned. From somewhere above him, walls exploded. He didn't hear it; he felt it. A shift in the air, a mild compression. He knew the sensation well. One of the contracts was blasting, loosening rock or collapsing a part of the mine where all the ore had been coaxed free. But bare seconds after the explosion, Clinton turned to stare down the drift behind him. His heart began to pound. He heard a sound, but not with his living ears, not right away. He heard on a deeper level. Something was wrong. And something was coming.

The blast threw Clinton Harris backwards over the mule and into the wall behind him, slamming the life out of the drift's few yellow bulbs. A hurricane of air howled around him, ripping at his slicker and snatching his hat and carbide from his head as it roared out of the drift. He clapped his hands over his ears but the fury was all around him, inside him, giving him the sensation of being trapped inside of a long trumpet blast. It disappeared just as quickly. Then silence clapped down, heavy and cold.

Clinton lay in a heap on the far side of the tram with a scattering of iron ore piled on and around him. He pressed his quivering hand to the floor of the mine and felt its solidness as a reassurance. A ragged pain ripped at his left chest. He was alive, swaddled in utter darkness. He braced himself to sit up, grunting. He breath wouldn't come. Ribs, he thought. One, maybe two, broken. He pushed himself up on his forearms and wiped a shaking hand across his face.

The air was still moving, a persistent breeze.

His mind grappled for an explanation. What had blown up? All the miners used dynamite, but how much would it take to cause a blast big enough to throw him over a tram? What was happening up there?

Clinton rose to his knees and felt heat on his cheek. He explored the cut sending warm blood down his face. He wiped this blood onto his slick and listened. Dead stillness. Whatever happened killed the power, and without power even the chug of the Layne and Bowler had disappeared.

Darkness saturated the room. He reached out across the floor and found a rail of track that would either take him to the trams waiting by the shaft or off down the drift to the chutes. The absence of both light and sound made it impossible for him to know where he was. The breeze grew stronger. *Something else* was coming, pushing air before it. What could—

One thought took form like a terrifying specter in Clinton's mind. It couldn't be that. Not that.

They caved a room.

Then there was wind.

It could be. It could be the lake.

Dank, swampy Foley Lake lay a thousand feet northwest of the mine's shaft. It brooded in winter, covered with a heavy frozen lid except in the middle where the spring that fed it didn't allow deep ice to form. The lake was treacherous, swallowing a half-dozen of Foley's residents during Clinton's lifetime, people who had forgotten exactly where the spring was and ventured onto the skin of ice that veiled it. The thrust of water exploding into the drift from above would shove air in front of it like breath through a straw. Clinton had read the stories of the too-few miners who survived such things.

He rocked back on his heels, his face tilted upward toward utter blackness. If it was the lake, if it was pouring in the drifts, it would take the whole mine.

A crash of metal from behind him jolted him to his feet, his left chest wailing. Seconds later another crash, then a third, and underneath the thunder of water rushing. Water, pouring through the chutes. Water, pouring in from above in a torrent.

Clinton's legs turned soft. He dropped to his hands and knees and scrambled away from the sound and rammed head-first into a tram. He grabbed it, pulled himself to his feet, and scrambled down the length of the trams until he felt the cool brass of the mule under his palms. He bent back down to all fours and crawled forward on the rails until he found the gate stretched closed across the entrance to the shaft.

An iron ladder was bolted to the inside of the shaft and stretched up the 200 feet to the light and air of the surface. The ladder was just beyond his reach, behind the closed gate. If he started climbing, he might make it. Even with his ribs, he might make the top before the shaft filled up.

Clinton pulled himself up using the gate for balance. The restless air chilled the blood on his face. Was the cage still on the surface? Or was it at one of the drifts, filling up with men to bring them to safety? Did the men know what was wrong, that death was in the mine? Or were they standing in the dark, feeling the air move around them and waiting for the lights to come back on? Clinton felt the solid iron of the gate under his palms. All he had to do was trip the lever, open the gate and climb. But what about the men? What if they didn't know to get to the shaft and get themselves out?

Just ten or so feet from him, a rope dangled. The rope sounded a whistle that howled through the mine to mark the end of a shift, but the welcome moan of the whistle liberating them from work at the end of the day became a harbinger of doom if it sounded outside of shift changes. If Clinton jerked the rope and kept pulling now, fully an hour before the shift was over, the men would know they had to get out. Searching for the rope in the darkness would take precious time, but without it the men above might drown where they stood.

Mud and water smashed into Clinton's shins and twisted him around. His feet shot out from under him and he slipped down onto one knee. The lake was pouring into the room from the drift behind him in muddy waves, slamming against his legs like a clay sledge. It was cold, so cold, and smelled of rot. The icy mud hit his groin and he gasped, tried to regain his footing, and fell again. The pain in his side wouldn't let him breathe. In seconds he was soaked to his chest. He grabbed the gate and used the heavy grating as leverage to pull himself to his feet.

The men. Faces flew into Clinton's mind, then just one. *Henry.* Henry was on contract 13, working on the 135-foot level. If the cave in was on the 165-feet level, Henry had a chance. He would run if he knew there was danger, run and climb the ladder that spanned the full length of the shaft and escape to the sun above.

The mud crawled up Clinton's body, each wave hitting higher. It was filling the room with unimaginable speed. There was a current in the flow, a force pinning him against the gate as the muck moved past him and fell like a waterfall into the pit landing. If it weren't for the closed gate in front of him, the mud would shove him down into the cage's pit and drown him there.

Clinton scaled across the gate and down the wall of the station, feeling frantically for the long rope. Nothing. He slid farther down and felt again. There. His heart ricocheted in his chest, pounding with the rhythm of the water pulsing through the chutes. The sound in the drift outside the room rose higher, drowning out the gasps of his own terrified breathing. He looped the rough coil of rope with both hands and pulled with all his strength.

The whistle howled. On the surface every head turned toward the entrance to the Foley mine.

Clinton clung to the rope and resisted the force of the current. His feet slid toward the pit anyway. The rope bit into his hands as he felt the lower half of his body dragged toward the hole. Then the current eased, then stopped all together. The pit was full. Clinton's mind grappled with the implication of the mud filling that gaping void so quickly.

His legs were numb with cold. He tried to pull them back under him, and his chest tightened in terror when he realized that he could not. The mud cemented him. He let go of the rope with one hand and tried to tug his right leg free. He lost his balance, which almost cost him his gripe on the rope. He clutched it. The whistle needed to keep blowing. They had to keep hearing it. He couldn't stop warning them of what he knew.

Clinton inched down the wall, sliding through the mud with his legs heavy and slow as in a nightmare, and found the gate. He kept tension on the rope with one hand and tripped the lever with the other, shoving the gate open. He leaned into the shaft, using the rope to keep his balance, and felt along its inner wall.

The ladder was there.

Clinton clung to an iron raiser of the ladder with one hand and the rope with the other. He wouldn't loosen the pressure on the rope; he couldn't let go of the ladder. He stood that way, anchored by mud, caught between hopes. It took a few moments before his racing mind hit on a solution.

He pulled the rope around his waist. There was enough to go around, with some to spare. He tied a simple, one-handed knot to secure the rope around his middle, then, clutching the ladder tight with his left hand, he used his right hand to try to free his legs. He was desperate to get away from the cold and tried clawing his leg free. The mud surged. Clinton grabbed his right leg at the knee and pulled, straining against his own body, ribs screaming, eyes squeezed shut and making small explosions of color behind the closed lids. His leg slid free with an obscene slurp. Water came in on top of the mud and he lifted his leg high, lunging toward the ladder. He caught his foot on the ladder step and stood bandy-legged as he jerked his left leg free. He climbed until the rope tightened noose-like around his middle.

The whistle wailed on.

He breathed. The pain in his side was distracting and he let himself wallow in it. A thought flitted across his mind that if the cage came down the shaft while he stood on the ladder, he would be crushed into the pit below him. But the mud was rising with every breath he took. They wouldn't send the cage so deep when his situation was already hopeless. They would send the cage to the higher drifts and lift those men to safety. He bet his life that they would be so wise.

The mud was getting thinner.

The lake's muddy bottom oozed through the drifts and now the water came more quickly, rising to his chest. Sounds in the shaft were flat, its natural resonance muffled and displaced. Clinton leaned higher, the rope digging into his skin, and stared up into the blackness above him. As muddy water clambered up his body like a living thing he forced himself to imagine a heroic rescue underway. Men rushing into the shaft, climbing down the ladder, pulling miner after miner out of the drifts and helping them climb to the safety above. He clung to the solid length of iron that might have saved him if he had started climbing at the first. Now it was

X

too late. He was stiff with cold. The lake was fast. He would never be able climb faster than it did.

So fast.

The water closed over his hands, then seemed to reach his neck in one surge. Clinton's breath froze, cold and terror stopping up his lungs. He closed his eyes for one moment and allowed himself to think of Jane, of little Michael. A wave of grief swept across his soul, a sorrow for his life, the balance of which he had forfeited in the blind hope that others might be saved.

He made himself concentrate on the howl of the whistle, of the men being snatched from death, the families clinging to their rescued loved ones—fathers, brothers, friends. The water climbed up his face eagerly. He clung to the ladder and felt the tension of the rope around him. He willed himself to remain still. He had done the right thing, he was sure. Men would be saved.

Clinton Harris remained there, his upward gaze unblinking, as the February waters of Foley Lake closed over him.

CHAPTER ONE

Spring, 1984

Dust rose in small puffs and whirled along the road's edge, driven by a steady southern breeze. The narrow strip of blacktop was coated by the red dust since little traffic zoomed past to swirl it away. The land was mostly flat, with wide hay fields pushing up against the ditches on either side of the road. A distant oak savannah spread along the western side of the pavement, its many trees disappearing over the edge of the horizon where the land dipped down and away.

A faint trail jutted off from the blacktop to the east and followed the lay of the land across a stretch of yellowing grass. Somewhere in the distance a soft *tink* drifted up and blended with the song of birds and the persistent chirping of unseen crickets. A hundred feet from the highway, a sign lay face-down at an angle on the bare, uneven ground. The breeze was catching its edge and rocking it, making it tap *tink tink tink* against the hard ground. The toe of a worn leather boot caught the edge of the sign and lifted it, turning it over. The fading sign was riddled with bullet holes and spray paint had almost obliterated the signs single message: No Trespassing.

The wandering man sighed as he eased the sign back onto its face and moved on. The trail turned and wound through a growth of struggling birch trees before it straightened and plunged into a sea of Canadian thistle. The man moved along steadily, never losing the way though the path disappeared for long stretches.

At the base of a steep hill, he hesitated for the first time. He gazed up the incline and stuffed his hands into the pockets, then he turned and looked back down the trail. The branches of the sparse trees hung limp in the still morning air. The grass around his feet was stunted and pale, not the rich, vibrant green typical of the miles and miles he'd walked to get here. He squinted against the glare of the sun. He could go back, he knew, walk away across the yellow fields, use the trail to escape to new lands and forget he had ever known this one. But even as he thought it, he found himself turning again and climbing up the rocky embankment.

After a short, intense struggle he crested the hill. He looked up, made a small sound in his throat, looked away. It took determination to look back again.

On the flat stretch of ground in front of him, the rusting remains of a mine head frame thrust upward. It intruded on the horizon, jutting up three stories in height, an aging, trapezoid skeleton. The man doffed his hat, gripping it with both hands. He swallowed convulsively as he moved toward it. The frame's massive right door hung askew where it had jumped off its track decades before, creating an open triangle large enough to allow a child to walk through unhindered. A heavy cattle gate was bolted across the sliding doors.

He stopped at the entrance of the mine and, reaching out with a trembling hand, took hold he cattle gate's crossbar. Once his fingers curled around the iron, he gripped with his other hand and leaned forward, folded his arms across the bar, and rested his forehead on them. His breathing slowed. It was done. He was here, and as he remained in that posture, head on his arms, he knew he would never fully let go again. A heaviness released in his chest, a deep, long sigh. Now he wasn't sure why he'd been so afraid. It really was like coming home again.

Eventually, the man stood straight. He wiped his wet face on the back of his sleeve and angled his head upward. The mine shaft blocked out the sun where he stood. He skirted its side, around the charred remnants of the crumbling ruin at one edge of the field and followed the curve of the hill until he could see the lake. It was swampy, full of reeds and cattails. He let his gaze go beyond the water, well beyond its far side.

In the distance, the small city of Foley Lake sat still and hazy in the early morning sun.

Chapter Two

A rush of cold air chilled Butch's skin as he closed the diner's door behind him and looked around. The diner was empty, save for two old men reading a newspaper in a back booth and a little girl clad in cutoff jeans and an oversized t-shirt, perched on her knees atop a red stool at the counter in front. She was huddled down and intent. Curious, Butch crossed the room and took a seat at the opposite end of the counter where he could see what she was doing. The girl looked eight or nine years old, her sandy-colored hair dangling around her face where it had escaped her ponytail. She was bent over a red plastic tray lined with glass pepper shakers, coaxing pepper from a can and letting it spill into the shakers until it filled them to the brim. Next to her, freshly filled saltshakers stood in perfect rows on a tray of their own.

A woman emerged from the kitchen, wiping her hands on a worn pink waitress uniform, a name tag reading *Hi, I'm*

May pinned at an angle across one breast. She flashed Butch a smile.

"Can I get you a menu?" she asked.

Butch shook his head. "Just coffee, thanks."

May filled a mug and set it in front of him. "How about a piece of blueberry cobbler?" she asked. "Baked it fresh this morning. Picked the blueberries myself."

"Sounds good. Let me try a piece of that."

May swirled away, returning with an enormous piece of blueberry cobbler. As she slipped the plate in front of him Butch looked at the size of the cobbler and raised his eyebrows at her. She shrugged. "It's been quiet today. Might as well enjoy it while it's fresh."

Butch picked up a fork and dug in as the waitress watched him with keen interest. He nodded. "Ummmh. Hmmmhn," he intoned. "Fresh blueberries."

May smiled. "Fresh just last summer," she said. "I canned those myself."

"Hard to beat fresh canned, that's for sure," Butch agreed.

The little girl sat back with a big sigh and looked at the shakers with satisfaction.

"Finished," she said. May set the coffee pot down and joined the child at the other end of the counter, bending to look at the shakers closely.

"Good job, Lowie. You hardly spilled any."

The child nodded proudly. "And no sneezing."

May nodded. "You know, that's right. I didn't hear one sneeze this time. How did you manage that?"

"I held my breath."

"Smart girl," Butch said.

May straightened up. "She is. She's my heir apparent. She'll take over this place for me someday. Right, kiddo?"

Lowie turned to face Butch. "Right now, I'm just the condiment girl. But I'm working my way up."

Butch chuckled, but Lowie's guileless expression sobered him. He furrowed his brow thoughtfully and nodded. "I can see that. Looks like you're off to a good start."

The waitress went to the cooler and pulled out an orange soda. She handed it to Lowie.

"Here you are, my dear. You sure are cheap labor." Lowie accepted the can with a smile.

"Are you sure about the ketchup?" she asked. "I could do them before I leave."

"No, honey. I had a little time so I did them right after the lunch crowd left."

Lowie hopped down from the stool. "Alright, then. See you tomorrow." She whirled away and disappeared with the tinkling of the door's bell.

May smiled after her, and then looked over the tray of perfectly lined rows. She picked up a shaker and noted that it was filled to the rim, then twirled the lid off and dumped half of the pepper back into the pepper can. She put the lid back on it and set it back on the tray, picked up the next shaker and did the same. Butch watched, his coffee hovering between his mouth and the counter. May glanced up at him and smiled shyly.

"I know. It looks deceitful. But it makes her happy to help, and makes me happy to keep her coming in."

"And the ketchups you filled up after the lunch crowd…"

"There hasn't been any kind of crowd in this diner for….well, in recent memory. I just forgot to empty the bottles after she filled them yesterday."

Butch laughed out loud, forking more cobbler into his mouth. May smiled and studied him, her head tilted like a curious puppy.

"You from around here?"

"Just passing through," he said. "But I wouldn't mind picking up some work if there's any to be had. Odd jobs, repairs, that kind of thing. You know of anything?"

May twirled the cover onto a shaker and sighed. "Lord knows I'm not hiring. It's been so slow I fired my cook a while back. Couldn't afford him anymore." May looked over at the men sitting at the corner booth. "Hey Emil, Vinny, you know if anyone needs a handyman?"

Emil answered from behind the classifieds. "Best ask Lane."

Vinny dropped the sports page and nodded. "Yup. Lane knows. Find her down at the courthouse."

Butch set his coffee cup down and slowly wiped his mouth with a napkin. "Lane?"

May nodded. "Yeah. Lane takes care of the city, maintenance and such, whatever the town needs. Just go to the clock tower and city hall is right there. If anyone needs some work done, she will know."

Butch stepped out into the sunlight, the taste of blueberry still in his mouth. He glanced back toward the mine. Lane was still here. Why? Why did she stay? He struggled against a snarl of emotion that coiled inside him, making his jaw clench. *It doesn't matter.* He told himself. *Get a grip. Stay focused.* But even as he scolded himself, his feet turned away from the mine of their own accord and carried him off toward Foley Lake City Hall.

Chapter Three

———●●———

The little city was a paradox. The stores were open, but empty. The streets were narrow and neat but crosshatched with jagged cracks punctuated with potholes. A small park in the middle of town sported a spotty turf, an empty jungle gym, a vacant sandbox. In the window box of the hardware marigolds grew in a neat row, but only two bloomed while the rest looked like they couldn't be bothered. All indications were that someone was paying attention and keeping things in order; still, the entire scene crumbled at its edges.

The clock tower poked up in the distance, its square pinnacle tapering into a narrow rod where it stood like a sentry over the squat city buildings that surrounded it. The black iron hands of the clock read 4:27. Butch glanced at the sun. It was not more than a little past two. He stopped and watched the clock, waiting. A minute passed, then two, but the thick hands stayed frozen in place. He moved closer and spotted the shreds of grass and straw from an abandoned sparrow's nest in the frozen cross section where the hands met.

He pulled open the door marked CITY HALL in fading black letters and stepped inside. The interior was dark but not cooler and smelled stale. Fans whirred overhead, achieving little beyond blowing around the dull air. Three short steps up and the entry opened into a foyer. To the left a sign read MEETING ROOM AND RESTROOM and a faded arrow marked the passage to an empty hall. To the right, a small, square room fronted by a glass wall was occupied by a heavy, broad-faced woman some years beyond middle-age, her hair pulled back in a severe knot and her bag-like dress dark at the armpits. She was working on an aged typewriter, striking the keys with sharp jabs that made the keyboard jitter. The door was propped open by a short stack of encyclopedias. Butch lifted the worn and dusty baseball cap from his head and stepped through.

"'Scuse me," he said, "I'm looking for Lane. Can you tell me…"

"Mike!" the woman bellowed without warning. Butch jumped, creasing the bill of the cap clamped in his hands. "Mike, come out here, someone's lookin' for Lane!"

There was a muffled reply from inside the interior office and the door popped open. A narrow head poked through, thin gray hair plastered flat by sweat.

"Dorothy, you have got to get Harvey over here to fix this air conditioner. I got three fans blowing hot air, it's a convection oven in there and I can't even hear myself think. I can't get any work done."

Dorothy shook her head and reached for the phone. "I can try, but I told you once we got past fishing opener Harvey won't leave his boat 'til November."

Butch stepped forward. "I can fix it."

Dorothy paused, the phone cradled against her shoulder. "This young man is looking for Lane."

Mike looked at him hopefully. "You know something about air conditioners?"

Butch smiled. "A little. Enough to fix most of them." He reached past Dorothy and offering his hand to Mike. "My name's Butch Brown. I'm looking for some work, odd jobs, that kind of thing. The fellas at the cafe said I should talk to Lane."

Mike shook Butch's hand with enthusiastic, premature gratitude. "Well, Lane isn't around, but if you know air conditioners, I bet I can give you some work right now. Come on in and have a look."

Butch followed Mike into the interior office, a medium-sized affair overstuffed with filing cabinets and a large metal desk. A small, unshaded window faced south and the summer sun streamed in uninhibited, adding to Mike's misery. The bottom of the window was blocked by the useless air conditioner. Butch stepped to it without a word and lifted the cover from the face of the machine. Mike dropped into his chair and began fanning himself with a legal pad. He watched Butch work.

"What luck you happened in. I've been dying here," Mike said. "What'd you say your name was?"

Butch squatted to look more closely at the inner workings of the air conditioner. "Brown," he replied. "Butch Brown."

Mike shifted restlessly in his chair and pulled a handkerchief from his pocket, swiping it across his forehead. "Can't say I know of any Browns around Foley."

"I guess I had some relations here years ago, but not anymore. I'm just passing through."

Mike nodded. "Your people must have left a long time ago. Name doesn't ring a bell at all. Are you staying at the hotel?"

"Right now I have a little camping spot by that old mine up on the hill."

Mike stopped fanning. "You're camping at the mine?"

Butch glanced back at him. "Yeah. It's a nice spot."

"A nice spot, huh. You are new. That mine is…" Mike broke off. Butch glanced back at him. "The mine is what?"

"Depends on who you ask, I suppose. Some folks think it's haunted. There are lots of stories floating around about it."

"Is that so?"

"Yeah, well, that place has enough bad luck to give birth to a few tall tales. Still, it is private property."

Butch turned and faced Mike. "I don't want to cause any trouble."

Mike shook his head dismissively. "I reckon if someone wants you to move off the property, they'll let you know. It's not my business."

Butch nodded and snapped the cover back onto the air conditioner's face. He turned the knob and the machine chugged, hiccupped, then purred to life.

"Well, I'll be!" Mike exclaimed. "You got it working!" Butch stepped out of the way as Mike stood and reveled in the cold air pouring from the vent.

"What do I owe you, Mr. Brown?"

"Just call me Butch. Let's see. Does ten sound fair?"

Mike grinned. "Ten dollars. Done. I assume you take cash?"

"That would be fine."

Mike stepped through the door to the outer office, closing it behind him to trap the cold air. Butch could hear his muffled voice yelling down the hall. "Dorothy, are you in the Ladies? Where's the key to petty cash?"

Butch circled the room, shutting off the fans strewn about on file cabinets and end tables. The room grew pleasantly quiet as the fan noise faded. Butch browsed the photos scattered throughout the office. He made a slow circle around the perimeter of the room, studying each; there were several of Mike at different venues over the years, giving speeches, cutting ribbons, the evidence of time passing in the cut of his jacket and the thinning of his hair. From among the business-like images one stood out, and Butch felt his heart clutch at the sight of it. It was old, black-and-white, and fragile with age, a faded group shot of miners at the entrance of the Foley Mine. Some of those early miners were little more than boys, clad in soft hats with carbide lamps clipped to the front, eyes hard and determined, shoulders sagging with fatigue. Names of some of the miners, hand-printed in blue ink, were fading from the photo but most were nameless. They were just miners, lost to history. There would be few in Foley Lake who would know any of those faces anymore.

Butch stepped back again, pondering the image of the old photo among all the newer, and realized that there was not one image of Mike with a family. The snarl of emotion shifted again, threatening to rise. Butch swallowed and felt it slide slowly back down. The unfairness of it galled him.

How quickly the dead were forgotten.

Chapter Four

Dawn came in perfect stillness, and by the time the sun fully crested the hill it bore down with a fury, making the shadow cast by the mine shaft sharp and hard as iron. Butch woke restless and early. He walked out into the fields of crab grass and Queen Anne's Lace that grew from the hard soil surrounding the mine, leaving the shaft behind and striding out towards the lake. Three hundred yards from the mine, the land began to feel softer under his boot. Four hundred yards and mud oozed up and marked each successive step with a dull, wet print. Twenty-five more yards out and he couldn't go any farther, his boots sinking deep into the muck, though the water of the lake itself was still more than a hundred yards off.

He stood still, gazing at the ground under his feet. This is where they made their mistake sixty years ago. The engineers measured off the distance between the mine and the lake and set a limit on how far they could blast, supposing that the underground drift would still be well away from the lake's muddy bottom. But somewhere between the lake at the edge of town and the mine far below was a spring that kept the mine flooded and the swampy lake from drying up completely. No one understood the true nature of that spring. It had lain in secret, saturating the ground that reached out like a soft finger toward the mine below it. They blasted too close to that hidden finger and it poked through, crumbling the ceiling of the mine and sending most of the lake into the drifts and tunnels of the Foley.

Butch turned, suddenly eager to be away, and tramped back up the hill. At his campsite he stripped, folding the clothes and balling the socks before dropping them in the grass and stepping his bare feet back into the boots. He walked around the mine and carefully skirted a patch of wild rose, mindful of the thorns, to the ridge overlooking a small pit that lay on a flat slab of land fifteen feet below. This hole was the only sign that the mine company briefly considered making the Foley an open-pit mine. They'd begun digging away the overburden, the soil and earth that lay over the precious manganese ore far below, since the Foley refused to give up the lake she'd swallowed in the flood and no pump they tried could keep her dry enough to continue as an underground mine. They didn't dig far, however, before the extent of the flooding became more obvious. Every scoop of earth they removed was replaced by water within a few days. Once the whole project was abandoned the bottom of the pit filled up and produced a clear pond. The assaulted land around it covered with the exposed rocky soil healed and grew thistle and weeds. The pond never got much attention from the local kids as a swimming hole. The struggle to navigate the steep decline to the water line and its proximity to the abandoned mine protected it from the incursions of local kids. The walls of the pit were steep, but there was enough slope on the near side to negotiate, and Butch slid his way down on the heels of his boots, managing to stay on his feet mostly because the consequences of riding down the hill on his bare backside were too unpleasant to ponder. The slag spilled him onto a narrow ledge of solid red ground a bare six feet wide like a giant step at the edge of the water.

Butch kicked the boots off and squatted at the edge of the small reddish pool, reaching down its vertical bank and swishing the boots back and forth to rinse away the mud he'd collected on his morning walk. The pit itself was remarkably full considering Foley Lake's infrequent rains. The mud loosened and dissolved from the soles of the boots, and satisfied, Butch set them aside. He stood and stretched, relishing the feel of the sun on his naked torso, and stepped down into the water.

A second later, he was drowning.

He had been thinking of a lake, with a compassionate slope that eased a person into the depths. This was an unnatural pool formed by men, and stepping into it was like stepping off a cliff. He plunged down, the water swirling closed over his head. Butch knew how to swim, but even so it took him a few moments to get his wits about him and stop flailing. The water was frigid, unaffected by the sun's charms, and as he kicked to the surface he suddenly understood why the pit stayed full. The water was cold because it was flowing fresh from the deep coffers of the earth, from a hidden spring that jealously guarded the ore below. He kicked for the surface and broke through to the heat and light of the summer air, his every sense was alive to the cut of the icy water. He rolled over on his back and kicked out toward the center of the pool, rolled again and breast-stroked back to the edge. His feet tingled and went numb. He ducked under the water, freezing his sinuses and earning a stabbing headache. He surfaced, gave in to a loud groan of pain, and chuckled; he rolled over onto his back and floated face-up along the pit's edge, staring up at the flat blue sky.

Suddenly Butch felt hairs along the back of his neck stand on end. He turned to face the mine, scanning the ridge above him. The top of the shaft itself was just visible. He could see nothing out of the ordinary, but still, something up there made a hard pit of anxiety form in his stomach.

Imagination. He chided himself. *Brain freeze. Get a grip.*

"This mine is private property, you know." The sound of a woman's voice behind him was so jolting that Butch gave out a small yelp as he spun around. A smallish, slender woman in her late twenties stood at the edge of the pool, arms folded. Her sandy blonde hair was pulled back in a low, no-nonsense ponytail, her t-shirt and jeans worn, but clean. Her face was unreadable.

Butch gaped at her. Her even gaze and her silence finally prodded a stumbling response from him. "Oh. Private," he stuttered. "I don't mean to cause any trouble..."

The woman shook her head. "No sense trying to explain anything to me. I said that it was private property, not that it was my property. Are you Butch?"

He nodded.

"My father told me you were handy and looking for work. I could use some help today. Are you available?"

Butch blinked. "For what kind of work?"

Lane shrugged. "Honest work. Hard work. If you are accustomed to any other kind, just say so, and I'll find somebody else."

"Yes, sure, I'll take the work, whatever it is." Butch was suddenly, unbearably aware that his feet were sending frantic s-o-s signals zinging up his legs. He started dog paddling to the edge of the pool. "If you don't mind turning around..."

Lane turned silently and started scaling back up the hill. She spoke over her shoulder. "You should know that from up by the mine, a person can see a long way down into that water."

Butch scrambled to the far side of the pool and tried to pull himself onto the bank on arms weak with cold, and when they gave way he fell face-first into the damp red mud.

Chapter Five

Butch stood several feet behind Lane as she worked the lock on the door to the city garage. She'd walked up the hill from the city rather than driving and she marched down from the mine without a word, her ponytail swinging. Butch followed, silent and meek. The fact that this woman had seen him naked made him reluctant to initiate a conversation with her. He kept a respectful distance, pulled his baseball cap down low, and kept quiet.

She led him through the city to a squat white building on the same block as city hall. The words CITY GARAGE painted on the building's concrete exterior were fading from constant exposure to the elements. Lane bent for the garage door's floor-level handle, but Butch was quicker. He grabbed the handle and lifted, the sound of reluctant rollers creeping into action reverberating inside the darkened building. Lane turned to look at him for the first time since leaving the mine. She studied him for a moment, but Butch wordlessly ducked his head and stepped back. Lane nodded her thanks and stepped into the cool shade of the garage.

Snapping on the interior lights did little to push back the darkness. Dust motes floated freely on the sunlight that streamed in through the open door. Lane stepped to a tarp and pulled it off an eight-foot pile of assorted boxes and bins, driving the motes into a frenzy.

"Well, here it is. Part of it, anyway."

Butch took a deep breath, glad to have the silence broken. He scanned the pile. "Okay. What is it?"

"You name it. Parade stuff, flags, stolen bikes that were never reclaimed, old park benches, highway cones, broken signs. Everything the city didn't want or know what to do with got thrown in here. And you and I are going to clean it out."

Butch pushed his hat back and squinted into one of the boxes. "Well, it doesn't all look like junk."

"I disagree, but the city council is on your side," Lane replied. "So, we are having a garage sale."

Butch reached into the box and lifted out a single roller-skate, its leather straps stiff with mold. He shook his head. "A garage sale?"

"I know." Lane rubbed her forehead as if she were fighting a headache. "It sounds like a bad joke. I wish it was. I talked to the council members about cleaning this building out so we can use it for winter storage. I told them we needed to get rid of this crap." She lifted the bike tire missing several spokes and lofted it into a corner. It landed with a clatter. "They just hate to throw away anything that someone else might be foolish enough to buy. So, they decided to have a garage sale. I need to sort this stuff, clean up everything that looks like it's *not* junk, and get it ready to go. The sale's in three weeks. Fourth of July is in five weeks. There's no way I can get this done, get ready for the Fourth, and keep up with the rest of my work." Lane turned to Butch. "I only need you until the sale, but I need you here every day until then. You interested?"

Butch bent to set the roller-skate on the floor and gave it a push. It limped forward, dragging its musty leather behind it. "Am I interested in three weeks' steady work? Sure. Sounds like an adventure," he said.

"Well, you have the right attitude," Lane replied. "We'll see how long that lasts."

Chapter Six

Lane let the screen door slam behind her. She'd suffered under her father's rebuke her entire life for slamming that door, and now she rebuked Lowie, but for some reason there was a disconnect between the knowledge that the door shouldn't be slammed and the action of closing it quietly. Lane stopped inside the doorway and noted with some relief that both her father's and Lowie's shoes were missing. She would have the house to herself, at least for a little while.

The old house's narrow halls and creaking floorboards gave Lane the security of the intimately familiar, and the tension of the day begin to give way. She dropped her keys on the counter on her way through the kitchen and mounted the stairs two-by-two. The house was old by most standards, built in the recession years after World War I, and its narrow halls and small rooms bore the marks of that conservative time. She had been raised in this house, and, other than a brief interlude that resulted in Lowie's birth, never left it.

Lane stepped into the bathroom and turned on the shower, leaving her clothes in a dusty pile on the floor while she stepped under the stream. The hot water hammered against her back, pounding away at the ache across her shoulders. She washed her hair twice, letting the lather of the shampoo carve trails down her abdomen and thighs, and when she emerged from the steaming bathroom fifteen minutes later she felt soft and new.

Lane scooped her dirty clothes up and opened the hamper to drop them in. The trousers her father had worn the day before lay on top of the pile. Frowning, Lane reached down and pulled them out. The cuffs were covered with red dust.

Hematite. She knew what the redness meant—she had some of the same dirt on her own clothes after her brief morning trip to the Foley Mine. She'd noticed some of the fine red powder on her father's shoes a week or so before, but when she tried to coax a clear answer from her father as to why he had been to the mine, he scowled at her and told her he had *not* been to the mine. She pushed the trousers back down deep in the hamper and dropped her own clothes on top. No point worrying about her father tramping around up there when it was clear he wouldn't give her an honest answer as to why.

Lane found a pound of hamburger in the freezer and put it in the microwave to thaw. She heard small, lively footsteps on the front porch and heard the screen door close with a profound slam.

"Lowie!"

Lowie appeared in the hall behind her, her eyes bright in her tanned, clear face. "Sorry," she offered. "I keep forgetting."

Lane shook her head, but ruffled Lowie's hair in greeting. "What did you do today?"

Lowie plopped into a kitchen chair and rested her chin on her hand. "Nothing much. I helped May at the diner, mostly. Can we work on the tree house after supper?"

Lane pulled two cans of condensed soup and a jar of green beans out of the cupboard and set them on the countertop. She turned to face Lowie, shoulders slumping. "Ah, Low, I am so pooped."

"You always say that!" Lowie protested.

"It's always true. I work six days a week, Mary Louise."

Lowie plopped into a chair at the kitchen table, dropping her chin back on her hands with a frown. She knew better than to push a point once her mother invoked her full name.

"What did you do today, anyway?" She didn't try to hide the pout in her voice.

Lane pulled the can opener out of the drawer and went to work on the cans. "Worked in the garage. Gotta get ready for that sale. The new guy helped me."

Lowie sat upright, fresh interest in her face. "The guy Grandpa told you about? The serial killer?"

Lane chuckled. "Grandpa was kidding about that. I don't think this guy is a serial killer."

"But he's staying up by the mine, right?"

"That doesn't make him crazy, Low, just short on cash." The microwave beeped and Lane lifted the mushy red ball of burger out, dumping it from the plate into the skillet she had heating on the stove. The meat sizzled and sputtered. Lane jabbed at it with a spatula. Lowie sat back and tapped the table thoughtfully. Finally, she sat forward. "Is he nice?"

"I guess. He works pretty hard."

"Where's he from?"

"I don't know."

"What's he do for a living?"

"I don't know."

"How long is he going to stay?"

"I didn't ask."

Lowie frowned. "Gosh, Mom, how do you know he's *not* a serial killer?"

Lane laughed. "Well, you've got me there. I guess he could be stark raving mad. But as long as he hangs around until that garage is cleaned up and squared away, I don't really care."

The screen door slammed. They both turned toward the hallway, where Mike emerged just seconds later. His hair was rumpled and sweaty, his tie pulled askew.

"Is supper soon?" he asked. Lane shook her head.

"Half an hour. I got a late start."

"Hi, Gramps," Lowie greeted.

"Hi, sweetheart," Mike answered without looking at her. He nodded toward the hamburger searing in the pan. "Just let me know when it's ready," he said. "I have some work to finish." He turned and stepped through the kitchen toward the hallway and his waiting office. Lane watched him go, his frame bent and thin, his pant cuffs stained with red. Lowie stood and crossed the kitchen to Lane, putting her hand in her mother's.

"Is he okay, Mom?" she asked quietly.

Lane pulled her gaze back to the hamburger, giving Lowie's hand a gentle squeeze. "Sure, Low," she said, probing the meat with the spatula. "Why wouldn't he be?"

Chapter Seven

The old dog hobbled across the open expanse of grassland, his gray-pink tongue lolling over the blank spots in his gums where teeth used to be. He panted from heat and exertion, the motion of having to methodically lift his ruined left hip with each step making the travel slow and tedious. The break was old and poorly healed, and the joint wouldn't bend, leaving his back limb frozen in a perpetual "z." The bare patch where he had licked away the hair on the constantly aching hip added to his derelict appearance. But he moved with purpose, slowly and systematically making his way toward the soft glow of firelight up ahead.

By the time the sun settled behind the horizon, the streets of Foley Lake were deserted. Now, in this late-night hour, it was easy for the dog to slip through town, unobserved except by an occasional stray cat. Even those strays didn't pay him much notice, crouching with ears flat when they first saw him coming, then dismissing him with a tail-flick of feline contempt. He stopped to sniff around a few garbage cans, but found little of interest so he kept moving, limping along through town and away toward the mine and the small flame in the distance.

He wasn't quite tall enough to see over the grass, being of primarily terrier descent, although any number of breeds might have contributed to his overall composition. He plowed through the turf, his face rubbed raw from the sharp grass brushing past his nose. No matter. He pushed through until he finally caught a glimpse of what he had dragged that stiff left hip all night to see.

He was there.

In the distance a low bonfire burned. The form of a man lay curled into a sleeping bag a few feet farther on.

The dog stopped, listening. His hearing was still good, at least. The quietness of deep night greeted him. Satisfied, he moved forward as quickly as his rolling gait would allow, swung in a wide arc around the man and the fire, and made for the mine's gated entrance.

There was just enough space for him to wiggle through the bars of the cattle gate and into the mine. Once inside, he sniffed back and forth across the chipped and aged concrete floor, searching. Finding nothing, he returned to the gate. He found a spot just inside the entrance and turned a tight circle, then lay down with a sigh. He angled his face toward the man, intent on watching the still form. And he did watch for a while, until old age leaned down like a heavy weight and sleep took him.

CHAPTER EIGHT

"Oh, *crap.*"

Dave pulled to a stop in front of the used car lot and looked at the control panel on the squad's dash. The aging Crown Victoria still had a pretty good air conditioner, and it was on full blast. Still, the air around the lot was so saturated the stink it was making its way through the vents. Spot waited impatiently on the curb at the edge of the lot while Dave made a show of retrieving his tape recorder, notebook and camera from the seat next to him and bit his bottom lip, trying to force a straight face. He wasn't in any hurry to step out of the squad and into the aroma of the sun baking liquid manure into the shining surfaces of thirty used cars.

Dave hated cows. He hated everything to do with them. He'd done his time in cow hell, spending every summer between the ages of seven and fifteen working slavishly on his grandfather's dairy farm. He was grateful beyond words when his father, long since abandoned by his mother, remarried a cheerful and spoiled city girl who was like-minded in Dave's disdain for all things bovine. Although the woman could be petty and demanding, she won Dave's everlasting affection when she motivated his father to abandon the rigors of farm life for the clean, fresh air of electrician's school. Dave had not set foot inside a barn in twenty years, and he hoped to never smell the scent of cow droppings again. Yet here he was, downtown in his own little city, and wouldn't you know but the smell had come to him.

And though his lip stung, he could barely keep a straight face.

He felt roughly the same way about cows as he felt about Spot. He and the car salesman were both home-grown Foley Lakers, and during their growing-up years Spot, a mean-spirited show-off and two years Dave's senior, never missed a chance to harass, terrify, or otherwise humiliate young Dave. Spot left the city the year before Dave did, and when Dave returned to Foley Lake in a uniform, he thought he was coming back to a Spot-free city and could reclaim some of his dignity. He was sick to his stomach when his old nemesis returned to open the city's only car lot less than a year later.

But now things were coming around.

Someone had sprayed Spot's Lot with liquid manure. And not just sprayed. Drenched. Doused. Machine-gunned. Every car on the lot had been so thoroughly soaked with the soupy brown manure that it was difficult to discern the color or model of the individual vehicles. Spot called 9-1-1 to report the "vile act of outright vandalism" early that morning. Dave, the only full-time cop in the city's payroll given its humble tax base, had taken his time responding. He told dispatch to tell Spot he had to run to Crow Wing to pick up some paperwork and that he would look into the vandalism when he returned. That wasn't true, of course, but sitting in his office, knowing Spot was fuming—literally and figuratively—was just too satisfying.

A small scattering of people stood along the two sidewalks upwind of the lot to point and chuckle. Dave slipped out of the squad, closing the door quickly to preserve the interior from a thorough drenching in the smell, wishing he could have killed just a little more time. Spot waited, hands on hips, his left side covered with a long, brown smear of manure. As soon as Dave got out the squad, Spot started marching toward him. Dave held his hand out. "Stop."

Spot hesitated for a moment, then kept coming. Dave dropped his free hand to the gun on his belt.

"You do not need to come any closer to me than that. Do you understand me?" Spot glanced on Dave's hand resting on the gun and stopped.

"Took you long enough to get here."

"I knew you weren't going anywhere." Dave nodded at the manure on Spot's side. "You didn't duck fast enough, I take it?"

Spot glared. "No, *Dave,* I wasn't here when it happened. I slipped and fell in…in it. "He started moving toward Dave again. Dave's grip tightened around the handle of the gun.

"Spot, you get any closer and, by God, I will shoot you. Man, you *stink*."

There was a ripple of laughter from the onlookers, and Spot's face sank into a deeper shade of red. Dave cleared his throat. "Just stay there and tell me what happened."

Spot glared. "I came to work this morning, and my cars were covered in crap. Then I fell in it. That's what happened."

Dave turned his head away, gnawing that bottom lip. He gave himself a moment to be sure he could open his mouth without laughing. "You weren't here? You told the dispatcher you knew who did this."

"Of course I know!" Spot roared. "Everybody knows! Chuck Larson did this!"

Dave frowned. "Chuck? Now why would Chuck want to spray crap all over your cars?"

"Because, Sherlock," Spot's snide voice made Dave's blood pressure spike, "Chuck is the only farmer within thirty miles that uses a liquid manure spreader."

Dave nodded, thinking. He wanted to proceed carefully. That Spot's wife was carrying on with some kid working as a hired hand out at the Larson farm was common knowledge; how much Spot knew, and how he planned to respond, were still in question. Dave twirled the pen in his fingers. "Well, Chuck may *own* the only liquid manure spreader around, but maybe he isn't the only one who *drives* it. He's got a couple of young fellas who work for him. Any reason to think one of them might have it out for you?"

Spot scowled. "Man, what are you talking about? Why would some redneck farmhand want to do this to my cars?" Dave stared at Spot, incredulous. He snapped off the recorder, put his pen away, and closed his notebook. He walked back to his squad as Spot followed.

"Where are you going?" Spot demanded. Dave opened the squad's door and tossed the notebook and recorder across to the passenger seat. "I'll go talk to Chuck and see if he's got anything to say. In the meantime, you get those cars cleaned up, and I mean today. They keep smelling up the city street and I'll ticket you for public nuisance."

Spot's blazing face faded from the squad's rear view as Dave rolled away, steering with one hand as he retrieved a new air freshener from the Crown Victoria's glove box. He would get to Chuck's for a visit, eventually. First, he had more urgent business. Even through the heavy perfume of the air freshener, he could smell cow. He headed over to Crosby to see if Gunther Lundgren might be able to fit the squad in for a thorough detailing.

Chapter Nine

Through the window of his home office, Mike watched Lowie in the morning sun, watering the rose bushes her grandmother had loved. She watered the base of each bush, careful to avoid the leaves as Lane told her, chattering away to the plants as she worked. She'd read that plants liked conversation, and she was a veritable font of words, so the relationship between Lowie and the rose bushes grew based on her assumption that if she talked long enough, eventually there would be actual roses. She was completely undeterred by the fact that despite three years of her careful tending, the bushes never once flowered.

Mike sighed as he watched the child tending bushes that were too far gone to make good on their promise. She was so like Lane in some ways—pretty, hardworking, pragmatic. Yet she had a charming, dreamy quality that her father, gone these eight years, also possessed, and Mike knew that was what Lane both loved and feared in the child. It seemed inevitable that Foley Lake would be too small for Lowie before long. Foley Lake was too small for anyone with dreams.

Turning away from the window, Mike dropped slowly into his desk chair. The sun shone in through the window and reflected on the glass of three photos hanging on the adjacent wall, obscuring the image in each. It didn't matter—Mike knew the photos by heart. They were three black and white snapshots of three distinctly different cities, all bearing the inscription Foley Lake. In its early years, every time the little city tried to grow roots the mine company would send a surveyor to bore holes under the main street, only to discover that rich deposits of iron lay under the city proper. Within weeks the city would be uprooted, the buildings lifted onto sledges with enormous jacks and dragged off their foundations, the iron below worth infinitely more than the wooden shacks above. The stores and homes were simply emptied, moved, and dropped down on a new plot of unbroken sod, the wooden sidewalks stripped loose and replanted on the new town site, the women fussing about the clotheslines and garden plots and the graveyards left behind. But the miners never complained. All the land belonged to the mine company. The store was a mine store; the houses were company houses. So, the men moved their families, moved their churches and sidewalks and chicken yards, leaving behind the unnecessary and the dead, bending their backs to the work and meeting their wives' complaints with stony silence. The town didn't matter. The town existed for the mine. It was, in every respect, a mine town.

Three times. It wasn't unusual for a town to be moved so that the iron under it could be mined, but the upheaval caused by such a move was usually short lived. In a year or two new garden plots had appeared, new streets had been pounded smooth, new chicken yards scratched clean by the constant action of claw and beak. But in those early years, Foley Lake didn't get the chance to settle. Three times the city was uprooted and recreated. It made Mike wonder why the mine's surveyors didn't have the foresight to bore some holes and check the new city site before the buildings were moved. For whatever reason, the little city had stood on three banks of Foley Lake, settling in, building up, moving on. No other city on the iron range had a more scattered and transient legacy.

The chair slowly swiveled back toward the desk. The contents of a large manila envelope lay there, spilled out across the stained oak. Mike gathered the papers together and slipped them back into the envelope. Some of the papers had markings in Chinese script, so utterly foreign to Mike's Midwestern experiences that it may well have come from another planet. It didn't matter that he couldn't read those words. He wasn't reading any of the material, not anymore. He slid the envelope under some other paperwork in the bottom drawer of the desk, then closed the drawer and locked it, dropping the key into his trouser pocket. He stood slowly and looked back out the window. The words no longer mattered. Only the doing mattered, and the question of whether the little city of Foley Lake had the fortitude to withstand what was about to unfold.

Chapter Ten

Lane was impressed.

When she pulled her aging pickup onto the concrete pad in front of the city garage early the next morning Butch was sitting on the curb, waiting. He labored hard all that first day, working without hesitation or complaint. During the lunch break he disappeared, but he was back before the hour was up. She'd paid him at the end of the day in cash, as agreed, knowing that if the man was a drunk, paying him before the job was complete was a mistake. Once he got some money, he might end up so thoroughly pickled that he would be useless. But here he was again, sober, scrubbed, and ready for another day. She unlocked the garage door and he bent and pulled it open, unapologetically chivalrous. Since he had proven that he was in possession of at least reasonable intelligence, she told him that she would trust his good sense—anything he thought truly valuable should be brought out to the driveway for cleaning and pricing, and everything else would go into the dumpster. She told him to work along the west wall, and she would work along the east. With luck, they would meet somewhere in the middle within the week.

The garage was a jumbled museum of the town's history. Ancient street signs for streets that no longer existed, campaign banners for town government races long since decided, and coils of wiring that wouldn't pass an electrical code anywhere in North America were strewn and stacked throughout the garage's cavernous interior. Butch discovered an entire shelf covered with old garden rakes, spades, and hoes, every one of which had a broken handle. Lane found a musty, sagging box filled with fliers reassuring Foley Lake's residents that fluoridation in the city water was good and was not a communist plot to poison them all. Butch and Lane were passing each other with armload after armload of useless junk on repeated trips to the dumpster.

Despite intermittent streams of sneezing and being covered with grime, Butch didn't show any sign of slowing down when Lane said it was time to stop for lunch. She went to the truck and pulled out her small cooler, taking a seat on the grass in the shade of the building. She lifted out a sandwich, carrots, chips, and a cupcake. She arranged her meal around her neatly, setting each item in a precise spot in front of her. Butch sat a few feet away and pulled an apple from some unseen place, biting off a chunk and chewing slowly. Lane ate, stealing glances at Butch as he took each slow, small bite of the apple. He noticed her stolen glances and chuckled. She felt her defenses rise.

"What?"

He shook his head, still smiling. "Nothing," he replied. Lane turned back to her lunch, irritated.

"Can I ask you a question?" Butch asked.

She shrugged. "Suit yourself. I may not answer it."

"Fair enough," He replied. "I was wondering how a girl—woman—like yourself ends up doing maintenance for a city like Foley Lake."

"Why do you ask?"

"I like stories."

"You like stories," she repeated flatly. She couldn't decide if he was making fun of her or not. Butch picked up on her suspicions and smiled.

"Look, I travel. I go all over, and I meet a lot of people. But I've never met a woman city maintenance worker before. So yes, I like stories. They are really all I have to show for all the walking I've done."

Lane gazed at him a moment, then—"My husband's gone, my father's the mayor, and I needed a job. *End* of story."

Butch nodded thoughtfully. "I can see the logic in that."

She was less than halfway through her sandwich when Butch stood up and tossed the remainder of his apple, nibbled cleanly down to the core, into the dumpster. He went back into the garage. Lane stopped chewing and listened. She heard the sound of items being moved around, and a few moments later he emerged with an ancient canvas tarp and threw it into the dumpster. He turned to go back into the garage.

"Hey, you don't have to keep working, you know. It's lunch break."

"It's alright. I would rather work than sit," he said simply.

"But it's lunch *break*. You're supposed to sit. You know. And have lunch."

Butch lifted his cap, wiping the sweat from his bald pate. For the first time Lane noticed that his eyes were a clear blue.

"I had lunch, and it was plenty," he said, replacing the cap. "If it's all the same, I'd just as soon keep working." With that he turned and disappeared back through the doorway.

Lane picked at the remains of her lunch. Every sound that drifted out from the garage felt like condemnation. After a few moments she tossed her leftovers and walked the cooler back to the truck.

She couldn't decide what she felt. She reached over the side of the pickup and put the cooler in the bed, then kicked irritably at the back tire, gazing down the row of weary houses lining Main Street. The garage marked the transition between the city's business district and its residential neighborhoods, with its ancient company houses and sagging bungalows. Lane studied the bleak homes, the small, empty yards, and an ache of longing welled up inside of her. She had a clear memory of virtually every house on the street, of the housewives who had been friends to her mother, of overnights with school chums long gone, of Sundays spent pedaling her old, red banana-seat bike from porch to porch to say hello and maybe receive an offer of home-baked cookies and lemonade. But she had watched that life, the life she had wanted for Lowie, fade away and what had taken its place was an indefinable longing that permeated the city and infected Lane with its ache. *What am I still doing here?* she thought. Maybe she was a fool for hanging on, like her husband had told her. Maybe she really did owe Lowie a better chance somewhere else, somewhere free from Foley's perennial angst.

The wind shifted, pushing toward her through the trees lining the street. She stopped kicking and leaned against the truck, listening. The song the wind made as it passed through the leaves soothed her restlessness like a lullaby. She closed her eyes and exhaled. When she opened her eyes again, the sun had emerged from a bank of clouds, and the nameless yearning melted into nostalgia for the sweet familiarity of a hometown street.

When she rejoined Butch, they worked together steadily, putting the garage to rights and making light conversation until well past supper.

Chapter Eleven

The old dog sniffed around the campsite, looking for a piece of hotdog bun he had seen the man throw into the tall grass the evening before. It took time, but eventually his search was rewarded—he found the scrap covered with ants and snapped it up, insects and all.

He needed water. He walked to the edge of the bank leading down to the pit and looked down at the gleaming surface of the pool below. He knew he might make his way down the bank, but he would never be able to reach the water. The bank was steep and covered with loose slag, and he was far too old to challenge it. He turned and walked along the edge of the clearing, looking toward the swamp of Foley Lake. It was a long walk, and we was likely to be just as thirsty by the time he made it back up the hill. In the end he settled for upending a bucket that the man used to shave that morning and failed to empty, and so he drank shaving cream with the water, and was thirsty enough that he didn't mind.

He climbed back inside the gate and lay down. Despite the heat of the day he curled into a ball, the coolness inside the mine's entrance so deep and damp that it made him shiver.

The old dog dozed, but the moment he heard the noise rising up out of the darkness behind him he snapped awake. He lifted his head and turned toward the place where the ground disappeared thirty feet away. A song drifted up from the depths, one of metal pounding rock, a sound so faint only a dog could discern its ring.

The dog felt the hairs along his spine rise and he stared into the darkness, a soft growl rumbling in his throat.

Chapter Twelve

He's early.

Emil Kangus heard the low hum of the pickup's engine long before he arrived at the crosswalk. He sped up his pace, the *kunk-a-chunk* rhythm of his metal walker increasing in meter as he hurried. The crosswalk was at the end of the block, and if his ears didn't fool him—and they never did—the truck was less than four blocks away and closing fast.

The early morning streets of Foley Lake were quiet and largely deserted, Emil's bent frame the only one visible, the hum of the oncoming truck the only sound. Emil moved steadily north along the edge of First Avenue, an unbroken line of brick and brownstone buildings blocking his view of the truck moving toward the intersection from the west. But Emil knew the pickup was there because he could hear it, and because it was there every morning, six days a week, because young Buddy Anderson had accepted a job as foreman at Steward's Wood Products in Brainerd, thirty miles away.

That made Emil dislike Buddy. Not that the kid was unique. Foley Lake had no industry, so most of the kids in Buddy's generation left the minute they turned eighteen for the promise of work or school in the surrounding cities. Of the few that stayed, most, like Buddy, drove every morning to a job outside the little city in order to survive.

Emil despised that kind of disloyalty. The reality of Foley's dying economy aside, he expected the kids raised in Foley Lake to remain in the city and care for the previous generation. Nevertheless, they fled, packing up in the weeks before high school graduation and leaving immediately after, aided and abetted by parents who wanted their kids to escape Foley Lake and not to look back. That fact ate at Emil, became a constant source of frustration and irritation, especially because he was helpless to stop the exodus that even included his own two sons. They'd fled not only Foley Lake but Minnesota, ending up in California and Washington state, visited by their mother every year until she became too ill to travel. But Emil never condescended to make any of those trips. And his sons, more like their father than either would ever admit, refused to step foot in Minnesota. As a result, the Kangas men had not seen each other in thirty long years. So, despite the fact that Buddy was one of the few that had stayed, Emil turned some of his impotent rage against the kid in the shiny black pickup.

The hum was growing louder. Emil cursed silently, heart pounding with exertion, his feet shuffling as fast as he could make them go. The Anderson boy was obviously speeding, judging by the high-pitched drone of the engine. Speeding through town, speeding to make it to and through the intersection before Emil arrived to step foot between the solid white lines that defined the boundary of the crosswalk. Emil lifted the walker rather than using it for balance, carrying it out in front of him, nearly running. He reached the edge of the old Woolworth's building and paused for just a second to slam the walker back down onto the concrete, his thin arms quivering from the effort of carrying it. He rounded the corner of the building and, a second later, stepped off the curb and into the city's only crosswalk.

Emil felt a deep satisfaction as he heard the sudden deceleration of the truck's engine. He kept his head bowed as he shuffled along, but out of the corner of his red-rimmed eye he could see Buddy Anderson scowling down at him from behind the genuine leather steering wheel. Buddy allowed the truck to creep up to the very edge of the crosswalk before he stopped. Emil, suddenly old and frail, didn't seem to see him. Instead, he was slowly, painstakingly making his way across the vast expanse of the crosswalk.

Shuffling along at a microscopic rate, Emil caught his breath. He heart slowed to its usual steady plod, and the morning breeze cooled the beads of sweat that had risen on his forehead. He glanced up, noting with immense satisfaction that Buddy was leaning his head on the steering wheel in a posture of utter defeat.

Just once, Buddy had driven through the crosswalk before Emil had gotten up the curb on the other side. Emil put in a call to Dave, the snot-nosed son of Foley Lake's only electrician who had grown up to be Foley Lake's only police officer. Emil carried on so long and loud that Dave finally promised to have a personal talk with Buddy, threatening him with a ticket for public endangerment if he strayed into another crosswalk while any part of Emil's frail being was still within its sacred perimeter. For his part, Buddy was willing to obey. He had no intension of taking Dave's advice about using one of the two dirt roads out of town that would allow him to avoid Emil altogether. Buddy kept his truck immaculate; it would never see a dirt road. The price he paid to keep the truck's gleam was sitting at the crosswalk for a full ten minutes while Emil tottered across. Buddy waited. With two drunk-driving charges on his record he didn't need any more trouble with the law or the DMV.

Ka-chunk.

Shuffle, shuffle.

Ka-chunk. Shuffle.

Shuffle.

The moment Emil had both feet firmly on the far curb the truck roared forward. Emil cackled under his breath. As Buddy disappeared from sight the old man picked up his pace, moving down the street with ease.

Emil knew he probably didn't need the walker anymore—it was a remnant of a mild stroke he suffered four years before. But he discovered that the moment he started using the walker, people made assumptions about his eyesight, his hearing, and the quality of his mind. The result was people were more careless with gossip when he was within earshot, more inclined toward patience and generosity, and more forgiving of his irritable and demanding nature, blaming the stroke and never seeming to recall he was at least as mean before the stroke as after.

"Good morning, Mr. Kangas."

Emil felt an icy jolt hit his heart that set it to wobbling in his narrow chest. The woman's voice was just behind him. He kept moving, hoping his failure to respond would be interpreted as senility. Instead, she caught up to him and leaned forward into his field of vision, her frizzy gray hair brushing his face.

"I said, good morning, Mr. Kangas!" She shouted this time. Emil stopped and scowled.

"Well, good morning," he snapped. He shuffled forward. Willa Magdich did not see this for a brush-off. She would take any occasion to talk to Emil. She seemed to think that just because he'd been friends with her late husband and worked on the same contract with him in the mine six decades before, she had a unique claim on his time. She was a constant visitor when Ida was still at home, stopping by with fresh baked coffee cakes and lefse, but even then Emil avoided her. Her blue eyes were unnaturally bright, and she had a peculiar habit of not blinking, a characteristic that made Emil feel like she could see into his very soul. He disliked her, but not with the disdain he felt for most. Rather, he found her presence mildly spooky, like a reminder of a very bad dream.

"How are you feeling today?" She shouted. Emil cringed. He stopped and glowered at her.

"No need to yell, Willa, I'm standing right next to you."

"Oh!" Willa beamed, smoothing her rebellious hair with her palm. "Well then, how are you?"

"I'm fine, thank you." Emil's reply was curt, but, he thought, satisfactory. He turned away and began making his way down the street again, thoroughly irritated when she fell into step with him.

"Glad to hear it, Emil," she said cheerfully. She was silent for a few moments, then chirped. "I am going out to the cemetery today to visit Peter. Would you like to come?"

Emil stopped. Willa stopped also, looking at Emil expectantly, hopefully. Emil rotated his body around to face her.

"Willa," he began. "I got a plenty good look at Peter the day I dug him out of that mine. Do you know what being buried for five months in a wet, black mine will do to a man? The only thing worse than the look is the *smell*."

Willa stepped back, ice-blue eyes wide at the sharpness of the attack. Emil shuffled forward a step to drive his point home. Willa didn't back away, though it is doubtful that it was courage that planted her feel to the spot. Emil leaned in, so that Willa could hear the faint clack of his dentures as he spoke. "If I spent my days visiting every rotting corpse that died in the Foley Mine," he muttered crudely, "I would have long since lost my mind. Not that it looks like it has done you any good."

Willa made a little "Oh!" of surprise, her icy eyes melting in dismay. Satisfied that he had made his point, but not feeling particularly glad of it, Emil turned away and shuffled on down the street, leaving a horrified Willa alone to sort and repack her emotions however she saw fit.

The sun gained altitude. It leaned down on Emil, turning the armpits of his button-down shirt damp. He gained the end of the block and looked north to the brown brick high school where he'd ruled as principal for over forty years. The building was closed now, encircled by a sagging chain link fence meant to discourage vandals. The districts started the practice of closing the smaller schools and bussing kids into the bigger, fancier schools in the nearby towns, and it was only by Emil's influence, and later, by a sheer force of his will, that Foley Lake High escaped the same fate for as long as it did. But the year after he retired the school was closed for good, and he told himself he no longer cared. He was faithful while the school was in his charge. It wasn't his fault that his successor, an inept man if ever there was one, had undone forty years of work and driven the school into the ground in a year's time. Administrating in a school was all he had known. That and mining. And after he spent four years working in the mine and another nine months helping to reclaim the bodies of his friends and coworkers—all but one—he knew he would never enter another mine as long as he lived.

Emil was gasping. The force of his memories had prodded him until he was tripping forward, chasing the walker down the street. He stopped, leaning into the hard rubber handles, catching his breath. He'd been moving so fast, caught in the memory of sights and smells no living soul should have to carry, that he didn't pay attention to where his legs were taking him. He was poised at the edge of the last sidewalk in Foley Lake's northern proper. There was nothing between him and the rusting head frame looming in the distance save a slope of ankle-high weeds. He stared up at it, felt a familiar wave of anxiety, and quashed it. It didn't matter now, anyway. There were few alive who knew, and not many who cared. But that head frame had not changed in sixty years. It loomed, visible from almost every street of the city, never letting him forget that one way or another, it would eventually come to collect his soul.

CHAPTER THIRTEEN

Lowie was completely enamored with Butch. A man who shaved all of his hair on purpose, who didn't own a car yet had been all across the country, and who was brave enough to sleep just outside the entrance to the mysterious and exotically frightening iron mine had all of the ingredients of a hero. Halfway through the first week Lane made Butch understand that when they worked, she would supply his lunch each day, a fact he accepted with simple thanks and no argument. Every afternoon Lowie's job became searching the refrigerator for whatever Lane assembled for a midday meal and delivering it to the garage. After the child ate with them, she would follow along at Butch's heel offering what help she could and asking endless questions about his travel. For his part Butch was good-natured and accommodating, regaling Lowie with tale after tale of his many adventures—his time spent with a traveling circus taking care of an aging elephant named Elvis, his months battling forest fires as a smoke jumper in California, his stint at a state mental hospital helping brain-injured patients learn to color. Lane tried shooing Lowie away from the garage, telling her to stop grilling Butch with questions, but Butch never seemed to mind, and soon Lane was listening as well. It was as if Butch had lived a hundred lifetimes to their one, having seen places most people they knew would not have been able to find on a map.

From time to time, Lane would ask a few questions of her own, gently prying. She asked about his family. He said his mother was alive, but he was furtive about his father. She asked about where he grew up and was told he moved back and forth between his parents, who divorced when he was young, and so he never really had what a person would call a hometown. She asked where he might go after he left Foley Lake. South, he said. Northern winters were just too hard on a man who liked sleeping under the stars. He didn't have a particular destination in mind but wherever he went, he would be leaving Foley Lake no later than fall.

In the mid-afternoons, Lane would send Lowie to the cafe to get some drinks, and while Butch worked silently nearby she would review his stories in her head, imagining places and people, wondering. Her husband always talked about leaving Foley Lake, about going to see how people lived elsewhere, what they did, who they were. Lane was fascinated by the idea of leaving, but she never saw it as a real possibility. For her, the idea of living anywhere else was like gazing at a beautiful painting of a landscape, something contrived that could be considered and admired but never experienced. The harder her husband pushed to leave, the harder Lane pulled back to stay, until even the glue of Lowie's infant existence wasn't enough to hold them together.

Butch asked Lane a few questions of his own, although most were less pointed than Lowie's. He asked about her school years in Foley Lake, about favorite teachers and class trips and prom. He asked about the rest of her family and grew quiet when she told him her mother was twelve years' dead of cancer and that she was an only child. But Lane noticed Butch seemed to be gathering at least as much information through observation as through questions. She realized that he watched her as she worked, not with cold appraisal or lust, but with a sort of admiration, an appreciation for her abilities that bordered on pride. She wasn't sure what to make of it, but it was so genuine and freely given she found herself enjoying his attention. Not that she was interested in him beyond the help he could provide in getting the garage sorted out. She simply appreciated his calm, self-effacing manner and his kindness toward Lowie. That is what she told herself each morning while she gazed in the bathroom mirror, studying to understand what it was he saw when he looked at her.

It didn't take long for Butch to work similar magic on Mike. The older man served as mayor of Foley Lake for more than thirty years, and Butch always seemed to know just the right questions to ask to start him talking about the city's history. Moreover, Butch didn't seem to ask out of mere politeness, but he was genuinely interested in Mike's long diatribes concerning who owned which businesses, what became of families that no longer resided in the area, and the politics of running a small town almost single-handedly for thirty years.

Butch's stories and questions had the effect of ingratiating him into the life of the Harris family, although it was Lowie's incessant nagging that led to the hiring of Butch to finish the girl's tree house. Lane had undertaken the project two summers before; however, the physical nature of her work and the needs of their household kept her busy and exhausted. The tree house had remained a work-in-progress for too long. Lowie's ninth birthday was the end of June, and she was determined to have a tree house sleep-over party. Butch agreed to take a look at the project and let them know how much he would charge to finish it.

Lane was hoping that he would agree to the work, both to take the pressure off her and because it gave her another opportunity to have Butch around. She wouldn't fully admit to herself that she found him intriguing. She hadn't spent time with any man since her husband, a result of Foley Lake's perennial famine of eligible bachelors, and she hadn't realized how much she craved male company. Besides, she told herself, it was good for Lowie to be around a man closer to the age her father would be if he was still in their lives.

Lane was mashing berries to make a pie when she glanced up through the kitchen window and saw Butch walking up the driveway. Her insides flashed heat like a burst of sparks from a candle wick, and she chided herself for the sudden warmth of her cheeks. Down the entryway hall there was a soft knock at the screen door.

"Come in," Lane called.

Lane heard the screen door open and close quietly, but Butch didn't appear. She looked down the hall and saw him standing just inside the front door, hat in hand.

"You can come in, Butch."

He stared down the hall at her, then turned back toward the door.

"Why don't I go on out to the backyard," he said. His voice sounded thick. "I want to have a look at this tree house I've been hearing about." Without another word, he disappeared back through the door.

Lane stopped mashing the berries, frowning. Through the window she watched Butch stride across the front yard and disappear around the corner of the house.

Mike walked into the kitchen and looked around. "Did I hear Butch come in?"

Lane nodded. "Yeah. But he went back out. He was going to have a look at the tree house." Lane went back to mashing berries, a small frown on her face. "You know, he seemed a little uncomfortable about coming inside."

"Well, I suppose it feels different seeing you outside of work." Lane stopped the masher in mid-stroke and gaped at her father. "What is that supposed to mean?" she asked. Her father only smiled mysteriously.

"Nothing at all. I'm just glad he found the house."

Lane went back to mashing. "All that means is that you gave him good directions."

"*I* didn't give him directions."

Lane scooped the mashed berries into a pie shell. "You didn't?"

"Of course not. He's not *my* guest."

Lane set the half-empty bowl down, frowning, and started to speak, but Lowie thundered down the stairs and burst into the kitchen, cutting her mother off completely.

"He's here! In the backyard! C'mon!" She loped across the kitchen and out the back door, letting the screen slam. Lane shook her head, quickly finished filling the pie shell, and followed Lowie and her father outside.

They found Butch standing in the backyard staring up the wooden ladder at the tree house. Lowie bounded across the yard, closing half the distance between herself and Butch when she stopped suddenly and changed direction.

"Hey! There's a dog out here!" Lowie yelled.

The ancient terrier sat on his haunches at the edge of the yard. Lowie closed the distance to the dog and fell on her knees, petting him.

"Lowie!" Lane shouted. "Get away from that dog!"

"He followed me down from the mine," Butch said. He leaned his back against the ladder and watched Lowie. The terrier was licking her chin as she pet him.

"He's yours?" Lane asked doubtfully.

"I have no idea where he came from. I caught him pilfering jerky out of my backpack the other day up at my campsite. He's so old he can't even chew it. I had to give him a hot dog instead. I didn't have the heart to run him off. I'm surprised he followed me all the way down here, though, because he can barely walk."

Butch chuckled at Lane's grimace as the ragged dog's tongue slobbered Lowie's face. "He seems gentle enough," he said. "I doubt that he'd hurt her."

Lowie lifted her face away from the licking and turned to Butch. "What's his name?" she asked.

"Hmm. I don't know. He hasn't told me yet," Butch replied.

Lowie tickled the dog's ears, cooing. "What's your name, huh, boy? Why didn't you tell Butch your name?" The dog wiggled closer to Lowie until she pulled back.

"Peeuuuu, you stink," Lowie said. She turned and looked at Butch. "Can I give him a bath?"

Butch grinned. "Be my guest."

***

Butch said he'd finish the tree house, which already had part of a floor and three walls framed in, for fifty dollars and a hot shower. Lane agreed and volunteered to add supper into the deal if Butch happened to be there in the evenings. Butch went to work, carrying an armload of wood up the ladder and cobbling together the assorted lengths and bits.

Lowie disappeared into the house for towels and scented soap and lured the old dog to a small tree. She tied him up and turned the hose on him. The poor creature shivered as

67

Lowie soaped and rinsed him three times, filling the yard with the scent of strawberry. She scrubbed him dry with a towel, then went to work with a comb, scissors, and a length of pink ribbon. By the time Lane called that supper was ready Butch managed to frame in the fourth wall and begin work on the roof. The dog was thoroughly scoured, and Lowie was stepping back to survey her handiwork. She smiled up at Butch.

"What do you think? Nice and clean, right?"

Butch bit his lip. Lowie had clipped away the matted hair in clumps and then tried to even up the leftover strands, leaving the impression that the unfortunate dog had been run down by a lawn mower. She'd chopped out crooked bangs, and snipped the hair all around his muzzle so short it stood out in bristled tufts. The terrier sat in the middle of the yard, ears and tail flat. He seemed to know that the last vestiges of his canine masculinity were rinsed away with the fruit-scented soap and the neat pink ribbon tied around his neck.

"Well," Butch managed, "he looks pretty."

Lane emerged from the house and crossed the yard to them. She was about to say something when she noticed that the sodden lawn foamed with pink bubbles. She snapped up an empty plastic bottle and wheeled around to face Lowie, her eyes flaming. "Young lady, what happened to all my strawberry bubble bath?"

***

Mike made his way into the kitchen just as Lane put a kettle of beef stew on the table. He had slipped down the hall to his office just after Butch's arrival, emerging only at the sound of Lane's call that dinner was ready. He closed and locked the office door firmly and wandered back down the hallway, with his hands stuffed in his pockets and a distracted gaze that make Lane feel a strange sense of foreboding. But he treated Butch with genuine hospitality and listened carefully to Lowie's telling how gentle the dog was, how badly it had needed a bath, and how well he took to the hose and ribbon. Lane saw to it that the girl didn't gloss over the use of a whole bottle of strawberry bubble bath, a fact that nearly cost Lowie dessert.

They debated names for the dog over pie. Lowie liked the highly inappropriate Rowdy or Tiger, while Lane favored the spiteful and equally inappropriate Bubbles. Never known for his personal creativity, Mike offered Sleepy, Dopey or Doc, and was quick to point out that any one of the dwarf's names would serve. Butch thought Stinky or Bandit was fitting. In the end no accord could be reached, so Lane opened a can of tuna for the nameless dog, who gummed the soft, oily meat and fell asleep in the shade of the porch.

After dinner, Butch accepted Mike's offer to drive him back to the mine, knowing that if he walked he would have to carry the exhausted terrier up the hill. They climbed into Mike's Buick and bounced over the mine trail in companionable silence, the dog sitting on the seat between them. Butch was surprised when Mike stopped the car where the trail narrowed and shut the engine down.

They followed the path up the hill. The dog sniffed around in the tall grass at the edge of the camp, retrieved a graying bone from its hiding place, and hobbled toward the head frame. Mike followed, watching as he slipped through the gate and settled down in his usual spot just inside the entrance. Mike stood at the gate, gazing through the small gap into the darkness behind it. When he spoke, he turned his head so Butch could hear him.

"You ever hear of the Lee Mine?" he asked.

"No," Butch replied.

"The Lee Mine was by Tower, up on the Vermillion Range. It was a good mine, lots of ore. Big, too. About 300 men worked there, most with families in the town just down the road. One night it disappeared."

"The town?"

"The mine. The whole mine. The company found out that a fur trader had filed a claim against the mineral rights on the land. He said the government gave the land to him two decades before. So, the company waited until the last shift ended, ran a train up there in the middle of the night and shipped out everything. Office, compressors, two engine houses, cars, even the rails the train wouldn't need on its way out. Everything was gone. And within a year the whole town died because there wasn't anything in the city that didn't depend on that mine." Mike fell back into silence and ambled to the edge of the clearing that looked down at the lake and the city in the distance.

Butch gathered paper and kindling from his stores just inside the burned-out frame of the old office building and set about making a bonfire, but he kept a close watch on Mike. He wasn't sure how to read the man's mood. He lit the fire and nursed the small flame until it sank into the wood and its survival was sure. The sun slipped away; dusk pressed down. Mike finally turned back and stood at the edge of the firelight.

"It's been a long time since I was up here last," he said simply.

"I can't imagine much changes up here," Butch replied.

Mike shook his head. "That's the truth. Nothing's changed. It's always the same."

Inside the mine, the dog growled. Butch and Mike both turned in the direction of the gate, then looked at each other.

"I reckon he's dreaming," Mike said.

Butch nodded. "I reckon so."

"You know, the shaft is still open," Mike noted. "It's a long drop, and half filled with water. You might want to keep an eye on him. It'd be a shame to lose him down that hole."

"I think he has the sense to stay away from the shaft itself."

Mike sighed. "I suppose you're right. Still, it'd be a shame."

The older man said his goodnight and turned back down the trail. Butch watched him go. Minutes later he heard the Buick's engine start, then fade as it descended the hill. He settled back and stared at the flame, thinking about the strangeness of grief. It's an odd thing. It hangs on a man like a second skin, clinging, becoming the medium through which the man feels every other sensation in the world. Over time it becomes a part of him, and once that happens, he doesn't recognize it as something separate from himself. It grows into him. And soon the world sees him through that gauze of pain, unable to recognize it as something unnatural, and never understanding what it costs a man to bear up under its weight.

Chapter Fourteen

Lane heard a loud knock and a soft curse come from the direction where Butch was working. The process of cleaning slowed down as they discovered more and more items too valuable to discard hidden among the worthless junk that crowded the garage's shelves. Lane told Butch that the work might stretch out awhile, given the growing nature of the garage sale. She nodded agreeably when he said he had decided to stay the whole summer in Foley Lake.

Lane walked toward the back of the garage and found Butch sitting on his heels, rubbing the back of his head.

She frowned down at him. "What happened?" she asked.

Butch scowled. "I guess I just found a mirror under this bench."

"Spooked yourself, did you?"

"Wouldn't it spook you to see a mug like mine staring at you from a dark corner?"

Lane chuckled as she walked away. Butch crawled back under the bench and gently worked the mirror free from its hiding place. It was large and oval, two feet by three-and-a-half, and once he walked it out to the garage door and wiped away some of the dust, he saw that it had a rich black walnut frame. He propped it up against the wall where the sunlight shone through the door and stood back to admire it.

"Throw it," Lane said from behind him.

He gapped. "*Throw* it? It's a beautiful old mirror. You don't just throw something like that!"

"The glass is screwed up. It's all dark. Just throw it."

"The glass is dark because it's old. It gives it character. That's what makes it so interesting to look at."

Lane sighed.

They had been having conversations like this one all week, ongoing debates over the potential value of some of the items. Generally, they were things that Lane wanted to trash, like a red Schwinn bike missing its seat and both tires, some ancient, assorted fishing tackle, and now, most likely, a mirror. Every two or three days, Lane would give Butch a ride to the mine with his latest find, and she didn't begrudge him one item. The more he took with him, the less she had to spend on tipping fees at the county landfill.

Lane liberated a sawhorse, its back broken in two, from under a tangle of old garden hose and carried it out to the dumpster. Butch was still in the driveway, the mirror forgotten, as he held up the listening end of an animated conversation with a short, stocky brunette. The brunette had a camera in one hand and a note pad in the other, a bright yellow pencil tucked behind one ear. Lane noted the mild look of shock on Butch's face as the woman pelted him with friendly conversation. After a little consideration she decided a intervention might be in order.

"Hi, Gigi," Lane said as she approached. The other woman winced.

"Uhg, Lane, please, it's Eugenia now. No one calls me Gigi anymore."

Lane sighed. "Oh, right, I keep forgetting. What brings you down here?"

Eugenia waved the camera. "Gonna do a short piece about the garage sale. Your father told me about it over at city hall just now. Great idea, just great. Out with the old, in with the new. Mind if I get a few pictures while you work?"

"Suit yourself," Lane replied. "I see you've met Mr. Brown."

Eugenia raised her eyebrows and pulled the pencil from behind her ear.

"Brown, is it? Your Mr. Brown here was reluctant to tell me his name. Seems he's the shy type. Where are you from, Mr. Brown?"

Butch shifted uncomfortably. "Out east."

Eugenia scribbled a quick note. "Hmm. Where out east?"

"Northeast. I was in Pennsylvania most recently."

"Really? And what did you do there?"

Butch shrugged. "Odd jobs."

"Interesting. Is there a Mrs. Brown?"

"Yes."

Lane was surprised by the jolt of disappointment she felt. Eugenia looked up at him with interest. "Oh?"

"She's my mother."

Eugenia rolled her eyes. Despite the humor, it was clear that Butch wasn't comfortable answering questions. Lane turned to her. "Gigi—sorry, Eugenia, I heard something people are saying around town, and I was wondering if you might be able to clear it up."

Eugenia turned to face Lane, sliding the pencil back behind her ear. "Well," she replied, "I'm not much for gossip, but if I can help you out, I will."

Lane smiled. "You know Spot Malloy, down at the car lot? Well, I heard something about his wife—"

"Sandy. Yes, it's true. She's been fooling around with some guy north of town. He works on the Larson farm and he's some years younger than she is. I hear he comes from either Fargo or Minot…"

Lane listened silently as Eugenia launched into the detailed play-by-play of Sandy's illicit affair, describing how Sandy's poor, cuckolded husband, Spot, was being made the fool and was the only person in Foley Lake wholly ignorant of his wife's activities.

Lane smiled faintly as Butch slipped away, phantom-like. Although she could hear him moving things about in the garage, he never reappeared to risk another encounter with Eugenia, and later Lane would have no memory of the reporter snapping a picture of him. That is why she was startled the next morning when a clear headshot of Butch appeared just below the fold on the front page of the paper, next to a long story about the all-city garage sale.

CHAPTER FIFTEEN

Warren stood under an ancient oak, listening. He knew no one would dare follow him. He had gained a reputation for madness, and though it was patently untrue that he was unstable, he allowed the rumors and speculation to continue. It gave him room. People left him alone. Over the last decade even his mother learned to let him be, though she craved his company and hung at the edge of his consciousness, like a small, buzzing fly.

He waited, perfectly still, as his father had taught him. No sound, save the usual workings of bird and cricket, rose from the field at the edge of the woods. Satisfied, Warren stepped deeper into the tree line and let the shadows swallow him.

He moved with remarkable stealth for a big man. He bent under low branches and side-stepped dried twigs and leaves, moving so quietly that he startled several squirrels as he passed under the forest canopy. He never took the same route to his stronghold twice in a row, so even though he had made this trip hundreds of times over the years, there was no trail leading to his destination that might give it away. His father had taught him how to be careful when he was only a boy.

When Warren reached the stand of red oak, he stopped again. The forest held a deeper quiet, the air pungent and damp. The morning paper had brought a revelation. It was a sign, and he needed to act to be sure the legacy of the Milford name remained intact. A man had to do whatever was necessary in his own defense, once he confirmed what he'd already come to believe. Something in Fool's Lake had wakened the dead. Something had disturbed a slumber long held. And it was up to him to put what did not belong in the light of God's own sun back underground.

Chapter Sixteen

Levi Johansson rolled his truck up to the bunkhouse and shut it down. The farmstead was quiet; both the main house where the Larson's lived with their brood of sons, and the bunkhouse Levi shared with two other hired hands, were dark. It was well after midnight and entirely moonless, the night in the barnyard pushed back by a single yard light that hung above the barn doors. A cloud of bugs floated around the light, and bats darted in and out of sight as they fed.

Levi reached under the driver's seat and fished out a cardboard pack hidden there. He pulled out a cigarette and replaced the pack, then stepped out of the truck, closing the door quietly. He lit the cigarette and took a long drag, ignoring a pang of guilt. Sandy didn't really like it when he smoked.

Sandy. The boy prided himself on his overt disdain for mushiness and sentimentality, but when he met Sandy he suddenly understood every love song he had ever heard. She was sweet and soft, and she was older than he was by almost ten years, a fact that he found deeply exciting. And she needed Levi. Malloy, the idiot she had married, was destined to ruin her life. That's what she had told Levi during their secret meetings in a cheap, out-of-the-way motel outside Crosby, and what she had been telling him since early spring, when he first arrived to work the summer season on the Larson farm.

Levi strolled across the barnyard, smiling to himself. What a summer it had been. He was making decent money, money he had planned to use for school to learn diesel mechanics in the fall. But now he had Sandy, and if he was going to get her away from Foley Lake, he would need every penny of the money he was earning. And getting her away from this place was a given. He would get her out of Foley Lake and set her free once and for all from the mistake she had married.

He took a final drag and crushed the cigarette out between his fingers. How he hated Spot Malloy. He hated the fact that the man shared a name with Sandy, hated the fact that he had any manner of right or claim over her. Every time he thought of Malloy looking at her, or reaching for her with those fat, white, manicured hands—he flexed his fingers into fists and kicked at a stone, sending it clattering across the yard. The very idea of the man touching her was more than he could take. He wanted to beat the pompous fool to a bloody pulp. But Sandy wouldn't let him do that. Spot, she said, didn't matter. He was less than nothing to her. She just wanted out. And she wanted Levi.

She wanted him. He would get her out of there. They had a plan.

Levi yawned and turned back across the yard to head for the bunkhouse. Five a.m. would come early. He needed some sleep.

As he crossed under the barn light, he heard a solid *thump* from somewhere above, and a small black form fell to the ground next to him. He stopped, frowning, and probed the form with the toe of his boot. A bat? He bent for a closer look. The bat lay dead at his feet, its mousy face twisted up at an impossible angle.

Levi looked up toward the light. Did that bat just fly into the barn? No way. Bats flew in drunken jerks and swooping, unpredictable angles, but they didn't run into things. Ever. They had an uncanny ability to avoid anything solid. One had found its way into the bunkhouse weeks before, and he had tried to kill it by knocking it out of the air with a shovel. It had managed to avoid his wild swings for a half-hour before Terrence Larson trapped it in a blanket and crushed it under his boot.

Levi straightened up. Out of the corner of his eye, a flash drew his attention.

In the distance, a pillar of light was leaping into the night. A column of orange and blue shot silently upward like a lightning bolt in reverse and stretched toward the sky. It pulsed once, then drew back down toward the ground and disappeared.

Levi stared at the space in the distance where the light had been. It was coming from the direction of the city, or maybe toward the north of the city, up by that old mine. Had something exploded? Maybe, but then why wasn't there any sound?

The boy shook his head and blinked, wondering if perhaps these late nights were getting to him. He turned back toward the bunkhouse.

Whoop.

A few feet further on a second bat tumbled to the ground just in front of the barn door. Levi looked back in the direction of the light. Silence fell. A sudden, overwhelming urge to be out from under that endless black canopy, with stars looking down like a million eyes, filled him and Levi ran to the bunkhouse, slipped inside, and with a mild sense of shame, locked the door behind him.

Chapter Seventeen

The first of the brown paper bags showed up the morning after the story about the garage sale ran. Lane arrived to find Butch sitting on the concrete pad next to the single bag, a look of profound amusement on his face. The bag contained a pair of men's loafers, used but clean and polished, several hand-embroidered dish towels, and an aging blender. A folded note of plain white paper was tucked inside the bag.

Lane parked the truck and walked up to the garage, and Butch pulled the note out of the bag and handed it to her. It was folded in half, Lane's name written in a lovely cursive across the front. She frowned. "What does it say?"

Butch shrugged. "I don't know. It's addressed to you."

Lane sighed and unfolded the paper, reading aloud. "Lane, the all-city garage sale is a great idea. Please add these things to the sale and use the money however you see fit. You can count on us to come the day of the sale and pick up a few items. Please greet Butch for us. Sincerely, Mayda M." Lane refolded the note.

"Mayda M. says hello," she said dryly. "I guess having your picture on the front page puts you on a first-name basis in this city."

Butch nodded. "Well, tell Mayda M. I said hello back, won't you?" he said primly. "I would tell her myself, but I have no idea who she is."

Lane rolled her eyes. "Mayda Moser. Why in the world would she think to send stuff for the sale?"

"Well, the newspaper said it was an 'all-city' garage sale, right?"

Lane thought for a moment, then her eyes widened in horror. "Mayda thinks 'all-city' means everyone in the city is supposed to contribute…oh Lord, Butch, you don't think other people will think the same thing, do you?"

***

Five hours into the workday the sun blazed down on a menagerie of bags and boxes dropped off at the door of the garage. Butch chuckled with every delivery, and with the enthusiastic greetings from a steady stream of townspeople. Lane had long ceased thinking it was funny, as all the protests she made against the stream of deliveries were dismissed as humble gratitude by the enthusiastic and generous Foley Lakers. Lane's dismay grew as she realized that she couldn't simply throw away the donations people were bringing; the items were not junk. They brought the best of their used appliances, books, winter clothes, homemade jams and pickles, and all manner of stitched, knitted, embroidered, and crocheted handiwork. By noon she had a headache from the heat and from clenching her jaw in frustration. When Butch offered to treat her to lunch at the air-conditioned diner, she readily agreed.

The diner was full. Nearly every table and booth was occupied, and all of the stools were filled. The merry hum of lunchtime chatter and the clinking of dishes and plates were punctuated by the ding of a small bell from the kitchen that signaled an order was ready. May zoomed into view, plates balanced precariously on an overloaded tray.

"May, what is this?" Lane asked. "Did a bus break down on the interstate?" May's narrow face glowed and she stopped at a nearby table, shuffling out plates like a blackjack dealer.

"I don't really know," she replied over her shoulder. "It's been like this all week. I had to call Wally back in to help. It's like folks just remembered that we're here."

Lane shook her head and moved toward one of the few empty booths in the back of the diner, sliding wearily into a seat. Butch slid in across from her and studied her as she brushed some loose hairs away from her face. She had gotten used to his scrutiny, but not the flush of heat it evoked each time.

"What?" she asked irritably.

"It must have been hard to grow up in a town where everyone knows your name."

She shrugged. "Not particularly. That's the way it's always been."

"But you couldn't have gotten away with anything. No mischief at all."

"I never wanted to get away with anything. I did what I was told."

Butch laughed. "Uh-huh. You were one of those really good, really boring kids who never broke a rule?"

In a flash, Lane's mind filled with a series of scenes—memories of walking away from the school in the middle of a school day, slipping through the pine trees that grew in clumps behind the gymnasium to avoid being spotted before she could disappear; sneaking out her bedroom window for midnight trips to Crosby for beer and a late night swim; the heavy taste of warm, humid air in Danny's back seat, the shadow cast from the moon over the Foley's head frame obscuring the car in deeper darkness. Funny to think that Lowie was conceived very near the spot where Butch slept each night.

Lane shook her head. "I didn't say *that*."

Butch grinned and leaned forward, folding his hands on the table. "Do tell."

Lane smiled, shaking her head. "You sure are interested in ancient history."

"I like stories, remember?" he replied.

Lowie appeared, a small apron wrapped twice around her waist, her hair pinned up in a miniature replica of May's loose bun. A pencil stub was tucked behind her right ear, and she held a full glass of water in each hand. She carefully set the glasses down in front of them and plucked the pencil from behind her ear, holding it to a small note pad. "Hello, folks. Can I help you today?" she asked sweetly.

"Hey, look at you!" Lane pulled Lowie into the bench with her, giving her an affectionate kiss on the cheek. "Don't you look official!"

Lowie tolerated the snuggling with a grin. "May said I could get the drinks and take some orders as long as I stay away from the kitchen. Oh, if it's okay with you," Lowie blinked up at her mother, beguiling. "Is it okay, Mom? I was still going to bring you lunch."

Lane sighed. "Having you earn a little of your own money? Yes, you need to learn how to take care of me in my old age."

Satisfied, Lowie hopped out of the booth and raised the pencil. "What'll you have?" she asked.

"A burger and fries, I guess," Lane replied.

Butch nodded. "Raw onions on mine, kiddo."

"Two burgers and fries? Easy!" Lowie trotted away, trying to replant the pencil behind her ear.

The diner door opened and closed, opened and closed. Neither Butch nor Lane, caught in a good-natured verbal wrestling match over the nature of Lane's memories, paid attention to it. It was the curious plunge in the noise level that alerted Lane to trouble, and it was Lane's sudden lunge out of the booth, yelling some indiscernible warning, that alerted Butch. He ducked instinctively, just as a man's thick fist shot out from behind him and glanced off the back of his left shoulder. Butch flew out of the seat and grabbed the man by the back of the shirt, hurling him forward across the table onto the floor. The man landed face down but sprang back to his feet and spun around with respectable agility, considering his lumberjack frame. Even crouched into a low wrestler's stance ready for another attack, it was clear that he was at least four inches taller than Butch.

"Warren!" Lane shouted at the attacker.

Patrons from all over the diner leaped from their seats, taking their plates with them, and moved back against the walls where they could watch in relative safety. Warren glared at Butch, his dark eyes flaming.

"*What are you doing in this town?*" he roared.

Butch met Warren's glare, unblinking. His answer was low, but there was no mistaking the danger in it. "Mister," he said quietly, "you don't know me."

There was silence, just the briefest of moments when the vapor of time became solid, locking the two men in an epic, invisible battle. Lane as she stepped between them.

"Warren! What is your problem?" she demanded.

Warren blinked. He slowly straightened to his full height as he stared down at her.

"Lane."

He wasn't addressing her but making a connection in his mind. His eyes narrowed at Butch. "How dare you—"

Lane glared at Warren. "How dare he *what?*" she asked sharply. More silence, thick and heavy. Lane glanced back at

Butch, who didn't take his eyes off Warren. "Do you know each other?" she asked.

"No," Butch replied.

Warren tore his glare from Butch and scanned the crowd. Most people looked away the moment he tried to catch their eye. He seemed outraged to find them there.

"Fools!" he bellowed. "You have no understanding!" The diner's patrons froze, mesmerized by the dramatic tension in the room. Warren turned back to Butch, his eyes brilliant with the passion of a zealot. He pointed a thick finger at Butch's face.

"This city is going to burn."

"That is enough!" Lane shouted. She stepped toward Warren, and though she was roughly two-thirds his size, when she clamped her hands on her hips and scowled, he dropped his arm. He loomed over her with a stern, authoritarian frown.

"I am disappointed, Lane, in the company you keep."

"You need to leave," she said firmly.

Without a word Warren turned and stalked toward the door. Lowie, cemented where she stood with a glass of water in each hand, stared up at Warren with a mixture of fear and awe. Warren saw her and paused, then turned back toward Lane.

"Lane Harris, you of all people know the dangers of living in Fool's Lake," he said. With that he stepped to the door and was gone.

The room came alive with an electric surge of chatter as diners returned to their tables. Lane collapsed into the booth and grabbed the single remaining water glass. Butch slowly slid back in across from her. He watched her hand tremble as she gulped the water.

"Is that a friend of yours?" he asked. It was meant to be a joke, a piece of gentle sarcasm to lighten the mood. Instead, Lane slapped the glass back down on the table and leaned forward, her eyes blazing.

"I was about to ask you the same thing," she said, a razor's edge in her voice. "You said you weren't from around here. How do you know Warren?"

Butch leaned back in the booth and sighed, shaking his head. "I don't know who he thinks I am, but he is no friend of mine."

Lowie stepped up to the table, her face pale under her summer tan.

"Mom?" She asked a thousand questions with that one word.

The emotion on Lane's face shifted in a blink. She turned to look at Lowie. "Everything's okay, Low. Mr. Milford is just having a bad day." Lowie searched her mother's face and Lane gazed back, all anxiety and anger safely locked inside her calm features, hidden where the child's probing eyes wouldn't see. Finally, Lowie nodded. "Okay," she said simply.

When they left a half-hour later, their food largely untouched, Lane's headache was back with a vengeance. She

ignored Butch and he, sensing her mood, chose for himself
the far reaches at the back of the garage, where he worked
among the dark remnants of the city's long forgotten past.

CHAPTER EIGHTEEN

Mike sat on the trunk of a fallen tree and lifted the shoe off his foot. He carefully peeled back his thin black sock, revealing a seeping wound. The blister had risen and burst during his protracted morning walk. The brown loafers were designed for a quiet life under an office desk rather than the rigors of overland hikes. Mike ignored the pain as long as he could, unwilling to pull his mind free from the maze of memories it had been traveling all morning, until the constant distraction of the offended skin forced him to take a look. Now that he saw the extent of the damage, putting the shoe back on was out of the question. He pulled the sock free and lowered his foot carefully onto the turf. His skin was shockingly pale, his toes gnarled in the yellowing grass. He wiggled them, letting them explore the ground, mildly amused that he had nearly forgotten the pleasing effect of summer grass on his sole.

Mike liberated his left foot from its packaging, tucking the damp socks into the toes of his shoes, and set them on the tree next to him. He stood and walked in a slow circle, experimenting with the feel of his pampered feet in the weeds, finding the sensation agreeable. He turned back to his thoughts with small, mincing steps.

The trail around the perimeter of the lake had plagued his dreams for a week. Each night he found his dream-self walking fast down the path on an overcast day, the air heavy with the threat of rain. He was a child again in those dreams, and full of boyish anxiety to find his father. His sense that an unseen threat lay just ahead was overwhelming, yet something compelled him to keep moving forward. He wanted to call out for his father, but all he would manage was a small whimper, too weak to travel beyond the canopy of thick green above his head, and even as he dreamed, he knew that he was walking the wrong direction. It was the middle of the day. He father would be at the mine. But Mike was moving westward on the trail, away from the mine, away from his father, and toward some nameless threat that lurked in the trees up ahead.

Mike woke that morning with the dream still fresh in his mind, complete with the anxious desire to see his father, though he didn't understand the feeling. He was a baby when his father died, and he had no memory of the man. The blend of anxiety and confusion grew into a restlessness that compelled him to seek out the trail. Arriving at the office early, he lied to Dorothy, telling her he had to go to Brainerd for the day on city business. He drove his car out of the city limits, doubled back on the little-used side road, and hid the sedan in a stand of poplar trees a half-mile from the mine's entrance. He sprayed himself with a heavy coating of bug spray and walked toward the lake, cut northward into the tree line, and began to search. He didn't have to look long. The trail was still visible. He had been walking it ever since.

He didn't know what he had expected. When he was a boy, the trail had been beautiful, winding along the banks of the city's namesake lake. Even then, the lake was little more than a swamp, but to Mike it was a wonder, an oasis of untamed nature rich with turtles and snails and swift, harmless snakes. Mike knew in an abstract way that the flooding of the mine by this same lake killed his father, but he held no grudge. The man was a storybook figure to him, only one more character in a tale peopled by men who seemed larger than life. Mike grew up hearing the legends about how his heroic father had sacrificed his own life to signal the miners on the surface that the mine was in trouble, and how he had tied the siren rope around his waist, his dead weight causing it to wail for hours and hours after the lake filled the shaft completely, the black water swirling. Not that it mattered—the only man to escape the flood was Emil Kangas, and he survived because he had been called to work on the surface just minutes before the mine ceiling collapsed and let the lake through. No other life was saved; no heroic rescue flowed from the wail of the emergency signal. Clinton Harris' sacrifice was for naught. Still, the people recognized the act for what it was, and Mike grew up in the warm glow of their hero worship. He never had to introduce himself to anyone. Everywhere he went his name was known. Fathers of the boys he grew up with encouraged their sons toward friendship with him; parents of the girls encouraged crushes and later, dates. His teachers sat him at the front of the class. He was the team captain for every sport he tried. He was chosen homecoming king.

So, though he grew up fatherless, Mike felt no real loss, surrounded as he was by friends and family members who doted on him. He didn't feel any connection to his father as a man or as a parent. It was the stories that Mike connected to. Workers had spent most of a year digging out the bodies of the dead miners, and when they found Clinton, it was said that he was entombed in mud, upright at the foot of the ladder inside the shaft, rope tied about his waist. That was hard fact attested to by the mine's own records. But the real story existed off the record. It was said that three times the men digging Clinton free fled the mine, spilling out of the cage at the surface in terror, demanding to know why the emergency siren had been pulled. Each time they were told that no emergency had been raised. They were told they were hearing things and sent back down to finish retrieving the body of Clinton Harris. The story went on that they wouldn't be down for more than an hour or two before the cage would reemerge on the surface, vomiting white-faced miners trembling into the November sun. The whistle, they insisted, someone pulled the whistle. The captain tried to reason with the men, reminding them that the whistle was still disconnected, but by the end of the day those men left the mine, and Foley Lake, altogether. The captain blamed their odd delusion on fatigue and stress, and the next day he assembled a new team to finish extricating Clinton Harris from the belly of the Foley. By then the legend had taken root, and Mike Harris grew up hearing, and telling, campfire ghost stories about his own father's haunting of the mine.

A sharp prick jarred Mike out of his musing, and he leaned against an oak to pull a thorn out of his soft heel. He had been following the trail as it sloped upward, skirting the edge of a tall hill that rose sharply on the trail's right side, an odd upward surge of the land that was the result of waste rock from the mine piled high and left to settle. When he was a boy the slag was small and loose, having collected little topsoil, so it's only vegetation consisted of clumps of hardy crabgrass and the ever-present poplars clinging tenaciously to life. But in the fifty or so years since then, annual cycles of dying vegetation had worked into a layer of compost, richly covered by red sumac. Mike gazed up the hill's steep slope, wondering at the ache of excitement it aroused in him. There was a spot, he knew, at the top of the hill, where the slag was firm and level, as if it were pressed flat by the palm of a massive hand. As a boy Mike had pushed some of that rock into a heap on the top of that summit, fashioning for himself a throne, and he passed many hours on that seat presiding over the city and the mine. Now he studied the hill, wondering if being sixty and barefoot could keep him from its summit. He decided to try the slope.

He struggled upward, using the stems of sturdy sumac for handholds, earning bruises and cuts on his too-tender feet, and glancing back once in a while to find that the passage of time and the onset of adulthood had not lessened the thrill of scaling what still seemed to him to be a great height. It took a full twenty minutes to reach the hill's rounded summit, which included a few stops wherein Mike stood with his hand on his aching back while the other clung to a branch, his gray hair standing at wild angles like an aging billy goat.

He achieved the summit with a breathless thrill and craned his neck to see the city on the other side. The trees had grown tall along the top of the hill, hiding the view. Crossing the summit from end to end was a walk of less than two minutes, even with the tangles of vegetation he had to push through. The sumac was hip deep and grew everywhere; the hill was capped with red and green that suddenly fell away on the far side like a waterfall.

The entire city lay at his feet, its street's neat lines running in perpendicular rows, one to the next. It was almost a half-mile away, but he could make out the stores and houses easily. He could even see the mailboxes on the street corners, small squares of blue. He turned and walked along the edge of the summit, mindful of how quickly it dropped away, and the lake appeared below him. He could see down into the tangle of weeds growing just below the surface. Mike lifted his eyes and scanned the horizon, miles of yellow and green, and a rush of memories from his boyhood flowed through his mind. He loved this spot. It had served as a touchstone for him, that place where he could stand and overlook the entire city and know that every person and every thing he had treasured most in the world was within his vision. He felt a deep yearning for the days when his life had been so manageable he could take it all in just by standing in one place. He had always meant to show it to Paul, when the boy got a little bigger. The chance never came. The child was gone too soon.

He turned around and crossed back along the hilltop. The mine's head frame stood high in the distance, and the ground falling away between the two hills gave the impression that Mike and the shaft were separated by a great gulf. Mike turned his back to it and began to search.

He couldn't find it. The rounded mound he had built by piling slag years before was gone, though in his mind he felt like it should have been too large to be defeated by the onslaught of time. Realistically, he knew the mound was only four feet square near the edge of the slag hill that overlooked the city—unless—was that it? Mike chuckled as he squatted stiffly and raked away some of the grass with his fingers, then slowly lowered himself to the mound, body arguing with the effort it took to bend. The sumac on the hillside in front of him was high; he could barely see over it when he sat. He shifted around, trying to get comfortable. It was impossible to sit upright with his knees at the ninety-degree angle—his legs had grown far too long. Instead, he stretched out. His back sent little shots of pain radiating up his spine, like something in there was spurring a nerve. As he settled in the pains quieted. A light breeze pushed at the leaves around him and made a sound like a soft purr. The sun was beginning to wane; everything below him softened and turned golden.

He reached into his pocket and pulled out the small cloth handkerchief Lowie had given him as a Father's Day gift two years before, soft cotton with his initials carefully stitched in one corner with her childish hand. She was turning nine soon, the same age Lane had been when they lost Paul. He wiped his brow and replaced the handkerchief. Time was so funny. He hadn't felt its passing. Still, it went. He sighed, rubbing the palms of his hands over his aching thighs. His body was getting old. He didn't know what to make of it. He was shocked, sometimes, when he looked in the mirror and saw the aged face, alien and weary, staring back at him. He was trapped in a strange old man's body. Inside, he was still a young father who wanted to give his own son the world. Inside, he was still the boy that scooped worthless rock into a throne.

Chapter Ninteen

Lane smiled through the screen door. In the backyard she could see Lowie embark on an energetic and utterly futile quest to teach Butch's stray how to fetch. Lowie playfully bounced a tennis ball on the ground, and Bones—the name Butch gave the dog because of his propensity for finding old, graying bones and carrying them back to the mine—wagged his ragged tail with interest. But when Lowie gently lobbed the ball across the grass and ran after it with enthusiastic shouts of "C'mon, boy! C'mon, Bones, get the ball!" the mutt watched the ball bounce on the turf, looked at Lowie curiously, and sat down. Lowie tried every trick she could think of to make the game enticing, throwing the ball over and over, only to end up retrieving it herself.

The ball rolled to where Butch worked at a set of wooden sawhorses, pounding old nails out of boards he found in the city garage to use for the tree house. Butch bent and picked the ball up, tossing it to Lowie. She caught it handily and threw it back. In seconds Bones' lesson on fetching became a game of catch under the waning summer sun.

Lane watched, wringing the dish towel lightly. Mike glanced up from his paper and looked at her. "What?" he asked.

"Do you ever wonder about him, Dad?"

"Wonder about who?"

"Butch. Who he is. Where he came from before this. Why he's here. You know, he never tells us anything about himself."

Mike went back to scanning his paper. "I thought you said he talks about himself all the time. He's sure told Lowie enough stories."

Lane stepped back to the sink and lifted a dish out of the drying rack. She swiped with the towel thoughtfully and stacked it with the others on the shelf. "He's told us about some of what he's done, not who he is. I mean, where did he really come from? Does he have a family? And where he's going after this? I mean, what are his intentions? He talks a lot, but he doesn't say anything specific."

Mike looked at Lane, a good-natured smirk on his face. "Could you be wondering about his eligibility?"

"Oh, *please.*" Lane snorted. Mike's eyes twinkled mischievously, and he raised his brushy eyebrows, bouncing them up and down. Lane shook her head irritably and turned away from her father's teasing. "I was just making a point."

Mike folded the paper and laid it on the table. "I am just making a point myself."

Lane kept her back to him. "Which is?"

"Which is how much you need to know about the man has everything to do with *your* intentions. If you just plan to be friends, and you expect to see him go in a month or two when the weather turns, then you already know enough. He must have reasons for not saying more, and maybe that tells you everything you need to know." Mike stood, stretched, and moved to the back door. He watched Butch and Lowie tossing the ball back and forth while the terrier slept under the sawhorses. "Either way, my dear, a man has the right to keep his own counsel." With that Mike stepped out and let the door slip closed behind him.

Lane leaned against the counter, thinking. Lowie's girlish giggles and Butch's deep, resonant laughter floated in through the screen. An image flashed before her, Warren's blazing eyes. Slowly, Lane turned and put the towel down. She pulled the top drawer nearest her open and lifted out the phone book. Feeling vaguely like a traitor, she opened the book and began turning pages.

Chapter Twenty

Butch sprayed clean water from the hose over an array of old tools, each deemed worthy of saving for the garage sale. Lane had been gone all day, mowing somewhere in the city, and Butch was enjoying the quiet of working alone. He was so lost in thought that he didn't hear Mike's approach until the man was only a few feet from him in the driveway, holding a familiar brown paper bag. Butch released his hold on the sprayer and nodded a greeting to Mike.

"Hello, Mayor. What brings you down here?"

"Well, son," came the good-natured reply. "Sometimes a man volunteers, and sometimes he gets drafted." Mike handed over the bag. "I believe it's a cheeseburger. With onions, by the smell. Lowie says to tell you hi, and that she got busy helping at the cafe so she couldn't bring this herself."

Butch chuckled as he took the bag. "Good of her not to forget," he said. He laid the hose aside and took a seat on an upturned box.

Mike bent and inspected the tools. "There are some nice things here. Useful. Did you find all of this stuff in that garage?"

"Yessir. There's a lot of good stuff in there. Lane would have me throwing the whole works, but there's nothing wrong with most of it that a little soap and water can't fix."

"Well, I reckon that's true with a lot of things. Stuff gets a little messy and folks just want to give up on it."

Butch regarded Mike thoughtfully. The older man's face sagged, his skin newly loosened by weight loss and lack of sleep.

There was a soft rustling at the edge of the garage and the ancient dog emerged from the shade, toddling to Mike, lifting his ruined back end with each step. Mike pulled up a crate and sat on it. "Well, look at this. Followed you down from the mine, huh?"

"I don't know how he does it," Butch said with a shrug. "I wake up in the morning and he's nowhere to be seen. But not an hour after I start working, he shows up. Hard to believe he can make it down the hill with that bum hip."

Mike reached one hand out, and the terrier trundled closer and sat in front of him, thumping his tail on the pavement as Mike rubbed his ears.

"How old do you suppose this dog is?" Mike asked.

Butch chuckled, unwrapping the cheeseburger. "No way to know. As old as it takes to get bad eyesight and worse hips, I guess. Nothing wrong with his hearing, though. He hears everything." Butch gestured with the burger. "I appreciate you bringing this by. You didn't need to come all the way down here."

"I was out walking anyway," Mike said. "Not much happening at city hall right now, and no sense sitting there doing nothing. A little city like Foley Lake doesn't like too much handling."

"I guess not. I reckon a city can just about run itself, as long as there aren't any surprises."

Mike's jaw clenched. "Surprises?"

"Yeah. You know, change throws people off. They cling to the past. I reckon that's how this building ended up so full."

Mike studied Butch, then nodded and looked away with a sigh. He nudged an old sand shovel with the toe of his shoe. "Had anyone told you about the mine you sleep in front of?"

"No sir. Don't believe that has ever come up in conversation."

"That old mine was the heart and soul of this city for more than two generations," Mike began. "Best iron ore in the world came from the Foley. There's manganese in it. Makes the ore burn hotter, which makes the metal stronger. That's why it was so valuable. The mine opened and the mine company built some roads and houses for workers to live in. Workers brought their families, and they built schools, stores, churches, you name it. Did you know that the high school here was the most expensive school in the world when it was built? In the world! Cost four million dollars, all of it paid for by property taxes the city got from the mine. Now you can barely build a gymnasium for that, but back then, it was a lot of money. The mine put Foley Lake on the map. It was a boom town, like the old gold mine cities."

"My great-grandfather moved here to farm, but he ended up in the mines. He came from England. Most of the people here are from all over Europe and the Scandinavian countries. The mine companies would recruit immigrants to come, just to keep cheap labor. Not that it was a bad thing since most of the people who came from other countries had it better here than they had ever had it before. But it was dangerous work."

Butch fiddled with the burger cooling in his hand. "Especially if you happened to work in the Foley?"

Mike sighed. "Yeah. I guess you have heard a few things. Forty-eight men were in the mine the day it flooded. Forty-eight, and every one of them drowned."

The old man turned and gazed down the street. Butch watched him, searching, aching that so little remained of the confident leader, the young father. Bones lay on the concrete in front of Mike and dozed off with his chin resting on his shoe. Mike shifted in his seat, careful not to disturb the sleeping dog.

"My father died down there. He wasn't supposed to be working that day. He was there because someone else called in sick, and he died at the very bottom of the mine. All those men. It took them nine months to get the bodies out. They had to try to pump the lake dry before they could pump the mine out, and then they had to go in with shovels and take out the mud that had filled up the drifts, digging out one wheelbarrow load at a time. They got it cleaned out, but something was wrong. Maybe it was the lake, or the pumps. They were never able to keep it dry. If the pumps weren't going full capacity every minute of the day, it refilled with water. Nine months to get forty-seven bodies. They never did find John Milford. You know his grandson, I believe."

"We've met," Butch said dryly.

"So you have. The war had kept demand for the iron high. The war ended, and so did the demand. The mine company shut off the pumps and walked away. Now the people here say the mine is bad luck, that it's cursed or what have you. They remember the bad things and forget that the work and security the mine gave their fathers and grandfathers are the reason any of them are here at all. They don't want anything done up there, no changes made. The head frame should have been leveled years ago, and the shaft itself sealed. But they won't have it." Mike chuckled, a humorless sound. "Not exactly a progressive bunch."

"I suppose they get comfort from the familiar."

"Yep. You said a mouthful there."

They sat in quiet, each man's mind sorting through thoughts and images. Finally, it was Mike that broke the silence when he stood.

"There is another reason that I came down, Butch." Butch looked at him expectantly, so Mike took a big breath and began.

"There's been some talk around town about you and Lane. Folks seem to think there's, well, a relationship starting between you."

Butch gaped. Mike shifted uncomfortably. He had never been good at this "concerned father" business. Louise had always been the one to interfere when interference was needed. Mike rubbed the back of his neck and sighed, a defeated sound.

"Look, Butch, I don't have a problem if you are interested in Lane. And God knows she has never given me leave to take a stance anyway. But I hear your plans are to leave Foley Lake in a few months, and if that's still true, then I guess I would just ask you to be careful giving folks reason to say too much. You might be passing through, but Lane, she's still got to live here. Does that make sense?"

Butch nodded.

Good Lord, could this be more awkward? Mike thought. He stood and turned to leave.

"Mike."

Mike turned back, and as he did, he couldn't help feel a flash of amusement about the redness in Butch's face. "I wouldn't hurt her," Butch said. "I never—I mean, I'm not sure what would give anyone reason to talk."

Mike grinned. "This is a small town, son. People don't need much of a reason."

Mike left without another word, and Butch watched him go, wondering at the fact that a father would still feel obligated to protect the reputation of a grown daughter. But never having had a child, Butch could do no more than imagine what such obligations would feel like. He took a bite of the cold burger, relishing the snap of fresh onion. An image of Lowie flashed in his mind. She sure was a sweet kid. She was the very picture of her mother, except for those green eyes. Lane's were hazel brown. But Lowie would be pretty when she grew up. Not beautiful, but pretty, like her mom. After all, Lane looked just like that when she was a girl.

Butch's stomach flip-flopped and suddenly the burger turned thick and dry in his mouth. He spit it into his hand and gagged. The terrier stood and looked at him, alarmed. Catching his breath, Butch tossed the remains of the burger to the dog as he tried to regain control. He stood suddenly and snatched up the hose. He turned the sprayer on and bent forward to drink, swallowing big gulps of the water, then took off his cap and turned the hose to spray his bald head. The cold of it made his breath come in small gasps. *Enough,* he told himself. *No more of this. It's obscene to think about her in any way beyond friendship. People are talking. Time to get a grip. Time to get the job done.*

Chapter Twenty-One

The hammer hovered midair, trembling. Lowie held it aloft with both hands, her face tight with tension, as she stared at the nail eight inches below the hammer's quivering head. The wood all around the nail was pocked with nickel-sized dents from misdirected whacks, and two nails bent beyond salvation lay discarded in the corner. One of Lowie's fingers throbbed dully from an attempt to hold the nail with one hand and hammer with the other. Now Butch was holding the nail near its tip, keeping it upright on the tree house's last loose floorboard.

"I don't like you holding it," Lowie said. "I might hit your hand."

"Let me worry about my hand," Butch assured her. "You worry about the nail. You don't need to slam the hammer down. Don't force it. Just let it fall." Lowie nodded, but lifted the hammer and held it a few inches higher. She stared at the nail.

Butch chuckled. "You're holding your breath. Let it go. And let the hammer go. It wants to hit the nail, just let it do its job." Lowie nodded again, hesitated, then blinked. She exhaled. In a flash the hammer dropped and hit home, the nail slipping halfway into the wood. Butch, both hands intact, rocked back on his knees and nodded approvingly. She dropped the hammer three more times to drive the nail home.

"That's it," he said simply. Lowie looked at the hammer with new respect and laid it carefully aside. She sat back on her haunches, arms wrapped around her knees. "This is the best tree house I have ever seen," she said.

"It's a good one, and I have seen a few," Butch agreed, gathering tools.

"It's better than what my mom could have done, I think."

Butch scratched his head thoughtfully. "Well, now, I wouldn't be so sure. Your mom is about as handy as they come. What she lacks is time, not ability."

"I guess. She says it's hard to be the mom and the dad."

"I imagine that's true. Hand me that little saw, will you?"

Lowie picked up the saw and handed it over. Butch gave her a wink. "I know what it's like to have one parent, Low. My folks were divorced when I was just a little older than you are. I didn't get to see my dad much either."

The girl shrugged. "I don't remember mine. I was a baby when he died."

Butch slowly lowered the lid of the toolbox and snapped it shut. "Is that right?" he asked.

"Yeah. Not even a year old. I don't remember him. Mom says you can't miss what you never had."

Butch nodded, thinking. "I'm not so sure about that. Seems like I miss a lot of things I never had."

Lowie tilted her chin toward him curiously. He shook his head before she could ask.

"It's too hot today to talk about old pains. I need to cool off. I'm going to go for a swim."

Lowie's eyes widened. "Do you mean at the mine?"

"Sure," Butch replied.

"But my mom says it's a bad place to swim. A lot of people have drowned there."

Butch chuckled. "Does that make it a bad place to swim," he asked, "or does that just mean some people are bad swimmers?"

Lowie scrunched up her brow, thinking. "You have a point," she said finally.

"Well, then," Butch responded, standing and stretching his back. "Would you like to accompany me to the mine for a swim?"

"I'm not allowed."

"You're not allowed to the mine, or you're not allowed to swim?"

"Both."

"Hmm. That is a problem. However, I don't see it as insurmountable."

The scrunch pulled at Lowie's features. "In-what?"

Butch chuckled. "It means we'll find a way to get you swimming," he said. "But first, we have one piece of official tree house business to take care of. Every new house needs a housewarming gift. And I have the perfect thing." He stood and fetched a soft, bulky package wrapped in brown paper from the corner of the tree house and presented it to Lowie with a flourish. Lowie giggled and took the package, unceremoniously ripped the paper off. Her eyes widened and the paper fell to the tree house floor.

"Oh, *cool.*"

From below the tree house Lane's voice drifted up. "Butch?"

"Up here."

"Can you come down?" Butch and Lowie looked at each other. Something in Lane's voice dampened their mood. Butch winked at Lowie. "You best stay here a minute." Lowie nodded.

Lane moved back toward the house as Butch descended the ladder and stood with her arms folded loosely over her chest as if to ward off a chill. Butch stepped to her and waited. A good deal of the trust she had given him disappeared after the fight at the diner, and he couldn't tell if their budding friendship would weather the blow.

"Marlys Milford died this morning," she said flatly.

"Who?"

"Warren's mother."

Butch frowned. "Wow. I didn't know she was sick."

"She wasn't, as far as I know. It was suicide, I guess. She cut her wrists in her bathtub. Warren said he stepped out early this morning and when he came back, he found her dead."

Butch's face hardened. "Well, isn't that convenient." Lane stiffened and turned to face him.

"Don't start," she said coolly. "I don't know what the problem is between you two, but I've known Warren my whole life. He isn't a murderer, and he certainly wouldn't kill his own mother."

Butch sighed and stared out over the yard. Lane shifted uncomfortably. "I could use your help for the funeral. We need to block off parking at the church and close a couple of streets to help move traffic through during the procession to the cemetery. There will be a lot of people."

Butch nodded slowly. "Can do. But I didn't get the impression the Milfords had that many friends."

Lane turned to move back toward the house, speaking over her shoulder.

"They don't. The whole town will come to the funeral, though. They wouldn't want to miss the potluck."

Chapter Twenty-Two

The funeral was indeed well attended. Not only were there mounds of potluck dishes to choose from, but there was a mountain of curiosity about why and how Marlys Milford arranged for her own demise. Rumors were whispered from pew to pew that Marlys had a drinking problem and had killed herself in a fit of alcoholic depression, or that she was tormented into suicide by unrelenting and terrifying visits from her dead husband. Most unlikely was the rumor that Marlys had a secret lover no one had ever seen, and the mysterious man had spurned her and caused her to seek solace in death. Warren remained silent, and as he had already made it clear to both Dave and the funeral director that he did not want the issue discussed, the entire city was left in a tense, delicious state of unsatisfied curiosity. One thing that everyone could agree on was that Marlys had never looked lovelier than she did in her casket, clad in the light blue brocade dress that Warren had chosen for her, her wiry gray hair tastefully pulled into a soft bun at the top of her head.

Butch made a point of staying out of sight. He dutifully helped Lane move traffic barriers into place to route the sparse, non-funeral traffic away from the church and cemetery, but when he wasn't needed, he melted into the trees behind the church and watched the goings-on from a distance. He noticed that Lane had worn appropriate funeral clothes, but she didn't go into the church. Instead, she stood outside next to the hearse, hands folded, eyes red. She wouldn't look Butch in the eye. He, she was certain, wouldn't understand why she felt the need to weep when a mother—any mother—died before her time.

The funeral was a short affair, with the pastor reading the obituary and talking in the most broad and general terms about what a good, albeit troubled, woman Marlys was. He drew the service out as long as he could, but within half an hour had repeated himself several times. He offered to let anyone who had something to say about Marlys come forward and speak, looking at Warren hopefully. Warren returned his look with a cool, even gaze. The pastor cleared his throat, sighed, and quickly gave a benediction. The graveside service was even shorter, with the pastor making a few half-hearted attempts at extolling Marlys' virtues before committing her to the hereafter.

At the cemetery, Butch took up a post next to the short, sturdy maintenance shed. He leaned against the building and watched Warren's face as people lined up and moved slowly past the casket at the end of the service. Warren was surprisingly tolerant of the handshakes and muttered condolences, and the usual hesitation to get within his reach seemed to be overridden by a communal desire to comfort the affliction of one of their own.

Lane lingered by the hearse until most of the crowd headed back to the church for the luncheon. She approached the casket and paused, one hand resting gently on the polished wood, then, stepping toward Warren, reached out and caught him in a hug. Butch could see the flash of confusion on Warren's face, then a softening of features and a boyish look of pleasure.

Butch felt a sickening flush well up from his belly and fill his face with heat. Lane backed away from Warren and grasped his hand, saying something as Warren stooped to listen. Finally, he nodded and she released his hand, then smiled up at him before turning away. She moved up the road to where her truck was waiting. Butch's pulse thudded as his old enemy gazed after Lane, watching her go, before he took a final glance at his mother's coffin and walked away.

Chapter Twenty-Three

"Oh, you have *got* to be kidding me."

Lane slowed the truck to a stop. Both sides of the streets leading to the city garage were lined with cars. It was not yet seven in the morning and the sidewalk that fronted the city garage was peppered with people of all ages, shapes, and sizes, clad in shorts and t-shirts and tennis shoes, faces scrubbed and ready to shop. All heads turned as they rounded the corner, a small cheer erupting at the sight of Lane's familiar green truck.

Butch chuckled. Tensions between he and Lane had slowly eased in the week since the funeral, and most of their former camaraderie had returned. She had fallen into the habit of picking him up on the road as he walked to the garage, a good sign, he thought, though he still sensed a loss of trust in her. Her genuine astonishment at the garage sale crowd was the first unguarded emotion he had seen in her since the day of the fist fight at the diner.

"You have got to be kidding me!" Lane repeated, more forcefully this time.

Butch grinned and waved at the crowd. They cheered again and he laughed out loud. "These must be all the people you said wouldn't show up, right?"

Lane shook her head as she eased off the brake and nudged her way up the concrete pad as the crowd parted to make room for her. When she stepped out of the truck a light applause started, then a ripple of laughter. She grinned self-consciously, unlocking the padlock and pulling the door open quickly, as if she had purposely kept them waiting rather than being the victim of an early morning invasion.

The moment the doors opened people flooded into the garage and fanned out, surrounding the numerous tables Lane and Butch had set up in the days before the sale. Whatever friendly conversation had sprung up on the lawn outside of the building came to an abrupt halt as the townspeople got down to the business of hunting for bargains. Lane set a small metal box on the card table she planned to use as a checkout stand and opened it, wondering if the neat stacks of ones, fives, and tens would be enough change after all. Butch stood by to answer questions and to handle heavy items that needed loading. Lane slipped away for a moment, and soon the light, breezy sound of a polka danced through the garage. The shoppers lifted their heads at the sound of the music as Lane reappeared. She shrugged.

"It's the only station that will come in."

The lively, old-timey tunes inspired a new surge of friendly chatter. Within minutes, Lane was taking money and making change as citizens lined up to pay for their finds. More than once the ladies of the town asked Lane how things were going, giving Butch a meaningful sideways glance. Although Lane pretended she didn't catch their meaning, they saw the soft blush of her cheeks and nodded approvingly.

The morning unfolded into a supple June afternoon. After the initial surge of shoppers, the pace eased and folks gathered in small groups scattered here and there, exchanging greetings and good-natured gossip, showing off purchases, lingering. A few of the men helped Butch move tables out onto the yard in front of the garage, the ebb and flow of foot traffic as easy as the breeze that ruffled the corners of hand-sewn linens and the edges of simple cotton skirts. Lane watched Butch move comfortably through the gathering as shoppers greeted him by name, his brief appearance on the front page of the paper making him something of a celebrity. His manner was soft and even, never rushing, never hesitating. *He fits here,* Lane told herself. *That's what it is. He belongs. How is that possible?*

As the day waned, an odd, rhythmic *cunk-chunk* floated in through the open garage door.

"Lane!" A man's voice demanded. Lane jumped, dropping coins that rolled in several directions across the concrete. Framed by his walker, Emil's diminutive form cast a long shadow.

"Lane!"

Many of the shoppers moved around to the back side of the tables, putting the furniture between themselves and the old man. Conversation died, but folks went on with their browsing, peaking at Lane seated behind the change table and Emil standing over her.

"What can I do for you, Mr. Kangas?" Butch detected the same tension and—was that fear?—in Lane that seemed to have infected the rest of the crowd. He found it fascinating that a woman who would stand toe-to-toe with Warren Milford would be intimidated by the bent form leaning against the walker for support.

"Young lady, what is your father up to?" Emil demanded. Lane shook her head in confusion, and she shoved a rumpled flier at her. She scanned it, frowning.

"I don't know anything about this, Mr.—"

Emil was like a weasel waiting to seize and shake every word. "You! Don't! Know!" he repeated, snatching the flier back. "These fliers are being posted all over town like Christmas decorations, and you mean to tell me that you and your father live in the same household, and you don't know why he would call a special meeting?"

May, a bundle of small garden tools in one arm, raised her eyebrows and gave Lane a questioning look. "What meeting?" No one was pretending to shop anymore. All eyes were on Lane, the warble of the polka music in the background the only sound.

Lane shrugged. "The flier says there's a town meeting at the city hall tonight at seven o'clock."

Avis stepped forward. "I didn't hear of any town meeting tonight. I should know, Willie's on the council."

"I don't know what to tell you," Lane said. "It just says there's an informational meeting. City business, I imagine. He didn't say anything about it to me." Emil smacked his walker on the concrete, reminding Lane he was still awaiting an answer. She scowled. "Why don't you go and ask him directly?"

"I would, young lady," he snapped. "But Dorothy tells me he stepped out and won't be back until the meeting tonight—"

"Well, then I guess you will have to wait until tonight to find out, just like everyone else," Lane replied evenly.

Emil opened his mouth to say something else, but snapped it shut, his dentures making a hollow sound. With a sudden and surprising about-face, he *cunk-chunked* his way in double-time, back out of the garage and down the sidewalk.

The crowd watched him go before it broke into a buzz of conversation. Butch stepped to Lane's side. "Who is that guy?" he asked.

"Emil Kangus. He was the principal here for something like a thousand years. He was a holy terror then, too. I still have nightmares."

Butch nodded toward the flier. "What's this about?"

Lane was still frowning, watching the crowd. "I have no idea," she said quietly, so only Butch could hear. "My father knows the sale was today. I'd bet he decided on having a meeting tonight because he's got some news he doesn't really want to deliver, and he's hoping people will be too distracted or too tired to bother with a meeting."

Butch frowned. "You think so? He had to know everyone being in one place would mean any word about it would travel fast."

Lane shook her head. "If he wanted to get people there, he would have come down here himself and handed out fliers. No, he was hoping they wouldn't notice. Something's up." Some of the groups began to thin out as shoppers moved off down the sidewalks, chattering about the meeting.

"We'll wrap up early tonight, even if we have to chase people out of here. I don't know what's going on, but I don't want to miss this."

Butch shrugged. "Whatever you say, boss."

Chapter Twenty-Four

The atmosphere at the city hall was so ripe with anticipation and curiosity it was almost festive. An hour before the meeting was scheduled to begin crowds left the garage sale, many going directly to the courthouse and filling the lines of folding chairs that Mike and Dorothy had crammed into the meeting room. By the time Lane arrived with Lowie in tow at quarter of the hour even the front seats were full and citizens were jockeying for good positions along the walls around the room's perimeter. Lane, exhausted from being on her feet all day, was irritated when she realized she would have to stand.

Dorothy was milling through the crowd with a tray of homemade cookies, and plastic cups of red Kool Aid were everywhere. Mike was at the raised table at the front of the room, shuffling papers. His shirt bore dark, damp circles under his arms, his hair in the wiry fray that was becoming a habit. He glanced up at the wall clock and quickly scanned the crowd. He spotted Lane, giving her a nervous smile and a nod. She returned the greeting with a questioning frown, and he turned away.

The excited hum of small talk taking place all around her told her that no one else in the room knew any more than she did about the nature of the meeting. Lane was mildly nervous and peeved at being left out of the loop. She found a section of wall to prop herself against and folded her arms, waiting. Lowie leaned against her with a sigh.

Across the room Butch slipped in and found a spot just inside the door. Lowie waved at him and he nodded back to her, but made no move to get closer to them.

Mike took his seat at the head of the table as other council members made their way through the crowd to their seats. Mike smacked his gavel, and the room fell silent. Unnerved by the plummeting of the noise level, Mike looked around the room for a few moments, his mouth hanging open, then cleared his throat before he began.

"This isn't a regular council meeting, as you all know, so we won't bother with the formalities. Except, of course, to thank Dorothy and the Lutheran Ladies League for the refreshments they provided tonight."

Dorothy stood up, curtsying, her broad face beaming. The crowd obliged with polite applause. She sat back in her chair, flush with pleasure. In seconds the room was silent again, and Mike looked out over the faces. He rubbed his forehead fitfully.

"Well, we might as well just get to it." He picked up a bound ream of paper and held it up. "This is a series of requests, evaluations, and permits issued to the Shanghai Mining Company. They have purchased the Foley mine, with all its mineral rights, and a few days ago I got word that they have decided they are planning to reopen it as soon as possible."

The room enjoyed a few seconds of stunned silence before pandemonium kicked in.

"Reopen the…"

"Mine! That's not possible, is it?"

"…not safe! Too many people have died there, that place…"

"…the money! This will bring jobs, we need…"

"…Shanghi? I've never heard of…"

Sound rolled over the room like a wave, surging forward, rebounding off the far wall, washing back. Mike rapped his gavel impotently. Lane was speechless, and Lowie looked around in wonder at the adults suddenly coming undone.

"Mike!" The shout was so loud and pointed that the room quieted and all eyes turned to Emil. He stood in the middle of the room, walker overturned and eyes ablaze. He pointed a bony finger at Mike.

"Young man, you know good and well that the mine can never be reopened. And you, above all people, know why!" Several voices called out their assent.

Mike sighed. "It's done, Emil. The company is from China. They want the iron ore. They're building like crazy over there."

"Foreigners!" Emil wailed. "They sold us off to the Commies!"

There was a collective howl of rage from most of the gray heads in the room. Mike banged the gavel again. "Settle down!" he bellowed. "They are not selling us off to the Commies. It's a commercial venture, a legal one. This is not bad news, folks. Foley Lake is a mining town. Always has been. The mine is what founded this city."

The crowd quieted, considering. Mike pressed the advantage the lull gave him. "They are planning to operate the mine as an open pit. It will be safer than the underground mine was. Another thing. They have agreed to give hiring preference to the people living in Foley Lake."

Bob Limming popped up from his place near the heat register. "Mike, how long have you known about this? I ain't heard a word about it. How come you haven't brought this up?"

"Confidentiality, Bobby," Mike said simply. "A company has the right to keep things quiet, and that's what they chose to do."

Chuck Larson stood near the back of the room and doffed his aging John Deere cap. "I don't know what you all are so upset about. I think this is great news. I have five boys who are gonna need jobs if they want to stay in this area, and Lord knows they won't make it farming. If the mine is hiring, maybe they can stay."

Mike nodded enthusiastically. "See that? That's just what I'm talking about. Jobs. A chance for the families who want to stay here."

"They can't just come in and do this!" Emil insisted. Lowie stared at him, fascinated by the bulging veins at the sides of his neck. "No one can decide what's best for us and make changes without telling. I say we put it to a vote!"

The noise level swelled as people shouted their assent. Mike slammed the gavel so hard that the head flew off and sailed across the room, smacking the face of the clock hanging on the wall twenty feet away. All eyes turned back to Mike and silence fell. He looked at the gavel's stem in shock, then gently laid it on the table. He folded his hands, his voice calm and reasonable. "There is nothing for you to vote on. This isn't a decision that the city gets to make. It's done. The mine will be reopened."

The room erupted in a new wave of sound. Lane shifted restlessly and looked toward Butch. Someone else stood in his place near the wall. He was gone.

Warren stood abruptly. He filled the middle of the room with the mere fact of his presence, and a stone silence fell as all eyes turned toward him. He gazed evenly at Mike, but his dark eyes were electric.

"I knew something like this was going to happen. I could feel it." He turned and looked around at the faces in the room. Few returned his gaze. "That mine is not to be disturbed." His voice was low but commanding. "This town cannot allow it. If we do, then we will deserve the ruin that follows."

Mike fiddled with his stack of papers. "I understand how you feel, Warren. Truly, I do. You and your family have more reason than most for not wanting the mine disturbed. But it doesn't belong to us." He lifted his head and looked out over the crowd, speaking louder. "The mine is not ours. It never was. It belongs to the mine company, and they have sold it to these Chinese folks. There is no decision we need to make here. The purpose of this meeting is purely to inform you of what's going on. That's all I have to say."

Mike picked up the stem of the gavel out of habit, sighed, and dropped it back onto the table. "I don't know about you folks, but I've had a long day. You're dismissed. Good night."

He stood, gathered up the ream of papers, and disappeared out of the back door behind the council table. The rest of the city council took his cue and funneled out behind him. In seconds the stunned populace of Fool's Lake sat staring at an empty table.

***

"Just what is it that your father intends to do, young lady?"

Lane hadn't made it to the curb before Emil caught her by the sleeve and gave it a firm jerk. Lane had been on the receiving end of heated questions and cold looks from the moment her father and the rest of the council evaporated from the meeting room. Worse, the sidewalk clogged with people spilling from the town hall made her own hasty exit impossible. But being physically accosted was too much, and Lane snatched her arm away and turned to face her assailant. Emil glared up at her through his wild tangle of eyebrows. She towered over Emil, but she was irritated at how much he intimidated her.

"Well?" he insisted. "What is it he's planning?"

"I honestly don't have any idea. The mine reopening is as much a surprise to me as it is to anyone," she responded stiffly.

"You mean that I should believe that you and your father live in the same house but he never discussed this business of the mine reopening with you?"

"No, never. Ask him yourself."

"I would ask him, but he didn't exactly make himself available for it!"

"I was in the same room you were, Mr. Kangus." Emil glared at her for a moment, then waved his hand at her dismissively and turned away.

Lane strode down the street toward home, Lowie's hand firmly clasped in her own. Lowie had to trot to keep up, but she didn't complain. Instead, she looked up at her mother's face, questioning. "Mom? What's going on?"

"I'm not completely sure, Low."

"Do we have to move?"

Lane glanced down at Lowie without breaking stride.

"No, of course not. Why would you think that?"

"Everyone says if the mine is ever disturbed all the people that died there will get angry and bad things will start to happen."

Lane scowled. "Who's 'everyone?'"

"The kids at school."

"That's ridiculous. The people who died at that mine aren't hanging around Foley Lake waiting to cause trouble."

"Not even Uncle Paul?"

Lane stopped. A small group of people approached and she faced them, an open dare. They passed by, whispering as soon as they were out of earshot. Lane looked down and the girl and sighed. "Lowie, I don't know what's going on. Okay? But your Uncle Paul isn't a ghost. And he isn't mad about anything."

"But some of the kids said he might not be dead," Lowie protested. "They said he was never found, and he might still be alive, but a monster now, and waiting to get revenge."

Lane gaped at Lowie with genuine shock. The child's round, clear face was upturned and fearful. Lane crouched down to get on her daughter's level. "Who is saying that?"

"All the kids do."

She was both horrified and touched that Lowie had clearly chosen not to tell her about the childish rumor to spare her feelings. "Do you think it's true?" Lane asked gently.

Lowie shook her head slowly, but the doubt in her face betrayed her. Lane brushed her fingers across Lowie's cheek, sweeping back loose hair. "Lowie, listen to me. That kind of talk is foolishness, made up by ignorant people who can't deal with reality. Uncle Paul is dead, okay? He died, and it wasn't anyone's fault. He was just a little boy when it happened, not much older than you are now. He isn't a monster or a ghost. He certainly is not still wandering around Foley Lake waiting to hurt anyone. He was just a kid. Okay?"

Lowie nodded.

Lane stood and glanced around at the people still streaming down the streets. "I didn't know about this ahead of time," she said. "There are no ghosts in this city, but there are plenty of fools. Don't worry. The adults will figure it out. Okay?" Lowie nodded, uncomforted.

"Good," Lane said. She continued her march, Lowie's small hand clenched firmly in her own.

Chapter Twenty-Five

From the ridge above the rock pit, a man looked east. He had been squatting, elbows resting on knees, the fingers of his right hand gently twining around a piece of crab grass that jutted up from the crust of the earth near his feet. Though the setting sun was at his back, he gazed into the distance intent on the far horizon.

The daytime birds had already settled into their nests and the evening critters had not yet begun their nightly serenade. The transition from day to evening was coming early, and the strange quiet added to the sense of expectation in the man's watching. Nothing stirred on that far horizon, the peerless silver of a June evening stretched out before him. But the pale eyes watched, intent, a form unmoving except for the finger twirling a single blade of grass.

The change happened in seconds. The man dropped the grass and shaded his eyes, straining to see across miles of open sky. He gave a satisfied grunt, stood and stretched. Without another eastward glance he limped to an ancient, dented toolbox lying open in the dirt, pausing long enough to roll up the sleeves of his dirty blue shirt, and fished out a worn hacksaw. He stepped to the barred entrance of the mine shaft. Grabbing one the bars of the old gate he ran his hand up and down its length, feeling thoughtfully. Choosing a spot, he laid the teeth of the saw against the bar and went to work. The *zip-zing* of the saw echoed deep into the shaft and the cold and black reaches of the mine itself.

Far east of the little city of Foley Lake, a gray cloud no bigger than a man's hand hung low on the horizon.

Chapter Twenty-Six

Lane walked into the house and stopped, listening.

"Dad!" She called. Silence. She released Lowie's hand.

"Go on up to your room," she commanded.

"But Mom—"

"Mary Louise, do not argue with me. *Go.*"

Lowie turned away with a pout and mounted the stairs. Lane walked through the kitchen and into the living room.

"Dad!"

Mike appeared from the hallway. She turned her back on him and marched into the living room. He followed, stuffing his hands in his pockets, and leaned against the frame of the living room doorway.

"I knew you'd be angry," he said simply. She rounded on him, eyes blazing.

"You had to know I was going to take all kinds of crap for this. But you didn't give me even the slightest warning you were going to drop that kind of bomb on the city. Worse, you took off and left Lowie and me to face all those people alone. You just threw us to the wolves."

Mike sighed. "Was it that bad?"

"It was bad enough!" she snapped. "Why didn't you tell me about this? Huh? And don't give me that line about confidentiality, because I'm not buying it."

"I didn't tell you because at first I honestly didn't think anything would come of it," Mike said wearily. "The mine company has had the mine for sale for years. Every now and then someone would ask about it. Nothing ever came of those questions. But things changed fast this time and, before I knew it, the sale was a done deal."

"'Before I knew it'? What is that supposed to mean? Don't try to tell me this whole deal snuck up on you. What gave you the right to keep it quiet when you knew the sale was going to go through?"

"Maybe I should have said something, I don't know…"

"Oh Dad, come on!" Lane railed. "You can't tell me you didn't cooperate somehow to get the mine reopened. Why? What is it they offered you? Money?"

Mike straightened up, pulling his hands out of his pockets, his temper flaring. "Oh, Lane, please. Don't tell me you believe I wanted money—"

"What was it then? Will you get your name in the papers?" Lane spewed, eyes flashing. "Maybe get your picture taken with the head of the mine company? What are they going to do for you, huh, Dad?"

"They promised to go into the mine and bring me back your brother."

Lane was struck silent. Mike turned away from her, gazing across the room to the window framing the darkening sky, and crossed to it. The glass still radiated the warmth of the absent sun. He felt a thick welt in his throat, like something he couldn't swallow. The quietness of his voice filled the room in a way that Lane's yelling hadn't. ""That was the only think I wanted. I told them I would do whatever I could to help them get the mine, but they needed to go in before they did anything else and look for Paul. They promised that they would."

Lane felt a chair solid against the back of her knee and she let her legs fold, dropping her weight onto it. She had spent much of her life forging a barrier against the knowledge that her brother still lay at the bottom of the Foley. Now her mind was flooded with memories and images she didn't want, and the yearning for Paul that had never entirely faded.

"Dad," she said. "It's been twenty years. After that much time…"

Mike turned back to her. She ached to see the age and sorrow that hung on him like a shroud.

"I'm sorry if you felt I threw you to the wolves. I didn't mean for you to get hurt by this, or Lowie either. But forget you are my daughter for a moment, Lane. Talk to me parent to parent. Imagine Lowie in that dark place, alone all these years. Imagine what it would do to you, after a decade, after two decades, knowing she was just out of reach. Look what losing him did to your mother. *I want my boy back.* And I don't care what it costs this town." He stopped for a moment, his sharp Adam's apple rising and falling like a piston, losing ground in the battle to control his emotions. "He is in that mine, but no one can find him. I don't accept that. I want my boy, Lane. I want him back so I can know where he is."

Mike fell silent, gazing back out the window. Then he turned, and stuffing his hands deep into his trouser pockets, he crossed the living room and faded back down the hall.

Lane stared at a bare patch in the carpet in front of her. Silence settled over the house like a pall. No words came to her mind, just a sound, a soft and steady whirling, like the turning of a waterwheel. She looked up at the two faded school photos that hung on the living room wall. One was of Paul at eleven years old, taken the spring before he died. The other was her own image at nine. She frowned and wondered why she had never noticed it before. She had many school pictures taken over the years, but it was the one taken just before that black summer Paul disappeared into the Foley that stayed on the wall. For some reason, once there were no new pictures of Paul, there were none of her, either.

Chapter Twenty-Seven

Lane woke up to the rumble of thunder. Not because it was loud. It wasn't. She woke because it *was* at all. She lay in bed, listening to the first few tentative splats of rain against the house, then the rhythm as more drops fell and sounded out the old memory of the pattering against eves and windows. Lightning flashed. The breeze grew restless and floated in through the open window, carrying the scent of dust, the snap of fresh ozone.

Lane got out of bed and slipped into Lowie's room. The girl lay sprawled across the covers, her boneless form limp on top of the blankets. Lane coaxed the bedspread out from under the sleeping child and covered her. Realizing she could feel drops against her bare legs, she turned to the open window where a spray of rain had ridden the breeze through the screen. She slid the window down and locked it, then returned to her own room.

Lane's window faced west, opposite the prevailing breeze, and she pulled the sash all the way open. The wind gusted and she felt a sharp rush of fear, watery and loose in her chest. Storms always did that to her, spooking her heart into a hard gallop. She stood her ground, forcing herself to stay in front of the open window, telling herself it was just the strangeness of the day acting on her. The success of the garage sale followed by the news of the mine reopening, the notion of finding her brother, and now this odd cloudburst, a phenomenon considered all too common everywhere except in Foley Lake, combined to give her a sense of the surreal. Lane pressed her face against the screen and took a long, slow breath, letting her senses reawaken to the aroma of wet streets and sodden grass. She crawled back into bed and lay on her side to face the window, telling her heart to slow and join the rhythm of the storm. The lightning and thunder gave way to a steady patter of rain.

Lane drifted. Somewhere deep inside a dream as dark as ink, she heard her brother call. His voice was distant, muffled, miles away, but it was getting closer. She felt exposed and vulnerable, and curled her knees to her chest against his approach. She didn't want him closer. Something was wrong with his voice. It was Paul, but deeper, a man's voice, an old, old voice full of the gravel of bitterness and regret. She tried to tunnel down to where that voice could not find her, but to no avail. She could not escape the sound and it began to pulse, to resonate, now distant, now deep inside her. She woke with a start to find Lowie standing at the edge of her bed.

"Ah, Low," she gasped. "You scared the crap out of me."

"Sorry, but it woke me up."

Lane heard fear in the child's voice. She pulled herself up into a sitting position. Lightning flashed and thunder answered, and Lane felt her own pulse rise.

"It's just a summer storm."

Lowie shook her head. "No, it was the—"

Bong.

A low, heavy chime sounded somewhere in the darkness outside of the window, followed by a sharp crack of thunder. Lowie sprang onto the bed and scrambled for covers.

"See? *That* woke me up. What is it, Mom?"

Lane stared out the window, mute. A few seconds later, another chime, another burst of thunder. "It can't be," she said.

Lowie cradled the quilt against her neck. "Can't be what? Mom?"

"How many times—" Another chime.

"Seven, I think. Do you know what it is?"

Lane untangled herself from the sheets and stepped to the window. She could see lights popping on inside houses all along the street, and figures moving just behind the brightened panes. Another chime. Without turning, Lane spoke. "Lowie, what time does my clock say?"

"It says midnight," Lowie replied. She pushed back against the pillows, digging her narrow shoulders into the softness. "Can I sleep with you?"

"Yes," Lane said absently. *Bong.* She turned away from the window and looked at Lowie's small, frightened face, a tiny white oval framed by pillows. She swallowed the tremor in her voice. "Don't be afraid, Low. It's just that old clock on the tower. I guess it has decided to start working again."

Chapter Twenty-Eight

For sixty years, the earth under Foley Lake had turned hard against the aspirations of new-fallen rain. The promise of life and vitality a steady drizzle might bring to a land and its inhabitants was lost in Foley Lake, hitting the ground and running off as if it had been poured down on a sheet of plastic, filling ditches and swamps that turned dank and rotten with the return of the summer sun. The soil around the city wouldn't accept the moisture, at least not enough of it to make the land thrive. The plants and trees didn't die; they didn't grow either. They remained stunted and yellow. Local wildlife had long since abandoned Foley Lake for the green fields a few miles down the road, and each October hunters applied for hunting licenses a county over so that they might have a chance at getting a deer come November.

It hadn't always been that way. The land had been rich, covered with thick forests, vibrant fields of virgin timber stretching out like a green swaying ocean. Loggers came through, sturdy sawyers hacking away tons of wood, binding it into heavy river rafts and sending it downstream to build mansions in St. Paul and factories farther south. The sawyers moved through like locusts, swarming one forest after another and leaving behind a blank and barren landscape. But the land is strong, and its strength was never just in the forests. The rains came and the land sprouted anew, hiding its scars under a fresh layer of green.

Then men came seeking gold and found iron instead, and the land, newly green on the surface, was suddenly valuable for what it stored underground. Miners slipped into the earth to root out treasure. They dug and blasted and drilled and shoveled, following veins of the finest iron ore in the world. And the earth gave it up, but not without cost. Every mine exacted its pound of flesh. Miners were crushed by full ore trams. They were blown up when their charges fired too soon. They were buried under mounds of rock and earth. They lost their footing and fell down shafts through eons of blackness. Perhaps somewhere, someone believed it was an even trade, a few lives lost for a wealth of buried treasure. The miners accepted the risks in exchange for the warmth and security of a company-owned house and enough credit at the company store to keep food in the bellies of their children. And there on the surface, when the rains came, the land opened wide to the moisture and drew it in.

But not in Foley Lake. Something had turned the land hard against the rain, and an entire generation of Foley Lake children grew up without the memory of blue-white storms cooling the night, of waking to the freshness of scrubbed summer air. The adults accepted it as a penance and acted as if the land they lived on was unlucky rather than offended.

In a stroke that changed. Lightening split the sky, and when the rain fell the land drank it greedily. The older folks grew restless. They didn't know what a sudden, unbidden shift in the attitude of the ground under them meant. Did something wake beneath the surface, something ancient and heavy with thirst? What woke it? And most importantly, if the land was no longer the hard shell that kept rain out, then what remained to keep their secret hidden within?

Chapter Twenty-Nine

Mike stepped lightly down the sidewalk, avoiding the cracks that were still dark with moisture. He whistled, a light, tuneless sound, his jacket flung over his shoulder and held by his trembling hand. As he passed storefronts, he called out greetings, so intentionally careless that no one noticed the rapid-fire pulse in his neck produced by his hammering heart.

The streets and storefronts glowed, washed clean by the wind-driven rain. The air was pungent with the morning-after smell that was the norm for Midwestern summer mornings in every other part of the region. Mike stopped whistling and slowed his step. In the park across the street, the plum tree was covered by tiny white blooms. He had almost forgotten that the tree could make flowers. He stopped and stood gazing, savoring the vision of his little corner of the world rendered whole by a common summer storm.

Nudged from his reverie by the sound of distant voices, Mike set off again and rounded the corner to the city square. A small crowd had gathered around the courthouse. All heads, most some shade of gray, were turned up to the clock tower. Mike stopped and studied the face of the clock, unchanged but for the fact that the hands had moved. The clock read 7:54. Mike looked down at his wristwatch.

7:57.

He grabbed the knob on the side of his watch and gave it a gentle backward turn, making it agree. Then he shook his sleeve down and marched forward.

"Good morning, folks," he said lightly. He didn't slow, though he knew he would never make it to the courthouse doors unmolested.

"Mike!" Emil yelled. Mike stopped with a sigh.

"Yes, Emil, what is it?"

The old man scowled, waving at the clock. "What do you intend to do about this?"

"About what?"

"About this clock!"

Mike turned and looked at Emil squarely. He knew he shouldn't, but he couldn't resist. "What about the clock?"

Emil's face blazed. "It's working! Didn't you hear it last night? Woke up the whole city!"

Mike looked up at the clock and smiled. "Yes. Now that you mention it, I did hear that old chime last night. Nice to have it working again." Mike turned and made for the door, ignoring a murmur of irritated conversation from the crowd. Emil stalked forward, walker smacking the pavement.

"What do you plan to do about this?"

Mike pulled the door open, stilling the tremble in his hand, and turned to face Emil. "What would you have me do?"

"I don't know! Explain it! Why would the clock suddenly start working again?" Mike shook his head and opened his mouth to answer, but Emil cut him off. "It's the mine! The mine is being reopened and this clock is giving us a sign that it ought not to be! It's an omen!" A murmur again, this one of assent. Mike didn't try to hide his irritation.

"Oh, get over it, Emil. You are far too old to believe those ghost stories. Nothing about the mine is cursed. It's had its share of bad luck, that's all. Shame on you for scaring these people." Emil's face went slack with shock. Mike turned to the crowd huddled shoulder to shoulder just beyond Emil's hunched frame.

"Shame on all of you. You're scaring the young people, you're scaring each other. This clock working isn't a sign. Or maybe it is a sign, a good sign. Why does everything have to be bad news to you people? The clock works. Consider it a gift."

The crowd stirred, its collective eyes turned down, some in shame, others in anger. Mike stepped through and let go of the door, but as he turned Emil caught his eye with a dangerous glare. He pointed a bony finger at Mike. "There will be blood on you and your family, Mike. You just remember that."

"Go on home, Emil. Quit stirring up trouble, now." Mike closed the courthouse door firmly, but once on the other side he turned his back and leaned against it, catching his breath. It wasn't as bad as it might have been, but he knew he would be getting calls all day. He didn't care. Calls were easy to dodge.

He climbed the steps and sighed with gratitude that Dorothy's chair was empty. He would deal with her hysterics later. He slipped into his office, closed the door, and let his suit coat slide out of his grip to the floor. He pulled the office chair to him and lowered himself into it. Alone in the silence, he sat back, gazing up at the wall.

His eyes wandered over the pictures of the miners. Dark men, strong and dark. Men born of the earth and returned to it, swallowed by it, vested in the mine in life and in death. Those chambers pried open could work magic, maybe. They would see.

Mike opened his desk drawer, pushed aside a stack of papers, and withdrew a faded school picture. He lifted the picture in front of him and held it, the tremble returning in force. He inhaled, one deep breath, studied the face of the boy, and let the breath go. This time he did not put the picture back in the drawer. He propped it against his plastic inbox and made a mental note to pick up a frame later down at the hardware.

Chapter Thirty

●•●

Lane stood in the middle of the garage, rubbing her eyes irritably. She stifled a yawn and surveyed the hodge-podge of goods left on the tables after the sale. She had to admit that the whole affair had been far more successful than she had expected. They had made nearly two thousand dollars, a vast amount as far as she was concerned, on what she'd considered worthless junk. The Salvation Army in Brainerd was sending a truck to pick up what was left. She and Butch would spend the day boxing the items up and returning the tables they had borrowed from the church and the VFW over in Ironton.

Lane scanned the table and her eyes lit on two small jars gleaming like red jewels on the end of one table. She smiled as she picked a jar up. Raspberry jam. *This* would come home with her.

"Knock, knock."

Lane jumped and wheeled around to see Dave, clad in his dark blue uniform and silver badge, leaning into the door of the garage. He grinned. "My, you're jumpy. Guilty conscience?"

"Hey," she greeted. "Not guilty, just raw. I didn't get much sleep last night. I'll warn you of that right now. And if you're looking for some jam, you're too late. These last two jars are all mine."

Dave stepped through the door, scanning the tables. "Yum. I haven't had homemade since my granny died. But I am actually looking for damage reports."

"Damage?"

"Storm damage."

"From that little cloudburst last night? I would hardly call that a storm."

"I know it. But I got a call from Amy in dispatch over in Brainerd early this morning. The weather service told her they think a tornado touched down here last night."

"You're kidding."

Dave shook his head. "That's what I said. But she insists that the weather service saw it on their radar at about three o'clock this morning. And the radar doesn't lie."

Lane chuffed through her nose. "I don't know anything about radars, but I think we would know if something that violent had happened in our own city."

"Exactly what I told her," he replied, with a tone of vindication.

"What'd she say?"

"She told me I'm an idiot."

"I guess that probably ended the conversation."

"Yes, it did," Dave replied with a sigh. "Maybe I am an idiot. Willa called this morning to say that some of the chain link around the school yard is down. I don't know if that's because of last night or if it's because the fence is so old. But I would appreciate it if you could prop it back up and keep your eyes open for anything else that's wrecked. I'm mostly just curious, but if a tornado did touch down here, we have to think about why our sirens didn't go off."

Lane nodded. "Will do. Any thoughts on the clock working again?"

Dave frowned. "No. I stopped over at the city hall and went up to the clock tower for a look. There isn't anything out of place, no obvious signs of tampering."

"Aren't you going to investigate it? You know, file a complaint, dust for prints, all that detective stuff?"

"What would I charge the person with, if I did find him? It's not vandalism. It's just the opposite. The clock was broken and now it's fixed. If I had to guess, I would say it's someone's way of making a statement about the mine reopening. Making a sudden decision to fix something that's been broken for twenty years is weird, but it's not a crime." Dave picked up a wrench from a small pile of unsold tools, turning it over in his hands. "So, how are we doing with, you know. The whole mine thing."

Lane shrugged. "If by 'we' you mean me, I'm fine with it. Why wouldn't I be?"

Dave raised his eyebrows. "A person could see how another person might be bothered by them reopening a mine where family members—"

"Couldn't care less one way or the other," Lane cut him off. "I think people are getting worked up about a lot of nothing. Anyway, I won't believe they are actually reopening the place until I see a load of ore roll out its front gate."

"That's not what I mean. The last time we were up there…"

"The last time we were up there a tragedy happened and a bunch of little kids let their imaginations run away with them," she snapped. "And it didn't help that the adults acted like what the kids heard and saw was real. They made things a hundred times worse with their own stupid fear. What they should have felt was guilt. They didn't seal that shaft. They've earned every ounce of their fear, as far as I'm concerned."

Dave nodded, silent. He turned the wrench around in his hands and lay it on the table.

"On that note," Dave said, "I need to get back to work. If you hear anything about storm damage, give me a call." He turned and headed for the door.

Lane sighed, regretful of venting her anger on her old friend. "Hey," she said. Dave turned in time to catch a sparkling jar of raspberry jam Lane lobbed to him. He looked at her, questioning.

"In memory of granny," she said. He grinned and, with a final wave, was gone.

Lane was packing a second box when Butch arrived. He was uncharacteristically late, rumpled, and sporting dark rings under his eyes.

"Sorry I'm late," he said.

"You look exhausted."

"I didn't get much sleep last night. That storm was really something."

"Oh, jeez, I forgot about that. You usually sleep outside."

"Yeah, well, not last night. I took cover in the head frame."

Lane shifted uncomfortably, the memory of a chorus of children's screams rising in her mind. Her stomach tightened into a cold knot. "You slept *in* the head frame? Butch, you know that the shaft is still open, right? I mean, wandering around in there in the dark is a bad idea."

"I don't wander, believe me. I know the shaft is open. But I didn't want to sit in the rain, and the downside of not having many responsibilities is not having many options. At least I stayed dry. It's almost time for me to be moving on anyway."

"Oh. I've been meaning to ask you about that."

"About what?"

"When you planned to leave. The Fourth of July is coming up fast, and there's a lot to do to get ready for the fireworks. If you're game to stay, I could give you a couple more weeks of work."

Butch raised his eyebrows. "I didn't realize that Foley Lake had fireworks on the Fourth."

Lane chuckled and looked out the open garage door to the street beyond. "It's a big deal here. The city council kicks in a pile of cash for it. It's a pretty good show, actually. We get folks from all over the area coming to watch."

"Hmm. I could use the money, that's for sure. Yeah, I'll stay if you need me."

Lane turned back to her packing to avoid meeting Butch's eye. "Good. And we have a couch, you know. It's old and uncomfortable, but it's better than sleeping in the rain. Next time the weather turns on you, come down to the house. You can stay there for the night."

Butch nodded slowly. "Okay. Thanks."

They went to work. And though the rains continued night after night for weeks, Lane never repeated the offer. And Butch never again broached the subject, though he thought of it often in the dark, wet nights when he lay in his sleeping bag on the cement floor, listening to the skies over Foley Lake pound furiously on the metal roof of the head frame.

Chapter Thirty-One

Dave glanced back at Chuck standing in the driveway near the house, the two smallest Larson boys playing at his feet. He didn't ask Chuck directly whether the manure spreader was used to spray Spot's cars; rather, he asked Chuck if he himself had done the deed, and Chuck's honest denial was all he was looking for. Dave knew a crime from a prank, or even from a childish and ill-advised attempt to strike out at someone who seemed to hold all the cards. None of the cars at Spot's Lot were permanently damaged. Dave had waited to talk to Chuck because he intended to let the issue drop, knowing that the only real potential for crime would depend on how Spot reacted when he finally figured out what was going on between Sandy and the farmhand. But given the fact that Spot was a self-absorbed moron who was largely oblivious to anything that didn't occur on his car lot, it could be a while.

Dave snapped his notebook shut and put it in his pocket, telling Chuck he figured the issue would work itself out, when Chuck called young Levi out of the bunk house. Dave sighed as the boy walked across the barnyard, refusing to meet his eye, his dark-tanned face a deep shade of crimson. Dave knew that Chuck was thoroughly honest; he would hand the boy over without question if he thought Levi had done wrong. But instead of forcing a confession he prodded Levi to tell Dave what he had seen in the night skies a few nights before. The boy relaxed and related the tale of the blue-white flash of lightening that seemed to come from somewhere around the old mine. The boy left off the detail about the bats, not desiring to look ridiculous. Not that it mattered to Dave. He had been hearing similar stories for more than a week.

Chip Borken called to say that he had been driving along Route 30 at about midnight, when a tall man wearing a long white coat stepped out of the ditch onto the side of the road. Chip shot passed the figure, and by the time he turned the car around to go back, the man was gone. Several complaints had come in of a small, strange light, no bigger than a flashlight's beam, spotted moving around buildings and through yards. The fire department in Crosby had rushed to Foley Lake three different times when people called to say lightning had set something ablaze. A search would turn up no evidence of a fire; the firemen, all volunteers, muttered irritably and made unkind references about the collective intelligence of the people of Fool's Lake.

Dave didn't know what to make of it all. It wasn't just the strange sights that couldn't be accounted for; an edginess was growing in the city, a strange anxiety that made people jumpy and irritable. Dave was responding to neighbors bickering about barking dogs and overgrown grass, minor incidents that had tempers flaring. There was a tension that seemed to be building toward something. And he himself wasn't immune to the change; he checked and rechecked his sidearm and made sure a round was chambered in the shotgun he kept between the squad's front seats. The Fourth of July was only a couple weeks away now, and Dave knew that the city faced some irritability every year before the big fireworks display. But this was different. This wasn't the kind of tension that led to anything good.

What had changed in the city? The announcement of the mine reopening? The repaired clock chiming out the hour? The weather? What did any one of those things have to do with the others? Not a thing, in his book. It was all coincidence. There was no common denominator, no source that he could point to.

But then why was it all so terribly familiar?

Dave felt a tightening in the pit of his stomach. The look on his father's face as Dave, a panic-stricken boy of nine, related the tale of Paul Harris' plunge down the mineshaft still haunted Dave twenty years later. His father was a man who put stock in signs and omens, a man for whom nothing ever happened by coincidence. He warned Dave to stay away from both the mine and the Harris family. Cursed, they were.

There was no doubt. Any family that lost three family members to the same mine in two generations had to be. And Dave, practical as his father was superstitious, couldn't help but wonder if there wasn't some truth to what his father told him.

Amy's voice from the squad's police radio interrupted Dave's thoughts. Three cows had escaped their pasture and were taking a leisurely stroll through Avis Anderson's garden. Dave picked up the radio handset and told Amy to call Bob Moe to let him know he best come and get his cows out of the Anderson garden before Dave got there, or Bob would be picking his cows up with a rendering truck. He pulled over to the side of the road and glanced back to see if it was safe to make a U-turn and caught a glimpse of the head frame in his rearview mirror. It occurred to him that there was one thing he knew for a fact had changed. The mine had a new resident. And things seemed to have gone from bad to worse since he arrived; even Lane was questioning whether the man was who he said he was. There was no way the stranger could be blamed for most of what Dave was seeing in the city, but his instincts still niggled at the fact that the man arrived just before things started to fall apart. Maybe it was time he drove up to the mine to have a talk with Mr. Butch Brown.

Chapter Thirty-Two

Lowie stood at the edge of the field of wild grass, holding Bones to her chest. She was out of breath, partly from the exertion of carrying the little dog up the hill, and partly because the long shadow cast by the head frame stretched toward her across the flat plain of Butch's campsite. She looked down at where the shadow stopped, the hard edge running in a horizontal line, inches in front of the toe of her shoes. She clutched Bones to her chest and slid her feet back.

She had never been this close to the mine. She had never disobeyed her mother's strong and repeated warning to stay away. But her errand was important. Butch was a stranger to Foley Lake, and in his ignorance, he had put himself in mortal danger. She had been hearing conversation after conversation at the diner since the night of the storm, talk that the city was on the cusp of disaster because of the mine reopening and that Butch had taken refuge in the shadows of a sleeping beast. She couldn't tell Butch what she knew with her mother around; her mother wouldn't like what Lowie had to tell. Climbing the hill herself was a desperate act, but she wouldn't see Butch suffer under the weight of Foley Lake's curse if she could stop it. She made up her mind to seek out and warn the man in the one place she knew they wouldn't be disturbed. On the way she spotted Bones floundering in the tall grass, whimpering when he stepped on his left hip. He licked her chin in gratitude when she picked him up and curled him against her chest.

She was careful to avoid looking directly at the head frame. After all the stories she'd heard, she couldn't help but think that even a glance could bring anything less than horrid luck. And she, a Harris, was tempting the fates already by coming so near to the mine. The sun was warm and high. Bones wiggled in her arms, and she put him down. He trundled across the campsite, stopping to glance back at Lowie with a wag of his tail, and disappeared under the gate.

There was no sign of Butch. Lowie skirted the broad shadow and moved to the left, toward the burned-out miner's dry. She looked inside the crumbling frame. It was empty, except for the stores of wood and kindling. She turned and crossed back the way she had come and gazed down the slope toward town, thinking. What would she do if she couldn't find him? Could she risk waiting one more night, knowing he was sleeping virtually on death's doorstep?

"Hello there, Miss Lowie."

Lowie wheeled around with a squeal to find Butch standing in front of the head frame, leaning against the gate. He laughed.

"I never figured you for the skittish type."

Lowie clamped her hands over her racing heart. "Where did you come from?"

"I just came up from the pit. Had to get some water." Butch nudged a full bucket of rusty-looking water with his toe.

"I didn't see you coming up the hill," she said.

"Well, then, we need to work on your powers of observation. What can I do for you?"

"What?"

"What are you doing here? I thought you weren't allowed."

Lowie swallowed hard, regaining her composure. "There's been some talk around town. I came to warn you."

"Warn me?"

"Something bad is going to happen."

"To who? Me?"

"Maybe, yes. Because you don't know."

"I don't know what?"

"You don't know what it's like to be from Foley Lake."

Butch lifted his hat and rubbed his head. The girl stood at the edge of the campsite, solemn, waiting to see if she would be taken seriously. He nodded. "Then I guess we better talk."

Butch waved her over to the cold campfire ring and settled himself in the grass. Lowie hesitated before stepping into the shadow of the shaft and sitting across from him, legs crossed.

He waited for her to begin. She took a deep breath and plunged forward.

"There's a ghost in Foley Lake."

She waited. He didn't laugh, roll his eyes, or interrupt her. Encouraged, she continued.

"He's been here for years. People see him sometimes, walking around at night, or if they come up here after dark. He died here. He's mad they are reopening the mine. Folks have been seeing things, and they say he's back—"

Butch held up his hand. "Wait a minute. Who is 'he?' Who is haunting the mine?"

"Clinton Harris."

Butch frowned. "Your great-grandfather? I thought Clinton Harris was a hero. Didn't he try to warn people to get out of the mine when it flooded?"

"Yeah. But it didn't work. They say he gets angry every time someone disturbs this place." Lowie shifted uncomfortably. "They are worried that he is going to be upset by the news about the mine. And they say if anything happens, it will happen to you first because you spend so much time here."

"Lowie, let me ask you a question. Your great-grandfather died trying to save other people, right?"

Lowie nodded.

"Would you say that he was a good man?"

"I guess so."

"If Clinton Harris was a good man, why would you think he would be a bad ghost? I mean, a man who would give up his life to try to save other people, a man that good, would be good even after he died, right?"

"But if he's angry…"

"Even if he is angry, would that make him bad? Good men get angry sometimes, especially when other good people get hurt or are in danger."

Lowie's smooth brow knit together thoughtfully. "I guess that's true. Maybe that would be right for ordinary ghosts. But this ghost…" Lowie looked back up at the shaft, a flash of fear on her face.

"What?" Butch gently prodded. "What is it that scares you so much?"

Lowie turned to him, her green eyes tragic. "This ghost kills kids."

CHAPTER THIRTY-THREE

Lane steered the lawn mower into the cemetery shed and shut it down. She stepped off the machine and stretched, her back objecting to the long hours she had been spending on the rider. The rain continued night after night, filling the air with restless, distant thunder that was having a wearing effect on the nerves of Foley Lakers. Last night's storm raged for two hours. Dave stopped Lane on her way to the cemetery to ask her if she knew of any damage and told her that folks had begun calling his office to complain about the weather.

Lane yawned and rubbed her eyes irritably. The grass, inspired by rain, was flying out of the ground, and she found herself falling behind in her other work because of the extra mowing. She wasn't sure what she would do when Butch left and she no longer had his able assistance to help her keep up. The Fourth of July was only two weeks away, and she couldn't see how she could be ready for it, even with his help.

The old town cemetery was an attraction, and people would stop by to mill through the headstones dating back to the city's founding. Lane couldn't let it go wild. Butch's promise to be gone by fall drifting into her consciousness, giving her heart a strange little leap. She clenched her jaw. *The man has every right to go and no reason to stay,* she thought as she slammed the shed door, locking the mower inside.

The sun was slipping below the western horizon, casting long golden rods of light between the trees standing sentry over Foley's dead. The earthy smell of freshly cut grass, made stronger by the late day dew, filled the air as Lane followed the path through the cemetery. She had every intention of heading home for a late supper and a long soak in the bathtub, so she was almost to her mother's grave before she realized her feet were taking her there. She crested the small hill on which her mother was buried just as the sun sank below the horizon.

A soft layer of clipped grass lay over the gray headstone, and Lane gazed at it for a moment before she gave in to impulse and knelt. She swept the grass away from the stone with her fingers.

"Hi, Mom," she said quietly. In a flash the image of her mother's thin, dying face filled her mind. She squeezed her eyes shut. Why couldn't she ever think of her mother without thinking of that? For fourteen years she had known her mother as a vital and healthy woman, a gentle dynamo, always finishing a chore or just beginning another. For nine months Lane had known her as pale and dying, life seeping out of her day by day. Why was it always the face of her dying mother that came to her?

She opened her eyes again and sat back on her heels, silent. She rarely talked at these graveside visits, feeling no compulsion to fill the air with words. It wasn't comforting to talk. Alone in the stillness, feeling the old ache, not thinking—that was what gave her solace.

It was hard for her to remember what it was like to be a mother's daughter. It seemed like too much time had passed since she was the child and someone else the parent. She wondered sometimes if Lowie would ever feel that way, sitting at Lane's grave, trying to remember what it was like to be cherished. A torrent of grief and pain surged through Lane, driving her to her feet. No. Not Lowie. Lowie would never have to wonder.

Paul's grave lay farther down the slope, silent in the blue dusk. Lane walked to it, needing to put some space between herself and the thought of dead mothers. She stood over the head stone. Its size had always irritated her. Paul had been a boy, and there was no need for such a big stone on a boy's grave. Besides, the grave was a mockery. Her father had insisted on burying an empty casket. No satin pillow for her brother. His little corpse lay cold and bare at the bottom of the Foley Mine while a pristine, empty white satin pillow moldered six feet below her feet.

Lane shivered, clutching her arms around her. *Such morbid thoughts tonight,* she chided herself. A new image rose in her mind, that of her father's haggard, weary face the night he told her of the new search for Paul's body. She had gotten so accustomed to seeing Mike bearing up under the weight of his grief for Paul that it had become normal to her. When she was in high school the senior class had put on *A Christmas Carol,* and she had been bothered by the long chain Marley's ghost was forced to drag through eternity. In that image she saw her father, adorned with grief, forging the chain with his ongoing regret and self-abasement. For years she had believed that when her brother plunged into the mine, he had taken his whole family with him. She was an adult before she realized it wasn't her brother's fall into the mine that had ruined them. It was his failure to ever come out.

Lane stooped at her brother's grave and dutifully swept away the fresh clippings heaped against the stone. Her finger brushed something dry and stiff below the grass. She reached down and lifted a small bouquet of Queen Anne's Lace. She slowly stood, staring down at the white wildflowers. They were little more than weeds, the stems tied together with a graying shoelace. She looked back up the hill. There was no such bouquet on her mother's grave, which ruled out Lowie, because the child's innate sense of fairness would never allow her to bring flowers for one grave and not the other. Besides, Lowie always brought wild violets. And Mike, on his rare journey to the cemetery, only brought roses. So who, she wondered, would come to visit her brother's empty grave bearing a bouquet of Queen Anne's Lace?

It was dark when Lane reached her truck. She stopped at the edge of the drive and lofted the dried bouquet she had carried out with her into the long grass in the ditch. For reasons she couldn't define, she didn't want to leave them dead and crumbling on her brother's grave.

Chapter Thirty-Four

Rain fell every night for weeks, always arriving after midnight with a flash of lightning, and always giving way to the warmth of the sun and cloudless blue skies by morning. The banks for Foley Lake expanded, reclaiming territory long since ceded to cattails and sedge. Lane found herself dealing with plugged storm drains and ankle-deep mud puddles in the middle of town, and Butch's true nature as an all-around handyman proved to be an invaluable asset. Still, the sixty-hour weeks were getting to her as she struggled to keep Foley Lake from drowning in its own sewer.

Sundays became sacred. Lane slept as late as she could, though try as she might, she never really could stay in bed past sunrise. On the third Sunday after the storms started, she awakened slowly and turned onto her side to gaze out the window. The sky was the soft golden blue of early morning. Her eyes wandered to her dresser, to a small box wrapped in bright red paper. Lowie's birthday was still a week away, but the gift was already waiting. She'd bought the child a heart-shaped locket, like the one her own mother had gotten her for her ninth birthday. She had worn the locket religiously, though the thin chain occasionally turned her neck green, until the silver plating had worn off in large patches and grew dull. Lane kept the locket in her jewelry box, and Lowie would take it out sometimes and admire it. The child seemed endlessly impressed by the fact that her grandmother and namesake had given her mother the gift, cheap though it was. Lane was determined that the locket she bought for Lowie would never tarnish. She found one fashioned of white gold and paid far too much to it. Inside, she had placed a tiny picture of herself on one side and Lowie on the other. A memory of her mother wafted through her mind, riding a ribbon of sadness. The locket she received as a child had always been empty. She wore it for years without ever realizing there was supposed to be something inside.

She pulled herself out of bed and made her way downstairs to the kitchen. Lowie was at the kitchen table with a variety of candy and small gifts scattered in front of her. Lane stopped and watched the child for a few moments, so intent on her work, so beautiful and simple in the golden light of the summer sun rising outside the windows. She felt an ache to hold onto the moment, to hold Lowie safe in it forever, to capture that picture and the small piece of contentment and lock it in her heart as a talisman against all future pain. Instead, she crossed the room quietly and satisfied herself with giving Lowie a kiss on the top of her head.

"Morning, Lowie-girl."

"Morning," Lowie replied, distracted. "Mom, we need more stuff for the gift bags."

"You have plenty. Besides, why do you have six bags? Only five girls could come, right?"

Lowie nodded. "Five girls plus Butch," she reminded. Lane chuckled.

"I don't think Butch will be hurt if he misses out on the jawbreakers and cherry lip gloss." Lowie looked up at Lane, her mouth a small, thoughtful "o". Then she sighed and began to split one pile of treats into the five other piles.

Lane moved across the kitchen and lifted the glass coffee pot from its burner as she glanced out the back window. She gasped, suddenly wide awake. She pulled the back door open, the coffee pot still in one hand.

"Lowie, look at this!"

They stepped onto the wet grass, staring at the rose bushes that lined the backyard. Several of the bushes were blooming, the tight new blossoms of red and yellow unfurling from among the deep green leaves promising a riot of color in days to come. Lowie leaped off the stairs and bounded to the closest bush, bending to smell the fragrance of a deep yellow bloom. Lane followed behind her, bewildered.

"They look like they did when I was a kid, when my mom was tending them. What would make them bloom after all these years?" she wondered aloud.

"The rain?" Lowie offered.

"But you've been watering them."

"Maybe there's something else in the rain that they needed."

Lane shook her head. "Maybe," she agreed.

A rustling under the bushes drew their attention and a gray, furry muzzle popped out. Lane and Lowie laughed.

"Looks like we have a visitor," Lane said.

Lowie dropped to her knees and tickled the end of the dog's nose. Bones' tail slapped happily, making the entire lower bush tremble.

"C'mon, Bones, come out," Lowie coaxed.

Bones retreated into the bush, sniffing and searching. Lowie bent down to peek under the leaves. "What are you looking for, Bonesy? Did you lose something?"

The dog emerged from the bush with his trophy in his mouth, tail wagging, and sat in front of Lowie. On the ground in front of her he dropped the top half of a gray human skull.

***

Lowie sat at the living room window, arms twined protectively around Bones. Occasionally a word or two of the conversation between her mother and the policeman road in on the warm breeze blowing through the screens.

"—don't know for sure, he just comes and goes—"

"—Butch at the mine? Just wandered up there?"

184

Her mother couldn't give much of an account for the dog, Lowie knew, but it seemed to her that Lane wasn't really trying. They had been out there a long time, talking. Lowie stayed inside, partly because of her mother's admonition to do so, and partly out of a desire to keep Bones out of reach of the law.

"—a man missing eight or nine years, from over by Brainerd. But this looks older—"

Bones had fallen asleep, his snores a throaty wheeze. The child didn't know what fate the law dictated for dogs who brought home bits of human skeletons, but she wasn't going to allow Bones to come to a bad end if there was any way she could protect him. She looked down the driveway and wondered how far she could get with the lame dog if she just made a run for it. Maybe she could take him out into the woods to turn him loose and give him the chance to go back to wherever he came from. But even as she thought it her arms tightened around the dirty-gray mutt. She might be able to run into the woods with him, but she knew she wouldn't have the heart to drive him away even if it was to save his life.

"—don't think it could be, do you? My father—"

"—too large, I think. He was only eleven, right?"

The sound of the back door opening made Lowie jump. Bones woke up. He yawned and tried to slip off Lowie's lap, but she held him firm.

"I better get a good look at him, I guess, so I don't end up trailing the wrong mutt." The policeman was speaking as he followed Lane into the living room, a brown paper bag dangling from one had. Lowie knew the skull was in it. She had seen him put it in there.

"What are you going to do with him?" Lowie blurted. Officer Dave seemed not to notice. Instead, he knelt in front of her and lifted Bones from her lap. "He's a little guy, isn't he?" Dave said absently. "Scruffy, but not too skinny. Have you been feeding him?"

"Of course we have!" Lowie retorted. "He's our dog. We feed him every day!"

"Lowie!" Lane snapped. "That's enough! What is the matter with you?" Lowie didn't respond. She just crossed her arms over her chest, eyes filling with tears.

"He's not our dog, Dave, but yes, we feed him sometimes. He pretty much comes and goes, but like I said, he belongs to Butch if he belongs to anyone."

"Butch will be mad if you do anything bad to him." Lowie managed to push the words out through the tight knot in her throat. Lane's face lit with realization. "Is that what you think, Lowie? That Bones is in trouble?" Lowie nodded, wordless.

Dave patted Bones' head and handed him back to Lowie. "He's not in any trouble, kiddo. He's just doing what dogs do. Actually, I'm going to deputize him. Make him an official police dog. Then he can help me find the rest of this fellow," he lifted the brown paper bag, "and figure out who he is."

Lowie eyed him suspiciously. "You aren't going to hurt him?"

"Nope," Dave said, getting back to his feet. "I'm going to follow him. See if he'll lead me to the place where he found the skull."

Lowie sighed, squeezing Bones to her with one arm and swiping away tears with the other.

"Lane, I'd like to talk to Butch about this, and one or two other things as well."

Lane frowned. "What do you mean?"

"Nothing, really. I think I'm the only one in Foley Lake that hasn't actually met the man yet."

"Are you kidding? You've never met Butch?"

Dave shook his head. "I've been trying to catch up with him for a while and I keep missing him. But now it's not just an issue of a social call. I need to know if he has any sense where this dog has been going." Dave turned back the Lowie. "Miss Lowie, maybe I should deputize you, too. I want you to be on the lookout. If you see this dog with any more bones, or if you find a bone lying around, have your mom call me. It's important for me to find all the bones he's been collecting these last few weeks."

Lowie nodded, giddy with relief. "Oh, that's easy," she said lightly. "He has a whole big pile of them up at the mine."

***

It wasn't until Lowie led Lane and Dave to the pile of skeletal remains that the dog had gathered at the mine that Lane realized there was only one way Lowie could have known they were there. When they returned home, she sat the child down and grilled her about when she went to the mine, and what she did there. Finding out that Butch knew about the trip to the mine did nothing to improve the situation. She ordered a crying, repentant Lowie to her room with no hope of supper. Then she went on a quest to find Butch.

Chapter Thirty-Five

The sun was quartering in the western sky by the time Lane returned to Butch's camp. She'd looked everywhere in the city for him to no avail. No one had seen him all day. Coming back to the mine was her final effort to locate him before her anger cooled. She didn't want to calm down. This man, this *stranger*, had endangered her daughter by failing to report Lowie's visit to the mine. She liked Butch, that was true, but the reality was that she didn't know him or his real intensions at all. If he was avoiding Dave, something was wrong. A man who steered clear of the law simply could not be trusted.

She stood by the fire ring, trying to decide what to do. He wasn't here, that was plain. She sighed, deflating as she realized she wouldn't be able to give vent to her anger tonight. She turned to leave when the smallest glint of silver dangling near the head frame caught her eye.

The chain going into the head frame was cut. Not just unlocked and opened but cut in the middle, creating two worthless ends of chain too short to wrap around the gate and affix a new lock. The glint of silver was the freshly revealed steel from the series of nicks and cuts in the chain's links. Lane frowned as she examined the jagged edge of the link. Whoever had broken the chain had sawn it rather than using a bolt cutter, an odd and clumsy way to cut a link. Butch most certainly wouldn't have bothered cutting it with a saw, seeing as it was easy enough simply to climb over it. Lane dropped the chain and it rattled against the door of the head frame. The gate had been pulled open enough to easily slip inside. She leaned against it and peered in, but the interior of the mine gave up nothing as little light filtered in past the door frame.

Lane had not been this close to the shaft since the day her brother died. Her parents would not allow it. Not that she hadn't been to the mine; she had been a regular visitor in her teen years. The mine drew kids like a magnet. Adults avoided it. It had a spooky history, and every child in town had been roundly warned by his or her parents to stay away from it, making it the most natural place for teens to gather with beer-filled coolers. But she had always stayed away from the head frame. All the kids had. Even with all the posturing the teenage boys made, the teasing and shoves and challenges to each other's bravado as they competed for female attention, none of the kids had ever challenged another to enter the head frame. It was off limits, anathema, unthinkable.

The stories she had heard over the years were the result of rumor and superstition, neither of which carried much weight in her mind. Still, she felt a wave of apprehension. She might be tempting some unseen fate just by standing near the gate. Yet Butch had been inside the frame; many times, in fact. That he remained untouched should be clear evidence that those fears were unfounded. Instead, the announcement of the mine reopening had stirred the anxiety of the whole city. Rumors and superstitions that had been put to rest over the last twenty years erupted in force. And she wasn't immune. She had recently noticed there were very few areas in Foley Lake where the head frame was not a constant, looming presence as she went about her work.

Suddenly she was disgusted with herself. Why had she allowed this place to frighten her for so many years? What did she think would happen if she went inside?

Her anger reemerged. There might not be anything she could do about the superstitions dividing Foley Lake, but she could do something to conquer the irrational fear of the mine that had plagued her since childhood. She rolled her shoulders back, lifted her chin, and stepped around the gate.

Nothing happened. She stood in the cool interior of the head frame, listening to the silence. No ghostly laughter, no hysterical screams. She took a big breath, unaware until that moment she had been holding it, and edged forward. There was an old beer can laying on the concrete floor of the mine, and she kicked it. It disappeared into the shadow but she heard it bounce off the back wall of the frame. It didn't sound like it went very far. The building wasn't as big as it looked from the outside.

Lane squinted to make out details of the head frame in the dim light. She crept forward, shuffling her feet a few inches across the cement with each step. The grind of her shoes on the concrete was the only sound. The fear that had been a wall to keep her out of the building faded almost completely, and she moved forward with more confidence. A stone lay in front of her, and she kicked it as well, sending it sliding along the surface of the concrete. It tumbled across the floor, then the sound broke off completely. She stopped. If the rock didn't hit the opposite wall, where did it go? An exquisite awareness rushed over her. It had to have fallen down the shaft.

What am I doing? she thought. *Am I trying to get myself killed?* Her fear spiked and she began to tremble. She needed to get out, to get away from the mine altogether. There was a difference between courage and stupidity, and moving forward in the dark toward a chasm she couldn't see was the latter. She would have to be completely nuts to keep moving blindly, not knowing where the shaft was.

Before she could turn back, she realized there was a square on the floor six or seven feet in front of her, not so much a hole as a deeper darkness. She squinted, trying to make out the edges of the shape. She slid a little closer. It couldn't be the shaft, probably wasn't, because it was much smaller than the gaping abyss she had imagined since she was a kid. It was unremarkable, about twenty feet square. Perhaps it was just a big stain from some piece of equipment that used to sit here, and the shaft was farther on. She shuffled forward.

Then the void was directly in front of her, and not more than two steps would bring her to the brink. She could feel chill air rising from it. It was the shaft, then, although it didn't look anything like what she had expected. Some internal instinct warned her back, but she squelched it. She wasn't going to go much closer. She just wanted to peek in, to see if she could make out anything beyond the solid edge.

A blast of air exploded out of the shaft, blowing Lane backwards with its power. She tripped over her own feet and fell onto her back as the wind crashed into the metal roof directly above her to peel a strip of the rusting steel loose and send it clattering. Lane sat up, her heart slamming. Light diffused by the setting sun fell into the timber frame through the new hole in the roof, and Lane could see the shaft clearly, its harsh lines and inner blackness. Horror washed over her and she rolled over, and with a sob crawled as fast as she could toward the doors. She gained her feet at the opened gate and tumbled through it into the dusk.

Lane didn't stop running until she reached the truck. The violence of her shaking made it hard to open the door. Once inside she slapped the door locks closed and seized the steering wheel with both hands, helpless to regain control of the gibbering stream of thoughts that plunged through her mind.

At home she slipped in as quietly as she could and climbed the stairs, legs watery and weak. Every sound made her jump.

Lowie didn't come out of her room and Mike was nowhere to be seen. She went straight to her room, stripped off her red-stained clothes and pulled a bulky sweater over her head, then got into bed and yanked the blankets up to her neck despite the heat. She kept her lamp on and lay awake for the rest of the night, wondering if her superstitious fear wasn't foolish after all.

Chapter Thirty-Six

The Foley Lake Journal
June 25, 1984

The Disappearance of Foley Lake

Eugenia Larson, Reporter

While our fair city struggles with the news of the reopening of our storied mine, something has been happening underground that none of us would have suspected. The recent rains have certainly greened up the city and swelled the banks of our namesake lake. But literally overnight, nearly one-third of the lake has disappeared.

This reporter spoke with a geologist from the University of Minnesota who said that most likely, the soft spot underground that led to the mine's flooding sixty years ago has given way under the pressure of our nightly rainfalls, once again spilling thousands of gallons of water into the underground tunnels. The geologist said that while the missing water might give the lake a strange appearance for a while, once the mine filled to a certain point both lake and mine would find "equilibrium" and the lake would refill over time.

What does this mean for Shanghi Mining's plans to reopen the mine as an open pit? It's hard to say, and the mine's new owners aren't talking. So once again Foley Lakers are left in limbo, our fates at the mercy of forces outside our control. But chin up, fellow townspeople! We have endured worse, and we will overcome. It takes more than a little underground flood to be the undoing of this city, as we have already proven in generations past.

Chapter Thirty-Seven

Dave sat in the shade of the mine's head frame, waiting for the little dog to emerge. He had taken the skull and the other remains he collected to Bemidji himself, walking them into the offices of the Bureau of Criminal Apprehension in two large brown grocery bags. The coroner he had spoken to on the phone had taken the bags from him and dumped them unceremoniously onto a metal table. Dave stood by silently, waiting for a simple confirmation that the remains were all human. Instead, the doctor breathed heavily through his nose as he poked at the bones with the end of his pen, separating them into piles by some system of categorization mysterious to Dave. Then the man said something that Dave had not entertained as a possibility.

"You have more than one body here."

Dave had driven all the way back to Foley Lake with the Crown Victoria's light bar flashing, the implications of what the coroner said ricocheting around in his mind, an urgency to organize a formal search pressing his heart against his throat and his foot against the accelerator. But the two-hour drive gave him space to ponder the reaction the people of Foley Lake would have if they knew that somewhere near their city nameless bodies lay rotting. Whatever fears already plagued the town would not be helped by that kind of news. How much more difficult would it make his job if word of the bodies leaked out to neighboring cities and groups of the morbidly curious showed up to wander Foley's woods in search of the corpses? He shut down the light bar and eased off the gas, rolling quietly into town, firm in the decision that he would give himself three days to try to find the bodies before he went public.

That evening he devised a plan to follow the gray terrier as best he could. The dog had to be making repeated trips to the bodies' location, so simply trailing him might be all Dave needed to do. If that didn't work, he could call Minneapolis and find out if they could send some search dogs to help him look. But first he wanted to try to handle things himself and protect the little town from invasion by outside forces and all the drama a large search would bring.

After a restless night, he was up before dawn the next morning. Luck was with him when he arrived at the mine at sunup; Butch was nowhere to be seen, but he found the dog curled up just inside the head frame. It regarded him with a friendly but guarded wag of the tail, the wizened gray face looking him straight in the eye in a way that Dave found disconcerting. Dave took up his post near the remains of Butch's campfire and wondered where Butch had spent the night. Everywhere Dave went it seemed as if he had just missed the man.

By mid-morning the sun was baking into Dave's dark blue uniform, causing him to seek refuge in the shade offered by the head frame. The sun continued its climb and the shadows shortened. His stomach gurgled. He silently chided himself for skipping breakfast and not thinking to pack a lunch. He kept peeking around the edge of the building at the gated entry, wondering how long the old dog would sleep.

About noon the gate rattled softly. Dave leaned out from behind the head frame and watched as the dog emerged, blinking in the bright sun. It stretched and yawned, then made a slow circle around the edge of the camp, sniffing in the tall grass until its search was rewarded with a hot dog that Butch must have left for it. The terrier stretched out on his belly in the grass and gnawed the meat as Dave watched. *Man, that dog is old,* he thought as he watched it work to chew the soft meat. Bones finally stood, still swallowing, and turned to look Dave fully in the face. Acknowledging him once more with a brief wag of its tail, it turned and started jogging down the hill toward town.

Dave hadn't expected Bones' sudden departure. He pulled himself to his feet and, with pinpricks rushing down his legs, he staggered down the hill in pursuit. It was a wonder to Dave that the terrier seemed to have any sense where it was going, since the grass was well over its head. Yet it kept on the steady track toward town and Dave felt his heart sink. He wanted to avoid being seen following the dog and risk questions as to why he was doing so. Suddenly Bones took a hard left and moved away from the city proper and toward the lake. Dave's legs began to complain about the labor of walking through the tall grass and his uniform soaked up the warmth from the sun. He wiped away sweat that threatened to roll into his eyes. His plan had been to keep a respectable distance so that the dog would be free to go where it wanted without feeling threatened, and he quickly realized that wasn't going to be a problem. The dog moved fast. Keeping Bones in sight was the real challenge.

The dog pushed into the deeper foxtail and disappeared completely, the only evidence of its location the movement of the grass through which it waded. It made Dave think of a shark, the way the foxtail waved and separated to mark the passage of the dog below its surface. Then, suddenly, the grass grew still.

Dave stopped, resting, and scanned the plain of long grass and weeds in front of him. Nothing moved. He took a deep breath and held it, listening. There was no sound at all—no labored panting, no rustle of movement. The grass stood straight and high. The dog wasn't there.

Dave cursed under his breath. How did that little mutt, with its wheeze and odd gait, manage to outsmart him? He turned in a slow circle, scanning. There, three hundred feet behind him, he saw the dog slip toward the banks of Foley Lake.

He didn't waste time trying to figure out how the dog had gotten around him, lifting his legs high as he struggled through the grass, trying to catch up. He was sucking down gulps of air by the time he broke out of the grass and onto the old trail that wound around the muddy, newly widened northern edge of the lake. The ground was open and soft from the recent rains, and Dave trotted along, holding his gun belt in place with both hands. The dog was still a hundred feet ahead when he slipped off the trail and into a thick stand of chokecherry.

Dave tried to push his way through the branches of the bush and was rewarded with nasty scratches on his face and hands. There was no forcing his way through. He stepped back out onto the trail and walked its edge until he found a break in the brush that allowed him to shove his way into the tree line and was frustrated to find that the far side of the chokecherry stand was not much thinner. He had to use his arms as brush guards for his face as he plowed through the foliage, hooked branches clawing at his ears and neck. He shoved forward blindly about twenty feet, then broke thought to taller trees and more open terrain. He stopped and scanned the woods in front of him. The dog appeared in flashes between the branches and brush up ahead, like a mirage.

Twenty feet in, Dave noticed that something didn't look right. Twigs were snapped and dangled from trees like broken fingers, their leaves wilting. In a few places brush was pressed flat, lying twisted against the ground. A little farther and Dave's way was blocked by a fallen pine tree, broken in two, the pungent scent of its sap perfuming the air. He climbed over it, only to be stopped a few feet farther on by an uprooted poplar lying at an angle across his path. The tree was big, its trunk easily as wide as Dave's waist. He was falling farther and farther behind the dog, which weaved in and out of the vegetation with ease. The fallen poplar was too high to crawl over. He scanned for an alternative route he saw the pine and poplar were not the only trees down. There was a wide swath of fallen trees in front of him, uprooted, broken, twisted into halves. Dave sighed. So there really was a tornado touchdown in Foley Lake. He would have to call Amy at dispatch and apologize. He smiled to himself. Maybe a dinner date would help smooth things over.

Crawling over the poplar was out of the question. Dropping to his hands and knees, Dave found a path under the tree and crawled forward. He was surprised to find that on his hands and knees, the way was clear and easier to navigate; no wonder the little dog could move with such speed. Up ahead, the dog had stopped and was searching back and forth at the base of another uprooted tree. It stopped its searching and turned to face Dave, a dirty bone in his mouth.

"Good dog," Dave chanted. "Good, good little scavenger." The man crept forward as Bones sat down and waited quietly, and when Dave reached for the bone, the dog willingly gave it up. Then, bone in hand, Dave stretched forward and looked at the base of the downed poplar.

"Oh, my God," he said.

***

Mike was late for supper, and he sat at the table with his rewarmed food as he filled Lane in on Dave's find. It seemed that Bones had discovered part of an old cemetery. Dave had arrived at city hall, muddy and animated, and asked Mike to pull up the oldest city records he had. While Mike searched files in a dark storage room in the town hall's basement, Dave filled him in on the details of the find. Three ancient graves, ripped open by the roots of fallen trees, and at least four additional patches of sunken, rectangular ground Dave suspected of being more graves. The cop had found little by way of markers, except one round stone that bore the initials "CM" and some indiscernible numbers that might have been a date. Dave had already put in calls to the Bureau of Criminal Apprehension and the archeology department at St. Cloud University, where the bored-sounding professor on the other end of the line told him that the dog had probably discovered the burial grounds for Foley Lake's original settlers. The professor promised to send some graduate students to have a look at the site and offer advice as to the best way to proceed.

When Mike finished talking, Lane leaned back in her chair, shaking her head. "Wow," she managed. "What a weird find. But I don't understand—the original town site was on the west bank of the lake, right? And we know there were cemeteries on the east and south banks, because those bodies were moved to the new cemetery a long time ago. But this cemetery was on the north side. It's a long walk from any of the old city sites to where you say this cemetery is. Why would the people who set up the original village put the cemetery so far away?"

Mike forked a couple of bites of food into his mouth, nodding. "I wondered the same thing," he said through a mouthful.

Lane grew silent, considering. She leaned back in the chair and rubbed her eyes. When she looked up again her father was watching her, frowning.

"Are you okay?"

"Yeah. I'm tired. I can't seem to sleep lately. You said the oldest city maps you found are from the mine company, right?"

Mike nodded. "There aren't any earlier, as far as I know."

Lane raised her eyebrows. "What if the cemetery was here before the mine? The professor said this was probably *an* original gravesite. But what if it's *the* original grave site?"

Mike pushed his plate away and shrugged. "The mine bought the land from the federal government. No one owned it before they did. If someone was here, they would have been squatters."

"Well," Lane said, "what now? Are you going to let people know about this, or do we just wait until the college sends someone up to see if we can find more information?"

Mike chuffed through his nose. "Eugenia saw Dave's squad outside the city hall and stopped in to see what's happening. I expect by tomorrow morning, the entire city will know exactly what that little dog found in the woods."

Chapter Thirty-Eight

Warren paced.

A copy of the newspaper lay folded on the kitchen table. He laid it face down so he didn't have to look at it, although the headline burned itself into his mind the moment he clapped eyes on it.

The Dead Rise in Foley Lake.

He didn't know what to do. Nothing had rattled him like those words. Even the return of the man and Lane's failure to recognize him hadn't terrified him the way the newspaper story did. Then there was last night. He felt his face burning with humiliation and shame. The bed sheets he'd washed in the early morning hours hung snapping in the sharp breeze out on the clothesline.

He knew this day would come. He had known it since he was thirteen. His dreams were plagued with images that terrified him, of brutal hands moving slowly, pushing a plank back to its very edge; the horrifying pallid skin and blank stare framed in blackness; that same look on his mother's face when he finally forced the bathroom door open. He was utterly abandoned. No one was there to help him now. He would have to figure out the signs for himself.

Warren's pacing brought him into his mother's room. He stood in the middle of the tiny space, the narrow bed, the neat dresser on which she had carefully arranged a few favorite items. Those things had gained a thin layer of dust since her death. He picked up an ornate bottle half-full of the perfume he bought her for Christmas two years before. She had been so pleased with the gift and the show of affection it represented. He knew he hadn't been considerate of her feelings for many years, and though the perfume was only a token, she treasured it. She had sworn she would wear that perfume only on special occasions, but she wore it regularly, just a tiny squirt discernable when he had reason to stand very close to her. She treasured the gift, although within days he slipped back into his old habits, his silence and brooding, and he continued to ignore her until, maybe, she questioned whether she existed at all. Maybe that was why she made the decision to leave him for good. He didn't know, couldn't know for sure. She never talked to him about it. She used to talk incessantly, but in the months before she died she had stopped. He didn't question why. He was glad for the silence. Now silence was all there was.

What was he supposed to do? What did it mean, the discovery of dead bodies among the trees? Was it a sign? And what of the mine flooding again, the backwards flow of the lake seeping into the lower drifts and shaft of the Foley? He glanced at the empty corner that had been filled by the three small boxes of his father's belonging, things his mother had warned him away from but seemed unable to throw away. His first act when he came home from her funeral was to scoop up all three boxes and march them out of the house. He wanted to be free of them. He felt a stir of uneasiness as he dumped them unopened into the big metal trash can, but he put both hands on the top box and shoved them to the bottom. That night a strong wind swept over his house, downing a tree, tipping the garbage cans, and scattering trash across the yard. He'd picked up everything he could find; papers, sketches, small tools, an odd gear it took him weeks to identify, and repacked them in brand new boxes, stacking them back in the corner. With every bow to pick up a scrap his mind chanted *forgive me, forgive me.* The next night he heard the cursed announcement. The mine would be reopened. Once again, the Milfords would have what was rightfully theirs, theirs by *blood*, ripped from them. And he knew that the news demanded that he make a choice between acting like a coward or acting like his father's son.

Suddenly Warren was sinking down, down, into the endless blackness, the stench of death rising to meet him. The vision was so sharp a tide of nausea welled up inside him and he clenched his fist closed over the perfume bottle, snapping the delicate glass neck. In seconds the room was filled with the scent of his mother, and the nausea was replaced by the ache of deep loneliness. He set the broken bottle back on the dresser, the ruined top beside it.

In the kitchen he stopped in front of the sink, staring out the window. The sun was slipping toward the west; it would be dark soon. He reached out and clicked on the heat under the coffee pot to rewarm what was left of the morning's brew, then drew the shade. He moved in a circle around the house, window to window, pulling each shade low, completely blocking the view of the outside world. Soon the dark would come, and he would begin another long vigil.

The scent of the perfume wafted softly from the bedroom down the hall, and he took comfort in it. It was almost like she was there. He knew it was possible. The dead never did seem to stay down long.

Chapter
Thirty-Nine

The birthday guests arrived in a flurry of car doors slamming and knocks at the screen, and within twenty minutes the quiet of the summer day disassembled into the riotous confusion of chattering pre-adolescent girls. Lane had been walking around in a haze since the incident at the mine and despite her assurance that she only had a mild summer flu, Lowie followed after her with a worried frown marring her young face. During that first sleepless night Lane decided she did not want to discuss the mine at all, not with anyone; she extracted a sound promise from Lowie to never step foot on mine property again, and then let it go. Lane simply could not, would not assimilate what happened at the mine—the desire to get close to the shaft, the force in the blast of wind that pushed her back—into her framework for believing that her brother had died in a freak accident. Still, the memory of that day picked at the edges of her logical and pragmatic understanding of what had actually killed him, keeping her awake and making her heart pound whenever an image of the head frame's interior emerged in her mind.

Lane stayed away from Butch all week, afraid he might perceive the apprehension on her face in that disarmingly intuitive way he had. But today she wouldn't be able to avoid him. She would have to disconnect from him as best she could, lest he notice her inner turmoil and say something that made her lose the fragile grip she had on her emotions.

The girls moved together as a giggling, chattering knot, flitting from room to room, reminding a bemused and overwhelmed Mike of a flock of birds moving through the air with perfect dips and switchbacks as if directed by an unseen hand. The noise level dissolved when the girls whirled up the stairs to see Lowie's room, the muffled chatter wafting down from above.

A bright glint of light in the driveway drew Lane's attention, and she turned to look just in time to be nearly blinded by a brilliant orb flashing through the window. Using her hand to shield her eyes, she realized Butch was walking up the driveway, the large oval mirror he carried throwing shards of sunlight toward the house.

Butch's arrival drew squeals of delight from the girls, who spotted him from Lowie's window and flooded down the stairs and out the front door toward him in a wave, Lowie riding its crest. Lane took her time following them. By the time she came out of the house Butch's advance had been stopped and he stood surrounded by the girls, the lowered mirror resting against the top of his boot.

Lane had ceased to be surprised that all the adults in town seemed to know Butch, but she hadn't expected a giggling, squirming herd of almost-fourth graders to recognize him. Yet they all greeted him with toothy grins and girlish flirting. A mild sort of competition emerged for Butch's attention, though all the girls seemed to defer to Lowie as having the superior claim. They stooped to look at themselves in the mirror, vamping and pulling faces.

Lane approached, feeling awkward. She had been leaving notes for him taped to the door of the city garage, telling him what she wanted him to work on that day and making excuses for needing to be in another part of the city. But he met her with an easy smile, and she felt a ray of hope that he would take the notes as face value and not question her reasons for avoiding him.

The girls parted and created a path for her to get closer. The giggling and the questions dried up as the five sets of bright, curious eyes looked from Lane to Butch and back again, clearly expecting something to happen.

Lane smiled politely and nodded to the mirror. "Is that the one you found in the garage?"

"It's the same. I sanded the frame and put on a fresh coat of stain. That cleaned it up a bit. "

"Wow," Lane said. "It's beautiful."

"I'm glad you like it," Butch replied. "It's for you." The girls drew a collective gasp and gapped at Lane. She stared at him for a moment, then shook her head. "Um—oh," she stammered.

"It's for the family," he explained.

Lane was irritated to find her cheeks growing hot. "That wasn't necessary." The words had more bite than she meant them to, but Butch seemed oblivious.

"Well, I can't take it with me when I go, and now it really *is* too nice to throw away. So if you could find a place for it, I'd be appreciative." His reasoning inspired a new eruption of giggles from the girls. Butch turned to Lowie. "As for you, Miss Lowie, seeing as how it is your birthday, your gift is in the garage."

The girls turned en masse and raced to the garage, slamming the door open. The building did little to muffle the squeals inside, and a few seconds later Lowie emerged astride a most remarkable bicycle. It was a hybrid of sorts, composed of the reclaimed frame of the red Schwinn Butch had rescued, its rusted fenders replaced by the freshly painted blue fenders from Lowie's outgrown bike. Brand-new black rubber tires were mounted on the recycled rims, each spoke hand-painted red and blue alternately. The bike's white banana seat was spotless, thought clearly not new. A bright yellow basket was strapped to the handlebars and filled with a bouquet of wild daisies. Lowie beamed as she rode the bike down the driveway and onto the road while the girls ran behind in her wake.

Lane stared after her, wistful. "Butch, it's so weird. I used to have a bike just like that one. The banana seat, the basket…it's crazy. I loved that bike."

Lane turned and realized that Butch wasn't looking at Lowie. He was gazing at Lane, watching her remember.

***

Butch carried the mirror into the house and propped it against the wall in Mike's office. Lane wanted to hang it in her bedroom, but she wasn't about to have five little girls going home and telling tales of Butch doing *anything* in her bedroom, so the office proved to be the best solution to keep the mirror safe until the party ended. She served sloppy joe sandwiches and chips for lunch, lit the candles on the cake, supervised games, and wrote a list of who gave Lowie which gifts so that the girl could write thank-you notes the next day. Sometime during a game of Blind Man's Bluff, Mike slipped up behind Butch and said something quietly. Butch nodded and both men disappeared, and Lane didn't begrudge them the escape.

Chapter Forty

Butch stood patiently behind Mike as the old man fished a small key out of his trouser pocket and tripped the padlock. The narrow wooden door, tucked away at the back of a dark corridor in the courthouse, creaked open to lament its long disuse. Butch followed Mike up a narrow staircase that ended in a small landing, then watched as Mike crawled spider-like up a ladder bolted to the wall and push open a trap door on the ceiling. He followed Mike up and emerged through the floor to find himself inside Foley Lake's clock tower.

The inside of the clock tower was a small, mostly vacant square just big enough for Mike and Butch to stand comfortably. From the ground, the tower looked completely enclosed, but Butch saw a number of gaps in the horizontal vents in the tower's walls that allowed a partial view of the square below. Butch moved around the perimeter of the room, peeking out at the city from every direction.

"Interesting, isn't it?" Mike said. "It's a whole different view of the city."

"Yeah. Funny how everything looks so neat from up here."

"Despite Lane's best work, that is truly an illusion," Mike chuckled. "Butch, you've heard some of the wild stories going around town, some of the ghost tales and such, right?"

"Lowie told me a doozie the other day," Butch replied. "Which?"

"Something about her grandfather haunting the mine. I was surprised she would get caught up in that kind of story. She's a smart kid."

"Yeah. That old story started right after the flood. I think every place that suffered the way the mine did is bound to breed some kind of legend. But you probably noticed that kids aren't the only ones in town that are worried. That flood killed forty-nine miners, and there was one body they couldn't get back out. Some adults believe there is a ghost here, or some kind of evil that hovers over this city."

Butch clucked his tongue. "I can see the kids believing such things, but you would think adults would know better."

Mike nodded. Silence fell for a few moments while each gazed out his respective corner overlooking the city.

"Did Lane tell you she had a brother?"

"She told me she was an only child."

"Did she?" Mike sounded vaguely hurt. Butch turned, taking in Mike's profile. The light filtering in cast the old man's shadow across the wooden floor. "I suppose she was, after we lost Paul. She had an older brother who died when he was eleven years old. He was at the mine with a group of kids, though they weren't supposed to go up there. My wife and I told them over and over that the shaft was still open. But they didn't listen. Well, my mother told me the same thing, and I went up there. We should have known. That place drew kids all the time. In a way I suppose it's amazing that no one got hurt long before that day. Paul went into the head frame on a dare. He fell in. It was an accident, from what we understand."

Butch stirred. "From what you understand?"

Mike paused, choosing his words. "The kids that were at the mine that day said they could hear—*something*—in the shaft with Paul. None of them could describe exactly what they heard. Some said voices, even laughing. Others said screams. A child's screams."

Mike broke off. Butch waited. When he spoke again, his face sagged with the weight of the memory.

"The kids ran. By the time they made it back to the city they were hysterical. We went to the mine, into the head frame, and looked everywhere. There was no sign of my son. Not a trace. We searched the entire city, the woods, the lake, and engineers from up by the Vermillion range came down and searched the shaft. They couldn't find him. He wasn't there."

"Are you saying he didn't fall in?"

"They found some blood and—" Mike paused, swallowing hard. "They found hair on a pile of debris at the bottom of the shaft. No, he fell down there. I have no doubt about that. But why wasn't he there? He couldn't have walked away. Where would he have gone? It's almost impossible that he would have survived the fall. They took some of the debris out in order to look for him, until it just got too unsafe. We never found anything else. We didn't find anything."

"That doesn't make sense," Butch said slowly. When the old man didn't reply, Butch leaned forward, a wave of agitation sweeping over him. "They can't have been as thorough as you think. If they looked that hard, as hard as you say, and he was there, they would have found him."

The older man didn't answer.

"You don't believe the ghost stories…"

Mike blinked. "No, of course not. But for twenty years I have been trying to make sense of this. Children don't just up and disappear. And losing a child, not even having his body, well, it just destroyed my wife. She was never the same after that. And me, I've wracked my brain trying to put the clues together. I just can't figure out a logical explanation for what happened to my boy."

"What clues?"

"Some things that didn't makes sense. There were some odd scuff marks on the concrete at the edge of the shaft. Scrapes, or drag marks. And there was some writing in the dust on the floor in there, too. I didn't see it right away, and by the time I did some of the letters were gone from all the footprints of people who came to help. It said 'priceless,' I think."

"Priceless?"

"That's what it looked like to me. Other people thought it just said 'price,' or maybe 'penance.' No one knows for sure."

Butch moved across the room and found a crevice that looked out toward the mine. He stuffed his hands into his pockets, stilling a small tremor that vibrated up from his core.

"Penance," he said quietly.

Mike nodded. "Things got pretty tense around town for a while. Folks had some good reasons to be nervous. Their children running down that hill, terrified, hysterical. Folks didn't know how to react. After Paul disappeared there was an exodus of sorts from the city. Several families just up and left. Mostly they were families of kids that had been at the mine that day. I guess I can't blame them. Strange things were happening. People insisted there was a ghost, a miner in a white slicker, walking around the city at night. Some of those children had a time getting over what they heard inside the shaft. Screams, they said. Inhuman screams. There were rumors the whole city had gone evil. Kids had nightmares, some claimed to see strange lights and sounds coming from the mine—well, you know how things get out of hand. But after a while the talk died down and things went pretty much back to normal. But now..."Mike turned his gaze back to the little city below him. "I don't know. Marlys Milford kills herself, people who have been friends their whole lives are turning on each other, there's talk about seeing that ghost again, that little dog turns up with a skull, and all those bodies—well, folks are just about at the end of their ropes. And this old clock just sounding out the hour, after years of nothing—I don't know what to do about it, Butch. I don't know if I can stop it.

"Stop what?" Butch said.

"Stop this city from flying into pieces."

"Maybe you shouldn't try."

Mike raised his eyebrows and looked at Butch. Butch met his gaze. "Maybe things just need to take their natural course."

"What would that be?" Mike asked. "How does something like this have a 'natural course?'"

"I don't really know. But I do know this. If you bury something, you better to bury it dead. If you bury it alive, it won't stay in the ground."

"Now you're the one talking about ghosts."

"I don't believe in ghosts," Butch replied. "At least not in the sense you mean." He turned abruptly and nodded toward the gears and works for the tower's clock. "Did you notice anything different about that old clock? Aside from the fact that it works now, I mean?"

Mike nodded, but he didn't turn to the clock. He didn't want to pull his gaze away from the quiet streets laid out before him. "It's clean," he said absently. "Someone took a rag to it."

"Well," Butch said. "I don't suppose a ghost would be worried about leaving fingerprints behind."

"I suppose not."

"Okay, then," Butch said. "Maybe the person was sending a message with stopping the clock, and now he's sending a new message by starting it. When, exactly, did the clock stop?"

Mike turned and looked Butch fully in the face. "The last time anyone remembers the clock working was the day that my son died inside the Foley Mine."

Chapter Forty-One

Lowie wasn't sure what woke her. She lay on her back on top of her sleeping bag, the blanket that had covered her thrown aside, frowning at the ceiling of the tree house. The battery-operated lamp her mother had given her to use was weakening, filling the room with soft shadows. Shanna and Kayla lay on their own sleeping bags on either side of her, their breathing the deep, steady rhythm of sound sleep. Lowie sighed and rolled over onto her stomach. Whatever had wakened her must have been part of a dream.

She was almost asleep when the sound came again. It was a rustling, like heavy material waving in a breeze. She propped herself up on one elbow, blinking in the dull light. Her sleep-numbed mind gave her an image of bed sheets hanging on the clothesline, waving and snapping in the sun. Yet she didn't recall seeing sheets on the line when she had climbed the ladder to the tree house just after sunset. Besides that, the air outside was perfectly still. Even if there were sheets on the line, they shouldn't be moving.

She sat up, listening. Nope, no wind. She yawned. There was nothing at all, as a matter of fact. No crickets, no frogs, no questioning *who-who* from the resident owls. The night was perfectly silent. So, when the sound of the fabric rustling and the light tread of footsteps on the grass rose, she realized the reason she could hear it so clearly was because she couldn't hear anything else.

Lowie crawled out of her nest between Shanna and Kayla to the hatchway in the floor. The homemade wooden bolt Butch had installed for her was in place, keeping the door from being pushed open from underneath. She listened at the door, wondering, and felt a jolt of fear as an image of Clinton Harris filled her mind, the whistle rope still tied around his waist as he gazed out from eyes rotted to empty sockets. She thought of her uncle Paul dead and abandoned at the bottom of the mine. In second grade Stu Webner, the boy who sat behind her, had drawn a picture of the mine's interior for history class. His great uncle helped him draw it, because he worked in the mine until it flooded. The drawing showed a long, skinny vertical shaft with two thicker horizontal drifts shooting out of the shaft's side. Stu had drawn an ugly, jagged hole at the end of the lower drift, where his uncle said the lake broke through, and standing in the drifts were rows of stick figure miners, all with big circle eyes and frowns. But in the bottom of the shaft Stu had drawn a smaller figure, eyes closed with two x's. When the teacher asked who the figure was Stu said it the rotting body of Paul Harris.

Lowie thought of that picture now. No miner, she thought, had the right to be a ghost—every one of them knew working in the mine was dangerous. But what of Paul? What had caused him to go into the shaft, and what had dragged him down into the black belly of the mine?

A cold shiver ran across Lowie's back. She told herself to get a grip. She was too big to believe in such tales, she told herself. Besides, even if the story was true, no self-loving ghost would take its vengeance on its only progeny.

She sat back on her heels, trying to think. Who would be down there at this time of night? Her mother? Maybe. It would be like her to walk out in the dark, in the middle of the night, just to check on them. In fact, her white cotton robe might make a rustling sound as she moved across the yard. She might be wandering back and forth under the tree house, locked out, unable to check on them and settle her own worries. And suddenly Lowie was ashamed of herself for being afraid.

She slid the bolt back and lifted the hatch halfway, as cool summer air wafted through the space. Holding the door for balance, Lowie leaned forward and peered down at a small patch of earth immediately below the hatchway.

"Mom?" she called in a loud whisper. She waited, listening. There was no reply. She leaned farther down, precariously balanced on her knees.

"Mom?" she called again, a little louder.

There it was. That rustle of fabric, the soft, fast stride of footsteps. Only something was wrong with the rhythm of the movement. Lowie Harris, who had been listening for her mother's step her whole life, suddenly realized it could not be her mother rushing toward the tree house's open door. The steps were wrong. All wrong.

A large man clad in a long, heavy, white canvas coat appeared in the square of earth below the hatch and stopped. Lowie gasped. The figure turned and looked up, and a strong yellow light on the man's hat hit the child's dark-loving eyes, blinding her. She leaped back, letting the door slam as she flung herself against the wall. She blinked in the darkness, trying to get her vision back. The rustling was getting closer. He was coming up the ladder. She threw herself forward onto the door just as she felt a solid bump against it. She slid the bolt into place and sprang back to her spot between Kayla and Shanna, crouching between them.

There was another solid bump against the locked hatch, then a slow scrape that chilled Lowie to the heart. Then nothing. After a time, the soft rustle faded back down the ladder. He was gone.

Lowie pulled her knees to her chest and hugged them against herself. She sat up for the rest of the night, keeping watch over her friends, her blanket pulled tightly around her shoulders as she prayed for the solace of first light.

Chapter
Forty-Two

Lane pulled a t-shirt out of the dresser drawer, tossed it onto the bed, and opened the closet to find jeans. The house was resting peacefully; her father was out somewhere and the restlessness that had been plaguing the house all morning went with him. Lowie collapsed onto the couch and fell asleep as soon as her guests left. Not that Lane was surprised. The child must have stayed up half the night goofing around with her friends, as tired and irritable as she was. Lane let her sleep and allowed herself the luxury of a long, cool midday bath.

She let the damp towel slip down to the floor and turned to pick up the t-shirt. In the periphery of her vision, she saw a glimpse of herself in the new mirror hanging on the bedroom wall opposite her closet.

She stopped what she was doing and turned to face the mirror, trying to comprehend what she was seeing.

Her skin glowed with a golden tan and her wet hair, far from the limp, plain mess she had always imagined, was vibrant and thick, chestnut streaked with honey. Her figure was statuesque, hips and breast full, waist narrow, thighs long and tapered. She was the image of feminine beauty, a siren, a goddess. She walked to the mirror, wondering if what she saw was a trick of the light. The closer she drew, the more beautiful her image became.

She turned away and ran for the door, scooping up the wet towel and wrapping it hastily around herself as she dashed down the hallway. She stepped into the bathroom, closed the door behind her, and pulled the towel away. She reached out and snapped on the light above the bathroom mirror.

Ordinary hair. Ordinary skin. Ordinary, everyday Lane.

She left the towel on the bathroom floor and walked naked back down the hall. Back at the mirror, she stood closer this time, studying her face. Her eyes glittered, deep hazel, surrounded by thick brown lashes. Her lips were pink and full, her complexion radiant.

She reached out and ran her fingers over the cool, smooth glass. As her skin brushed the surface, she felt warmth, then a sweet, deep ache of sadness, of desire, of yearning.

Lane pulled her hand away and stepped back, lowering herself to the edge of her bed. Tears flowed up from some deep place as the ache resonated inside her. What was that feeling? Love? More than love. This feeling made her long for something she couldn't define, ache for something she couldn't have. It was overwhelming in its force, and dangerous. Its power could take over her whole purpose for existing, had she known its source and the answer for its hunger. It was something like the way she felt for Lowie, but not. This feeling was steeped in passion and desire.

She gazed at her image. Tears streaked silver down her cheeks, the sadness beguiling, desire emanating from her as if her very essence longed for some unspoken tonic. An image of Butch's face flashed in her mind, the way he watched her, and a niggling memory struggled to come forth. But something inside her reacted like a door slamming shut, and the memory faded.

A word came to her. She stood and slipped back out of the room and across the hall to Lowie's bedroom. Lane lifted a dictionary from a Lowie's bookcase in the corner and took it back to her bedroom. She closed and locked the door, sitting on the bed where she could see herself in the mirror. She opened the book and began turning pages. There. That was the word she was thinking of.

Unrequited.

She read the definitions, committing them to memory; *Not reciprocated; not avenged or retaliated, Not repaid; unsatisfied.*

Unrequited. That was the feeling.

She stood and looked at herself again. There was no reason for the beauty she was seeing. But her stunning reflection wasn't what stirred her. It was the *unrequited.* She realized for the first time in her life how the word fit her.

She crossed to the window and looked out through the gauzy lace curtain. The street was quiet and empty. A wave of loneliness washed over her, and a sharp awareness of how successful she had been in building the walls of isolation that trapped her. She had become a princess in a tower, trapped by a dragon of her own design. She had never allowed herself to feel an ache over what might be, or long for what she didn't have. Yet somehow Butch had managed to capture the passion she refused to own in a bit of wood and glass and bring it right to her front door.

She gazed out of the window to the empty street below, wrestling with the ramifications of facing life if she were to slay the dragon. Who would emerge from the tower? Ordinary, average Lane? Or the woman in the mirror? She doubted that anyone would be able to see them as the same person. There was only one who might.

Chapter Forty-Three

Mike stood at the base of the tree house, staring up. His knuckles were white, clenched around the razor he held in his hand. His undershirt, fresh just moments ago, was damp with sweat and hung limp across his narrow chest. The sun was dodging in and out of clouds and blots of gray and gold chased each other across the lawn. The breeze rippled the dull black fabric of a flag hanging next to the tree house's rough frame.

A jolly roger. A worn, graying jolly roger, its grinning skull and thick crossbones fading and flaking from the old fabric. Mike had spotted the flag hanging next to his reflection in the bathroom mirror as he stood shaving, the tree house framed by the small bathroom window opposite the mirror. The next fully conscious thought he had was of standing at the base of the tree house, looking up at the pirate flag, the shaving cream growing warm and running in rivulets down his throat and across the tangle of gray chest hairs poking up at the top of the shirt.

A jolly roger. He didn't understand the appearance of the flag. Where did it come from? Had it been here long?

Was it Paul's?

He pushed that last thought away and scolded himself. No, of course it wasn't Paul's. The jolly roger he had given Paul was destroyed years ago.

The old fish house fort. Mike bought the little wooden shack when the kids were small, and every fall he told himself that as soon as the ice was solid, he would haul the shack out to the lake for a little ice fishing. But Minnesota winters are bitter, the days short and full, and he never got around to making use of the house. Paul, however, couldn't seem to stay away from it. Mike spent two years chasing the boy and his friends out the fish house before he realized that letting them use the narrow shack as a fort meant he no longer had to feel guilty about not using it for fishing. The shack became plaything, Lane's dollhouse, Paul's pirate liar. Mike spotted a jolly roger at a rummage sale and brought it home, and that old flag hung from the side of the fish house for the rest of Paul's life and for many years after, until constant exposure to the elements tore and tattered the fabric to shreds.

The ache in his hand from his extraordinary grip on the razor brought him back to himself. He relaxed his fingers, letting the cramped muscles loosen. He reached out and touched the ladder, and when the impulse to climb struck him, he didn't resist. His hands and feet felt awkward climbing rungs situated for a small girl, but he made his way up, pushing open the trap door at the bottom of the tree house and pulling himself through the floor.

Despite Lowie's frequent invitations, he had not taken the time to climb inside the house before. As his eyes adjusted to the dim light, he realized how much the girl valued the space. She had spent a good deal of time decorating the inside in the days since she and Butch finished it. An old rug covered most of the floor. A poster of two unicorns running across a stormy sky took up one wall, while three baby dolls, rejected as toys but deemed suitable for their aesthetics, were propped up in a box in a corner. A notebook, some pens and a scattering of books lay in the opposite corner.

Mike turned and looked through the window at his home. If it wasn't for Lane and Lowie, it would be unbearably empty, though he was aware of the deep wrong he'd committed by trapping Lane there by his neediness. He didn't know what else to do. He was drawing the life out of her, but he was helpless to stop himself. If he made her leave, she would find her own life, and he would fade into a limbo of despair.

He descended the ladder and walked slowly back to the house, grabbing a towel on his way through the empty kitchen to mop the cream from his face. He moved past the bathroom and down the hall to the closed door. He stopped to catch his breath, then opened the door and stepped though.

Paul's room was preserved as it had been the day he died. Mike had allowed Mary Louise to wash the scattering of dirty clothes that had been left on the floor, and to make the narrow bed, but beyond that it was untouched. He stood in the middle of the room, savoring the scene though it broke his heart anew each time he walked through the seldom-used door. An old pine dresser dominated one wall, still filled with the clothes Paul wore the summer that he died. On top of the dresser were two electric train engines, a yellowing picture of Old Faithful clipped from a magazine and pasted into a frame, a plastic Brier statue of an Appaloosa stallion. The bed sat exactly opposite the dresser, and next to it a small bookshelf held an assortment of paperbacks and comic books that the boy had loved.

Mike stepped to the shelf and reached in—his hand was trained where to reach, for he had long since memorized the placement of every book on the shelf. His fingers brushed the book he needed, and he pulled it out. It was *Treasure Island,* a special edition with notes from the author and a full-color drawing at the beginning of each chapter. He had ordered it from a bookstore for Paul's eighth birthday, and the boy loved it, reading it over and over again. Mike had never seen another edition like it. He rubbed his palm over the cover, thinking of all the times his boy had held the book, how even now he might somehow connect with some of Paul's skin cells or sweat or any other thing of him that could still be on the worn cover. He longed for that connection, any connection he could find to bring the boy back across the chasm of time and space that separated them.

A loud knock from the front of the house roused Mike from his ponderings. He left the bedroom, carrying the book with him, and crossed the kitchen to see Dave's head poking through the open kitchen door.

"Morning, Mike," he greeted. "Got a minute?"

Mike waved him in, offered him a cup of coffee, and took a seat at the table. He motioned Dave to take the opposite chair and waited. Dave dispensed with any niceties and got straight to the point.

"Have you ever heard of preemption?"

"Preemption. I don't know. Depends on the context you mean, I guess."

"In the context of land ownership. Ever heard of it?"

"Has to do with who claims the earliest right to land, I think."

Dave nodded. "Basically. Preemption was something people used during the earliest settling of this area. Originally the government held the rights to all the land, and preemption said that whoever settled a plot of land earliest has the first right to purchase it from the government when it became available for sale. It was used all over the country when territories gained statehood and the government wanted to settle the area."

Mike nodded. "Like homesteading."

Dave took a sip of coffee and shook his head. "Preemption came before homesteading. Before the land was officially ready to homestead, a few people made their way into the wild areas and worked the land, hunting, farming, whatever. But it was a hard life, because they were completely alone. No roads to speak of, no stores or doctors or law. Nothing but Indians and the wild animals, either of which might put an end to the settlers in a hurry."

"They were squatters, then," Mike said.

"More or less. But no one considered what they were doing wrong. The government didn't try to stop them. They wanted to get folks out here and get them working. So if settlers came out and they survived to clear the land and build a home, it couldn't be taken from them later. Eventually surveyors were sent into a territory, and they mapped the land, assessed its value, and let anyone living in the area know they should file for preemption so their land would be protected once homesteaders showed up. After that, the land was opened for homesteading."

"Very interesting," Mike said, gazing at the cover of the book he still held. "But this city was built on property the mine company bought from the government, so I don't see what it has to do…"

"Well, that's where you'd be wrong. The mine company didn't buy this land from the government. It bought the mine, including all the land Foley Lake sits on, from fifteen different men who filed for the land under preemption. And I think it has everything to do with the little burial plot out on the north end of the lake."

Mike raised his eyebrows. He stood slowly and took a clean coffee cup from the drying rack, poured the last cup of coffee for himself, and sat back down. "Go on."

"The mine companies knew there was iron ore in this area. There's iron ore under half the state. Mines up on the Vermillion range were getting ore with almost seventy percent iron content. *Seventy percent.* A lot of mines where lucky to see forty percent ore. This area promised to be just as profitable as the northern ranges. So, the companies sent their own surveyors to slip in here and bore test holes to find out where the good ore was and draw out maps showing the most valuable land. Now, the mines knew the government surveyors would do the same thing, test the land to find out how what was in the ground before they offered anything for sale. And once the mine knew what it had here, it didn't want to risk losing the land in a bidding war. So, they used preemption."

"They hired people to settle the land they wanted, I suppose," Mike said.

"Yep. They got a lot of it that way. They hired what they called 'entrymen' to claim the land, then the mine bought it from them at $1.25 an acre. It was illegal, but no one seemed to care that it happened. It was basically condoned."

"What does that have to do with the old cemetery, then? You think some of these entrymen were buried there?"

"The date on the stone I found was worn down, but it looked like 1849. That is almost ten years before the earliest preemption claims I could find. No, I think there were already some folks here when the preemptions were filed."

"So, people where settled here, but they either ignored the need to file preemption on their land or they didn't know they had to."

Dave nodded. "Or someone beat them to it."

Mike sat back in his chair. "You reckon the folks that were already here were the Milfords?"

Dave sighed. "You know what that family has always claimed."

"That the land was stolen from them, yeah. By the mine company, they said."

"Looks a little more possible, considering what Bones turned up out there."

Mike turned from Dave and gazed out the window. "When I was growing up Ruben Milford never missed a chance to try to beat me up. I couldn't figure out why he hated me so. My mother used to say that he was crazy, and that his father and grandfather had been too. They were always raving about how the land the mine sits on was stolen out from under them. But as far as I know, there was never any proof of that. Everyone just thought the whole clan was nuts. Everyone did."

"The initials on the stone I found were 'CM.'" Dave said.

"Could have been a Milford founding father, then."

"The Milford homestead is one of the oldest in the county," Dave added, "so one thing is true, that clan has been here longer than your family or mine."

"Well, that's all very interesting. But you can't prove any of it, can you?"

"Apparently there are some tests they can do on the bones to see if those dead people are related to anyone here. But it would take a long time and it would be expensive. And we need a living blood relative of the Milford clan willing to agree to provide a blood sample."

Both men looked at each other.

"This is going to stay a mystery, isn't it?" Mike said.

"Yep. Warren doesn't seem like the curious type. I doubt he'd cooperate. But we are eventually going to need to bury these folks somewhere."

Mike rubbed his forehead. The ache that had been there all morning was building. "How many graves do we have out there?"

"Looks like six, total."

"Well, that's going to cost something."

"Right. But we can't just leave them above ground."

"No, I reckon we have to do something for them."

Dave leaned forward. "You know, Eugenia is nosing around constantly, asking for details about those bodies. And I've gotten calls from TV stations in Minneapolis and Duluth wondering if the story here is worth their time. I don't know what to do about that. If I tell them what I know, I risk making our whole history a scandal. But if I stay quiet, it looks like I'm trying to hide something."

Mike laid his hand on the book and stared past Dave, out the back window to the tree house. The jolly roger flicked softly as the breeze ruffled past it. He thought about his father, his son.

"Tell them," he said. "Tell them everything you know. They can check the facts for themselves. We aren't keeping any secrets. Not for anyone. Not anymore."

Chapter
Forty-Four

Foley Lake lived for the Fourth of July. Most Minnesota cities celebrated every summer holiday with a verve common among regions that spent five months of the year in a deep freeze. But even among these, Foley Lake's fireworks display was a stand-out. The city designated twenty thousand dollars to the fireworks display alone, a scandalous amount for a council with an overall annual budget of less than two million dollars, and that extravagance was supplemented by money collected in fundraisers and bake sales and small metal cans scattered throughout the resident merchants, appealing to local shoppers to drop their spare coins in for the glory of Foley Lake's biggest event. Other cities in the area vested a good deal of time and effort in parades and other daytime diversions, but not Foley Lake. The collective effort of the city was completely vested in the night of the Fourth, when the sky turned black and provided the perfect palette to paint the night with fire.

Roger Dean ran the fireworks show, and Foley Lake was the envy of many a Minnesota town because of it. Roger was the state's greatest pyrotech, being the talent behind the St. Paul River fest in the spring and the Vikings Winter Wonder held on frozen Lake Mille Lacs every January. He was a hot commodity come July, and he had been courted by several bigger cities with budgets much larger than the little town of Foley Lake's, bake sales and tin cans notwithstanding. But Roger was faithful to his unwritten commitment to serve the small, backwards city; he was, after all, one of Foley Lake's native sons.

The awkwardness Lane felt around Butch melted into a shy self-consciousness every time she was around him. The image of herself in the mirror emerged every time he was close, and she found herself wanting to be that woman. Moreover, the man knew how to work. By the time the big day came every green space in the city had been mowed and raked, the picnic tables set up, the parking spaces outlined with a border of orange traffic cones and chalk, streets blocked off to accommodate the foot traffic, and extra trash cans stationed at regular intervals. A line of portable toilets stood like soldiers along the back edge of the park. A menagerie of vendors began to arrive late in the morning, their colorful trailers laden with the aroma of grease and sweets.

Roger appeared in the park early in the morning with his crew, setting up the equipment on the baseball diamond. Racks of mortars that held the fireworks stood in banks, and the perimeter of the diamond was cordoned off by a series of roadblocks, rope, and more orange cones.

Lane ducked under the rope and greeted Roger. He returned the greeting with an affectionate hug. "Hello there, Lane. How are you? How's that kid of yours?"

"We're just fine," Lane responded. "She's getting bigger, and I'm just getting older, I guess." Lane surveyed the scene, noting the homemade mortars racks, fashioned from rows of heavy vertical PVC pipe supported by wooden frames to keep them upright, stood at intervals along the edges of Roger's working area. Among the group of strangers Roger had working for him, Lane recognized a familiar face.

"Hey, is that Terrence over there?" Terrence Larson heard his name and glanced at Lane with a shy grin.

"The one and only. I get him from Chuck whenever they can spare him from the farm. He's good with the mortars, learned them last year. This year he's been learning how to program the fireboard to cue the mortars to fire off. You know, he programmed most of tonight's show himself." Lane raised her eyebrows and looked past Roger to Terence. "You did?"

The boy shrugged, blushing. "I did some of it."

"He did most all of it. And it's fine work, as you'll see in a few hours. By next year he'll be an old hand at this. I'll have him set up the whole show while I sit in the shade and drink iced tea."

Lane laughed. "Sounds like you're working yourself out of a job."

Roger nodded. "That's the plan." Terrence grinned and turned away, his face a bright red. Roger chuckled and nudged Lane with his shoulder as he walked away, a sign that she should follow him. He spoke quietly as we walked.

"Terence tells me there's been some trouble around town."

Lane shook her head. "No real trouble," she replied, and turned to watch a new vendor pull in to avoid looked Roger in the eye. "People have been jumpy since this whole thing about the mine reopening came up. There's been a lot of bickering and some problems with vandalism, trespassing, that sort of thing."

Roger slowly removed his sunglasses and used the edge of his shirt to rub the lenses, watching Lane out of the corner of his eye. "He said something about people seeing ghosts and whatnot."

"Well, you know that's nonsense. But it does seem like someone, or maybe a few 'someones,' are working hard to keep people around here off balance."

Roger fiddled with the glasses a bit longer, and Lane could see that he was wrestling with some internal decision whether to speak or remain silent. Finally, he turned and looked at her. "I know that a story told by a bunch of scared kids doesn't hold much weight with most people, but my little sister was at the mine the day your brother died up there. She was just an ordinary kid, not a particularly good liar. But let me tell you, that day she was terrified. Absolutely terrified. I've never seen anyone so scared."

Roger looked back over his shoulder at Terrence laboring away to set up a rack of mortars. "I don't know what those kids heard up on that hill. But whatever it was, it was real. I have never doubted that. And I have never understood why anyone—even you, my dear—would choose to stay and raise a kid in this cursed city."

Lane scowled. "Cursed. Honestly, you're worse than the kids are."

"Maybe. But to this day my sister won't talk about what happened. Ask her and she just gets this look on her face and walks out of the room."

"What happened to my brother has nothing to do with what's going on today. People are just superstitious—" she made a point of looking hard at him— "and they let their imaginations fill in every blank they can't account for."

"Well, maybe. Hopefully, whatever is happening now is the result of overactive imaginations. But the fireworks show will be over by eleven, and I plan to be out of here by midnight. This place doesn't feel right. I don't plan to hang around long enough to find out why."

Chapter
Forty-Five

Spot paced down the hallway of his precise three-bedroom rambler, a crumpled note in his hand. His short-sleeved button-down shirt hung open and loose past his ample hips, not quite hiding his stark white briefs. His pants lay where he left them on the bedroom floor, where Sandy, had she known her place, would have picked them up, folded them neatly, and placed them in a pile to go to the cleaners. But Sandy apparently didn't know her place, because Spot came home to the empty house, despite his repeated warnings to her that he expected her to be waiting for him when he arrived. He worked all day, toiling to make a living, and he expected her to show her appreciation when he came back home. But when he called out only silence greeted him, and when he went to the bedroom to take off his business pants and slip into some comfortable shorts, he noticed that his clean suit coats had been pushed back. He could see the wall safe, its thick door standing open.

The note in Sandy's graceful script told him that she was in love with another man and that she was leaving and never coming back. It also said that she wanted a divorce, and that he could keep everything else, but she was taking the cash. He sat stunned on the closet floor for a full minute, staring at the hollow safe where just hours before $11,384 dollars had been arranged in crisp stacks. Rage and grief compelled him to his feet. He left his closet and pulled hers open to find it full, but for a few notably empty hangers. He went to the dresser and, thinking not of Sandy in the arms of another man, but of the $11,384 that was to have been converted into a brand-new boat next spring, pulled open the drawers in search of a wooden jewelry box. Sandy kept her few expensive pieces of jewelry, including his mother's ruby necklace and the wedding ring she had stopped wearing the year before, in that box. The box was gone. His anger turned to panic when he saw that his own top dresser drawer stood ajar, the wood chipped and dented where it was pried open to defeat the lock. He searched frantically through the drawer, upsetting the order of the folded shirts, until his was satisfied that the Rolex he wore to impress wealthy clients, his grandfather's gold cuff links, a stack of silver dollars, and a voucher for two free dinner buffets at Grand Casino in Mille Lacs fifty miles away, were all gone.

Spot bolted out the front door, determined to make Foley's worthless excuse for a cop find Sandy and get back his property. It wasn't until he felt the stinging burn on the backs of his thighs from the hot leather seats of his Cadillac that he realized he still wasn't wearing any pants. He marched back into the house and, somewhere between the threshold and the bedroom he lost his resolve. He flung himself on the couch and bawled. A woman had robbed him. She duped him into trusting her completely. He was ashamed that he had let it happen, and grateful that both his father and his grandfather were long dead and had not lived to see that he had failed as a man by losing control of his own household.

He wailed and kicked for fifteen minutes until, his tantrum spent, he rolled over onto his back and wiped his nose across his sleeve He stared up at the ceiling, his breathing occasionally interrupted with angry hiccups. He should have known this would happen when she started talking about wanting to have a kid three years ago. He didn't want any kids, so he found her a job instead. The pitiful salary she earned from Bjork as a secretary was laughable, but at least she was making her own money. Apparently, making money wasn't her only interest. At some point, she got a boyfriend and she got greedy. And now he was left destitute. Except for the the car lot, the house, and $80,000 he had tucked away in annuities he never bothered to mention to her, he had nothing. She had broken him.

Spot pulled himself into a sitting position, gathering strength to get off the couch and find some pants. Across the room, a flash of mellow amber caught his eye. He pulled himself to his feet and shuffled across the floor, stopping in front of a glass-faced bar. He gazed down at the full bottle, then stepped to the side of the cabinet and slipped his hand in behind it, feeling for the solid metal of a key.

There it was.

He unlocked the glass door and lifted the unopened bottle of Red Label from the shelf. Thank God that the woman lacked any clear sense of what was valuable. This, at least, she had left behind.

Chapter Forty-Six

By nine that evening the park was packed full of loud, lively families, squalling children, clingy teenage love birds and gray-haired seniors parked in rows of wheelchairs, knitted lap blankets tucked tightly around their legs despite the summer heat. The vendors scattered throughout the park weredoing a lively business selling hotdogs, soda, and virtually anything that could be deep fried and served on a stick. The atmosphere was playful and light, and Lane realized for the first time how much the news of the mine reopening had truly affected attitudes within the town. She hadn't felt a sense of camaraderie among Foley Lakers since the day of the garage sale. The last month had uncovered a divisiveness, an ugliness she had not known existed. But now, through the magic of a warm summer evening, groups of friends gathered to celebrate the town's biggest holiday. Nearly every living soul that called Foley Lake home attended the fireworks show.

A small grandstand had been assembled in the middle of the park, where the city's leading citizens—usually Mike, some board members, a few business leaders, and their families—had the privilege of sitting. The rest of Foley's residents generally claimed space immediately surrounding the grandstand, setting up lawn chairs and spreading blankets on the grass to form an island of locals amid an ocean of tourists.

Lowie tugged anxiously at Lane's hand, trying to steer her though the crowd. Lane kept asking, then telling, the determined child to slow down; she simply could not negotiate the throngs the way her smaller escort could. She noticed that there was already a plague of trash collecting on her newly mowed grass. She sighed. A tug at her free arm stopped her and she turned to find Butch had fallen into step right behind her. She felt a surge of warmth were his hand gently held her wrist. She stopped, not wanting to pull loose from him, and jerked Lowie to a halt.

"Is there anything you need me to do?" Butch asked. Lane noticed he had cleaned up after the day's work and wondered how he had managed to get to the mine and back in such a short time. She shook her head. "Nope. We did our part. Now we get to sit back and watch."

Lowie looked back and saw Butch. Her face brightened. Grabbing his wrist with her free hand, she gave him a tug. "C'mon, Butch," she ordered cheerily. "You can sit with us."

Lane felt the questioning and amused gaze of most of Foley Lake's city council on her as Butch lifted the yellow twine that cordoned off the grandstand so she could slip under. She pretended not to notice, refusing to make eye contact with anyone. Before they had the chance to sit, Butch excused himself, skipped nimbly down the bleachers, and reappeared ten minutes later with two billowing clouds of blue cotton candy on cardboard sticks. He sat next to Lane, reaching one of the treats past her to Lowie. Lowie's eyes where shining as she looked at Lane questioningly. Lane's wordless answer was to pull a swath of feathery blue candy from the stick and poke it into her own mouth. Lowie grinned and snatched the candy from Butch.

Lane found herself sharing cotton candy with Butch, and she wondered what new rumors were being contrived by the scandalous fact that they were eating from the same cardboard stick. Maybe, she thought, she should have Lowie sit between them. But the thought didn't translate into action, because she was keenly aware of the way the cuff of Butch's pants leg touched the bare skin of her ankle. She turned to say something to Butch, careful not to move her leg as she did, and realized he was looking across the crowds to the far corner of the park.

***

Despite the stories that would emerge later, Spot didn't go to the fireworks looking for a fight. What he wanted was to find his wife. Had he been sober, he would have realized that

Sandy was probably already seeing Minnesota in the rearview mirror of her new boyfriend's pickup. But in his whiskey-dimmed condition, it hadn't occurred to him that the woman would be intentional about fleeing the moment her hands closed about the stacks of cash he had so lovingly placed in the safe. Instead, he had convinced himself that Sandy would stay for the fireworks, camouflaging herself among the throngs. The fact that he had put his Cadillac in the ditch on the way there and had been forced to walk two miles made him that much more determined to flush her out.

He weaved through the crowd, bumping into strangers' shoulders and hips as he marched on. He was utterly determined to get to the park's single shelter, because Sandy always saved a picnic table close to it. She did the same thing every year. Predictable, he told himself. Except today. She had to choose today to tip the apple cart and abscond with his boat savings. He shoved forward, earning scowls and a few curses. No matter. The shelter. He would find her there. He didn't have any delusions about wanting Sandy back. Now he could never trust her. He was better off a bachelor. He was glad, in fact, that she was gone. No, he didn't want her anymore. But God Almighty, he knew he wanted his money.

***

On the narrow strip of green that separated the gravel parking lot from the swings and teeter-totters, a line of people pushed their way through the crowd, bearing a series of picket signs made from slats and brightly colored poster board. They grouped into a tight knot in the midst of the crowd, then moved back and formed a ring. They held their homemade signs aloft and began to march in a slow circle. The rhythm of a chant made its way across the park. The words were indiscernible given the distance and the hum of the crowd. "What is that all about?" Lane wondered.

"It's about the mine," Butch answered, studying the scene. Lane glanced at him.

"How do you know that?" she asked.

"The slogans on the signs. 'Foley Mine is a Tomb' and 'Let Our Dead RIP,' stuff like that."

Lane squinted across the distance. "You can read that from here?"

Butch glanced at her. "Can't you?"

A white light flicked on and illuminated the picketers and Lane groaned.

"Please don't tell me that's a news camera," she said.

"That's a news camera," Butch replied. Then he added impishly, "It looks like a big one."

Lane turned and scanned the stands for any sign of her father. Her search was in vain. A bubble of resentment welled up in her when she realized that if anything was to be done, she'd have to do it herself.

Butch looked at Lane expectantly as she rose to her feet. "I better go and see what's happening," she said.

Butch nodded and stood. "I'm coming with."

"Good." She swiveled around and looked at Lowie. "Stay put and save our places. We'll be right back." Lowie nodded, face and fingers sticky with blue flecks of cotton candy.

***

Emil held firmly to the sides of his walker, staring owlishly back at the reporters who crowded around him, lights and cameras trained on him. He had memorized a short speech, and he gave it now, speaking loudly to be heard over the chant of his picketers.

"We want it publicly known that we will not stand for the reopening the Foley Mine by foreigners! Some of Foley Lake's dead are still in that mine, and that makes it a burial site. You can't desecrate a burial site! It's illegal! We won't stand for it!"

One of the reporters leaned in. "What about the mine reopening? What's the name of the company that wants to reopen the mine? When are they planning to reopen?" The reporter popped the microphone back out toward Emil, and his face fell when Emil snatched it out of his hand.

"I don't know the name of the mine company, boy, just that it's a communist outfit. And I don't know the particulars of just when and how they plan to open it back up. My point is that they can't open it at all. It's a burial site. And according to Minnesota law, that makes it sacred. If you want details, you'll have to talk to the mayor, hiding out by the grandstand over there. End of story." Emil flung the microphone toward the reporter and swung around, joining the circle of picketers. He trundled along in the small circle, stamping the ground with his walker.

Butch and Lane reached the ring of the reporters and the curious in time to catch most of what Emil said, and they felt the reporter's attention shift as they turned en mass toward the grandstand. There was a collective movement by everyone bearing a press pass. Lane glanced back toward the grandstand, her heart sinking. Whatever her father was guilty of, she didn't like the looks of the media hoard heading his direction. She wondered if he could slip off before the reporters dragged their cameras across the park.

Just then, the PA system, borrowed from the courthouse and strung through the park, crackled to life. Mike's voice asked everyone to stand for the playing of the national anthem. All over the park people sprang to their feet. This was part of the routine, a signal that the fireworks were about to begin, but it also slowed the migration of reporters. Lane smiled inwardly. *Way to go, Dad,* she thought. *You are paying attention.*

***

The music for the National Anthem began to play and a ripple of voices of those old enough to know all the words could be heard through the crowd. As the song wound down all eyes turned skyward. Everyone knew it was tradition for the first fireworks to erupt as the song ended, and they weren't disappointed. As the last notes played out, an enormous Roman candle burst from a mortar and filled the sky with red and gold, its heavy *whooommmpp* shaking the ground. The crowd cheered, babies wailed, and the show was officially under way.

***

Everyone was looking up. Everyone but Spot, who was still making his way across the park to the shelter where his clouded mind told him Sandy and his money might be waiting. He gave up trying to move around people and lurched through the crowd, turning slightly sideways so he could use his shoulder as a wedge. He ran into a smallish woman holding a toddler, almost knocking her down. The woman's husband caught her with one hand and caught Spot with the other, and without a word he picked Spot up by his shirt and the back of his shorts and threw him toward the shelter. A thin cheer of approval from the crowd followed Spot as he flew head-first onto the concrete floor of the open-sided shed. He lay face down and still, playing possum. His nose, which had suffered violence in his landing, bled freely all over the shelter floor.

Once he felt vaguely confident no more blows would follow, he sat up. His head reeled. Squinting in the darkness, Spot tried to orient himself. The shelter was a simple affair, a concrete pad surrounded by eight wooden beams, supporting a tin roof that provided succor from sun and rain. It didn't take Spot long to realize there were no picnic tables under the shelter he could use as a lookout to scan the crowds for Sandy, and even if there were, the line of bodies along the shelter's perimeter would make it impossible to see out into the crowd. Spot crawled to one of the vertical supports and pulled himself up to a standing position.

He looked across the park, dark and moving with its sea of humanity, and he groaned. This was no good at all. He couldn't shove his way through that crowd. He slumped back against the shelter's support and groaned once more. Nobody heard or cared. And if they did care, he would have to face the humiliation of telling them that his worthless wife had made off with his cash, his watch, and his grandfather's cuff links. His cuff links! He wouldn't even be able to report the theft of his property without admitting to Officer Davey Snotnose that his wife had duped him. He could imagine the look on Snotnose's face as he took a report. And eventually, the entire city of Foley would know that his wife had been fooling them all, having an affair while the entire town remained ignorant. He would be a laughingstock.

A new wave of outrage washed over Spot. No, he wasn't about to be a laughingstock, a town joke, and a byword. He would not have Snotnose laughing behind his back. He would not have the whole town know he had been deceived. He *would* find Sandy himself, find her and get his property back. A firework exploded in the sky, followed by two more in quick succession. The crowd cheered. His original plan was good. All he had to do was find a high spot from which he could survey the crowd and he was sure to spot Sandy's signature platinum up-do. But high spots were scarce in the broad, flat plain of the park. The only thing higher than a picnic table was the grandstand. Spot turned away from the cheering and moved toward the empty baseball diamond behind the shelter. If he couldn't go through the crowd, he'd go around. One way or another, he was going to get to that grandstand.

Chapter Forty-Seven

Terrence's heart leaped with every report of a mortar, and the scent of exploding powder suffused the air and made his soul sing. He stood behind Roger at the fireboard, the system that tied the fuses of every mortar together and cued each explosion according to the pattern he had spent weeks helping Roger design. He hadn't told his dad or his brothers about the fact that he had designed so much of the display, though he was bursting with pride over the fact. He wanted to wait until after the show, until after they all gathered back at the farm for the homemade ice cream his mother always made to celebrate the day, to hear what they had to say about this year's show. Then he would causally mention that he had been the brains behind most of it. And then he would drop the big news on them—that Roger had offered to train him to be a pyrotechnologist and had even mentioned the possibility of letting Terrence buy out his business someday.

His stomach wobbled nervously. He imagined the look on his dad's face when he made it clear that he had no intention of taking over the farm. Not that he didn't care about the farm. He did care. But nothing had moved him like painting with light. He could set the sky ablaze. Roger told him there was new technology being developed that would allow a pyrotech to time the explosions to music. To *music.* His mind soared with the possibilities. All he needed to do was finish his last year of high school and Roger would make him an official apprentice.

Terence was so absorbed in the workings of the computer and the cheering of the crowd that he didn't immediately realize that the movement he was seeing near second base was a problem. But when it hit him that there was a dark figure moving gracelessly toward the mortar stand loaded with the fireworks set to fire next, he raced across the diamond to intercept a very drunk Spot Malloy.

***

Spot was not at all happy to find one of Chuck Larson's boys standing in front of him, shouting at him that he couldn't come that way. He didn't know what the kid was saying, and he didn't care. The only thing that registered in his pickled state was that this must be one of the older Larson's, because the kid was huge. That didn't stop Spot from taking a clumsy swing at him, which the surprised kid dodged with relative ease. However, the second punch was a bigger surprise, quicker and better aimed, and sent the kid backwards, right into the rack of PVC mortars. The rack tipped, the kid fell, and Roger didn't see any of it until the computer was sending the signal to fire the first mortar of the finale.

***

Butch stood back and admired Lane's calm comportment as the microphones of three or four reporters stabbed forward to try to catch her words over the sound of the fireworks and the crowd's cheers. She did her best to respond to the questions that the reporters threw at her: Yes, her father was the mayor, but no, she didn't know any more about the mine reopening than anyone else. Yes, she supposed reopening the Foley would be dangerous, but then, wasn't mining always dangerous? She didn't know anything about the mine being considered a burial site or what the picketers wanted. One of the reporters, a middle-aged woman too old for her trendy bleached-blond hairstyle, pushed her way forward. "Is it true that the body of a little boy is still in the Foley Mine? The mayor's son? Wouldn't that be your brother?"

Lane felt her stomach suddenly grow heavy. She stared at the reporter mutely and not knowing what else to say or do, she slowly turned away.

Butch stood on the edge of the crowd, hands in his jean's pockets. It was too dark for Lane to make out his face and she was glad. She didn't want to feel his curiosity, or his shock, or even his sympathy. Instead, she slipped past him into the crowd, and didn't notice that when the reporters tried to follow her, Butch blocked their path.

Across the park, a firework exploded. Then another. Then two more, in quick succession. A woman screamed. A hundred voices started screaming, then a thousand. Lane turned in time to see a large rocket tumble horizontally across the field, cutting a path toward the crowd on its way to the grandstand. An ocean of bodies surged away, fleeing. The force of the mortar exploding knocked people flat. Lane turned toward the grandstand.

"Lowie."

Chapter Forty-Eight

Lowie was mesmerized by the fireworks above her, the ballet of light and sound that always made her think of Sodom and Gomorrah. She had heard the story years ago, and even though she knew that the cities were destroyed, and people died, she couldn't help but think that God's judgment must have looked like a fireworks show, brilliant and flaming and cosmic. She hadn't paid much attention to the fact that her mother and Butch hadn't come back; once the fireworks started, she was in her own world. But then she saw a few big explosions on the ground in the baseball diamond and heard screams as a wide streak of red and gold shot sideways along the ground into the crowd to her right. It burst, and the screams grew to howls of shock and pain.

In seconds, the world was pandemonium.

The baseball diamond was erupting in sound and color. The crowds nearest the diamond were fleeing in panic, as fireworks burst all around them. People all over the grandstand stood, as if on cue, and began to flood down the stairs, pushing, shoving, leapfrogging one another in an attempt to get away. Lowie watched the chaos in wonder, realizing for the first time she was completely alone. She stood up, then slowly sat back down, confused by the determination of the hoards around her to flee the grandstand. After all, ground-level was a battlefield, with rouge fireworks blazing across the turf. But she was at least fifteen feet in the air, and safer, she thought, sitting where she was. But the problem became apparent when a mortar sped under the grandstand and burst, blasting balls of flame through the gaps in the grandstand's seating, burning the back of Lowie's legs and sending her flying down the steps in terror.

Lowie landed amid chaos. Her ears were numb from the concussion of the mortar. The bare skin on the backs of her legs stung. She was being jostled and shoved. Suddenly she felt a hand clutch her arm and turned to see May's pale, terrified face, her lips moving, her free hand gesturing. Lowie clung to her. May turned and half-led, half-dragged Lowie away from the grandstand, away from the mortars, deeper into the crowd.

The whole world was elbows and backsides. Feet seemed to appear out of nowhere to stomp on her toes and ankles, her pink flip-flops offering no protection. Bodies slammed against her and knocked her to her knees and, for a moment, all she knew was the sharp pain of shoe leather against her bare skin. May jerked her back to her feet. A bare second later she saw an explosion of white light as an elbow came down hard on her right eye and cheek. Lowie felt herself slip out of May's grip.

Her head swam. Muffled sounds rose and fell around her, like people yelling into a long tube and channeling the sounds from a hundred miles away. She was shoved face-down, flat to the ground by the sheer force of the powers above her. She felt the sole of a tennis shoe stomp her ear and temple. She felt hands scramble across her back, grasping—was someone trying to find her?—but then the searching hands disappeared. Another foot stumbled over her arm, and then the weight of a knee dropped full force onto her back, shoving the air out of her lungs. She opened her mouth to gasp and tasted dirt and blood.

She was dying. The knowledge came to her in a detached sort of way, merely information. She knew she should pull her hands up to protect her face, but she couldn't move. The numbness in her ears was spreading, taking the feeling in her hands, in her feet, in her bruised, flattened chest.

Darkness pressed in. It grew completely quiet. The pain disappeared. Lowie felt peace wrap around her like in a soft haze. Grateful for the reprieve from pain and fear, she wasn't surprised when she realized she was lying face up, or that Butch was standing over her, gazing down at her with a supreme tenderness that flowed from him. He was engulfed in a soft, pearl glow, a circle of velvety white. People rushed past all around her, but no one was stepping on her now. No one entered the bubble of light and peace that surrounded her and Butch. He knelt next to her.

"Lowie?" he asked. His voice was bells. He lifted her up and looked at her face. "Are you alright, kiddo?" She smiled at him. *Yes,* she thought. *I'm alright now.* She sighed, content, and leaned her head against his chest. Darkness came to her—the darkness of sleep, or death—and though he wasn't sure which she was unafraid and leaned forward to meet it.

CHAPTER FORTY-NINE

The blanket wouldn't lay flat. The top edge was trimmed in blue satin and bent back where it had been awkwardly folded, and now it wanted to curl upward rather than lying back evenly. Lane fidgeted with it, willing the edge to flatten out, to stay down and away from Lowie's face. Every time Lane let it go it folded up, and she would be compelled to run her hand over it again, each time feeling the wisps of Lowie's breath against her fingers. The child's breathing was shallow, a result of some badly bruised ribs, the doctor had said. Lane fussed with the bed, the lights, and now the blanket, not sure what else to do with her overwrought nerves in the wake of the knowledge that she had come very close to losing Lowie forever. For her part, Lowie dozed, loose and noodley from the pain medication the doctor had given her. He told her that she must have been born under a lucky star, having survived being trampled under the feet of the panicking hoards with nary a broken bone. Many had not been so lucky. She smiled dreamily as he sewed six stitches into her forehead and told him she thought she might have been dead for a while, a statement that made the doctor smile and her mother burst into tears.

Lane's eyes kept flicking up to where Butch stood staring out Lowie's bedroom window. He had been there for an hour, since they had gotten home from the emergency room, silent and unmoving. She felt an ache of gratitude—and more, she acknowledged—toward Butch for rescuing Lowie, although he was thin on the details of how exactly that came about. He said only that he heard May screaming for the child and deduced the rest. But now Lane wasn't sure what Butch was thinking or feeling. He was steeped in silence, and some interior sense made her hesitate to disturb him. She stayed near Lowie and went back to work on the blanket.

Mike knocked lightly and slipped in through the bedroom door. He was pale and gaunt, his shoulders slumped in an attitude of exhaustion and defeat. He had spent nearly an hour in front of a bank of television cameras outside the overwhelmed hospital emergency room in Crosby. The reporters were looking for an explanation for the disaster at the fireworks display; instead, they found themselves filling Mike in on details, like the fact that eight people were injured badly enough to warrant hospitalization. Among them was Terrence Larson, who had been seriously burned and lost most of his right hand in the melee.

Mike crossed to Lowie's bed and studied her face. "How is she?"

"Okay, I guess," Lane replied. "The medicine seems to work. She isn't complaining about pain."

He glanced up at Butch. "How's our hero?" He asked with a wry smile. When Butch didn't respond Mike looked at Lane curiously. She shook her head.

Mike sighed. "I'll make coffee." He slipped out of the room, closing the door behind him.

Lane stopped fiddling with the blanket and stood. She crossed to Butch and put her hand on his back. "Butch?"

He didn't turn, but Lane felt him tense under her touch. "Why haven't you ever taught Lowie to swim?" he asked.

"What?"

"She said you didn't allow her in the water. Why not?" His voice was quiet, but there was an edge to it that couldn't be overlooked. Lane withdrew her hand.

"Because she doesn't know how to swim. She could drown."

"Of course, she could drown," Butch flashed. "She's nine years old and you haven't taught her how to survive in water." Though Butch kept his back to her, speaking over his shoulder, Lane took an involuntary step back. His words were quiet but heavy with anger.

"Why did you go back to your maiden name after your husband died?" he asked. "You didn't just change your own name back. You changed hers, too. Why?"

Lane's eyes narrowed. "I hardly think that's any of your business."

Butch turned to look at her, his face so hard Lane took a step back.

"You have been lying to me," he said. "You told me your husband left you. He didn't leave, he's dead. You said you were an only child…"

"I am an only child!" Lane whispered loudly, glancing at Lowie.

"You have a brother. Having a brother, even a dead brother, is not the same as being an only child. Why haven't you taught her to swim? Is it because you are afraid of water? What good is that, making her fear the things you're afraid of? You're crippling her. It's the same with not ever taking her outside this city, letting her see that there's more to the world than Foley Lake, letting her biggest dream be growing up to be a waitress in a dying town. It's because you're afraid to leave. But you know some day no matter what you try to do she is going to go. Or die trying, like her father did."

Lane was horrified. She angled away from him, torn between a desire to flee and a need to stand her ground.

"Is that what you want for Lowie?" he pressed on, "to leave her so reckless and unprepared that she can't survive the world away from Foley Lake?"

Lane opened her mouth to speak, but the words were blocked behind a sob at the back of her throat. She turned away from him and swallowed hard, scrambling to regain control.

She didn't hear his approach. He rested his hand lightly on her shoulder. His palm was broad and warm, big enough to cover the length from her neck to the gentle slope of her shoulder. Her hair was pulled up in her typical ponytail, and suddenly she was acutely aware of the warmth of his breath on the back of her exposed neck. When he spoke, his voice was tender.

"I'm sorry. I don't mean to make you cry. But you can't just erase the past, even if it's to try to protect her from making the same mistakes. You are a good mother. But if you are afraid of something, shouldn't that be even more reason to teach her how to face it?"

Lane swiped tears from her cheeks and turned around, rotating under Butch's palm. He didn't step back as she faced him, his hand still on her shoulder. She reached her hands up, letting them rest on his chest, and looked up at him, her face only inches from his. Impulsively she stretched up and into his arms, finding his lips with her own. At first, he returned the kiss softly, then more urgently. She wrapped her arms around his neck and clung to him, wanting to melt into him, wanting to belong to him. He pressed forward, letting the contours of her body fill the curves and voids of his own. The urge to sweep her up into his soul surged through him with a force that terrified him, and Butch jerked back, pulling himself free of the kiss, and pushed Lane away. He held her with his palms on her shoulders, his fingers wrapped tightly around her arms. Lane blinked, confused.

"No," Butch said firmly, as much to himself as to her.

Lane shook her head. "I don't understand."

Butch shook his head emphatically, stepping backwards and giving her a light push away, his expression one of horror and deep pain. "You have to trust me, Lane. This—this just isn't right."

She stepped forward. "But—"

"You don't know me," he said quietly.

Lane was trembling. She reached for him. "I know you. You're Butch. And you have been wandering all over, looking for a home. You have a home here, if you want it—"

Butch was suddenly, terribly angry. "No. No! You don't know me!" He pushed past her to the door and grabbed the knob, and without another word he was gone.

Lane stared at the closed door in front of her. She could hear his steps on the stair treads, then nothing. She couldn't hear him moving through the house. She couldn't hear the door open or close. It was as if he had evaporated.

She stepped to the bed and sat on its edge. A tear slipped from the corner of her eye and she swiped at it impatiently. She smoothed the soft blue trim of the blanket where it had been folded the wrong way for too long. It wouldn't lay flat. No matter how many times she tried to smooth it down, it just wouldn't lay.

CHAPTER FIFTY

He stood in the dim light of the head frame, waiting. Outside the sun beamed down from the summer sky, warming all it touched, but the cold air near the shaft was immune to the sun's charms. He looked toward the gate and the welcoming green and golden picture just beyond its frame. But he didn't move toward the light; if he did, and someone saw him, it would ruin everything.

He began to pace. The nervousness he felt when he slipped into the darkness hours before had eased up, and now he was getting bored. He hummed to himself, wondering how much longer it would be. How close were they? Had he fooled them? And what about her? Would she come? Of course, she wouldn't be easily fooled, but he thought she would come anyway. She was the bravest. He sighed and smiled a little to himself. That was one of the things he liked best about her.

A knobby stick as long as his arm leaned against the head frame's tin wall, a remnant of one of the many earlier visits. He picked it up and dragged it across the floor as he paced, looking

277

behind him at the fine line it left in the dust on the concrete. He carved random trails with it for a while, then found a spot near the wall where the dust lay thickest. Thinking of her, he began to write.

P…

R…I…

N…

A sound from the far back of the head frame made him jump. He wheeled around. It was a soft, heavy swoosh, like something solid rubbed itself against the metal back there. He squinted to see into the dim light. He heart kicked up a notch. He listened.

Nothing.

Imagination. He slowly turned back to the word he was working on.

C…E…S

The hairs on the back of his neck pricked up, and a wave of chills rushed down his spine. Something was watching him, something angry, dangerous. He turned to face the back of the head frame and peered into the shadow. Nothing. It was just too dark back there to see. He backed away, uneasy. There was a shift in the attitude of the air, and he was suddenly, completely aware that he wasn't wanted there.

He clutched the stick like a weapon. The ghost stories he had heard, the legends of death and terror, of miners who had died young and held a grudge against the living, sang though his mind. But he stood his ground, determined. They had been planning for weeks. He wasn't going to be the one to mess it up.

He could see the edge of the shaft dropping away into blackness fifteen feet in front of him, its square frame intersected by the plank. If something had slipped up from there, from the black depths below, he would have seen it. Wouldn't he? But that was impossible. Nothing was alive down there. No matter what stories the kids, and sometimes the adults, told, there was nothing hiding in the drifts below the Foley Mine.

He bent slowly to pick up a rock and threw it as hard as he could into its darkest corner.

There was a clatter of stone against metal. Silence returned and he waited. He couldn't see anything, yet he had a feeling throwing a stone was not smart. Whatever it was, it felt angrier. His heart hammered.

Nothing was there.

Something was there. He could feel it.

He saw only darkness.

The need to flee swept over him and he turned, running toward the gate and the welcoming sunlight beyond. He had to go, to get out from under the frightening gaze of whatever it was he had provoked. Something WAS there, and it wanted him gone. He couldn't oblige fast enough.

He made it to the gate and put one foot on the lowest rung to climb over.

From below the hill rose the sound of voices. Shouts. Laughter.

He stopped, listening. The sun at the gate melted into his chilled skin as the chattering of voices grew louder. He slowly lowered his foot. He couldn't leave now.

The children were coming.

Chapter Fifty-One

Mike pulled into the parking lot of the Good Trail Village Care Facility and shut off the ignition. He looked around the grounds of the old folks' home. That's what he had been raised to call places like Good Trail, because his mother had thought that "nursing home" sounded too depressing. He pulled the key free and sat listening to the tick of the cooling engine, surveying the neatly trimmed lawns, the cheery flower beds, and the handicap-accessible walking trails.

How he hated this place.

A cloud of despair hung over the campus, a sadness that no amount of landscaping could disguise. He sighed and got out of the truck, steeling his resolve. He had to go inside. He needed to talk to Will, to find out if the man could help him fill in any of the blanks in his mind. It was the questions that motivated this visit, and he felt a twang of guilt when he

281

realized that for the last eight months, family loyalty hadn't been enough.

As Mike reached the door he took a deep breath, knowing he would only be able to hold it for a few moments before he would be forced to breathe the air inside. He stepped through the door and into the dim lobby. A few residents looked up at him hopefully, then turned away in disappointment and irritation when they saw he wasn't someone they were waiting for.

Mike had long since memorized the way through the maze of halls that led to Will's room. He felt eyes following him and he tried to avoid looking directly at anyone, though he nodded in the direction of a few to hide the awkwardness that plagued him every time he walked through the doors. He set a quick pace and marched through the halls, zigzagging around walkers and wheelchairs without slowing. He passed a large picture window that faced the garden sprawled out to the edge of the parking lot he had just come from. He saw a familiar form outside of the glass and jolted to a halt.

Butch was walking across the parking lot. He moved with quick, determined steps, carrying a cardboard box in front of him. His face was turned away, his body at a right angle to the window where Mike stood, but it was undeniably Butch.

Mike stood staring with both hands on the window, until he realized that some of the residents and all of the nursing staff were walking, hobbling, and rolling past him with undisguised suspicion.

He bolted down the hall. He rounded a corner, looked at the room numbers to get his bearings, and trotted along, passing room after room until he came to number 331. He stopped at the door and looked inside.

Will sat alone in his wheelchair, his back to Mike, his face lifted to the sun and the light his eyes could not comprehend. He held a silver pocket watch in his right hand, his thumb traveling around the circumference of its face. Mike took a moment to catch his breath and gazed at the man who had once seemed so mighty to him. When Mike was a boy, he and Will had played a game of Will's own invention. It was tag, but in reverse. Will stood in the center of a room, leaning casually on his white-tipped cane. Mike tried to sneak forward and slap his blind uncle on the leg before Will could lift the end of the cane and poke him; it was a game that Mike always lost. Over the years Will's ears had learned to do what his eyes no longer could. He heard everything, even the sounds of a small, barefooted boy slinking forward on carpet.

And now, as always, Will sensed that he had an observer. He grasped one wheel of his chair and gave it a crank, turning to face the doorway and slipping the pocket watch into his breast pocket. Mike frowned. The man's wrinkled, worn skin was wet with tears.

"Who's there?" he asked. Mike didn't respond right away, but he stepped forward into the room. Will turned his head slightly. "Who is it?" he asked again. Mike quietly cleared his throat.

"It's me, Will. It's Mike."

Will sat back in the chair, fresh sadness flickering across on his face. "Well," he said simply, "Mike."

Will turned his wheelchair and hooked an empty folding chair with his right leg, nudging it toward his guest. Mike slipped into the seat. He watched while his uncle rolled past the empty bed and toward a small table pushed into the corner of the room and reached out his hand. The searching fingers found an insulated coffee pot resting on a tray, then felt out a small stack of Styrofoam cups. He freed two cups from the stack, expertly filling them to the brim without spilling. When he turned back toward Mike his face was dry and leathery. Mike accepted the coffee, wondering to himself if he had really seen tears at all. "You okay, Will?"

"I get along alright."

"I hear tell your roommate passed this spring."

Will nodded. "He died in April, in the first week. He wasn't a well man, but in the end things went quick. I just finished cleaning out the last of his things."

"I'm sorry to hear that. He must have been a good friend."

"That he was."

The old man sat back in his wheelchair and found Mike's eyes with his own in the same unnerving way Mike had seen his whole life, causing him to wonder once or twice if Will's blindness wasn't just some elaborate ruse. Mike tried to ignore the thought and studied his uncle's lined, weary features, the bright and empty eyes lined with red.

"You look upset," Mike said, leaning forward, trying to sound less agitated than he was feeling. "Did Butch say something to upset you?"

"How's that?"

"The man who was just here. Butch. He came to talk to you, right? About the things that are happening in Foley Lake?"

"Foley Lake," Will said quietly. He picked up his coffee cup with one hand and turned the wheelchair with the other, facing back toward the window, the sunlight on his face. "I've been hearing that name on the news lately. Some trouble with the Fourth of July. And the mine. I hear tell they are going to start working the mine again. As an open pit, I hear."

"Yep. Yep, that's a fact. The mine is going to be reopened. Folks are stirred up, some of them," Mike tried to gauge his uncle's emotions, choosing his words carefully. "The older folks, the ones who remember when the mine was open last, they're the most upset. They say the mine should never be reopened. They say to let the dead lay."

"I imagine they would." Will's voice was remote, as if he spoke from a faraway place.

"It's bad, to tell the truth. Property's been ruined. People are bickering, fighting about old hurts. These are folks that grew up together, known each other their whole lives. Some people swear they've seen something—I don't know— unnatural. And then there's this whole disaster at the fireworks the other day. I don't know what to do to settle things down."

Somewhere down the hall a woman's wail began low and rose to a swift crescendo. Other voices grew louder to be heard over the lament, voices pleading with the woman to be quiet amid a shuffle of footsteps. Slowly the wailing slid downward into a low moan. Mike turned to face the door, watching nervously as two male attendants wheeled a tiny woman, with fine white hair as fine as a newborn's, past the door. Each attendant held the chair's hand bar with one hand while the other clamped down on the woman's shoulder. Mike slowly turned away.

Will took a sip of his coffee. "How's Lane? And the little girl, Mary Louise? How is she?"

"Fine. Fine, they're both good."

Will nodded. "And the boy. I reckon you're still missing him."

Mike was rendered momentarily mute by the question. He searched Will's face, hoping for a clue about what the man was thinking. The soft lines and wrinkles betrayed nothing but the quietness that always seemed to run with an undercurrent of grief. Silence in the room was heavy, interrupted only by the renewed wails somewhere down the hall. Mike felt the heaviness in his chest, a feeling of oppression and great need. He leaned forward.

"Will, help me. I don't understand what is going on back home. It's not just the people. It's the city itself. Did you know we found a whole cemetery full of dead folks in unmarked graves by the lake? Those graves have been there for ninety years, now all the sudden they are too close to the surface to stay buried. People are talking of ghosts again, just like they did…" Mike broke off.

Will gazed out the window, unmoving, so still that Mike might have thought he had dozed off if it wasn't for his open eyes, unblinking. When he spoke, his words were soft and measured.

"I don't know what you want from me, Michael. The mine has taken a lot from that city, and the city has taken from the mine. It's like those creatures that live off the life of another creature. But in this case, who's the parasite, who's the host? I can't say. Maybe its mutual benefit and mutual destruction. Maybe reopening the mine would destroy the city or change in beyond recognition, but as I recall, there wasn't much worth saving in Foley Lake anymore. Destruction might be the only thing for it."

Mike shifted in the chair, frustrated. "What did Butch want?" he demanded. "What did you tell him about the mine?"

Will frowned, confused. "I don't know who you're talking about. I don't know anyone named Butch," he said. "But there is only one thing to tell about the mine, and that is that people died there. Some deserved to die, some didn't. But I don't have the power to go back and change what's happened any more than you do, so I guess we both best just find our peace with what has already come to pass."

Mike opened his mouth to object and found himself too weary to make the effort. He put the coffee cup on the tray and, using both hands on his knees for leverage, slowly stood.

Will turned to face him, finding his eyes in that uncanny way of his. He set his own coffee cup down and leaned forward in the chair.

"Let them open it, Mike. Let them open it all the way up. That place is like a wound that has festered for sixty years, and its rot has poisoned everything around it. It's time to make it give up its ghosts. Let him get it all cleaned out."

Mike sighed. He turned toward the door. Before he stepped through, Will added, "And tell that Emil Kangas to mind his business. I heard him shooting off his mouth on the television. I may be old and blind, but I could still give him a beating if I had to. That young fella was always a little too cocky for my liking."

***

Mike drove home in silence. He was ten miles away before Will's words, replayed in his mind, made him lean hard on the brake and jerk the sedan over to the side of the highway. He skidded to a stop, both hands frozen to the wheel.

It's time to make it give up its ghosts.
Let him get it all cleaned out.
Him.

CHAPTER FIFTY-TWO

Lowie moved around the yard with small, mincing steps. Lane watched from where she sat on the back step. She had not worked in the three days since the disaster the park. She couldn't do much anyway until the state fire marshal finished his investigation of how the fireworks had gone so terribly wrong. The prohibition against cleaning up the park became an excuse not to work at all. Traffic barriers had been moved by irritable townsfolk and left on the sidewalks. Trash cans overflowed. Litter was strewn everywhere. Let the city stay in disarray, she thought bitterly. She didn't care. She couldn't fix everything anyway. Not alone. Not anymore.

She studied Lowie. The child moved slowly, mindful of her injured ribs, with Bones at her heel. Every few minutes she looked back to be sure Lane was still there.

Lowie's life orbited around her. Why hadn't she noticed it before? If she moved or went back inside, Lowie would follow. No matter where she went—around the house, around the city—Lowie always tracked her down. And though she knew that eventually the child's world would grow larger and larger, it occurred to her for the first time what effect it might have on Lowie if the steadying force of her own presence vanished from her daughter's life forever. What if she disappeared from Lowie's reach? Would she find her own way? Or would Lowie spin out into cold and darkness without the centering pull of her mother's existence?

Is that what happened to her?

A memory flashed in her mind, of her father's old station wagon parked in the driveway. She could see it as soon as she turned the corner on her walk home from school. For months her father had been coming home early. She would walk in and find him sitting across from her mother, and when he saw Lane, he would look at his wrist watch and stand, reaching for his coat. He would say he had some work to finish down at town hall, but he would be back for supper. He would disappear without a word of explanation.

He never told fourteen-year-old Lane he didn't want to leave her mother alone, but the regularity with which she found him there when he should have been somewhere else told its own story. It was the *why* that had kept her stomach loosening and constricting. Her father would leave, and her mother would turn to her with a small smile curling the corners of her mouth and make small talk with her, asking how school was and whether she had any homework. Lane was accustomed to the small talk that led nowhere. But each day, before Lane could fashion a question of her own, her mother's gaze would be pulled toward the window, up and away. During those days her mother's attention always seemed to be directed away from Lane, outside the Harris house and skyward, toward some focal point Lane could not see.

Then came the day she came home to nothing. There was no car in the drive: the house, which was always quiet, was uncharacteristically still. They stayed away all night, and Lane, unwilling to admit she had been abandoned, stood by the living room window in the dark, waiting. She saw the night fold tight outside the glass pane, then loosen and open again, cosmic origami. She stared out at the brightening sky until she heard the alarm in her room begin to sound. The only thing she could think to do was get ready for school. So, she showered, and she dressed, and she spent the day waging an internal war to stay awake as she floated numbly through classes.

When she got home that afternoon, they were there.

Her mother, dressed in a soft pink bathrobe, sat with her hands folded on her lap. She was staring out the window, but the look was different. This wasn't her searching gaze, her wordless prayer. There was a blankness about her, and Lane recognized the presence of a strong drug. When she asked what was going on, her mother smiled and touched Lane's face and said she had been to the hospital for some silly tests that the doctor wanted to do because she had been feeling a bit worn out. Who wasn't worn out, she asked? Of course, she was tired. Every woman with a family found herself a little fatigued now and then. And while her mother spoke in that soft and disconnected fashion, her father wandered away down the hall with his hands stuffed down into his trousers pockets, his dark hair frazzled.

As Lane lay awake that night, something inside her snapped loose. She felt it go, an internal popping, and the slow easing of pressure as her insides began to unwind. A week later, the looseness made it hard to walk. Things were shifting, the spring that held her innards in place uncoiling. She said nothing to her friends or her teachers about what was going on at home. She took her cues from her father, whom she saw making wide allowances to care for her mother, but otherwise maintaining his normal day. She began to cook supper, usually sticking with grilled cheese and soup, though the meals generally went uneaten. She tried to figure out the washing machine, ruining loads of clothes. She began reading labels on the backs of the cleaners her mother kept in the hall closet as the house fell into disarray around her. But most of the time, she sat very still in her desk chair, textbook open in front of her as a stream of teachers prattled on about topics that held no practical meaning now that she was adrift. She designed a ridged schedule for herself and stuck to it, careful not to disrupt the cycles around her lest some new reality provoke more uncoiling and she flew into pieces.

Her mother shrank. The tension of chronic pain carved new lines into her handsome face. She told Lane that Lane needn't go to school if she didn't want to. She could stay home. But the thought of sitting across from her mother and watching the side of her face as she stared out the window made staying impossible. Always she scooped up her bag and said no, she needed to go; she had a science project to work on or an Algebra test that needed taking. She would plunge out the front door, marching down the street, arms folded tightly over her chest.

Neither she nor her father uttered a word about her mother's condition. The town found out anyway. People were kinder. Teachers told Lane she could skip certain assignments if she wished and gave her higher grades that she deserved. Her friends' light-hearted gossip and horseplay dried up in her presence. She couldn't escape what was happening at home anymore. It dogged her everywhere.

Then came the afternoon she came home and found her mother crying. She dropped her school bag and walked into the living room. Mary Louise lay on the couch, tears flowing down sallow cheeks. Her father sat in a straight-back chair watching her, wringing his hands.

She's had all the pills she can take, he said. No more until midnight. Lane glanced at the clock. 4:00 p.m. She looked at her mother's tears and her father's empty, wringing hands.

The looseness inside her constricted, pulling tight with a snap. Her jaw clenched. She marched to the medicine cabinet, pulled out the bottles, and examined them. She carried them back out to the living room and quizzed her father on which pills he had given her mother and at what time. She was outraged to find he had written nothing down and that his memory was fuzzy. She opened a pain killer and gave her mother one, helping her sip water through a straw to swallow it down. Then Lane turned to the phone and placed the first of many calls to her mother's doctor.

She took care of the house. She made sure the yard was mowed and raked. She learned how to really cook, how to keep track of medicine, how to call in a prescription. She knew what the signs of infection were and just how to balance pain pills so that she could give her mother something every two hours. No more waiting. She issued instructions to her father about what needed to be done each day before she left for school. His relief that someone had taken control was so complete it was almost palpable. He did what she said, stepping back to let her pass when they met in the hall or in a doorway. She realized that grief and fear could be empowering if one just knew how to harness them.

Sometime during the week she turned fifteen, she picked an outfit out of her mother's closet, chose a matching necklace and shoes, and carried them to the funeral home. She couldn't remember if they had done anything to acknowledge the birthday.

Lowie walked toward her, her hands hidden behind her back, a playful smile on her face. She stopped in front of Lane and presented her with a new rose, its bright yellow petals just beginning to unfurl. Lane accepted it, lifting the bloom to her face and inhaling deeply. Lowie sat on the step next to her and leaned her head against Lane's shoulder.

"Hey," Lane said.

"What?"

"As soon as those stitches come out, you are going to start swimming lessons."

Lowie's head popped up and she stared at Lane, wide-eyed. "Really?"

Lane nodded. "Yes, ma'am."

"Who's going to teach me?"

"I don't know. We'll find someone."

"Butch said he'd teach me."

Lane felt her heart slide down toward her stomach. "I don't know where Butch is."

"You don't?"

"No. I haven't seen him. Nobody has. I think he might have left."

"No, he didn't leave. He must be here somewhere," Lowie said confidently.

"You think so?"

"Of course. He didn't say goodbye," the child replied. "And he would never leave without saying goodbye."

Lane smiled. "You sound pretty sure about that."

"I am. I'll find him. When I do, I am going to ask him to teach me how to swim."

Lane leaned over and kissed the top of Lowie's head. Her hair was soft and warm. "Whatever you say, Miss Lowie. You're the boss."

Chapter Fifty-Three

His fingers were numb. He flexed them, folding his fists closed, then opened, then closed again. He had thought that after a while the cold would cease to matter; that, in time, he wouldn't feel it as much. Not true. The cold was always there, stiffening his joints, making his movements slow and clumsy. He never seemed to get used to the dampness, either. The chill below the ground permeated everything.

He thought about the sun, about the last time he'd seen it. When he left the mine, it was dark. When he came to the mine, it was dark. Days passed above while he shivered in the darkness. He missed the sweetness of a warm breeze.

No matter. He was close. He wasn't stopping until he finished everything he had come so far to do. He was tired and wanted to lay down and rest, somewhere above, somewhere warm and dry. He would. But not yet. Not while there was still work to be done.

A noise echoed down the drift from somewhere behind him. He froze, listening. He wasn't afraid, but he was aware. He listened for a long moment and, once he was convinced he was alone, he went back to work.

The sounds in the mine were different now that the shaft was almost full of water. He'd worried that when the lake burst its seams it would fill the whole mine again, and everything would be lost. Not so. The lake flooded the bottom drift and most of the shaft, but it hadn't reached to the top drift. Not that it wouldn't, he knew. At any moment the water could surge, and he would have very little time to get out, but then, nothing would matter. Maybe he wouldn't even try.

He was getting good at working in the dark. He felt along the wooden timber frame in front of him and found the wire loop hanging there. The small bundle slipped into it easily. He snugged it up tightly and checked the connections. Everything was intact.

Good. He turned his face away from the wall, down toward the long stretch of the drift in front of him, and though he couldn't see he measured the length in his mind's eye. He knew exactly how far he had to go to reach the end. Things were changing quickly now. It would all be over in a week. Maybe less.

Chapter
Fifty-Four

Lowie stood shivering at the edge of the pit. She had wrapped the towel tightly across her shoulders because, though she wasn't wet yet, goose bumps raised on her spindly arms and legs. Butch climbed down the bank in a small avalanche of rock and sand and joined her at the edge of the pit. He was wearing cutoff jeans and a t-shirt. He squinted down at Lowie.

"You ready?" he asked.

"I guess," she said slowly. The idea of coming to the mine and learning how to swim in the pit sounded exciting and exotic when Butch first agreed to it. Lane had been more shocked by the news that Lowie had tracked Butch down than she was by the request, giving a curt nod of permission when Lowie explained that the lake was useless now that it was half gone, and asked if she could accompany Butch to the pit for lessons. But now, shivering at the edge of the clear pool, Lowie was losing her nerve.

"All you have to do is jump in and swim to the other side. Grab the bank and rest a minute, then swim back. Like this." Butch stepped to the edge of the pit and made a big show of swinging his arms. "*One* banana, *two* banana, *three* banana, go!" With that he leaped off the bank and pulled himself into a neat cannon ball, sending water up in a huge explosion that drenched Lowie. He broke the water's surface and set off across the pit with the strong, confident strides of an experienced swimmer. Lowie watched in admiration as he turned a somersault under water and kicked off the opposite bank, crossing back to her in less than a minute. He stopped where she was standing and did another somersault, kicking water at her as he turned. He surfaced with a grin.

"Okay, your turn."

Lowie sighed and turned to the bank, making a great deal out of finding the best place for her towel. That done, she returned to the edge of the pit and looked doubtfully at Butch as he tread water, waiting for her.

"Can you touch bottom?" she asked.

"No way. That's cheating. Besides, there is no bottom, remember? It just goes down forever."

Lowie blanched. "Maybe I should start with something shallower. You know, so I can wade in."

Butch grinned. "But that's not swimming. That's wading. I thought you wanted to learn how to swim."

"I do, but…"

"Woman, the only way to learn how to swim is to swim. So come on in."

Maybe it was the logic of the response. More likely it was being called "woman" nearly ten years before the title could rightfully apply. But for whatever reason, Lowie threw herself forward and was over her head in icy water just one second after Butch spoke those words. He was so surprised by her sudden entry that he panicked for a moment, reaching under the water to pull her back up. She surfaced on her own, eyes squeezed shut and arms flailing in a wild dog paddle. Butch reached out and grabbed her elbow, helping her stay up. She opened her eyes and gasped. He grinned. "Atta girl."

"It's cold!" she wailed.

"That it is. Okay, you already have a rhythm going, so I am going to turn you toward the other bank and you just swim for it. I'm right beside you."

"Okay," Lowie replied, breathless. She was keeping her face out of the water, neck high and stiff. Butch slowly turned her. "Okay, now keep your arms in the water more. Don't lift them so high, they can't keep you up if you're grabbing air. Good, that's better. Now kick."

Lowie kicked and paddled, her breaths coming in ragged puffs, and made slow, steady progress across the pit. Butch swam alongside her, encouraging and instructing. He felt a surge of pride as he watched her strain forward, resolute despite her fear.

When they reached the opposite side Lowie clawed at the bank and Butch took her hand and directed it to a rock that jutted out of the wall's side. She clung to it, gasping. Butch gave her a few minutes to catch her breath, then helped her turn and aimed her to the opposite bank. She paddled back more slowly, fatigue and the cold water taking their toll. When she reached the opposite bank, she found a handhold.

"I did it!"

"You almost did it," Butch said. "You still have to get yourself out."

"Will you give me a boost?" she asked. Butch shook his head.

"Nope. You have to be able to get yourself out."

Lowie looked hurt. Butch chuckled. "It's generally a whole lot easier to get into a situation than to get out of it, Miss Lowie. But it's the getting out that can save your life. So find a hand hold, and pull yourself out." Lowie turned slowly back to the bank and looked uncertainly for a grip. The bank was only about a foot higher than the water, thanks to the recent rains, but it was sheer and mostly smooth but for an occasional rock or divot. She reached up higher on the bank and grabbed a handful of crab grass, but pulling herself up was impossible. She lost her grip on the grass and fell back into the pit, plunging all the way under. Butch tread water nearby and let her struggle to the surface on her own. She blinked the water out of her eyes and coughed, feeling a sharp rebuke from her ribs. She looked at Butch expecting him to help her. He nodded toward the bank.

"Try again."

She tried again. She was growing weaker by the moment. She grasped feebly at the bank and fell back a second time. She looked at Butch imploringly.

Butch was unsympathetic. "You have to know how to do this. You need to find a way out. Think, now. Your hands alone aren't enough. What else can you use?"

Lowie swallowed back tears, her hands and feet aching with cold. She reached up and grabbed on to the bank with both hands, and she let her toes scrape painfully against the edge of the pit, looking for a hold. In seconds she found a small ledge. She wiggled her toes into it and, using her arms to pull and straightening her legs, she pulled herself up, teetered for a moment, then threw herself forward and onto her belly on the bank. She wiggled forward, ribs protesting, until she was far enough on the bank to be safe. Then she lay still, her breath coming in ragged gasps. Butch pulled himself out and flopped next to her. She looked away from him.

He picked up on her mood, her new distrust. "Lowie, what would you do if you fell in that water, and I wasn't here?" he asked.

She blinked up at the sky. "Drown, I reckon."

"No. You would find a way out for yourself any way you had to, and live." She still wouldn't look at him. He sighed. "I almost drowned when I was your age, Lowie, or just a little older than you are."

Lowie turned her head and looked at him, resentment giving way to curiosity. "You did? What happened?"

Butch shrugged. "I don't remember. I was unconscious for a while. I fell into a lake and managed to get to the shore somehow. But that was why I decided to learn how to swim. I was never, never going to end up in the water again without knowing what to do. That's what I want you to learn. Today was lesson one. You can survive, and you can get out by yourself. That's a tough one, but after this, the lessons get easier. We need to do this every morning, Low, until you know exactly how to get yourself out."

Lowie lay back again, thinking, trying to grasp the hard lesson Butch was teaching her. She didn't know what to make of him sometimes. But she did know one thing—he was a man of action. If anyone knew how to react in a frightening situation, it would be him. Lowie rolled on her side so she could face him.

"I saw a ghost."

Butch had closed his eyes, the sun bright on his face. He smiled. "Hmm. Okay, I'll bite. When did you see a ghost?"

"On the night of my birthday. After everyone was asleep."

The frankness with which Lowie spoke rid Butch of the notion that she was setting him up for a joke. He turned to face her, a mild frown on his face.

"Like the ghost people have been saying is hanging around town? What did it look like?"

Lowie took a deep breath and sat up. He was listening. She knew he would. "Big. And fast. He was wearing a long white coat. And he had some kind of weird light on his hat. At least that's what it looked like."

Butch's frown deepened. "Fast? What was he doing?"

"He was walking around in the yard in the middle of the night. I could hear him from inside the tree house. I opened the door because I thought it might be Mom, but it was him. And then…" Lowie broke off, folding her knees up and pulling them to her chest. Butch waited.

"He climbed the ladder and tried to come into the tree house. I had to hurry to lock the door."

Butch stared at Lowie for a moment, then turned to look out over the water. The muscles of his jaw were working, and he had a deep, angry furrow in his brow. She wanted to say more, to ask Butch not to tell her mother lest her mother think she was going crazy, but she didn't dare. Something about his bearing had shifted. With the sharpness of a child's intuition, she knew that even a ghost had something real to fear in Butch Brown.

Chapter Fifty-Five

Dave leaned against the trunk of his squad, arms folded across his chest, watching the ruined Cadillac as it was coaxed from its resting place. The car had been wedged between two sizable pine trees with such force that both trees where bowed outward and the sides of the car scraped down to bare metal. It was a wonder that Malloy hadn't slammed directly into one of the pines and been killed instantly. *Shame, that,* Dave thought uncharitably. But Foley Lake would have been spared a night of terror and chaos, and few would really mourn one less used car salesman in the world.

The tow truck driver worked the winch at the back of his rig, wincing at the squeal of metal as the Cadillac came forth. Once the car was free of the trees Dave waved to him to stop, then scooped his camera up and snapped a couple more pictures from the road. He walked to the car and looked through the broken driver's side window. Glass fragments covered the leather seat like confetti, but otherwise the car was spotless. *Spotless.* Dave chuffed through his nose.

Spot had called dispatch to report his car stolen the morning of July fifth. He claimed he had turned in early, the car setting safe in his driveway, though he could not swear to the fact that he had taken the keys from the ignition. When he woke the next day, the car was gone. Dave felt a warm rush in his middle, and instinctively grabbed for the roll of antacids he kept in his breast pocket. He munched two tablets as he leaned through the window and snapped pictures of the car's seats and dash. He knew that Malloy had crashed the car himself, had shown up at the park drunk, and had started the fight with Chuck Larson's boy that led to the disaster. But he couldn't prove it. Several people thought it was Spot who went lurching into the baseball diamond that night, though none of them could, or would, swear to it. Terrance was not certain who it was that jumped him; all he could say for sure was that the man was surprisingly fast for how large he was, and that he reeked of alcohol. If Dave couldn't find some way to prove that Spot was at the park, he would never be able to nail him with any of the veritable litany of charges that should be brought against him, and drunk driving would only be the start. Still, charges would be meaningless if Dave couldn't prove Malloy was ground zero of the whole disastrous affair.

Dave walked around the passenger side of the car and the toe of his boot caught the edge of something solid in the tall grass. A rumpled paper book lay face down. Dave squatted and retrieved it, flipping it open at random. He stood slowly, turning pages, a sense of foreboding growing with every turn.

It was part of a yearbook from Foley Lake Elementary, dated 1962. The book was damp, the mimeographed pictures faded from exposure to the elements, but it didn't matter. He was familiar with the pictures—he had a copy of this same yearbook in storage at his father's house in St. Cloud, along with some other relics from his childhood. He flipped the book to the second-grade class, knowing exactly where he would find his own image, but when he arrived at the page he was so startled he physically jumped.

His eyes were gone. Someone had blackened them out with ink. There were black voids where they should have been.

Dave's heart started to pound. The pictures of many of the children in the book had been defaced somehow. Several bore a heavy single slash mark, while others were scribbled with a pencil. But only a few had been blinded and he was one of them. As he turned the pages forward he saw that most of the adults had been blinded as well. He felt his shoulders slump when he saw that Paul Harris' picture was scrawled out with a red pen. He flipped the page back and was relieved to see Lane's picture was untouched.

"Hey, off'cer?"

Dave jumped. Clyde squinted at him, lifting his hat to wipe sweat from his brow. "Can I finish hauling this Caddy in? I just got another call for service out on Highway 18."

"Go ahead, Clyde. I'm through with it for now."

The Cadillac lurched forward as the winch came back to life. Dave followed it out of the ditch and climbed into his squad, the yearbook in hand. He couldn't make sense what he was seeing, but he knew enough to see the defacing of the book as the work of a disturbed mind. He opened the book to Paul's picture again and studied it. The image was so marred that, had he not already known that Paul's picture belonged on that spot on the page, he never would have recognized him. The boy's face was obliterated. More, the bottom of the page had been ripped off at an angle, taking with it the last picture on the lower right corner.

Dave sat back in his seat. Whose picture had been on that spot on the page? He couldn't recall. He was two years younger than Paul, and although the school was small enough for him to remember most of the children, he could not recall who was missing. He set the book on the seat next to him and put the Crown Victoria into drive. The book probably had nothing at all to do with Spot or the events in the park; still, his instinct told him not to dismiss it. He turned the squad back toward Brainerd, waving at Clyde as he passed. He had a meeting with the sheriff, who had more than a few questions about what Dave had discovered since the events of the Fourth. Dave had few answers. And now, thanks to the rumpled yearbook, now he had a whole new set of questions.

Chapter Fifty-Six

<hr>

Emil sat in the blackness of midnight and stared out the window. He hadn't been able to sleep in the dark since the night the clock first reawakened. Now, every time he began to doze the deep chime sounding out the hour jolted him awake, a rush of pure adrenaline making his heart slam in his chest. And his heart resented it, the regular shocks to its rhythm becoming a tightness that made it hard to breath. Rather than being jerked out of sleep every hour, Emil had developed a habit of sitting up all night. He kept watch at his kitchen window, leaving the lights off lest a nosy neighbor notice them and question his newly acquired insomnia. He didn't want anyone's help or sympathy. He knew how their minds worked and he had no need to be pitied by the likes of them. He knew perfectly well that the people of Foley Lake considered him well into his dotage and that anything unusual about his behavior would be taken as a sign that his rock-solid mind was finally slipping. He wouldn't have it. So, he sat alone in the dark and silent house until the eastern sky began to turn pink. Only then did he feel tired enough to climb into his narrow bed and sleep.

He hadn't moved any furniture in the house in the four years since Anna had left their home for the last time and had gone to live at the nursing center in Duluth. The Alzheimer's that consumed her left her little more than comatose, and he knew that her time was near. It had been the most painful thing in his life, watching her mind disintegrate like a flower losing its petals, watching their fifty years together were slowly erased from her memory, but there was a part of him that envied her. She no longer had to bear the weight of fault for anything she had done in her life. The place where memories had been was now a gray void. When he sat alone like this, he wished he could do that, just wipe away regret like steam from a mirror. Because lately every time he was alone in the dark, memories of the mine and its horrid, secret ways flooded back, and he found himself wondering how he would escape the certainty that the mine would somehow find him in the end.

Down the street a dog barked. Emil turned toward the sound and listened. The dog quieted but the man remained still, head cocked. Finally, he shifted his weight and settled back into the chair. The darkness had an odd way of magnifying sound, and the effect wasn't lost on him. He noticed every creak the old house made, every pop of a closing car door down the street, every tick or moan he couldn't place. It was disturbing, the noise the night made.

It played on one's mind. Good thing, he thought, that he was not prone to being spooky. He was unmoved by the fear because he had faced down his demons already, years ago, in the rotting belly of the Foley.

He wasn't sure why he said yes when the company asked him if he would go down into the flooded mine and help bring out its dead. It certainly wasn't nostalgia that drove him. He hadn't a nostalgic bone in his body. Maybe it was a sense of duty, even obligation, although he didn't believe in survivor's guilt or any such thing. He had nothing to feel guilty about. He had been on the surface when the alarm whistle began to wail and in minutes the lake had filled the entire mine. Rescue wasn't an option; the very idea was absurd. Trying would have meant certain death. Scaling down the ladder to reach a handout for any miner that he might have helped probably would have killed him. He wasn't foolish enough to end his life on a vain hope, not then, not now. That's what he told himself for years afterward, as he lay sweating in twisted sheets in the wake of a vivid dream.

The smell was beyond foul. It had taken three months to pump out the mine, and to make it all safe enough to send down the living in search of the dead. There was no fresh air down there and the smell of decaying human beings, and of dead fish, beavers and turtles that had been swept into the mine when its swampy lake bottom poured into the drifts. The funeral home had suggested a spray to fumigate the wet tunnels, and all the workers were given masks. But no amount of fumigation could hide that stench, and the mask only served to cut off enough oxygen to make him feel lightheaded and disconnected from the task.

They worked in shifts, each crew digging on hands and knees and using hoses to rinse away sand and mud, sending it to the bottom of the main shaft where a giant Layne & Bowler pump lifted it out of the mine. The work was hard, hand-digging out the drifts in search of the buried souls. It took weeks to find the first body. After that they found them regularly, one or two at a time.

Nelson was found just inside the top drift. If he'd have run another 10 feet, he would have made it to the shaft and might have survived. Graves and Valentine were found together, clutching one another, and the foremen said most likely one got stuck in the cement-like mud that filled the drift, and the other stayed with him rather than let him die alone, though entwined as they were it was impossible to know which was the victim and which the hero.

Peter Magditch. Emil picked up his cup and swirled the cold coffee around inside it. Pete had been a good man. They were part of the same four-man contract, shoulder-to-shoulder laboring to mine out the ore, each earning his pay based, at least in part, on the other's work. Emil made good money with Peter, until Emil was enticed from his contract by the promise of easier work as a mechanic's assistant. He finished out the contract and found himself oddly touched when his team didn't fill his spot right away.

Emil knew where the body would be. He had seen Pete gathering up his tools halfway down the upper drift just minutes before the flood, as Emil made his way to the cage. Despite the force of the mud and water, he knew Pete wouldn't have gotten far. If anything, he would have run deeper into the drift, because he would have run toward the cries of the other men rather than away. That was the kind of man he was. Good. Peter was good.

The hose did its work, rinsing away mud and filth. Then, behind the stream, a pie-shaped patch of gray-white appeared with a sharp new scent of rot. A face. Or part of a face, distorted and foul. But Emil knew who it was, and as soon as the hose was shut off he stepped forward and started digging.

It took less than a shift to liberate Peter's head, shoulders, and upper torso. Emil worked steadily, refusing offers of help or suggestions that he take a break for some fresh air and let someone else dig. His fellow rescuers watched him bend to the task and they stepped back. All the men removing the bodies had worked in the mine. Nearly all had been in the tunnels when a friend, a brother, or a cousin was discovered. They respected the need of a man to liberate his own. They stooped nearby, keeping the hose at the ready, letting Emil root out his grief alone.

Once Peter was freed from his thighs up, Emil slipped a rope under his decaying arms. The other men each took hold of the rope, and as the boss said, *careful, now,* they pulled on the rope, trying to coax Peter Magditch from his hiding place. The body wouldn't budge. They tried again. Nothing. They released the rope and Emil went back to work, trying to feel what was keeping the man from coming forth. Hands deep in the heavy mud, his face only inches from Peter's rotting remains, Emil found the problem. A timber from the tunnel had fallen across the dead man's ankles and a pole was lodged under both knees. Pete's legs were jackknifed in the mud. Emil said he wasn't sure what to do. Boss handed him a drill. *What am I supposed to do with this?* Emil asked. Boss looked up at the tunnel's ceiling. *You can't chop. You can't shake the ground. All I got is a drill. Get him loose.*

Emil got him loose. He drilled and they pulled, and Peter came forth. But when the basket was set down and Peter's body, legs mostly intact, was laid inside, he was so stretched that his head hung over the top. And that basket was seven feet long.

Provoked to movement by the memory, Emil shuffled to the counter and refilled his coffee cup from an ancient percolator that hadn't been plugged in for hours. He returned to his chair in the kitchen, eschewing the comfortable living room with plush recliners and a picture window that faced the street, in favor of sitting at the kitchen window in a straight wicker chair. The window faced the back of the house, with its tiny yard and woods beyond. He wasn't concerned about anything that might come from the street. It was the woods that bothered him. He could never clearly see what might be lurking out there once the sun slipped behind the western horizon, especially now that the regular rain had provoked a new vitality in the trees. He spent each night staring out at the darkness, a cup of cold coffee at his elbow. And that's where he was when he saw the first flash of yellow light floating in the trees a hundred yards from his back door.

At first, he thought it was a firefly or something of that manner. The light was small, blinking. Someone sending a message, maybe, like Morse code. But no. It wasn't flashing on and off. It was moving, bouncing a little from left to right, but definitely moving forward. What looked like blinking was the light disappearing behind trees and reemerging as it made progress straight toward Emil's unlit kitchen window.

Emil's breath caught in his throat. He stood slowly and felt his chest tighten. The light looked like a small flashlight, but it was too high—unless the person holding it was carrying it over his head, which didn't make sense. It was blinking in and out like a strobe, making headway fast, and at the rate it was going it would close the distance to the house in a matter of minutes.

He cursed silently. Then one thought rose above all the others. *I am not going to hide. If he wants me, I'll be waiting.*

Emil reached back for his walker and pulled it to him, then clunked his way to his bedroom as quickly as he could. There he pushed the walker up against the wall and lowered himself slowly, painfully, to one knee. He reached under the bed, his hand shaking, groping blindly until he felt the cold steel metal box. He lifted it to his bed and shoved his dry, wrinkled hand between the mattress and frame. His fingers brushed a small key. He pulled it out and sprung the lock on the box.

The luster of the Colt .45 automatic caught a glint of light from the streetlamp outside the bedroom window. Emil ran his hand over the smooth metal, then lifted it from its box. He pushed the magazine release on the side of the gun and the magazine slipped into his waiting hand. It was full. The weight of seven gleaming bullets nestled into the cool steel of the clip was reassuring. He snapped it into place with a satisfied grunt. But when he grasped the action and tried to pull it back, it wouldn't budge. He struggled, clutching the grip of the gun with his right hand and tugging the action with his left. It was tighter and stiffer than he remembered and his hands, grown weak with age, could barely pull the slide. An image of the light moving quickly through the trees flashed in his mind and his heart gave a sharp lurch. Pain radiated out in a wave toward his neck and stomach. He struggled to his feet, his breath no more than short gasps. He clutched the gun in his left hand, bracing it between his knees, and jerked the slide with his right.

The slide gave way, slipping back along the length of its barrel and springing forward with a solid snap.

Emil stood bent over, leaning against the walker, the gun dangling in his right hand, his left arm curled up against the pain in his chest. His heart quieted and the pain dwindled. He slipped the gun into the waist band of his polyester trousers and turned back toward the kitchen.

The light was gone. Emil stared into the darkness, unsure what to do. He dragged the walker to the cupboard and fished around in a junk drawer for a flashlight, then went to the back door. He stood for a moment, listening. His heart gave a few painless wobbles as he considered the wisdom of his next move. The weight of the gun lay heavy and reassuring against his bony hip.

There was silence beyond the door. He unbolted it, pulled it open, and stepped through.

The backyard was empty save the dull yellow beam of Emil's flashlight. He made his way to the middle of the yard, the *cha-chunk-chunk* of the walker muffled in the turf. He stopped, listening. There was no sound, not even the usual crickets. But there was something there, or someone. He could feel it in the chilling of his blood. A presence watched from somewhere beyond the neat trim of his perfectly square lawn. Emil scanned the darkness for signs of movement.

"I'm here!" he called, his voice a sharp intrusion in the night. There was no response. Emil marched forward, holding the flashlight in his right hand and grasping the rail of the walker, so with each step toward the tree line the light swung up and down in a dizzying swath, shining up into the tree canopy, then down to the grass with the rocking of each step. He stopped at the edge of the tree line. "I'm here!" he yelled again. "If you got business with me, come on out here and let's finish it!"

A figure stepped out from behind a large oak tree only ten feet in front of Emil. It was a tall form clad in a miner's white slicker, his face hidden in the shadow of an aged hat fitted with a glowing carbide lamp.

Emil's heart exploded into rapid-fire in his chest as he staggered backward, the abandoned walker the only thing between him and the specter staring out from the trees. The figure stepped toward Emil and panic surged through the old man's veins as his grabbed at the gun in his waistband, fumbled with it, pulled it out. The end of the barrel shivered as it pointed toward the silent figure.

Emil stood in the middle of his yard, trembling, words tumbling through his mind in an incomprehensible stream. The miner didn't move, but a low, jagged chuckle floated toward Emil through the still and black night air.

Emil began to gasp, small gulps of air that couldn't make it past the tightness that clamped down on his lungs like a vise. The gun drooped in his hands, and the weight of it pressed his finger into the trigger. The gun fired into the ground in front of him. The shock of the recoil knocked Emil backward and he sprawled flat on his back, eyes wide open, mouth agape, staring blankly up into the vast endless depths of the black summer sky.

Chapter
Fifty-Seven

Mike pulled the hospital door open and stepped into the lobby. He had been laboring away on a press release about the Fourth of July disaster when Dorothy tapped on his office door and opened it. She filled him in quickly. Emil had been found in his backyard, where apparently, he had lain all night after having a heart attack. He was alive, but the doctors expected that would change within a day or so. And most curiously, Emil insisted on talking to Mike.

Mike didn't know how he felt about the fact that Emil wanted to see him. He had never really considered the man a friend. He was more like an ill-favored family member, someone whose presence Mike didn't seek out, but who he had learned to tolerate. And having Dave meet him at the doors of the hospital looking tired and irritable didn't endear him to the task.

Dave nodded a greeting and fell in next to Mike so that Mike wouldn't have to stop to talk to him, since it was clear he didn't intend to. Dave got straight to the point. "Do you have any idea why Emil would ask to see you?"

"Good morning, Dave," Mike replied.

Dave waved his hand. "Good morning. So, do you have any idea why?"

Mike shook his head. "No idea."

"Do you have any idea why he would have felt it was necessary to fire a gun last night?"

Mike stopped. "What?"

"About two a.m. we had a report of a gunshot in Emil's neighborhood. A county squad went over and checked things out, but it was quiet. They didn't see anything out of order. This morning when we got the 9-1-1 call about Emil. He was found lying in his backyard with a loaded gun in his hand."

"And he'd shot it?"

"We found a spent casing on the ground next to him."

Mike started walking again, more slowly. Dave walked with him, watching his face. "So, you don't know of anyone who might have been threatening him?"

"No. Not everyone loves the guy, but I can't imagine anyone making him scared enough to take out a loaded gun."

"Well, what about all the commotion about the mine reopening? Emil's been in the middle of all that. Any thoughts whether someone might have wanted to quiet him down, maybe scare him a little?"

Mike shrugged. "People are stirred up about the mine but I hardly think it's come to that. Besides, the folks that are most stirred up were stirred by Emil himself."

They arrived at the elevators and Mike punched the button for the second floor. They were silent on the ride up, but as the elevator doors opened, Dave spoke. "Mike," he said. "How much do you know about Butch Brown?"

Mike scowled at Dave. "Butch has nothing to do with this. He barely even knows Emil. Why would Emil shoot at him?" They emptied into the hall and stopped at the double doors that guarded the entrance to ICU.

"I don't know. But he's a stranger, and strange things have been happening since he got here."

Mike planted his hands on his hips defensively. "Like what?"

"Like what happened to Emil last night. Like the accident at the fireworks show, the mine being reopened, the storms—"

"Oh, for heaven's sake!" Mike exclaimed. "The mine is being reopened and you want to blame that on Butch? Or the rain? C'mon Dave, who do *you* think Butch is? A man can't be blamed for the weather!"

Dave studied Mike's face, openly intrigued by the passion inspired by his line of questioning. Mike waved him away and pushed the door open.

"His name isn't Brown, you know."

Mike stopped. "What?"

"Butch Brown. His name isn't Brown. I ran it through the computer. It's a fake."

Mike stepped back and let the door slip closed again. "Why?" he asked.

"I don't know. Could be any number of reasons a man wouldn't want people to know who he—"

"No. I mean, why did you run his name? A man had the right to his own privacy, so what reason would you have to do such a thing?"

Davy frowned, "Lane called me at the station a couple weeks ago and asked me to."

Mike felt his jaw clench. He gave Dave one last, hard look, and stepped alone through the doors where Emil lay waiting for death.

Chapter Fifty-Eight

<hr>

Mike walked into the clearing that made up Butch's camp and looked around. There was no sign of Butch, which didn't surprise him. Something had happened between Butch and Lane, which he understood from Lane's quiet anger and Butch's absence. But unlike Lane, Mike never doubted that Butch was still around. He wouldn't have left the city. Not yet. Something tied him here, and he would stay around until whatever the tie was could be severed once and for all. No, he was here somewhere. But Mike didn't expect the man to be at the mine and was glad he wasn't. The solitude was exactly what he needed.

He crossed to the campsite. Butch was a neat guest. The ash pile was surrounded by a circle of rock, forming a fire ring to keep live coals from spreading into the grass a few yards away. A bucket of old ashes and a small shovel waited just outside the ring, as did a bucket of clean water. Mike circled around the fire ring and glanced into the burned-out office building, then turned and crossed the campsite again, this time moving toward the gate blocking the entry to the head frame. The metal was brown and dark red like dried blood, making the gleam of newly exposed steel where the chain was sawn open stand out in sharp relief. He leaned forward, curving his body to avoid touching the metal, and peered into the shaft. He could see a patch of concrete, a scattering of dusty beer cans, and beyond that, nothing. Darkness met his eyes like a solid wall. If he wanted to know more, he would have to go inside.

It's the mine, Mike…there're things you don't know…your family. The mine. Keep it closed. Whatever you do, keep it closed.

Emil's warnings had sent a cold lash of fear down Mike's spine, their power undiminished by the weakness of the man who spoke them. Emil had stared up at him from the maze of tubes surrounding his bed, his eyes bright with terror as he tried to brush the oxygen mask away from his face with one withered hand.

Mike. Listen…

I am listening, Emil, just take it easy. Leave the mask, you need it.

…the mine…keep it closed…listen.

I'm listening. What about the mine? Leave the mask, Emil. I can hear you.

Stay away from it, Mike. Leave it closed. Your father…it took your son…

What about my son, Emil?

Leave it closed, Mike. He's come back...

Who's come back? Emil? Can you hear me?

...already here...

Emil?

More people will die.

With that the old man slipped into unconsciousness, his eyes sliding closed and locking the terror in them behind the sagging lids. When Mike left the hospital he marched toward his truck, rich with the conviction that he had to stop the mine reopening or risk certain death. But the drive from Crosby back to Foley Lake had given him twenty miles to turn Emil's words over and over in his mind. *Leave it closed. More people will die.*

It took your son.

He's come back.

Who was back? Who did Emil see the night before and what scared him enough to take out the gun? The man might be delusional, but there was something in the blend of fear and regret Mike saw in his face that was too familiar to simply dismiss. He had seen that look before. He had seen it in some of the old men who had known his father, men who weren't in the mine that fateful day. And on occasion he had seen it in Butch.

Twenty miles. By the time Mike rolled past the city limit sign in Foley Lake his mind was made up. Emil's warnings about the mine became clues to a truth he desperately needed to understand.

Now, looking into the yawning black mouth of the head frame that had plagued his dreams for twenty years, Mike found his resolve wavering. He clenched his jaw and grabbed the gate, yanking it open before he lost his nerve entirely.

Moving out of the sunlight and into shadow, he stopped and waited for his eyes to adjust. He could see little, but a sound sent his pulse into orbit. It was an odd *whoop whoop whoop,* a smallish thumping with just enough energy to send a soft echo through the mine. Mike's first thought was of the wings of a large bat. But his eyes adjusted quickly—he had always had remarkable night vision—and a stirring in the corner caught his attention. There, sitting on a pile of rags, was Bones. His tail made the soft *whoop* as it slapped the ground in warm greeting. Mike exhaled, not conscious until just that moment that he had been holding his breath. He bent down and patted his thigh. Bones took the invitation and waddled over.

"Hey, buddy, how are you?" Mike crooned, patting the dog's ragged head. "I didn't expect to see you. You gave me a scare for a second there." Bones sat on his haunches and panted, his expression bemused and friendly. Mike chuckled as he stood. Strange how perceptive that dog seemed to be.

Mike surveyed the shaft. Although Butch had attempted to clean up the outer campsite, he had left the inside of the shaft largely untouched. It was a broad and cavernous, dark despite the sunlight eking in through holes punched in the corrugated steel shell. The concrete floor was covered with dust and dirt, and a tangle of iron and cable lay decaying against the northernmost wall, some remains of the old cage cable that was used to raise and lower miners. Beyond that, the shaft seemed empty. Mike sighed, his hands on his hips, and scanned the emptiness for something like an answer. He wandered over to the square of concrete where, two decades earlier, mysterious scrawls in the dirt were left as the only evidence his child had been in the head frame. Priceless. Penance. Promise. Mike squatted and studied the layer of dust, as if it might still yield us a clue as to the meaning of that old message. The concrete gave up nothing. Mike stood quickly, turning away from the spot as a wave of frustration surged through him. No sense brooding over it. There wasn't time. He had to remember the reason he had come back to this horrid place to begin with.

It was hard to know exactly what answer he was looking for, because he was still unsure what the question was. But his conversation with Emil had stirred up a need to find some kind of clue to what was happening, and he couldn't get past the idea that he would find his answers in that head frame. Yet all that greeted him was rust and dust and ruined steel beams hidden under a canopy of shadow. The building seemed unwilling to yield a single clue.

Bones shuffled back toward the corner he had come from, and Mike watched him go. The dog curled up on his pile of rags, but this time Mike noted something propped against the wall next to Bones' nest that his maladjusted eyes had missed before. A rolled sleeping bag and a worn backpack leaned against the steel, lonely and out of place. Mike walked

toward them, provoking a new wave a thumping from Bones'
tail as he approached. The backpack was clean and free of
dust, proving it hadn't been left behind by a wayward hiker.
He could only assume it was Butch's. Mike squatted, one
hand on the dog's head and the other feeling the front of the
backpack. Feeling it, he reasoned, was not the same as
looking in it, which would be wrong and a full-blown
invasion of Butch's privacy. But feeling it, its soft, pliable
lumps here, a few hard blocks there, gave rise to new
curiosity, and Mike shoved his internal objections aside and
pulled the bag toward him, unzipping it as he did so. In
seconds, he had the bag upended, its contents spilling out
over the mineshaft floor.

A silver flashlight. Well, that was handy. He clicked it on
and scanned the rest of the contents. Tape. Pliers. A new
toothbrush still in its cellophane. A pack of batteries. A
plastic baggie filled with pictures.

Mike braced the flashlight it in the crook of his arm and
lifted the photos out of the baggie. There were only a few.
One featured an unfamiliar man and woman, though Mike
guessed by Butch's resemblance to the man that they were his
parents. Mike studied the man's face. Did he know him? Or
was it the resemblance to Butch that made him familiar? He
looked at the next picture, hoping for a clue. It was Butch as
a teen, husky with close-cropped hair, grinning as he leaned
on the hood of an El Camino. The last picture was of an older
Butch, bald and thin, standing unsmiling next to the woman.
The lady had aged noticeably. They stood in front of a tall

set of doors framed by the brick walls, the words, "St. Isadora's" etched into the door's frame.

Mike put the pictures back into the plastic and set them on the ground next to the backpack. He stood, flashlight in hand, and walked back into the deeper darkness. He shined the light back and forth, then up and down, scanning. The light bounced back off walls and fallen beams, then disappeared into a gaping blackness. He stopped. In front of him, framed by concrete, was the shaft.

This wasn't the first time he had seen the hole, the site of his son's demise. He had been there every day, all day, as the would-be rescuers flooded the hole with light and rigged cable systems to lower divers clad like astronauts in heavy canvas suits and helmets to the waters below. They searched daily while most of Foley Lake waited outside amid the clamor of reporters and television cameras, only to end each day in empty-handed frustration. After two weeks they called off the search, saying that they had looked everywhere they could expect Paul's body to be. But the mine waters were murky, and the shaft filled with sharp edges, bits of soggy timber, and hunks of concrete, an unstable and shifting mess designed to trap and kill divers. Mike vividly recalled the dive captain's cold consolation. "We're awful sorry, Mr. Harris, but we just can't risk the lives of our rescuers looking for a corpse."

A corpse. In one stroke, his living, vital, energetic boy was assigned that black label and an eternity alone in the obscure depths of the mine.

Mike stepped to the edge of the shaft and shined the flashlight straight down. The beam was swallowed in darkness not twenty feet beyond the concrete rim. He shuffled his feet closer to the edge, letting the light play around the perimeter of the hole. He had thought many times about stepping off the edge and joining his son, of feeling for just a moment what his boy felt, the weightless free fall. But it was the image of Lane's small face that always pulled him back. If he'd had only one child, dying would have been easy.

Bones whined softly. Mike clicked off the flashlight and watched the lines of the shaft disappear before he stepped back.

He returned to the backpack and squatted, cursing himself for dumping the bag with no regard to how items had been stored. Now it was impossible for him to replace everything as it had been and conceal his riffling. When he reached into the bag to replace the flashlight, his hand brushed something soft and papery. He pulled the flashlight back out and clicked it on to look inside. There, on the bottom of the bag, was a ball of white tissue paper.

Mike pulled the package out. It was neatly folded around the edges of a soft, round parcel. Tucking the flashlight under his arm, he pulled the tissue free.

Mike's world became a wide, white place. Later he wouldn't remember replacing most of the items back in the bag or zipping it shut. He wouldn't remember setting it back in its corner or patting Bones on the head as his left, closing the gate behind him. What he would remember was endless walking, his feet covered with red mud, and a small baseball cap clasped carefully in both hand.

Chapter Fifty-Nine

It was a full moon. And true to form, Artie was restless. He had been roaming the halls all day, the peculiar sound of his slow lope passing by Will's open door every hour. Now that the sun had set and the night shift had begun, Artie would soon slip out of his room where he had been feigning sleep and creep down the quiet halls, past the nurses' station to the big double doors that fronted the home's main parking lot. He would shove the doors open, doors that were wired to an alarm from the inside to foil such escapes by wayward residents and lope out into the parking lot for a midnight romp in the moonlight. The attendants would chase him down and steer him back inside, as he drooled and gibbered. Then Artie would get a shot of something soothing to help him sleep and would spend the night moaning impotently tied into bed with soft handcuffs made of cotton and Velcro.

Will waited. He stood next to the exit door in the dim light of the nursing home's hallway, listening intently for the buzz of the alarm he knew was coming. He had made up his mind after Mike's last visit that he needed to act, and telling what he had to tell by phone, seeing as how Mike hadn't returned his calls anyway, struck him as a bad idea. Besides, he felt sure somehow that the daughter needed to know as well.

Artie's restlessness was the sign that Will had been hoping for. He slipped on his light windbreaker and best loafers, folding the wheelchair that he didn't need and leaving it behind. He stepped silently down the hall to the emergency exit. His trouser pocket bulged with cash. Willa sent a five- or ten-dollar bill with every birthday and Christmas card she sent, and she had been sending cards for years. "Walking around money," as she would call it. Will smiled to himself. She sure was a weird woman. Sweet, but weird, and thoroughly rooted in the past. Will had few needs the home didn't provide, so he had been accumulating the cash for years, and now he hoped it would be enough to get him where he needed to go. It seemed a bit foreign, the feel of a wad of paper money in his pocket, his good shoes on his feet, waiting in the empty hallway next to a narrow and little-used side door. A prickle of nervous excitement made his senses sharp, so sharp that when the alarm sounded, he jerked with a start. Artie was bolting. All the exits were wired to the same security system, so Will's departure through the side door raised no further warning. He pressed the release bar and pushed the door open and stepped out into the warm night air.

Will leaned against the brick façade of the building and listened for the commotion in the front parking lot to cease. Artie was enjoying his romp, and from the sound of things the attendants were not in a big hurry to collect him. Their voices told Will they had formed a loose circle around Artie and were slowly closing in, letting the old fellow wear off some of his energy before they cornered him. He cackled as he loped about, a strange sound that was something between a growl and a cough, until the cackles turned to howls of rage as the old man was caught and towed back inside.

Fifteen minutes later, Will stepped onto the sidewalk and started moving. His absence would not be noticed for hours but there was no sense wasting time. He followed the edge of the building, his cane swinging in gentle arcs in front of him, until he felt the unmistakable solidity of the concrete sidewalk underfoot. He turned left, edged down the sidewalk twenty feet, and turned left again. Then he stopped, giving the ground a questioning tap with the cane's tip. The winding trails through the nursing home's extensive gardens led away from the home, looped around, intersected one another, and led back. Will knew them all well, and he knew that, judging by the sounds of traffic on most days, one in particular came very close to Crosby's main street. That was the trail he was headed for now. He wasn't entirely sure what he was going to do once he got to town in the middle of a summer night, but he would worry about that after he was clear of the nursing home. One way or another, he would make his way. It was time he saw for himself, metaphorically speaking, what in the world was happening in the little town of Foley Lake.

Chapter Sixty

Mike struggled his way up the hillside, sliding and grabbing hold of great clumps of sumac to steady himself. His breath came in ragged gulps, but he maintained a steady pace, climbing by the light of a full moon. Loose slag rolled out from under his weight, giving him the sense of scaling a mountain of ball bearings. He pressed forward, heart protesting with loud thumps. This was the hard part, he told himself. It was always hardest at the top.

Almost there.

He gained the summit of the hill, pausing to catch his breath before he dropped to his knees, and crawled around the edge of the hill to its northern slope. He pulled himself along with all the stealth his sixty-year-old frame could manage, though from the hillside, no one could have heard his movements. The moon gave a sprinkling of light, enough for him to creep with reasonable certainty toward the northern summit that he had been using as an observation post for the past three nights, enough to help him avoid tumbling down the slope in a manner that was not likely to be fatal but would create scrapes and bruises that would be painful and difficult to explain. He clambered onto the flat area, a broad, sandy impression, and situated himself among the sumacs. Legs curled into a stiff lotus position, he slipped the pink backpack he had borrowed from Lowie's closet off and withdrew three items—a bottle of water, a sandwich so mashed from the journey it appeared to be bleeding strawberry jam, and a pair of night vision binoculars. Mike set the sandwich aside, opened the water and took a long swig, then closed it and tossed it on top of the sandwich. He lifted the binoculars to his face and aimed them at the next hillside over.

The binoculars were a wonder. They cost a small fortune, but they lit up the landscape in shades of green. The old head frame stood out against the dark sky, and he scanned back and forth, back and forth. Nothing was stirring. Nothing had stirred, not since that first night, when he watched Butch enter the head frame at around midnight, not to emerge again until just before daybreak. Since then, he laid in bed each night, waiting for the house to sink into stillness so he could sneak out and stand lookout over the city.

Butch was working at something inside the mine. Mike didn't know what it was, and he had made up his mind not to ask lest the very question throw Butch off. Something told him that whatever the man was doing was important, vital even, and Mike had every intention of doing what he could to allow Butch to see it through. His suspicions were confirmed when he spotted Butch leaving the diner four days ago, moving stiffly and sporting a large bruise over the left side of his face. Someone was trying to stop Butch for accomplishing his mission. Mike wouldn't have it. He would clear a path for the man, whatever it took. So night after night he hauled himself up the hill just south of the mine, watching and waiting, ready to run interference for Butch if need be.

Mike lowered the binoculars and sighed. Nothing. He reached into his inside jacket pocket and withdrew the baseball cap, neatly folded in its tissue paper, and gently liberated it from the wrapping. He set the cap on his knee, one hand resting on it while the other hand lifted the binoculars to his eyes. He scanned the mine and the bare grasslands that fell away all around it. The night was still.

He turned the binoculars toward the city. How odd it looked at night. He couldn't clearly make out the houses on the farthest edge, in what used to be the wealthy district of Foley Lake, but he knew the neighborhood thoroughly. This had been where Mary Louise grew up, a pampered only child, in the years before she agreed to marry him. His arms grew tired, and he lowered the binoculars. Mary Louise. She had been a true beauty. He would watch her as she walked down the street to her father's law office where she worked as a secretary, her head up and shoulders straight. He wasn't alone in his admiration; every male head on Main Street would turn to watch her pass. She was ten years his junior when they married. He was an assistant city manager, ambitious by Foley Lake standards, and he promised her he would make her every dream come true. She quit her job and began to prepare for the arrival of the first of what would have been a houseful of Harris children; instead, years she wanted to fill with birthday parties and first steps echoed with the void of infertility. For a decade, every month brought new heartbreak, until the miracle of Paul's birth reawakened a joy in her that Mike had almost forgotten she had ever possessed. Lane's arrival two years later was icing on the cake, but it was Paul that Mary adored. Losing him killed everything that was most beautiful about the woman. After Paul's funeral nothing ever seemed to scare her. Nothing seemed to touch her at all.

How he wished she would have lived to see this day.

He ran his thumb gently over the rim of the baseball cap, savoring the rough feel of the cloth. A thrill ran through him. He should have known right away, he chided himself. Butch's interest in the Harris family and his uncanny knowledge of the town should have been dead giveaways. Yes, he should have guessed it. Butch's arrival in Foley Lake, at the same time the mine was going to be reopened, was no coincidence.

An image of Lane flashed in his mind. His poor girl. How would she react to Butch, if Mike's theory about him proved true? What would she say, once she understood why there could never be anything romantic between them? Would she accept him? Or would she push him away, as she had so many others? Lane, brotherless at nine and motherless at fifteen, pregnant at eighteen, married soon after. Eighteen seemed impossibly young for a girl to be married. He had wanted to tell her so, but she never gave him leave, never gave him a chance to try and help her direct her life. Instead, he silently walked her down the aisle, and five months later brought flowers to the hospital to woo his infant grandchild.

He didn't need to. Lowie never needed a token of any sort to entice her affection. She gave it liberally, freely, and in an abundance that belied her tiny frame. She, who had still failed to learn that life was savage, lived in a guileless bubble of goodwill. It seemed nothing bad could touch her. But the rest of them were easy bait for the bad fates. Sadness and loss lurked at the edge of every good thing.

Mike thought of Danny, rejected by Lane barely a year into their marriage, flying out of town on his beat-up soft tail Harley. A mile outside the city limits he drove into the blind spot of an eighteen-wheeler loaded with a massive mine generator and bound for the northern range. The trucker, behind schedule, made a hasty lane change without signaling. He sped through two counties with a bright red blood spot on the side of his trailer before the state patrol caught up to him.

Lane was dry-eyed at her husband's funeral, Lowie babbling and beaming in her arms. The day Mike helped her move back home, she set everything of Danny's on the curb for the garbage truck to collect, bringing nothing of her marriage back to her childhood home except Lowie. His heart hurt for his daughter, for her aloof observation of the world around her, her unwillingness to engage in anything that might provide a way for change and hope. She worked so hard to stay disconnected. Except with Butch. With Butch she was different, willing to take some risk. And yet it could never be. The way Mike saw it, that was the greatest tragedy of Lane's young life.

Mike lifted the binoculars and scanned the hillside again. Movement just east of the mine drew his attention. Two small does were scrambling along the bottom ridge of the hill, pushing through the brush. One of deer stopped and looked back the way she had come. Mike could see her ears flicking nervously, while the other danced and shifted by her side. Something must have startled them from their beds among the tall grass between the mine and the lake. Mike followed the direction of the doe's anxious gaze.

A figure emerged from the trees on the far side of the field, causing Mike to physically jump, a small grunt of surprise breaking the quiet. The figure was tall and slender, and moved across the grassy stretch toward the mine with ease even though whoever it was would have been walking in darkness. Mike lowered the glasses for a moment, squinting into the night, then raised them again in time to see the figure pause for a moment at the edge of a clump of brush and scraggly red oak. The figure glanced back the way it had come and hesitated, then turned and stepped into the shadow of the brush.

Mike waited a full five minutes to see the figure emerge from the other side. It didn't.

He lowered the binoculars, thinking. That didn't make sense. The brush pile was no more than twenty feet across. What did the guy do, lay down for a nap? He raised the binoculars again and scanned the brush pile, and the area around it. Nothing there stirred. It was movement from the west that caught his eye.

Another figure was moving quickly toward the brush. Mike frowned. This man must have been hiding in the grass, waiting for the first. He wouldn't have had time to make his way down from the mine. How did he know the first figure was coming? Mike watched closely. This man wasn't graceful, stumbling through the tall grass that sprouted from the mine's western slope, but he was making quick and steady progress toward the brush and the first figure lurking there.

The man slowed as he reached the brush, leaning forward, listening. He looked behind him, then peered into the bushes. He reached up and lifted a cap from his head, rubbing a smooth, round head.

"Butch," Mike whispered. Below, Butch replaced his cap, hesitated, then disappeared into the dense brush.

Mike watched. Stillness settled back over the landscape. He scanned. Nothing.

He lowered the night vision goggles, thinking. Butch *was* up to something, something important. And whatever it was, he apparently needed the cover of darkness to do it. Mike turned toward the city with its few streetlights, his mind alive with possibilities. He needed to do what he could to support Butch, regardless of what it might cost the city, or himself. If

Butch needed darkness to finish his business, then by God, darkness he would have.

Chapter Sixty-One

• •

Lane stopped at the edge of the clearing and listened. She heard little save the wind and birdsong, but she called out anyway.

"Butch?"

A moment later the gate to the head frame rattled and she spotted Bones wiggling through the bars. He limped toward her, tail wagging merrily. She bent to pat him. When she straightened up, Butch was standing at the gate and looking at her from the shadows.

Lane was jolted by his appearance. He was thin and pale against the dim background of the shaft's interior. His shirt and jeans were smeared with red mud, his face drawn and marred by a large bruise. He didn't speak, but he nodded to her and waited. Lane hesitated.

"I didn't know if you'd be here," she began. "Lowie said that she hasn't been able to find you for the last week or so."

"I've been around," he replied simply.

"Your face—"

"I fell," he said simply.

Lane nodded. "Well." The speech she'd rehearsed for the moment she saw Butch again evaporated. She was sure before she left the house that she needed to talk to him, to seek him out and make her request. But seeing him face to face and knowing that, perhaps, the weeks since the accident at the fireworks had passed at least as badly for him as they had for her, made her hesitate. Now she realized he didn't look like he was in any shape to do someone a favor.

"What do you need, Lane?" The question was pointed, but gentle. She gathered her courage.

"There's something wrong with Dad," she began. "He's acting strange. Really strange. I'm getting worried about him—about his mind."

"What's he doing?"

Lane stepped to the gate, shaking her head. "Locking himself in his room all day. I can't remember the last time he actually went to work. He keeps to himself, hardly ever eats. But then at night he disappears. He just leaves and I don't know where he's going."

"What does he say when you ask him?"

"Nothing. He talks but he doesn't say anything specific. Just gives me this strange smile and tells me not to worry, that I just need to have faith."

"Faith in what?"

"That's what I asked. But he smiles and walks away."

"Is he angry? Upset?"

"No," Lane leaned against the gate with a sigh. She was relieved that they seemed to fall back into a comfortable pattern of conversation so quickly. "No, just the opposite. He's happy. Giddy, even. Excited, like he's waiting for something."

"Like what?"

"No idea. He won't tell me. He won't tell me, he won't let me in his room, he even locks the bedroom door when he leaves."

Butch nodded, thinking. Lane studied his face. He had aged years in the few weeks since she had seen him last.

"Do you want me to have a talk with him?"

"I don't mean to make this your problem, Butch, but there isn't anyone else in town that I can trust with something like this, considering his position—"

"I get it. Where can I find him?"

"That's the tricky part," Lane replied. "He's wandering all the time now. You might just have to keep your eyes open and catch him when you can."

Butch nodded. "Don't worry, Lane. I'll talk to him. Things will get better soon. Real soon."

Lane frowned and looked at Butch. "Weird that you would say that."

"Why"?

Lane turned her head, looking down toward the city below the hill. "Because that is *exactly* what Dad keeps telling me."

Chapter Sixty-Two

The explosion of power and sound from the rifle's first report caught Mike off guard, sending a jolt of adrenaline into his system that made it hard for him to keep the rifle steady for the second shot. The first shot had been good, despite the trauma it caused his ears and nerves, but it was only one transformer. His real target was down the road. He thought that the quarter mile walk to the substation would calm him, but instead he had grown more jittery, and the rifle felt every twitch. The chain link fence around the substation looked blurry through the scope and the crosshairs jiggled up and down the transformer's length. When Mike squeezed the trigger all he managed to do was tick the edge of the transformer, and the bullet ricocheted off the squat electrical bus on the ground in front of it. He cursed his nerves and the ringing in his ears. Taking aim a second time he raised up onto his knees and willed himself to steady his hand. The jitter grew worse, and the angle was poor. His second shot missed the transformer entirely.

He sat back on his knees, considering. The echoes from the shot died away and a sudden silence took its place as the wildlife took cover from the onslaught of gunfire. Mike waited until the natural world decided it was safe to resume its doings before he laid the gun on the ground and began searching for the spent cartridges liberated each time he pulled the trigger. He crawled around on his hands and knees, spotting them on the edge of the clump of scrub oak about a foot apart, gleaming in the sun. They were still warm when he dropped them into his breast pocket. He needed a better angle at the transformer. He would have to move. He retrieved the gun, stood and stretched, and started walking.

The weight of the rifle in his hand felt like determination. It was a new sensation for him. He'd realized as he lifted the gun from the back of his bedroom closet that morning that he had been letting himself be pushed about by circumstances for far too long. Even in the matter of the mine reopening, he had been more of a pawn than a player, despite what the people of Foley Lake were saying. But now that he had his first real hope of getting his son back, he wouldn't stay on the sidelines. Time to be a man of action, he told himself. Time to start making things go my way.

The small substation stood a mile outside Foley Lake's city limit, its sole source of power. It sat in the middle of a wide square of cleared ground, the woods lined its edges on three sides, and the highway running along the fourth. Mike slipped into the tree line and spotted a deer trail that ran roughly parallel to the substation, so he followed it, appreciating the cover it afforded him as he bobbed and weaved around tree branches. It wouldn't do to have the mayor of Foley Lake spotted walking with a deer rifle so close to ruined electrical equipment. He couldn't risk the scandal, not now. Later, whatever happened, it wouldn't matter.

Mike's short-sleeved button-down shirt clung to him, dirty smudges across its front. He had scratches on both forearms and on his face from encounters with stray branches, and a few small twigs had taken up refuge in his disheveled hair. He'd parked a mile away and walked through the woods to the substation, swallowing up the trail in quick strides, stopping to crouch down in the underbrush as the occasional car passed by on the county road. He didn't have much time. Someone would be out soon to investigate any disruption of voltage, and it wouldn't take long to connect sound of rifle shots to the problem. He needed to finish this business and get back to the office to establish some kind of alibi before someone put his absence and the transformers' demise together.

The deer trail opened into a small hay field that reached to the road. Mike stopped at the edge of the tree line. All around the substation was open ground. He was at a right-angle to his target. Mike pulled up the rifle and tried to site the transformer in the scope, but the heavy canopy and the ongoing jiggle of his nerves made it impossible to get a good shot. He lowered the gun, thinking. He was reluctant to step across the open ground and lose the camouflage the trees afforded, but he had no options. The transformer lay on the other side. He needed to get to it.

He listened for the sound of a car engine. Hearing nothing, he lifted the Savage and ran the bolt, chambering a round, and clicked the safety off. After a few more moments to collect his nerve, he stepped into the open field. Moving quickly, head down and ears alert, he crossed the span in hurried strides. He stepped into the poplar trees on the far side of the hill—the stand that he had not closely examined in his concern over crossing the field—and nearly collided with the man waiting there before he realized his mistake.

Chapter Sixty-Three

Lowie stepped out of the air-conditioned coolness of the diner into the early August heat, too involved in counting her tips to notice the sharp difference. She was bone tired, as her mom would say, but happy; the diner had been busy all day, and just by serving drinks to people she had earned almost thirty dollars. After the diner closed, she stayed to help May clean up, sweeping and wiping tables and refilling ketchup and mustard bottles. May, her hair falling loose in curlicues around her pretty face, had given her another twenty dollars and a wink. "I don't know what I'd do without your help, Miss Lowie," she'd said. "You're a lifesaver."

Bones danced up the sidewalk toward Lowie, making playful lamb leaps and wagging his tail furiously. "Hello, Bones," she greeted him, stuffing the money back into her pocket. She bent to pet him. The little dog danced away, turning his body sideways toward her. She shook her head at him, too tired to give chase. "Mom's right," she said. "You are a little weird."

Lowie turned toward home, wanting nothing more than a shower and a bowl of Cheerios. Bones trotted back up behind her and whined. She turned around, bending to pick him up, but he dodged away a second time, putting four or five feet between them before he stopped. He gave a playful *woof* and bowed toward her. Lowie put her hands on her hips and frowned, confounded. Bones was not an emotive dog. She couldn't think of one time when he had barked or issued what seemed to be an open invitation to play. When she stepped toward him, he slipped away; when she stopped and turned back toward home, he trotted up behind her and woofed. Finally, he turned and moved up the block and opposite from the shower she longed for, and at the intersection he turned back to give her a long, meaningful look. Then he slipped around the corner and disappeared. Lowie considered for a moment before she turned and jogged after him, curiosity displacing fatigue.

An old man sat alone on a bench halfway down the street. Bones trundle up to him, circled his feet, and lay on the cement next to him. The old man reached down to give him a pat on the head. Lowie approached slowly, not wanting to seem rude. She stopped a few feet away from the bench.

"Come here, Bones," she called. "C'mon, boy. Let's go home."

The old man turned toward her and smiled. "Hello, young lady," he said cheerfully.

"Hi," she said shyly. "That's my dog there. Well, he's almost mine. Sorry if he bothered you."

The man raised his eyebrows. "Is that right? He's a friendly little fellow. What'd you say his name was?"

"Bones."

"Ah!" The man said, bending again to ruffle the dog's scruff. "Bones, is it? Well, he's a good egg. Been keeping me company all afternoon."

Lowie edged closer and studied the man's face. There was something peculiar about the way he looked at her. "You've been sitting here all afternoon?"

"Yes, Ma'am, Bones and I both have."

Lowie moved around to the front of the bench and noted the long, white-tipped cane the man carried. She recognized that he was blind, yet he tracked her easily, even when she wasn't talking. She found this intriguing. Forgetting everything her mother had ever said about avoiding strangers, she sat next to him.

"My grandpa says dogs are good judges of character. That's why he likes coming to our house. My mom says it's because we feed him tuna."

The man laughed. Lowie liked the sound of his laugh. It was vaguely familiar.

"Well, I'm afraid I haven't had any tuna to give him, so he must be attracted to my fine personality. Young lady, can I ask you a question?"

"Yes," Lowie said simply.

"Good," the man replied. "What's your name?"

"Lowie."

The man nodded, his face brightening.

"Now, let me take a guess at something. Lowie isn't your real name, is it?"

Lowie shook her head. It didn't occur to her that the man couldn't see what she was doing. He seemed to read the movement and went on.

"Would your real name, by any chance, happen to be Mary Louise?"

Lowie gasped. She did know this man! But how? She had no recollection at all of where they might have met.

"Yes!"

"And you mother is Lane, and your grandmother's name was Mary Louise, just like yours."

Lowie's gaped at him. "How did you know that?" she asked.

The man turned his face toward the street, tapping his cane lightly. "Because, dear girl, my name is Will Harris. You and I are family."

***

Lane's attitude migrated from astonishment to anger to chagrin when Lowie showed up at home with an old, blind stranger in tow. But it didn't take long for Lane to recognize Will, and she greeted him with a hug and an invitation to stay for supper that was stiff, but well-meant. Will accepted readily enough and refrained from requesting a place to stay overnight. That invitation would come, or it wouldn't, he

358

supposed, and if it didn't he would find a quiet corner away from traffic and sleep under the stars. Lane wondered if Will's arrival might have been somehow prearranged with her father, but when he arrived home, dirty shirt clinging to him and shoes covered with red dust, his face registered genuine surprise at the sight of his uncle seated at the kitchen table.

The conversation over dinner ranged from family history to town gossip, and for the first time Lane and Lowie were treated to stories about Mike's distant and mischievous childhood. Lowie gaped at her grandfather in shock when she heard that he had been kicked out of school for a whole week for putting four garter snakes in his teacher's desk drawer, an act that left the poor lady a hysterical mess and probably contributed to her early retirement. By the time they moved into the living room Lane found herself thoroughly enjoying the conversation, and realizing how little she knew about her father's past. Her amusement turning to shock when she heard Will's tale of posting bail for Mike after he was arrested for trespassing. He was caught trying to shinny up a drainpipe to steal a kiss from Lane's mother. The charges, leveled as they were by Mary Louise's father, were dropped when Mike called her from jail and proposed.

"Mary was a good woman, Mike," Will said. "You were lucky she said yes."

"I was," Mike agreed. "Especially since her father was a lawyer. I would probably still be in jail if she'd have said no."

Lane laughed. Will's old stories seemed to somehow bring Mike back to himself. She was reluctant to let the night end. Having the old man around seemed to be good medicine.

Lowie was curled up against her mother's side on the couch and had begun to drowse. She jumped at the sound of their laughter. Lane smiled down at her. "Alright, Miss Lowie, I think it's bedtime."

Lowie groaned. "But I don't want to miss any stories."

Lane ruffled her hair. "Well, what if Uncle Will stays with us for a few days? That should give you plenty of chances to hear his stories."

Mike shot Lane a look that she carefully ignored. "What do you say, Will? I can give you a ride back to Crosby whenever you're ready, but it would be nice if you could stay for a night or two."

Will smiled. "Well, if you're sure it's no trouble. I have plenty more stories to tell about this city and, especially, your father. Besides, I've hardly had a chance to know young Lowie here. And really ought to know what kind of stock she's bred from."

***

Lane called the nursing home the next morning. Will's absence hadn't been noticed until breakfast, and once the receptionist who answered the phone understood who she was, Lane found herself on the line with an embarrassed and deeply apologetic director. She told Lane that she thought Will's sudden departure from the nursing home might have something to do with the recent loss of his longtime roommate. Lane deflected both the apology and the excuse by simply announcing she would bring Will back when he was ready, and that she was sure he would find his room in order and waiting for him when he returned.

Ever hungry for stories, Lowie became Will's companion and guide around the city. Lane brought them with her to the cemetery one afternoon, and while she mowed Lowie led the old man from stone to stone, reading the names and dates aloud to him. Will regaled the child with stories about the people he remembered, and she was an engaged and adoring audience. Lane offered to drive Will up to the hospital in Crosby so that he could see Emil, who still tenaciously clung to life, but Will declined, saying he preferred his memories to the reality of tubes and wires. As the short visit stretched out into a week, Lowie reluctantly left her new friend for a part of every day to work at the diner. Will took to wandering around the city, Bones his constant companion, the two moving in tandem up and down Foley Lake's few streets. Lane worried at first, but it didn't take long to see that Will possessed considerable capabilities. His blindness was hardly a handicap. After a few days she left him to his own resources, wondering at the wanderlust that seemed to rule the lives of Harris men.

Will rapidly learned that, once he understood his mannerisms, Bones was more than adequate as a seeing-eye dog. The little dog walked near Will's right ankle, keeping the lightest of contact with his pant leg as they moved along, gently nudging him when he wanted Will to move to the left, and shifting away so that his furry body lost contact with Will's leg altogether when he wanted the man to move right. Will, who had long since learned to listen to the finer cues in the world to keep himself safe, quickly came to understand the dog's native ability to steer him clear of danger.

The memory of Foley Lake's layout was so emblazoned in Will's mind, and the city so unchanged, that the man found it easy to move about the stores and streets. But each day he found himself wandering down Foley Lake's last sidewalk, out toward the mine. He would stop when he felt the concrete disappear under his feet and stand facing the old head frame, leaning on his cane. Bones would circle his feet and lay down, his muzzle on the toe of Will's boot, and wait quietly for the man to contend with his own heart until he grew weary of the struggle and was ready to turn back home again.

Chapter Sixty-Four

Don't ever go back there. It doesn't matter what happened. What matters is that they never find out who you are.

Butch's eyes opened slowly, the swaying green cattails and the memory of water washing over his neck and head jolting him awake. He lay still, listening to his heart slam in his chest, the rush of adrenaline he felt every time he dreamed the dream of water making him tremble. He closed his eyes again and made himself focus on the solid ground beneath him. He reached out and felt the narrow stalk of the tall grass that surrounded him. *Grass, not cattail,* he told himself. Think. Focus.

He lay still, listening for a few minutes, wanting to be sure he was alone before he sat up. He didn't want to risk another ambush, having barely escaped the first. He stared up into the soft gray-blue of the morning sky framed by the tall foxtail that surrounded him. He understood why the deer had chosen this spot to bed down. The tall grass concealed him while the nearby tree line offered an easy escape from pursuers. He felt mildly guilty for taking over the spot. Oh well, the deer had many such beds, and he needed to move each night if he hoped to stay alive.

The sun had been up for a good twenty minutes. It should be safe. Satisfied, he pulled himself upright, peeling his body from the ground. He groaned—everything hurt. He turned and looked up toward the mine, then down toward the city. He stretched, rubbed his head with one hand, and lifted his face to the sun. *Please, please, help me. I need to know. I need to understand.* He listened for a reply and, hearing nothing, he looked down at himself he sighed. His shirt and jeans were crusted with mud and filth and damp from the early morning dew that settled on him. His hands stained red from mud and covered with little nicks and cuts. It wouldn't do for anyone to see him like this. It would invite questions, attention that he just didn't need.

After a thorough scrubbing in the pit, Butch carried a bucket of water up to the head frame with him. All his belongings were still there, and still intact. He was grateful. He dressed and retrieved a small mirror, a razor, and a small can of shaving cream from the burned-out office building. He propped up the mirror and ran his hand over the soft shadow of blonde stubble that had grown over the last week. Dangerous to let it get so long. He held the mirror with one hand, lathered and shaved with the other, and in ten minutes the sun was gleaming against his smooth pate as he dumped the soapy water at the edge of the campsite. He replaced the shaving kit and retrieved his small cooler, popping the lid open. One hotdog remained in the plastic wrap. He pulled it out and walked to the gate of the head frame, whistling softly. He waited a few moments, then bent and set the hotdog in the tall grass. He didn't pretend to understand the little dog's nocturnal habits; however, he was not in any position to judge. He turned and started his journey down the hill.

Fifteen minutes later Butch was at the diner, sipping a cup of hot coffee and listening to the lively chatter around him. May set a small plate before him, a slab of apple crumb cake hanging over the sides, and gave him, a wink. "Good morning, Butch," she said simply.

"Good morning," he replied. "This smells amazing."

"Good morning, both of you." A voice behind Butch made him freeze. May grinned. "Well, Mr. Harris, you are becoming quite a regular. Coffee?"

Will slipped onto the stool next to Butch. "Thank you, young lady." Will replied cheerfully. "Coffee would be perfect. And put this young man's breakfast on my tab." Will turned his stool toward Butch, his blank eyes bright. "It's Butch, is it?"

Butch's hand trembled as he lowered his fork, laying it carefully next to his untouched cake. "Yes," he said quietly. "Call me Butch."

***

Lane stuffed a load of clothes into the washer, dumped a scoop of soap over the top, and slammed the lid. She cranked the dial to turn the machine on, then grabbed up a full laundry basket and hauled it up the stairs. She emerged from the basement and crossed through the empty kitchen to the empty living room, dumping the load of clothes onto the couch. She started folding, snapping each towel irritably with a forceful flick of her wrists.

Where was everybody?

Lowie was still helping May at the diner, but Mike had neither called nor sent a message that he wouldn't be home for dinner, and there was no sign of Will anywhere. She had labored away all day in the city alone, feeling the lack of Butch's help keenly. She rushed home to thaw hamburger and make a large meatloaf, which had been baked to a brown brick and had since grown cold.

The screen door slammed, and Lane stopped folding and listened. The steps in the hall were slow and weary—it would be her father. He was still behaving strangely, but Will's presence seemed to have a steadying effect on him. At least he was out of his office during the day, though she still didn't know where he was spending his nights. She heard him pause in the kitchen, then come through to the living room, thin and disheveled.

"I hope you weren't holding supper for me," he said.

Lane angled her back toward him as she continued folding. "It's there if you want to eat."

Mike sighed. "Where is everyone?"

"Lowie's at the diner. I don't know where Will is—"

"There he is."

Lane looked up and followed Mike's gaze out the front window. Will and Butch stood on the street, with Bones waiting beside them. Butch was talking and gesturing toward the house. Will nodded. Butch turned and moved quickly down the street. Bones looked up at Will, then turned and trotted after the younger man.

Will prodded the ground with his cane, making his way up the driveway. Moments later they heard him come through the screen, closing it quietly behind him. "Hello?" he called.

"In here," Mike responded.

"It sure smells good in that kitchen," Will said as he entered the living room. "Sorry to have missed supper. Lost track of time, I guess."

"I see you met Butch," Lane replied.

Will nodded as he sought out a chair and sank into it with a sigh. "He is a fine young man. He carries a world of care on his shoulders, though."

Lane frowned. "What do you mean?"

"Well," Will said with a smile. "That's not my story to tell. I have my own story, and a man has enough to do if he can just tell his own tale. Besides, my story might help you make some sense out of what is happening in this little city. Maybe it won't. Either way, I need to talk, and you need to listen now, because this concerns both of you, and young Lowie as well. Anyone who carries the Harris name ought to know the truth. We Harris' have blessed this city in a lot of ways. But we are also the source of much of Foley Lake's suffering, far more than you would suspect. And it's time you knew what happened the day the Foley Mine flooded, how we've cursed ourselves by covering up what never should have been hidden in the first place."

Chapter Sixty-Five

"I was the one who killed those men. I caused the flood, or at least I didn't stop it. I could have, but I didn't try." Will held the pocket watch loosely in his right hand and his thumb traveled the circumference of its face. This was an old habit of Will's. Over the years, he had rubbed it smooth.

"The Foley was a good place to work. It was hard work, but a man could make a decent living. My father had worked there for almost twenty years. I started at seventeen. My brothers, Henry and Clinton, had been there for a few years before me. The company gave me a job shoveling rock and running the tram, and by the time I was nineteen your father had been promoted to skip tender and I took his place on the contract with my dad and brother—your uncle Henry.

Most all the work down there was by contracts where men worked together, three or four of us, and we chased down veins of ore and drilled and blasted and shoveled it out. We filled a tram, rolled it over to our chute and dumped it through to the level below. The skip tender would mark how many loads came down each chute before sending it to the surface in the skip. Contracts got paid by the number of loads dumped down the chute assigned to them. That was the way it was back then.

"Most of the men that worked at the mine were good men. Lots of them were second- and third-generation miners. Most had some family working in the mine, brothers and cousins, or family by marriage. So, we knew each other, tried to look out for each other. But John Milford, he was different. His family had been around for a long, long time. They claimed the land was theirs and that the mine company stole it from them somehow. That was just talk. Still, when the mine started making money, the Milford's got mean and bitter. And John, he was the worst of the lot, a cheat, a liar, and a thief. And he was so quiet when he moved. He could slither up behind you, even in the mud in the wettest parts of the mine, and you wouldn't hear a thing. My granddaughter has a word for the feeling you get from someone like that. She says it gives her the creeps. That's a good word for it. John Milford and his quiet, skulking ways gave me the creeps.

"Now, working in the mine was good money, like I said. And the year I turned twenty was an especially good one. The mine was producing, and we were all making a good living. I married Ida and we moved into Honeymoon Row. That's what they called that little group of houses miners could rent cheap. I don't reckon you remember Ida very well, Mike, but she sure favored you when you were a baby. She kept saying she wanted a little boy just like you. 'Course, all we managed was girls, but they turned out alright.

"My dad paid off his house that year. He bought Mom a new cook stove. Then he did something completely extravagant—he bought himself a silver pocket watch.

"He would stop and look at that watch through the store window in the evenings when we came home from the mine. It was about the most perfect thing I had ever seen, real silver with a heavy chain, etched with a picture of the sun coming up over a mountain. But it was expensive, a true luxury. He said it was a waste of money, but still he stopped and looked. In a way I wasn't too surprised when he showed up at church one Sunday with that silver watch chain dangling from his pocket.

"Dad loved that watch. Carried it everywhere. And we loved to see him with it. It meant security, you know. Nobody spent money on things like that when times were tough. But him buying that watch meant life was good. He would take it to work with him, carrying it in his inside pocket so it wouldn't get dirty, and at the end of the shift he would pull it out of his pocket just so he could flick it open, the sun glinting off its face, and one of the other miners would always say, 'What you got there, Frank?' and he'd say, 'Oh, just a little watch I picked up. Says it's time to go home.' It was like a game almost, but everyone played it, and it was alright. It was part of the rhythm of our lives. Home, the mine, the watch, back home again.

"Dad took sick the fall of twenty-three and died a week later. That was hard, standing at his graveside by my mother and Henry and Clinton, me hanging on to that watch the whole time the preacher was talking. The watch was a comfort to me, like a little piece of my dad, and oh, I treasured it. I knew it was supposed to go to Clinton. He was the oldest son, after all, and I was the youngest. But I just couldn't seem to let go of it, and Clinton must have understood, because he never once asked me for it. He was like that, though. Always looking out for me.

"I wish he had asked. I wish that he had insisted that I give that watch up. Because it was the beginning of the problems that finally took my eyes, flooded the Foley, and brought so much misery to this city.

"A few weeks after Dad died Lena was born. I was always sorry he didn't live to see her. She had such a headful of hair, black as coal, so much that Ida was already combing it and clipping in little bows before she was a week old. I can't picture her adult face at all, but whenever I think of Lena I see that thick black hair, soft velvet, with a little white bow clipped up on one side.

We kept working and the mine kept giving up all the good manganese ore. They said there were a million tons still under the ground. A million tons. Some men didn't like working in the Foley, saying it was a bad mine, too wet, too near the lake, but the engineers said she was alright, and they did inspections on her all the time. I didn't worry. We should have listened more carefully.

"I never dared to carry my father's watch into the mine the way he did. I was too worried I would lose it somewhere down in those dark drifts. I put it in my lunch box at the beginning of every shift. One day I went to leave at the end of my shift and my watch was gone. I looked everywhere for it, asked all the fellas if they had seen it.

"Now, times being what they are you may not believe this, but I trusted every man I worked with on my shift. There were fifty men that worked underground with me, and I saw the same fifty day in and day out. I would have trusted any one of them with anything. All but one. John Milford.

"Milford always seemed to be where he didn't have any business being. He'd sneak around. People lost track of things all the time when he was on shift, little things, never anything big. Whatever went missing had to be small enough to disappear into Milford's pocket or up his sleeve. Small tools, money, that kind of thing. The company heard plenty of complaints about him but they could never catch Milford at the thieving, so he got away with it, over and over.

"From the moment I realized my watch was gone, I knew Milford had taken it. While the other men where helping me look around the break room for it, Milford stood back with this tight little smirk on his face. I asked him if he'd seen the watch and he just shook his head. Stood there with his arms folded and lied. I started hating him right there.

"But I still looked, hoping that somehow, I had just mislaid the thing, that it would still turn up. It wasn't to be, and over the course of days and weeks I grew more and more convinced that Milford had taken the watch. But things turned ugly one day while we sat in the lunchroom, and Emil asked me if I had ever found that watch that went missing. Before I could answer, Milford gave this little snort, like a laugh he was trying to hold back, and I just lost control. I flew over the table into Milford, knocking lunch buckets everywhere and sending men scattering. I laid into him with everything I had.

"Now, keep in mind, I grew up tussling with two brothers. I was twenty-one years old and had been working like a mule in that mine for four years. Milford was already over forty and, even though he was strong, he wasn't a match for me. I saw red, like they say. I got him in the corner and punched and punched and punched him. Not a man tried to stop me—that's how popular Milford had become. I might have killed him and no one would have cared, but for Clinton coming in and pulling me off of him.

"He was a mess. I busted his nose, maybe his cheek bone, and cracked a couple of his ribs. But none of the guys who saw it all would tell the captain what had happened. They all claimed they didn't see anything. Milford himself wouldn't say a word. I guess what went down on record was that he had an accident, and no more. He was out for a whole week.

"When he came back, he acted different. No more skulking around, no more dark looks. He minded his business, kept his mouth shut. We thought he had finally learned his lesson.

"A few weeks later came my accident. One of my jobs every morning when we came on shift was to fetch the drill from the equipment room just off the main drift. The only light in there was a small bulb dangling from the ceiling with a chain pull to turn it on. That morning when I walked into the room and tugged that chain, the bulb exploded in my face. That was about all I remembered for a couple days, except the sound of my wife crying next to my hospital bed. I woke up confused. I couldn't open my eyes. My face burned like nothing I had ever felt before. I asked Ida what was wrong, if something happened to the baby, and why I had a bandage around my head. She started crying harder and ran from the room. I knew she ran because I heard her footsteps go and I could vision the sight of her, and all at once I knew. I wasn't ever going to see again.

"The light bulb was filled with kerosene. Someone had taken it out of its socket, drilled a small hole in it, and filled it up. Then that person put the bulb back, knowing I would be the one standing under it when it blew into a million pieces.

"They sent me home about a week later. We had to move in with my mother because I couldn't work anymore, so we couldn't stay in a company house. I remember sitting in the bed in the dark. Always in the dark. I listened to the noises of the day—cars on the street, Ida working in the kitchen, her and my mother talking as they hung laundry out to snap and pop in the breeze—and trying to vision it all in my head. I kept waiting for something to change. I couldn't take it in, this idea that I would never see again. I couldn't imagine how it could be true. Yet there I sat.

"Ida tried her best to comfort me. She would come and sit and hold my hand or bring the baby in and lay her in my arms. But I was so angry. I could tolerate Ida touching me but not the baby. The idea of those bright, clear eyes looking up into my blank face, the way she felt so dense and strong in my arms, her velvet hair on my skin—I just couldn't stand it. I gave her back to Ida and told her not to bring her back in anymore. Ida took the baby and left and she didn't say anything, but I know she was crying. I could hear it. There are no such thing as silent tears.

"Have you ever sat alone with your eyes closed and just listened to the sounds around you? You should try it some time. You would be amazed at what you can hear if you just get quiet enough. I learned very quickly how to pick up sounds other people might miss. Ida took to sleeping in a separate room with the baby, but I knew the baby was waking up for her night feeding before she started to cry. She made these little grunts that I could hear through the wall. I could sit at the table and know when the coffee was about to perk or when the potatoes were about to boil over. Time passed and winter came on. I listened to the sound of snowflakes brushing against the windowpane. I could tell how big they were just by the sound they made. I kept the window open in my room so that I could hear what was going on in the streets and I could tell what time of day it was by the traffic. That is why, no matter how sneaky he tried to be, I heard John Milford come to my window one evening about two weeks after New Year's.

"Henry told me that things had been going badly for Milford ever since my accident. There was no doubt in anyone's mind that he was the one who rigged the bulb to blow up in my face but there wasn't any proof. Since Milford had covered up his tracks so well, the company wasn't going to do anything about it. The miners started to settle things themselves. When Milford showed up for his shift and walked into the locker room, everyone else just walked out. Most days he found something bad in his locker, like a dead rat, urine, acid spilled and eating holes in his slicker. When he went to the cage—well, what you'd call an elevator—to go down into the mine, he was told there was no room for him, no matter how few men were aboard. He was told he had to wait and ride down alone. Same thing at lunch break. A few of the guys would stand at the door of the break room and tell him there wasn't any room for him. And he was having a little trouble staying clear of loaded trams, or getting out of the way of a blast, or keeping his dynamite from sweating nitroglycerin into the insides of his work gloves. Nitro against the skin will give a man a headache that would nearly kill him.

"Henry was in the company store when Milford came in and asked for a plug of the chewing tobacco under the glass on the counter. Clerk said there wasn't any, they were fresh out. There was a whole plug of tobacco under that glass, right where the clerk and Milford were standing, but the clerk says 'no, we're sold out.' Milford's face turned red, and he saw every miner in the store watching him, not one ounce of sympathy or support. He stomped out, alone, as always.

"Thing is, it wasn't just in the mine that he was having trouble. All around town everyone turned their backs on that man, and on his wife and boy. The wife raised chickens and sold eggs to the mercantile in town. They told her that they wouldn't buy any more from her, that they didn't need Milford eggs. She was overlooked and disinvited to pretty near every event that the ladies in town had going on, even at the church. The boy, Rueben, was big for his age and had always been a bully, but he took a bad beating in the school yard. A group of boys ganged up on him and gave him a thrashing while the teachers just turned their backs. Maybe the company didn't officially have evidence to charge him with any wrong, but the whole town found ways to let Milford know what they believed. His credit slips went missing. He couldn't buy any caps or dynamite or any other material unless he paid in cash. And his tally kept coming up short for the number of trams he and his contract filled. I reckon that happened in the bookkeeping somewhere, because Clinton never would have messed with the number of trams a contract filled. It got so that the other men on his contract wanted to kick him off because they were losing money on his account. Soon there wasn't anywhere he could go that he wasn't dogged somehow because of what he had done.

"Mad as I was, something about that didn't set right with me. I don't know if it was the image of his wife sitting there with her full basket of unsold eggs, or the boy coming home bruised and bleeding, or Milford stomping out of the store alone, but it bothered me that the whole city was taking vengeance on my part. I started thinking that maybe enough was enough. So I should have said something to Henry because of what he told me next. He said, 'Milford ain't seen the worst yet, Will. You ain't gonna be the only one sitting in the dark pretty soon.'

"I should have told him to stop right there. If I had, maybe things would have gone different. But then Milford himself came for a visit and that was what made up my mind.

"I was sitting alone in my room, in the evening after supper, with the window opened just enough to hear the traffic on the street. The wife was always complaining that I was making the whole house too cold, so I kept the bedroom door shut.

"As I sat there, I got that feeling I wasn't alone, that there was someone else in the room with me. But I knew that was impossible. The bedroom door was closed, and by that point, I had gotten sensitive enough that no one could sneak up on me. Then it dawned on me. The window. Someone was standing at the open window, out in the snow, watching me.

'Who's there?' I said. 'What do you want?' There was nothing, not a sound. I knew. It was Milford. Milford, slinking up to my window, come to take a look at what he'd done, to gloat.

"I got angry. Maybe I should have been scared, maybe I should have thought that he might come to finish me off. But I just wanted to get to him, throttle him, kill him if I could. I got up and ran at the window, stumbling over furniture and rugs, swinging my arms out to find the glass and smash through and kill the man. I ran into the wall and felt my way along to the window, cursing as I went. When my hands finally found the window, they landed on something cold and hard on the sill.

"My watch.

"I stood there for a full minute, feeling the weight of it in my hand, tracing my fingers along the etching, seeing that mountain in my mind. Then I visioned Dad's face the first Sunday after he bought the watch, how proud he was. I wanted my dad so badly right then, even more than I wanted my eyes back. I realized I was crying, tears running down my face, making little grunts in my throat the way the baby did on those nights she woke up hungry.

"I heard Milford walk away from my window. He didn't even try to cover up the sound of his feet in the snow. I realized that the man had stood outside my window and had seen me cry and figured that he got some kind of sick satisfaction about doing that because he wanted me to know he could still get to me. I stood there, shaking, clutching that watch. Part of me wanted to scream at him to come back so I could kill him, but I was beyond words. I didn't care after that what my brother and the other miners did to him. I didn't care that the whole city turned their backs on him, or what happened to his family. I wanted him to suffer.

"It didn't occur to me until much later that maybe he was sorry for what he'd done and giving me that watch back was the closest thing to an apology he knew to give. But by the time I thought of that, it was far too late.

"I was sitting at that very same window a few weeks later when the siren started sounding at the mine. I knew what it meant, and I knew Clinton had pulled the cord to set it off. My wife went up to the mine to find out what was happening and when she came back, she didn't come in to tell me. She didn't have to. My brothers were gone. I could hear her crying from the other side of the house, through all those walls and closed doors.

"There are so many things I regret about that time. So many things. I sat alone in that room day after day and held onto my watch, and slowly I began to see how much of what we suffered was my own doing. I could have stopped things from getting out of control. It was like some of those countries do. One throws a knife, the other gets a gun. One gets a gun, the other gets a bomb. It escalates. And as hard as it was to take, I had to admit that I could have stopped the escalation. I could have told Henry that I didn't want him to do whatever it was he was going to do. I should have pushed him to tell me what he was planning. But I didn't know, and to my everlasting shame, I decided to leave it to Henry and the men to know what best be done where Milford was concerned.

"That became the excuse I hid behind until three years later when Emil turned up in my driveway one night, drunk as a sailor, and told me about exactly how it came about. How the men had come up with a plan to trap Milford in the room they needed to blast at the east end of the drift. About how they tackled him when he was alone and tied his hands and feet, gagging him with a dirty handkerchief. How one or two of the other miners had seen what was going on but they turned their backs and walked away, letting Henry and the rest get their revenge without a word of protest on Milford's behalf. How two of them dragged Milford into the back of the room and threw him against the wall while Henry set the charges for the blast. They all knew they would be the ones digging his body back out. They knew no one would talk. They knew they would get away with killing the man without paying a price for it. Or at least, that's what they thought.

"Emil said he turned back for one last look at Milford lying there on his side in the light of a carbide lamp. He didn't struggle. Emil said that's what he couldn't get over. Milford wasn't even trying to get away. But he was crying. That's what Emil said. The man didn't make a sound, but he laid their and his face was wet with tears in those last few moments of his life. And you know what? I believe he was thinking the same thing I was thinking just a few weeks later. That he could have stopped this. That maybe, because he didn't stop, because he always had the need to strike back, he deserved what was coming to him. And I wonder if he thought about leaving the watch on my windowsill and whether his one effort at finding forgiveness was so completely rejected that he was about to die for it. That haunts me. I hope he didn't think that.

"They blasted the room. The lake broke through. And that was the end of everything, the end of the whole way of life we had known. The mine punished us all for what we had done, the innocent along with the guilty. And this city has suffered ever since. We were all fools, every one of us who thought that somehow, we wouldn't reap what we were sowing. And whatever curse seemed to plague the Milfords fell on the Harris' until eventually, both families had kin laying at the bottom of that mine."

Will paused and silence fell on the room. He slowly sat up straight and slipped the watch into his pocket.

"But I always knew it wasn't over. That mine has more yet to say. And the Milford's and the Harris', they have more reparations to make. And they are long overdue."

CHAPTER SIXTY-SIX

The chestnut mare flicked her tail, irritated. The weather had been changing all day and, as the sun slid toward the horizon, the air turned heavy and thick. The humidity covered the mare's narrow chest with sweat. She stomped her legs, trying to keep the bugs off. The deeper grass would offer more protection, she knew, but she wouldn't leave her post, though her tail was in constant motion. The bugs were at their worst when the humidity was high. She glanced back at her herd mates standing in a loose group, positioned head to rump to take advantage of each other's swishing tails. In the whole group, only the stout gray gelding watched her.

The chestnut headed the herd. When she was hungry, she led the others out in single file to the pasture to graze. When she was thirsty, she led them back to the water trough. She met any challenge to her authority with flat ears and a stinging kick. The rest of the herd respected her right to lead. Eons of wild existence had reinforced the drive to follow a leader, and thousands of years of domestication had not erased the need.

Tonight, the mare led the herd away from the barnyard as usual, leaving the shade of the broad loafing shed as the sun sank and the large yard light that hung over the barn doors ticked on. But rather than moving out to the south pasture where a tender new growth of grass was waiting to be grazed, she took them west. She trekked over the rolling hills until she reached the western edge of the field, then stood staring out across the fence into the trees. She had not allowed any of the herd to graze, keeping them together, warning any wanderers with a flattened ear and a snap of her teeth to get back to the group. The herd accepted her demands, standing quietly by, flicking flies and waiting for her mood to change.

The gelding had been raised in a stall and never felt secure away from the barn. He learned early that safety lay in the mare's leadership and, ever sensitive, noticed her concern with something in the trees. He kept a close eye on her, watching for some cue that trouble was at hand.

Darkness kept her from seeing anything, but something was happening in the woods. For all the years she had wandered the pasture, a low, steady buzz had risen from some source beyond the tree line. Summer and winter, night and day, a soft white hum drifted into the pasture, so familiar she barely thought about it anymore, but over the last few days that sound had been changing. Its tone sounded sharper, strained. And there was an acrid scent in the heavy night air she couldn't identify.

There was a soft pop. The mare's ears snapped forward and she froze as energy pushed through the trees, making the ground quiver. The gelding behind her snorted. There was a sharp crack and an explosion of white and blue light.

Enough.

The mare wheeled around, and pinning her ears she flew at the herd. They needed little convincing. The gelding spun on his heels and disappeared into the darkness, making for the safety of the barn. The rest of the herd, jolted by the sound and an explosion of sparks, fell in behind him as the chestnut mare drove them forward, teeth snapping. In the distance the glow of the barnyard light marked the way to safety and protection. The gray threw himself toward it, thundering across the soft turf until, to his horror, the light ahead dimmed, flickered, and disappeared.

Chapter
Sixty-Seven

Dave kept his hat on when Lane answered the door, so she knew there was going to be trouble. She opened the screen and frowned at him. "C'mon in, Dave," she said simply. "You know you don't need to knock."

Dave looked grim. "I'm on official business, Lane. Is your father here?" Lane nodded and stepped back to give Dave room. He slipped in past her and followed the hall into the kitchen. Lowie looked up from the apple she was attacking with a small knife, a scattering of curly peelings on the counter next to her.

"Hey there, Miss Lowie. What are you up to?"

"Mom's helping me bake a pie," she said.

Dave glanced back at Lane. "You have electricity here?"

"No. But I figured it will be back on by the time we need the oven."

"Don't count on it."

"Why?" Lane asked. "What's going on?" Dave tilted his head toward the living room and Lane led him in. Mike emerged from the hall, tucking his office door key into his pocket. "Morning, Dave," Mike said cordially. "How's business?"

Dave sighed. "Getting a little too eventful. Have either of you seen that Butch fellow around today?"

Mike and Lane exchanged looks. Mike shook his head. Lane shrugged.

"No," she said. "What do you want with him?"

"I just heard from the power company. One of the big transformers blew last night. That's why we lost power. They don't think it was an accident. A couple days ago someone shot a small transformer west of the city, then got to the substation and took some pops at the big transformer there. They hit the casing of an electrical bus and all the oil that cooled it leaked out. Last night it overheated and blew up."

Mike's eyes widened. "And you're blaming Butch? Why? Anyone could have done that."

"True enough," Dave said. "But I have a witness who says he saw Butch walking toward the mine with a rifle three days ago, just before sunset."

Mike opened his mouth to speak, then snapped it shut. Lane scowled at Dave. "Butch wouldn't do something like that. He's not the type to stir up trouble. Everyone knows he's been camping next to the shaft. Of course, he was walking out there. And as far as him having a gun—well, how do you know it was a gun? Maybe it was something else. Was this witness of yours close enough to be sure it was a rifle?"

"What do you plan to do to him?" Mike demanded.

Dave held his hands up in surrender. "Easy, now, both of you," he said. "I didn't say I was sure he did the shooting, or that he did have a gun, and I certainly don't plan to *do* anything to him at this point. But you both know he's not who he says he is. You said yourself, Lane, you can't trust a man who wants to run away from his real identity. And I've been looking for him for three weeks, but it seems I've always just missed him. I'd say he was a figment of you all's imagination if it wasn't for that picture in the paper."

Lane opened her mouth to object, and Dave shook his head. "All I'm saying is that some transformers were shot up, and that someone saw this man, who calls himself Butch, walking in the same area with what appeared to be a gun. You have to admit there's logic to me wanting to follow up on that."

Mike and Lane fell silent. Dave reached back and pulled out the rumpled yearbook wrapped in a plastic baggie. He handed it to Mike.

"Does this look familiar at all?" Mike glanced at the book and shook his head as he handed it to Lane. Lane looked at it more closely. "Isn't this a yearbook from the school?" Lane looked more closely at the page and frowned. "Where did this come from?"

"I found it a few days ago. A lot of the pictures have been scribbled out."

"What does that have to do with the power being shot out?"

Dave sighed deeply. "I don't know. Nothing, maybe."

Lane handed the yearbook back to Dave and turned to stare out the window. Mike shoved his hands deep into his pockets and studied the tops of his feet. Dave asked again if either of them knew where Butch might be.

"At the mine, I reckon," Lane said. She sounded weary.

"I checked. His stuff is there but he's not."

"What if he did shoot the transformers out, then what?" Mike asked.

"Then he'll be charged with destruction of property and based on the dollar amount it's going to take to fix the damage, he'll do some time in jail. Of course, if we find out he has a prior record, then it could be a long time."

Mike shook his head. "He didn't do it, Dave. He wouldn't have. It's not in him to do a wrong. He's a good man."

Dave tilted his head and gazed at Mike. "Well, Mayor, you sure have a lot of faith in a drifter with no name. You'll let me know if you see him, won't you?"

Without waiting for them to answer, Dave turned and let himself out. Mike waited until he heard the door close and spun around, hurrying back to his office. He returned with his shoes in his hand.

"Where are you going?" Lane asked.

Mike glanced out the window to make sure that the squad car was gone. "To the mine to warn Butch."

"But Dave just said Butch isn't at the mine, Dad. Besides, why do you have to warn him of anything? What? Do you think he did this?"

Mike pulled a chair to himself and dropped onto it, stuffing his feet into his loafers. He called into the kitchen, "Lowie!" He turned and looked at Lane, his blue eyes electric. "All I'm saying is that I need to warn Butch. He hasn't done anything wrong, and he doesn't need Dave slowing him down."

Lane's eyes narrowed. "What do you mean, 'slowing him down'? What exactly is he doing out there?"

Mike looked toward the kitchen and called Lowie a second time. The kitchen was quiet. Mike scowled. "I need Lowie to run to the diner and see if Butch is there."

Lane folder her arms across her chest. "No. You leave her out of this."

Mike stood. "Fine. But for Butch's sake, I hope you won't be sharing any more of your suspicions with the local authorities. I'll go to the diner first. If Dave stops back here, I went for a walk, and you don't know where. Can you do that much for me?"

He gave her a hard look, then disappeared down the hall and slammed the screen door behind him.

Lane went back to the kitchen and picked up the apple she had been skinning when Dave knocked. She skimmed the knife along its surface, separating the peel from the meat, sending it down in a spiral to the counter. The look in her father's eyes haunted her. Why the sudden change in his attitude toward Butch? Who did he think, or maybe even know, Butch was? Her father's behavior had become so secretive, even obsessive, and it was clear he knew Butch *was* doing something, something that somehow involved the mine. But what? What could Butch be doing out there that would invoke this kind of response from her father?

Suddenly Lane dropped the apple into its bowl and walked toward the back hall, pausing for just a moment before she pushed open the door to Paul's bedroom. The placement of every item in the room was so precise and familiar that it only took her a moment to spot the one thing out of place. There, on the dresser, a newspaper clipping was propped against the framed, fading school picture of Paul. She crossed to it and picked it up. It was the picture of Butch that Eugenia had taken just before the garage sale.

Lane lifted the picture of Paul and held the two images side-by-side. There was virtually no resemblance between man and boy, so why did she feel a nagging sense of connection when she looked at the two images? She tried to look at the pictures the way her father would, tried to imagine what he might see as he gazed from Paul to Butch. Slowly a frightening new idea began to solidify in her mind.

Butch was just the age Paul would be if he'd lived. And he had an uncanny knowledge of the city, and an unusual attraction to their family. Then there was the bike he gave Lowie, so strangely like the one Lane had as a child. And his attraction to the mine. The mutual hatred between him and Warren Milford, a man he claimed he didn't know. And what about the things she was seeing, her exotic image in the mirror, so beautiful? And what of the rain, the roses, the nagging sense of familiarity she felt so often when she looked into Butch's eyes? Lane blinked and gave her head a sharp shake. *No,* she told herself. *Stop it.*

She replaced the pictures on the dresser, thinking. It couldn't be. It couldn't be because it was impossible. Mike knew better, didn't he?

Didn't he?

Lane bolted from the room. She had to get to the mine to find her dad and to make him tell her everything he was thinking. He might be crazy. Maybe he was sick. But either way, she couldn't let him roam around that mine in search of Butch in his current mental state.

"Lowie, I—" Lane stopped. She realized that the stool Lowie had occupied was empty. Lane looked at the rug in the hallway near the front door. The place where the girl's shoes should have been was bare but for a ghostly shadowing of red dust.

Chapter Sixty-Eight

●●

The cane was worthless in the high grass. Will gave up trying to swipe it back and forth to find level ground shortly after they left the sidewalk, the weeds grabbing at it making it impossible to feel anything. He began to use it for a walking stick. He needed a third leg anyway, to help him keep his balance on the uneven ground. The sun was hot, and he sweated freely; if it wasn't for his conviction that there was more to the little dog than a mere pet, he would have turned back. Yet Bones seemed anxious, insistent that Will follow him. The man allowed himself to be led through the silent city, rendered mute by the power outage, and beyond its last sidewalk into the hills that surrounded Foley Lake.

Bones leaned firmly on Will's leg, confirming the direction he wanted the man to go. Will sighed and followed, not liking the way the high grass tugged at his loafers. He wondered at first if the dog might be taking him to the mine.

But eventually he deduced that wasn't the case. They seemed to be moving along the edge of the hill rather than straight up it, his left foot feeling a lateral angle, his right mostly flat. He stumbled several times, but Bones urged him on until Will found himself anxious to get wherever they were going as quickly as possible.

Will jumped at the unexpected slap of a twig against his cheek, and he stopped. He reached out, fingers questioning. A small bush stretched up on his right hand. He lifted his cane horizontally and poked it forward, feeling the elastic resistance of branches. He was at the edge of some kind of tree line. He slowed, holding one hand up near his face to ward off more surprise pokes, and swung the cane in a small arc in front of him. Bones moved in tandem with him, approving of the slower pace, until the dog stopped altogether and whined. Will froze, prodding the ground. It was flat and unremarkable, until, two feet directly before him, it suddenly disappeared.

Will lowered himself to his knees, and crawled forward, exploring the blank space where turf should have been. The edges of the hole were rounded and smooth, perhaps three feet across by the feel of things. Will lay flat down on his stomach, reached inside the hole, and was startled at the unexpected feel of cool metal on his palm. Even before he let his hand dance across the surface of the metal, he knew what it was, and he knew what it meant. His stomach sank. He slowly rolled over and lay flat on his back on the grass.

His useless eyes stared at the sun overhead, and tears filled them and slid from their corners down his leathern cheeks. Bones slipped quietly next to him and lay down, leaning against his side, and whimpered. Will reached out and stroked the little dog's head. "I know," he said softly. "I know. No need to lead me on, old dog. I have to do this part myself."

Bones sighed and rested his rugged chin on Will's chest, satisfied.

Chapter Sixty-Nine

— ●●● —

Lowie was thoroughly out of breath by the time she reached the mine. She had run all the way from the house, slipping out the back door as soon as she heard Mr. Dave talk about Butch being in trouble. She had to warn Butch to get away. In her youth she didn't concern herself with his guilt or innocence, only his freedom. She simply didn't believe he'd do anything wrong, and even if he did, he must have had a good reason.

She stopped at the edge of the clearing and tried to listen. "Butch?"

Nothing. She trotted to the fallen office building, then to the drop away down to the pit. The camp was abandoned.

From inside the mine shaft, she heard a noise. It sounded like a low moan. She trotted toward the gate, slowing as she neared the tall shadow of the head frame stretching out toward her. She cupped her hands to project her voice forward into the darkness.

"Butch!" She called. A scuffling, another soft noise. She stepped into the shadow of the gate.

"Butch?" Lowie's voice echoed off the metal walls and faded.

Silence.

She stood waiting, grasping the gate. It might have been a cry, like the sound someone might make if they were hurt. Maybe that was it. Maybe Butch was doing something inside and had an accident. An image flashed before her eyes of a wounded Butch lying cold and alone in one of the dark corners of the head frame.

Lowie climbed up on the rail of the gate and tried to peer into the darkness. Her eyes began to adjust, and she could make out some of the shapes within. There were cans, some twisted bits of metal, and some rumpled trash. She spotted something along the side of the far wall, just on the edge of the deeper darkness of the head frame's interior.

A movement. In the dark corner of the head frame, something shifted. Was it Butch?

A wave a fear swept through Lowie. She climbed one more rail of the gate and leaned in yelling, "Butch, are you there?" No answer. "Are you hurt?"

A soft whimper drifted back to her. She listened, straining, willing herself to hear. She couldn't get the picture out of her mind of her friend, crumpled on the floor, helpless, bloody. Suddenly her concern over Mr. Dave's hunt for

Butch took a back seat to the possibility that he might be seriously hurt, even dying. Maybe he didn't answer because he couldn't. She stepped down off the gate, took hold of it, and pushing away her mother's warnings with a force that was almost physical she took a deep breath and pulled open the gate to the mine.

The air inside the head frame was chilled. Lowie folded her arms across her chest and let her eyes adjust. Fear sharpened her senses, and she took in an acrid, earthy smell of unmoved air, the rustle of bats sleeping in the head frame's high loft.

"Butch?" Her voice floated up into the upper reaches of the three-story building, curling around and evaporating. Somewhere straight in front of her she heard the whimper.

She called again, shuffling forward on quivering knees. She scraped her feet along the top of the cement floor with each step, feeling along with the toes of her shoes to make sure the path was clear as each step took her into deeper shadow. Her heart pounded in her ears, the sound of blood rushing making it harder for her to hear. The cold grew deeper, and she untied the gray sweater from around her waist, ready to pull it on. She could see very little except the image of the yawning open shaft in her mind's eye. She crept along at a minute pace until the sound of shifting body weight in front of her made her stop completely.

There, just a few feet in front of her, lay Bones, wagging his tail in happy greeting. Immediately behind him was the yawning black mouth of the open shaft.

Lowie's heart plummeted. The dog was mere inches from a sudden and violent death. When he sat up to greet her, she sank to her knees, holding her arms out.

"Bones, *stop,*" she commanded. The dog stopped, his tail still, and gave her a wounded look. "Good boy," Lowie crooned. "Now stay." She dropped to her hands and knees and crawled toward him, heart slamming, snatching breath in short gulps as she silently willed Bones to remain immobile. And the dog did remain still, though his ears popped up and his tail began to beat the cement again as she neared. The cement was cold under her hands and knees, little pebbles and dirt cutting into her skin.

Bones stood and wagged his tail more vigorously, his bad left leg leaning on the concrete at the edge of the shaft. Lowie's heart erupted into a series of ungainly lamb leaps.

"C'mon, Bones," she called softly. "C'mon, now, come over here." Happy to oblige, Bones stepped forward as Lowie reached out and wrapped one arm around his girth, pulling him to her. She dropped her sweater and sat back on her haunches, hugging the dog to her chest as he licked her face, his rough fur smelling like dirt and a faint hint of strawberry.

Lowie cuddled Bones to her and looked around, the dog's friendly presence giving her courage. So, this was the fabled mine shaft. Bones was the source of the noise she had heard, not Butch bleeding in the dark. He wasn't here. She would have to look down in the city. She decided she would take Bones with her, carry him down rather than risk having him decide on more naps on the brink of certain death.

Relieved, Lowie twisted her body around and sat the dog behind her, between her and the gate beyond. She pointed toward the light. "Go, Bones. Go outside." Bones turned and slowly limped back toward the gate.

Lowie could feel cold air rising from the open hole. She turned back toward it, still on her haunches, her eyes wandering around the edges that defined the shaft. Here was the place of legends, the scene of countless ghost stories she had heard her whole life, and the center of Foley Lake's current unhappiness. She raised herself up on her knees, the cement cutting into her skin, and considered the precipice before her. Something odd caught her eye, an interruption of the smooth lines that framed the shaft. Some kind of cable or rope hung down into the shaft, snug in its corner, barely visible at first glance. It was a cord, smaller than a pencil, and it seemed to come from the back side of the head frame, trailing across the cement floor to disappear into the shaft. *Weird,* Lowie thought. Who would leave a cord hanging like that? She leaned forward and squinted into the darkness, trying to see where the other end of line went. It was no use. The gloom was unyielding. From deep inside the shaft, she could hear soft sounds—a drip, a faint tinkling of water moving—and suddenly she was awash with curiosity. According to the stories she had heard, water had filled the mine shaft to within a few feet of its top. Was it still that full? How much of the water had returned? Was it possible that the vast hole she had envisioned was more like the pit outside, clear and cold, but square like a pool? Could a person swim in it?

She considered, then decided that the question was important enough to pursue. She dropped her hands to the floor and crawled cautiously forward. What she saw was a disappointment. The faint light from the gated entrance only illuminated the top edges of the hole, which then turned to a solid wall of black and yielded no secrets. Even if there was water just ten feet below the shaft's opening, she wouldn't be able to see it. Lowie chuffed. She sat back on her heels and glanced behind her.

A rock lay within hand's reach. She picked it up.

The girl stretched forward again, a little farther this time, dropping the rock into the shaft. She had half-expected to hear a splash within seconds, so her eyes widened when the rock disappeared down the hole and she heard only silence.

Her awareness at how far down the soggy bottom of the mine really was reawakened her fear. The shiver returned. She crawled backward a few paces, then slowly rose to her feet. It wasn't until she was standing that she realized she had left her sweater behind.

She took a deep breath and walked forward, closing the distance between her and the shaft by less than half, then stooped to pick up the sweater. It was covered in red dust. She gave it a shake. *Mom's going to kill me,* she thought as she turned to leave.

An enormous man in dirty blue shirt stared down at her, blocking her exit, blocking out the light. He reached toward her with a muddy red hand. Lowie gasped and fled backward, feet skidding on the concrete. Too late she remembered the vastness of the black chasm behind her, waiting to swallow her in shadow.

Chapter Seventy

By the time Butch arrived at the mine, Lane and Mike were in the midst of an animated argument. He walked into the clearing and stopped, listening. Lane was on a tirade about taking Mike for a visit to the doctor over in Brainerd, and Mike was telling Lane that her inability to grasp the miraculous was the problem, not his mental health. Butch walked across the clearing and had nearly closed the distance between them altogether before they noticed he was there. When they saw him, they fell into an abrupt silence.

"What's going on?" he asked. Both turned to face him, Lane's eyes blazing, Mike's full of the eerie benevolence. "Nothing at all, son," Mike said, smiling. "Everything's fine."

"Do you know the cops are looking for you?" Lane snapped. Butch pushed his hat back on his head, a look of genuine astonishment on his face.

"Are they? Why?"

"Because they think you shot out some equipment along Highway 18. The whole city has lost power. That's why." Lane replied. Butch's eyebrows rose slowly. He didn't look at Mike.

"Well," he said slowly. "I did no such thing." Lane studied him for a moment, then believed him. She found herself oddly comforted that, despite the apparent hitch in her father's mental apparatus, at least Butch was innocent.

"See?" Mike said simply. Lane shook her head at him. "It's not that easy, Dad." She turned to Butch. "Dave says someone saw you with a gun yesterday. That's why they thought you did it. They thought you had a rifle, and a rifle was used to shoot the transformers."

"I did have a rifle," Butch said, "and it was the one used to shoot out the transformers. But I didn't pull the trigger."

Lane's eyes widened. "Wait. What are you saying?"

Butch shrugged. "Only that I found a gun a couple of days ago and I carried it back here. It was the gun used to shoot out the transformers. But I didn't do it."

"You *found* a gun?" Lane asked. "Did you report it?" Butch shook his head. She sighed forcefully. "Butch, do you think that Dave is going to believe you just happened to find a rifle? He already has his doubts about you."

"And whose fault is that?" Mike asked. Lane flushed. Butch noticed the new brightness in her cheeks and intervened.

"There's only one suspicion I'm concerned with right now, and that's about me shooting out the transformers along the highway. So, let's get the rifle and go to town and talk to Dave." He turned and walked toward the gate but stopped.

"Have you been in the shaft?" Butch asked.

"No," Lane replied. Butch looked at Mike and Mike shook his head. Butch frowned. "I know I closed this. Who else has been up here?"

"Dave said he came up here looking for you," Mike offered. Lane's eyes widened. "Lowie." Both men turned to her. "She left while we were talking to Dave. I thought she might have come up here to warn you, but when I got here it was only Dad."

Butch bolted into the head frame Lane and Mike on his heels. "Lowie!" he yelled, his voice booming off the metal walls. There was no reply. Butch snatched up his backpack and pulled out the flashlight. He walked back toward the shaft, clicking the light on as he went. Lane tried to run past him, and he reached out and stopped her. "Wait," he said. "You don't want to just run back there."

Lane clung to Butch's arm, her breathing a collection of ragged gasps. Mike crowded immediately behind them. "Lowie! Answer me!" Lane yelled. Her voice crashed in a circle around the shaft walls and returned to them.

As they neared the gaping hole Butch's flashlight caught movement. It was Bones, who had returned to the edge of the hole, wagging his tail.

Lowie's gray sweater lay next to him on the ground.

Butch felt a sudden weight on his arm. Lane's legs collapsed under her, and he stooped to try to support her, but instead he sank down with her, his eyes never leaving the sweater. He had the strangest pulling sensation in the middle of his body, just above his belly button. It felt like a long, taut string, like piano wire, pulling him backward through time. He was falling, but not down. He was falling horizontally, toward images that terrified him, memories that he had spent most of his life trying to erase. Now all he could do was let his weight fold down next to Lane's and it was only the high, piercing keen of her first cries that drew him back.

There wasn't any weight on his arm anymore. Lane had let go her grip and was crawling on hands and knees to the edge of the shaft. Butch flew forward and grabbed her, dragging her screaming backward from the abyss. He pulled her to him and held her as she railed, wild with rage and sorrow, throwing her fists against his chest. He clamped his arms around her, but he didn't try to stop the beating he was taking under her flailing fists. He deserved it, and worse. Much worse.

Mike walked calmly to the edge of the shaft and looked down. Butch watched him as he drew so close a half-step would be fatal, but he didn't reach for Mike. He couldn't fight for them both. Not anymore. If he had to choose, his choice lay sobbing in his arms.

Mike bent, picking up the sweater and reflexively patting Bones lightly on the head. He walked back toward Butch and Lane, studying the fabric.

"Don't worry, Lane. We'll get her." Mike said simply, though he seemed to be talking from a long distance. "She'll be fine. We just need to find her, get her out. We need to be quicker this time. That's the trick. It shouldn't have to take years."

Lane lunged at him, clawing the sweater out of his hands.

"This is your fault!" she howled. "You wanted the mine opened no matter what it cost! No matter what it cost!"

"Now, Lane," Mike replied, calm beyond reason. "You're assuming the worst. But she's still alive. Can't you feel it? She's alive down there. We just have to get her out."

Lane abruptly stopped crying. Her eyes raked over Mike's face, wild for any trace of hope. Mike nodded. "You can feel it, can't you? She's alive. And we know someone who found his way out of the mine, don't we?" He put his hand on Butch's shoulder. "Don't we, son? You know the way in and you know the way back out. It took you some time, yes, a *long* time, but you know. You'll show us the way to Lowie, won't you?"

CHAPTER SEVENTY-ONE

Lowie fell forever. Pin wheeling through the darkness, every muscle tense and ready for the moment of impact, she hit the side of the shaft and slide downward against it. She screamed as the flesh from her forearm to her shoulder was peeled from her body against the rough wooden planks that covered the inside walls of the shaft. She stopped tumbling and fell feet first, her mind blank with disbelief. She couldn't assemble a coherent thought about what was happening. Her mind was filled with terror, and the image of the big man whose sudden appearance had caused her to fall.

There was a tiny sliver of time that Lowie felt a sense of perfect clarity, and, in the small moment, she wondered what awaited her at the other end of her fall. It was then she heard it.

Plug your nose.

The voice was in her head, but not, small but imminently clear, and she took a gulp of air and clamped both hands over her mouth and nose with all her strength. A second later she slammed feet-first into the water, the force of the impact folding her legs at the knees and curling her into a tight ball. The water stung. Her frantic mind told her that the shaft was not filled with water, but acid.

The natural impulse to gasp took over, but her hands created tiny seals over her mouth and nose and prevented it. Momentum was still taking her downward and she kicked her legs frantically, desperate to get to air. Her downward plunge slowed. She let go of her nose and flailed her arms; she opened her eyes and they burned with the bitter cold of the water. She didn't know which way was up, but she kicked and clawed with all her might. The water was endless. She couldn't tell if she was moving. Her lungs begged for air, demanded it, and she had a fleeting thought that maybe, just maybe, there would be a little air in the water if she took one gulp. Just one. Nothing could feel worse than her heart slamming and lungs screaming the way they were now.

And suddenly there was air. She burst through the surface to cold, dank, wonderful air, gasping, gulping, she slipped back below the surface, and kicked up again, tried to scream, slipped back down. She barely made the surface again, her arms clawing at the empty air above her head.

Think. Butch's voice scolded her from within. *Get a grip and think.* She stopped flailing her arms and legs and forced herself into a rhythm. She was able to keep her head out of the water, struggling against hysteria. She looked around her, up, side, behind. Nothing. There was no light at all, save the small spastic dots at the edges of her vision from oxygen starvation and the shock of utter darkness.

She panicked.

"Help!" she screamed. *"Please! Help me!"* The force of the screams sapped energy from her frame, and she started slipping back under the water's surface. It wasn't any good. She couldn't scream, or she would drown. *Get a grip,* her mind chanted. *Get a grip get a grip getagrip!*

The memory of Butch's words gave her a small margin of calm. She found a rhythm again and made herself focus on it. Kick, kick, wave, wave. Her wild bobbing up and down decreased, and she began to tread water. She turned herself in a slow circle and swallowed down another wave of panic. *What is your first problem,* she asked herself? *What? What?*

It's dark, she thought, a sob convulsing her. She clenched her jaw the way she had seen Butch do. *You don't need light to breathe,* she told herself. *Think, now. What's your first problem?*

She shivered violently. Her arms and legs ached with cold, overwrought nerves firing constellations of pain through her body. The water. She had to find a way out of the water.

Lowie forced herself to take three long, slow breaths, then she began to kick herself around in a tight circle, eyes huge, looking for any sign of light. Blackness. She felt disembodied. If it hadn't been for the pain in her hands and feet, she might have believed she was dead. A deep, aching sob escaped her, but she pulled her feet under her, and dog paddled straight forward. When her fingers scraped something solid, she squealed and jerked her hand back. She trembled as she reached forward. A solid wall, slick and cold.

She opened her hand and pressed her palm onto rough wood timbers running horizontally, wooden braces that formed the sides of the shaft. One edge protruded and she braced her fingers on it, keeping a tenuous hold as she searched with the other hand. Reaching out and up, scared of feeling anything, terrified of feeling nothing, searching along the wall for a better handhold. Nothing. Her legs threatened to cramp but she kept moving. Stopping meant sinking. She had no desire to simply fade from the surface like a waterlogged twig.

Using one hand as a guide she followed the wall around. A small cord dangled down the wall and into the water and she grabbed it with both hands. She tugged gently and learned that it was loose at the bottom but secured somewhere farther up. She clung to it with both hands, and trembling violently, let her legs rest.

Holding the cord with one hand, Lowie moved a little farther down the wall. Under the water's surface her fingers brushed something sharp and heavy, and she cautiously slid her hands along it. She could feel a vertical bar, then a horizontal one, and another vertical. She knew immediately what it was. She'd found a ladder.

Lowie let go of the cord and grasped the ladder with both hands. Her feet found the rungs below her, and she stood on them, so overwhelmed at the feeling of something solid under her feet that she sobbed. Was it possible that the ladder went all the way up to the top of the mine shaft? She climbed, one rung, two rungs, three. When she had lifted herself so that she was only in water to her knees, the rungs above her stopped.

Lowie climbed another rung. She reached above her head, feeling. The wall was bumpy, and she could feel where the ladder's vertical supports had been bolted, but all that remained now where jagged iron fragments. Lowie climbed another rung, standing on one rung and holding the one immediately above it in an awkward squat. Slowly, carefully, she let go, leaning on the wall for support. She didn't know if the ladder continued above her, but she didn't have a choice. She reached up, searching with her hands. All she could find were the broken bolts. Carefully, legs shaking and weak, she stepped up to the top rung of the ladder.

There it was. Lowie's fingers scraped a ladder rung above her head and she grabbed it. She was stretched her whole length against the shaft wall to reach it, but it was there. She clung to it. She tried to pull herself up, but her arms were limp. That wasn't going to work. She needed to find a foot hold. She lifted one leg, swiping her sodden sneaker back and forth along the wall until she felt the sole catch on the bolt. She gathered her strength. Once she stepped off the rung, there would be no turning back. If the ladder disappeared again, she would be trapped against the wall and would have hang there until she fainted, which would plunge her back into icy water below. Her teeth chattered sharply. She tightened her hold on the ladder rung and stepped up.

Lifting herself onto the bolts moved her up enough to grasp the ladder three rungs higher. From there she managed to step up off the bolts and onto the bottom rung of the intact ladder. She stopped, clinging, trying to calm herself, trying not to think of how very, very long she had fallen on the way down. The climb upward would take hours. Her body ached, her feet tingled and pricked painfully. If she had any option besides climbing blindly up a slick and unpredictable ladder—that didn't include dying alone in the icy blackness—she would gladly take it. She reached up for the next rung.

In the darkness an image of Paul's picture rose before her. She wondered if he had plugged his nose before he hit the water, if he felt the pain and icy confusion of trying to know which way was up. His body had never been found and he was, in all probability, rotting away within twenty feet of where she stood clinging to the ladder rail. If she fell again, she would most likely end up rotting next to him for eternity. Her grandfather's deep sadness seeped into her consciousness, and she imagined her mother, years and years from now, walking aimlessly around Foley Lake with a far-away gaze and red mud on her shoes. A heavy sob rose in her throat and escaped her, and she leaned her head against the ladder rung and wept. She couldn't stand it. Not her mom. She couldn't allow her mother to suffer so. She *had* to get out, *had* to find a way back home. Her sobs slowed to gasps and hiccups, and she looked up into the blackness above her. With no other hope for salvation, she stepped.

Lowie moved slowly, steadily, giving each rung a small tug before trusting it not to come apart in her hands. Her fingers, stiff and numb, resisted every movement. The only part of her being that felt any warmth was her cheeks, where tears warmed salty trails down her face.

The stillness in the shaft was such that when Lowie felt the light movement of air against her body, she was instantly aware of it. Somewhere to her right the blackness felt more alive, like something was stirring, and she paused. What would cause that?

Breathing, she thought. *It feels like something breathing.*

She skittered up three or four rungs without testing them, eager to put space between her and whatever might be moving the air. Her heart slammed in her chest, and it was only near total fatigue that stopped her rapid ascent.

Getagrip getagrip, she chanted in her mind. *It's nothing. It's healthy imagination, like Grandpa always says.*

She moved eight feet higher before the ladder disappeared again. She stepped up as high as she dared without a hand hold, but to no avail. The ladder was gone. Had she been able to see, she would have noticed the missing section jammed at an angle in the water below her and realized that it was only by grace that she missed impaling herself on it in her original fall.

Lowie climbed down far enough to get a good hold on the ladder, put her arms around the rungs and her forehead on her arms, and rested. She imagined the children in her class, studying Stu Webner's third grade drawing of the mine just as she had, wondering where exactly Lowie's dead body had come to rest. She could see the poster in her mind's eye, the worn yellow construction paper and the cracking glue, the blackness of the mine's walls—boy, Stu had gotten that one right—and the smallness of the narrow drifts tunneling back into the far reaches of the earth.

Suddenly Lowie lifted her head. She reached out her hand and felt the wall to the right of the ladder. It was solid. She stepped down three more steps and felt. This time her searching hand happened across a heavy steel brace, and immediately below that, nothing. A hole. Lowie descended a couple more steps and there it was again, the slight feeling of air movement. A doorway stood just three feet from the ladder. It was a drift. She just knew it.

Lowie slid to the right side of the ladder, using her right hand to feel the edges of the open doorway. She needed something to hold to pull herself into the opening. She wouldn't risk launching herself at the door in the total darkness, as she didn't know if anything blocked the path into the drift. Her hand strayed across a bundle of cables, slick as bound snakes, and she tugged at it. It seemed secure enough. She would have to grab it with both hands, though, and to do that she would have to let go of the ladder and the only security she had.

Lowie hung sideways off the edge of the ladder, her right arm clinging to the cables, and wiggled the fingers of her right hand into the bundle for a better hold. She tried to loop her left leg around the vertical support of the ladder so she would still have some stability when she let go, but to no avail. The ladder was only a few inches from the wall, far too close to slip a leg behind. If she tried to force her leg behind it she could end up stuck. She would have to let go of the ladder, grab the cable with both hands, and try to keep her balance. She curled her body inward to balance herself. She tugged the cables as far as she could with her right hand and slowly, carefully released her hold on the ladder with her left.

It was the leaning that made her fall. If she had been able to stay upright, her right leg wouldn't have slipped leftward and kicked her own left foot off the rung. If she had been upright, she wouldn't have made such a clumsy grasp at the cable, or missed, and she would not have ended up swinging away from the ladder and toward the doorway hanging only by two fingers she had entwined in the cables for added security. But dangle she did, and the trapped fingers dislocated, and she screamed and grabbed at the cables, trying to lift herself to get her weight off her wounded hand.

Whatever it is that dictates the fates of little girls stranded and dangling in abandoned iron mines seemed to take a liking to Lowie Harris. That was why, at the same moment her howling fingers slipped loose from the cable, her flailing legs caught the edge of the doorway and propelled her forward into the drift rather than out and away from it. She landed just inside the doorway that had once opened to admit miners into the Foley's upper drift, knocked breathless, her legs hanging over the edge of the shaft. She used her elbows to pull herself deeper into the darkness of the drift and away from the drop and the acid-cold waters below.

Lowie crawled away from the edge and curled into a small, exhausted ball. She lay perfectly still, eyes wide open, wounded hand cradled against her chest. She didn't cry now. The throb in her hand might have had that effect on any other day, but she welcomed the pain. It wasn't just her hand that hurt anyway. Her feet ached and prickled with the most exquisite pain as nerves that had gone beyond cold in the water warmed. She'd made it into the drift. She imagined Stu Webner's drawing of the mine again, and for the first time she realized how much it mattered whether that little boy had gotten it right.

Chapter Seventy-Two

Warren used the broom in short, stiff strokes, raising puffs of dust from the floor worn smooth by years of similar treatment. He knew the dust would resettle on the floor the moment he stopped sweeping, as the lack of air circulation in the chamber didn't move it abroad. The sweeping sent it straight up and it came straight down, ready for another day. Still, he swept, following the protocol established by his father. Reuben Milford had set certain rules about how things should be done. No use unsettling things more than he had to. It was better to stick with the old ways than risk provoking more wrath than he might have already incurred.

He was sweating despite the cold and damp of the mine. Three lanterns softly hissed as they glowed with a deep golden light, filling the cavern. He might have replaced the lanterns with the newer, brighter propane lamps he used at home, but these lights had been brought down by his father.

Besides, the weak lamps didn't shine much light into the corners of the room. That alone was reason enough to keep them.

A sound floated into the room from somewhere down the drift, a low moan. Warren turned his back to the square opening leading to the drift, sweeping harder. He had never been able to just ignore the noises the way his father had, and he found no comfort in the dark walls streaked with red. The older Milford did. Reuben was never more at home than when he was a hundred feet under the ground. The land was theirs, he said, stolen from Milford's by the iron company and its minions. The Milford's may not be able to reclaim what was above, but it no longer mattered. They made good their claim from below, he told Warren, and from the bowels of the earth they could manipulate the fates of generations. Not all gods, after all, ruled from above.

Warren pulled a matchbook out of his breast pocket and approached the earthen altar silently, holding his breath. A brass candle holder was screwed to the wall just above the altar, and Warren struck a match and lit the candle. He blew out the match and checked his wristwatch. The candle burned one hour a day. His father had started the habit years before, when the stench of rot was so bad Warren had to flee into the drift to vomit in the darkness. The smell had lingered for a long time, and even now there were times Warren's stomach lurched uneasily as he touched the match to the candle's black wick.

The candle holder hung next to a brass hook that held John Milford's white slicker. Warren smoothed his hand over the fabric, thinking about the old man. If what his father had told him was true, the man deserved what he got. Still, the sound of the gunshot, the man's blank skyward gaze, his choked breathing, were fixed in Warren's memory now, and he would never be free of them. His father had been in the habit of donning the white canvas overcoat and lurking around the city two decades before, when the Harris boy first disappeared. The old man enjoyed seeing the town reduced to superstition and terror. But Warren didn't share his father's love of turmoil. He had donned the coat only to warn the people of Foley Lake they must change. Since that night with the old man, he had not used the coat again.

Warren looked down at the stone altar and bowed his head, paying his respects. The dead man's body had been preserved with the utmost care. Reuben had scrubbed each bone white and placed it precisely according to an anatomy book he had stolen from the library in Brainerd, and as he did, he told Warren again and again the tale of how, as a young man full of rage and grief, he first trekked into the black drifts of the Foley Mine to find his father. He knew the miners had lied about not being able to find John Milford. He knew they hated the man, jealous as they were about his intimate knowledge of the mine and all of her secrets, knowledge that John Milford was in the process of passing on to Reuben when the flood claimed him. The older Milford had shown Reuben how to gain access to the mine through the rarely used timber hole that lay two hundred yards from the main shaft. The timber hole was a tiny version of the main shaft, a three-foot square vertical tunnel that provided ventilation and a route to lower timber down to the mine without clogging up the main shaft. The small wooden shack that marked the timber hole's presence had long disappeared into a stand of brushy red oak, but Reuben remembered its location, and once the mine failed for good, he sought it out. The timber hole had been clumsily sealed with an oval cement cap. Ruben pried it away and lowered a rope down the chasm, measuring out the length until he felt it touch bottom, and determined he needed a ninety-foot ladder to reach the drift. He fashioned a rope ladder over the winter, answering his mother's questions about what the ladder was for with an angry glare, and that spring he slipped out under the cover of darkness and fed the ladder down the hole. He climbed down into the blackness and found himself in the damp tunnel of the mine's topmost drift. Though the flood had changed things somewhat, the waters had receded and Reuben quickly learned her new landscape. He lowered a wheelbarrow and shovel and lights into the mine—the very same lights Warren was still using—and, over the course of two summers, he excavated each collapsed room until he found what he was looking for. His father's rotted remains were indeed still in the mine. Reuben's suspicions of foul play were confirmed. John Milford was encased in mud, crushed under the weight of the lake, the skeletal arms still bound with filthy ropes, a sodden rag stuffed in his gaping mouth.

Warren had spent hours as a boy, shivering in the chill while his contemporaries played in the summer sun above, watching silently as his father took fine silver wire and wove the bones together. Reuben paid special attention to the injured places where breaks and fractures bore evidence to the violence done to John Milford at his death. Each fracture fueled Reuben's hatred of the men of the city. Each tiny crack fed his hunger for revenge, just as each trip to the mine crypt fed his sense of superiority over the fools who lived in the city and concerned themselves only with the needs of their pathetic little lives.

The bones had grayed over time. Warren thought his father probably would have taken the entire body apart and bleached each bone white again, but he himself wasn't willing. He gazed at the skeleton, remembering the sight of his father bending over the bones and caressing them with such care, and the nauseating blend of jealousy and revulsion it inspired. His father saw the emotion in the boy's face. He stood over Warren, his cold blue eyes freezing the child's blood in his veins and told him that the Milford's knew a traitor when they saw one. They had never hesitated to eliminate those who threatened the family name. If anyone—*anyone*—betrayed a Milford, the vengeance would be infinite. The dead would rise and hunt that person down and drag him straight to hell.

Warren clenched his jaw at the memory and turned away from the corpse. Another sound echoed up from the drift, a distant sob. He lifted his head to listen. The echo faded.

Warren picked the broom up and made a few more swipes at the floor before he put it back into its little nook. Three neat spools of wire were stacked atop a wooden box marked "Danger." A small, cloth sleeve lay neatly on the ground next to the box. He knew it was a bad idea to keep the blasting caps so close to the box, but he didn't like to leave ordinary things lying out in the chamber. Besides, the box was nearly empty now. The most dangerous work was already done.

Except for the niche the room was precisely square, twenty feet by twenty. Its earthen walls had been carefully scraped so that they were flat and pristine, a feat that had taken his father a decade to accomplish with a hammer and a small hand chisel. The old man had never believed in using a power tool when a hand tool would suffice. Warren respected his father's opinion and had never brought a power tool into the mine with him. He honored the tradition, though time was short. He knew that if he was to preserve the family name, he must be quick. The man had been back for months. There was only a short time left to act.

Even so, he had one task to finish before he could put an end to his grandfather's story. His eyes flicked over toward the corner of the room, and he quickly pulled them back. He bent to pick up the hammer and chisel. If any Milford was ever going to rest in peace, Warren had to finish the work.

The ring of steel against stone was a shock to his ears. He struck again and again, the sound bouncing off the walls of the chamber and out the doorway to echo down the length of the drift.

Chapter Seventy-Three

Butch felt numb. He had stood over the timber hole many times since that first night he followed Milford to it. He had deduced the fact that Milford was somehow getting into the mine, but a week of prowling around Foley Lake's moonlit streets by night, seeking a figure in a white slicker, produced nothing. Butch resorting to hiding outside Milford's house and following him from his front door. Milford was quick and difficult to follow. Butch lost him three different nights in the woods at the edge of the lake before he finally realized it was better to wait in the tall grass outside the mine for Milford to pass by and follow him from there. That's when he saw Milford slip down the timber hole. Then he spied on Milford for another week, watching him descend through the hole in the early morning before the sun rose and appear again after sunset, bent with exhaustion, hands and face muddy. But in the last week he had not seen Warren emerge from the hole, though he watched almost constantly. And though Butch was certain that whatever Milford was doing was bad, no amount of curiosity could compel him to descend the ladder into the black circle that led to the mine. Nothing, he thought, could ever convince him to do that.

Lowie. For her he was willing to risk the climb down. He wasn't sure he could survive without finding her. He knew Lane couldn't. And he could not, would not, have Lane live the life that Mike had, driven slowly mad by the pain of not knowing the fate of her child. They would find Lowie and they would bring her out, whatever the consequence, and they would have an end to their story.

The descent took a long time, climbing as they were through absolute darkness. Butch had his flashlight tucked into the waistline of his jeans. Trying to use it on the way down was to risk dropping it and having to wander around in the mine in utter blackness. The folly of all three of them going into the mine without telling anyone was clear to him. If Milford figured out they were there, all he would have to do was destroy the ladder from above, shove the concrete cap back over the shaft's opening, and walk away. The mystery of their disappearance, and Lowie's, would never be solved.

When Butch felt the firm surface of the mine floor under his boots, he reached up and helped Lane take the last few steps down. She was trembling so badly it made his heart ache. He waited for Mike to finish descending, then pulled the flashlight out. But he didn't click it on. Instead, he stood staring down the length of the drift in wonder.

Lowie lay still, a stream of incomprehensible gibberish flowing through her mind. The worst of the pain in her hands and feet had eased, though her dislocated fingers were still throbbing, and she wore a latticework of scratches and bruises across her body. She shivered intermittently, a violent convulsion that shook her whole being, but otherwise she was completely still, eyes wide in the blackness.

She was in the mine. She was in the mine. She would die here. There was no way to climb out. She hadn't told anyone she was coming here. They wouldn't know where to look for her. And they would never think of the mine.

She was going to die.

Yes. If you don't move, you will die where you lay. So move.

That voice again, the one that told her to plug her nose. She lay motionless, trying to think of whose voice it sounded like. A little like Butch, maybe, and her mom. But the voice was crazy if it thought it could make her move an inch from where she was. She had already forgotten for certain which direction the open shaft was. The blackness was completely disorienting.

Sit up. Get your bearings.

Another shiver racked her body and her teeth chattered. The ground she was lying on was wet with muck, sucking away her body heat. The voice was right. She needed to sit up, and maybe move to someplace a little drier.

Fighting a wave of nausea and dizziness, she eased herself up and leaned forward, pressing her good hand into the mud, breathing slowly. The swoon eased. She raised herself to her knees, and curling her wounded hand to her body, she reached forward with the other hand, feeling the ground in front of her. The muckiness grew more solid in one direction, and it felt like there was a mild incline. She slid her knees forward, then reached again, feeling, exploring. The ground in front of her was smooth and flat as slate. She inched forward. Abruptly, some deep instinct warned her of trouble. She froze. It was the air. It was moving. She slowly reached forward and felt the rim of a metal brace, then nothing. She was at the edge of the shaft.

She scampered backwards, heart slamming, whining softly. Not that again. Not again. She couldn't do it twice. She curled back up, struggling to breathe between hiccups of panic. She willed her heart to slow down, her breathing to quiet. By increments, she regained control. She had to get turned around. Raising herself back to her knees and reaching out toward her right side, took a deep breath and started searching.

She swept her hand slowly from right to left, exploring, learning. Her fingers brushed something smooth and flat raised above the mud, and she lay her palm across it. A rail. She felt to her left, then her right. There. Another rail. She knew there had to be two. She was sitting between rails, and the rails would lead deeper into the mine, away from another fall into the shaft. She began to crawl forward with more speed, trusting the rails to keep her safe and give her a sense of direction. The prospect of wandering aimlessly in the mine didn't occur to her. Her single-minded desire was to put as much distance as possible between herself and the icy black waters below.

A soft, metallic ring sounded from somewhere down the drift in front of her. Lowie froze. It came again, then again. It was the sound of work, of metal and stone. She listened, holding her breath.

There was someone else in the mine.

Someone looking for her.

She crawled forward on hands and knees, frantic.

"Help me!" she screamed. "Help me!"

***

Warren stopped pounding and listened. Had a voice echoed down from the drift? He stood frozen for a few moments, his senses on high alert. The only sound was the pounding of his own heart. He turned back to his work and raised the hammer, and as it fell ringing against the chisel the sound came again. He stopped. This time he heard it. It was unmistakable. It was the sound of a child's voice.

He swallowed several times, though his mouth had gone completely dry and all he managed were a few hollow clicks. He bent slowly and set the hammer and chisel down. The sound came again, a frantic sob. Warren's legs folded under him, and he collapsed forward, falling prone before the flat surface of the altar.

435

There was a light shining out of the wall forty feet down the drift. Lane and Mike saw the light as well, but Butch clicked on his flashlight and shined it on his face, pressing his finger to his lips to warn them to silence. He shined the light toward their faces to see if they understood. Mike nodded silently. Lane gazed back, numb, unblinking.

Butch reached out and took Lane's hand. On the climb down the timber hole, he thought he had heard an echo of something. The sound was faint and distant, but it also had a rhythm. It couldn't have been anything natural. Warren was in the mine. Butch glanced back toward Lane and Mike, feeling their nearness. He wouldn't be able to protect them both, if it came to that. He squeezed Lane's small, cold hand just a little tighter.

He started moving, clicking the light on to shine it immediately in front of their feet. The drift was silent now. They moved as quietly as they could, but to Butch every step seemed like a loud pronouncement of their presence. The light was shining from a wide doorway on the right side of the drift. Butch gave Lane's hand a squeeze, then released it, and she stopped. He crept forward and peeked into the room.

Three lamps filled the room with light. It was spotless and nearly bare, its only adornments a few lamps and a lit candle. An old white slicker, stiff with age, hung on the wall. Just below it a human skeleton lay on a raised bed of stone.

Butch slipped across to the skeleton, bending close for a better look. The bones were pristine, perfectly preserved, carefully wired together. Butch didn't understand the meaning of what he was seeing. Is this what Warren had been working on for the last week? Who was this? What was this? Had Milford stolen a body from somewhere? Whose? And *why?* His eyes followed the network of silver that held the body together. Evidently it had been crushed, judging by the amount of wire needed to keep it intact. He noticed the left hip had taken the brunt of the damage, the silver zigzagging across its broad pelvis. Butch stood up, suddenly afraid. He knew that Warren was mentally off-balance, but he never suspected the man was this disturbed. A mind that could conceive of doing something like this to a body would be capable of a lot of violence. And they had walked right into his lair. Butch had to find Lowie and get them all away from here before they suffered the same fate as this poor fool displayed in front of him.

A wail of despair jolted Butch free of his thoughts and he wheeled around. Lane and Mike had followed him into the room. Lane stood numbly staring, but Mike was on his knees. In his fascination with the carefully displayed skeleton on the stone altar, Butch had missed the smaller one strewn carelessly in the corner.

Mike was bent forward, hands extended over the body, moaning. He lightly touched the faded rag that must once have been a t-shirt, black with mold, over the top of a narrow rib cage. The pelvis and legs, still encased in rotten denim, had been pushed against the wall, breaking the spine. The skull was dislocated from the neck and lay at a right angle to the rest of the torso.

Butch sagged to his knees next to Mike. He felt like his soul flew away and left hollowness in its place. Mike grasped a skeletal hand and its shape dissolved at his touch, leaving only a collection of small bones that Mike gathered and cupped in his palm, clutching them to his chest with a groan. He sobbed then, tears and indiscernible words blending in agonized lament. Here, at last, was the long-sought child, the boy whose absence had rent an unbearable void in the universe of those who loved him. Here was the chance to see him, talk to him—not the memory of him but the boy who, in his degraded state, was still Paul. Butch reached over and placed a hand on Mike's shoulder, having no other comfort to offer. The searching and questions that broke upon his own heart over and over like the pounding of waves against the shore were answered in one look at this tiny, broken form. All this long time, the boy really was in the mine.

"No, no, no…" Mike rocked himself. "No, I don't understand…he got out…he got out…"

Butch felt a hand on his shoulder and turned. Lane's face was wet with tears, but her eyes were clear, the numbness gone.

"Help me, Butch," she pleaded. "I have to find her."

Butch looked at Mike, lost to a world of grief. Leaving him here would be risky and painful—asking him to leave, intolerable. Lane tugged urgently on his shirt. "*Please,*" she begged.

Butch nodded. His breath came back to him. He stood, picked up a lantern, and led Lane out of the room.

Chapter
Seventy-Four

He had known this day would come. He had known it most of his life. His first instinct when he heard Paul Harris' voice had been just to get out, to destroy the mine and flee Foley Lake for good, but he couldn't. The boy wasn't alone. There was a man standing silent in the drift just outside the shrine, blocking his escape to the timber hole. Warren saw his face in the light of the lanterns for just a moment, but he knew him from the pictures around town. It was Clinton Harris, come to take revenge for the life of his murdered grandson.

He'd had no choice but to bolt the other direction, running blindly down the drift. When he finally forced himself to stop, he backed into the wall and scrambled for the small flashlight he always kept in his back pocket. He couldn't breathe. An image of the detonator and wires came to mind, tucked safely in its hiding space behind the head frame, and he cursed himself for not keeping it closer. He would bring the whole mine down with himself inside of it rather than let them get a hold of him.

His father's broad, hard hands holding the plank, sliding it back until its far edge rested on the very rim of the shaft, destined to slip down at the slightest pressure.

He rocked his head backward, knocking it against the stone wall behind him. He deserved what they would do to him. He deserved every moment of what he would suffer.

Jealousy, his father said, was an evil trait. It led to the very first murder when Cain slew Able. It was jealousy that had killed John Milford, and jealousy plagued the family still. And Warren knew, as surely as it had caused the demise of Able, it caused him to go to his father twenty years ago, with news of what the Harris boy was up to.

Warren had been watching them for a week, the Harris boy and that curly-headed friend of his. He hid in the tall weeds next to the shaft and watched them as they dragged a plank of wood through the forbidden gate, laughing and trying to talk like pirates. Warren waited until they were inside, then slipped behind the head frame to peek in through the broken vent, lurking from the shadows as they slid the plank over the gaping shaft to form a bridge. He watched the nameless boy nervously hold the board as the Harris kid, the brave fool, stepped gingerly out onto it, taking little jumping steps to test its strength and balance. He watched all the long while it took the Harris kid to coax his accomplice out onto the board. 'Walking the plank,' they called it. Warren waited silently as they rehearsed over and over their dramatic rouse to scare the other children. Their bravado and their companionship chafed at him.

He strode home and told his father what the Harris boy was doing. He regretted that decision the very second he saw the look his news brought to Reuben Milford's eyes.

The child wept, and the sound echoed up the drift. Warren dropped the unlit flashlight, his limbs leaden. He slid slowly down the wall and felt the steel of the flashlight against his leg. He didn't try to pick it up.

The blood guilt was on him.

He followed his father the next morning to the head frame. His father left him in the shadows and moved the plank, then stepped back to Warren's side. They waited as Paul and the other kid arrived, their loud voices echoing around the shaft's interior, agreeing on details of their plan. When the Harris boy left, Warren was sure that the other kid would notice that the plank had been moved. He didn't even look at it. But he wasn't a total fool; he realized he wasn't alone. The rock he threw nearly struck Reuben. Reuben was angry then.

Small, wet sounds, like slithering, echoed toward him. Warren thought of the body in the chamber, of the altar he was trying to make for it. It wouldn't matter now. It was too late to seek atonement. He would not be spared.

Blood guilt. It was on him as he stood silently next to his father, the man's heavy hand resting on his shoulder as a warning not to interfere. He witnessed Paul Harris' fall into the mine and the other boy's howling grief; his knees weakened, and he swooned. His father let go of his shoulder and issued a single, stinging slap on the side of his head to sober him up.

Only one boy fell. Warren was sure that wasn't Reuben's plan. He watched as his father stepped forward. The other boy stopped screaming when he saw Reuben, his ashen face standing out in sharp relief against the dark backdrop of the shaft. The kid was clutching Paul Harris' baseball cap to his chest. Reuben walked calmly toward him. Warren, ear ringing with the force of the slap, wild with the weight of what he had wrought, could not watch this silent boy tossed like a rag doll into the mine after his friend. He followed his father out of the shadows.

Reuben lunged at the boy.

Warren lunged, too, right into the path of his father's hooked fingers.

In a flash the nameless boy came alive. He scaled the gate in two steps and disappeared down the hill.

Warren stepped back into the shadow. His father stood alone at the gate, curling his hands into fists.

***

Lowie stopped crawling. The mine was full of sounds—the dripping of water, sighs of air from the direction of the shaft, unidentified creeks and moans that seemed to drift in from in front of her, then back up from behind. She clung to the rail with her left hand and wiped her face with her dislocated and bleeding right. Her knees were raw from moving across the muddy floor, the cross sections of the rails jutting up.

The pounding had stopped some time ago. Now, in the disorienting darkness, in the bizarre, dreamlike mental state of utter terror, she couldn't be sure she had heard it at all. She tried to think about how long she had been crawling. It seemed like a long time. If someone was in the mine, why hadn't she gotten closer to him by now? If someone was looking for her, why hadn't they called out?

She pulled her knees to her chest and wrapped both arms around herself. She rocked back and forth, back and forth. It made her think of her mother, how she would still allow Lowie to sit in her lap sometimes, rocking her gently in the big, old, stuffed rocking chair in the living room. Maybe her mother thought she was already dead. Maybe it was true. Maybe this darkness, this cold, was what dead meant. She laid her head on her knees, rocking, rocking. One thing was for sure. The noises she had heard weren't real. No one in the world was looking for her.

***

The boy Warren climbed silently down the forgotten timber hole, his father descending above him. He followed meekly through the darkness to the end of the drift and stood by as Reuben swept the beam of his flashlight back and forth across the watery surface of the shaft, two dozen feet below the drift's edge.

The dead child lay against the wall of the shaft, pinned by the plank that had fallen with him. He was partially submerged, kept from sinking by a tangle of cable. Reuben fashioned a harness from rope and tied it to Warren, handed him a small flashlight, and told him to step off the edge of the drift.

Warren stepped.

The weak yellow beam of the flashlight shivered across Paul Harris' soulless face. Warren dangled against the wall above the child, but when he saw the boy's eyes were open he started to gag. He kicked his feet, desperate to swing himself away from the body, and managed to catch his foot on a curl of cable. He dropped awkwardly onto the scrap, struggling to find footing as the frigid water soaked his feet and lower legs. He grabbed onto a cable with one hand and planted a foot on the plank to steady himself, trying not to lose his hold on the flashlight and what precious little illumination it gave him.

His father issued a quiet order from above. Warren withered inside. He clicked off his flashlight and dropped it into the water. He hung on to the harness with his free hand and waited. The harness went slack. He looked up. The strong white light from his father's flashlight shined down on him.

Then it clicked off.

Warren's bladder let go. His urine mingled with the dank waters that reached up through the tangled nest of cable. It was punishment, he knew, for letting the other boy get away. Silent tears streaked down his face. He knew better than to make a sound. If he did, his father was likely to leave him there forever.

Hours passed before the flashlight reappeared. Warren held Paul's stiffening body against his chest as his father hauled them both up, never noticing Warren's shame, wet as he was from the shaft waters. He would rarely fail to notice in the decades that followed.

They moved Paul's body to John Milford's crypt, a blood offering to atone for the miner's own savage murder. Above ground, the search for Paul Harris dragged on day after day. The press arrived. Law enforcement converged. Confusion reigned and hysterical children persisted in their descriptions of more than one screaming voice in the mine. One child, a pale boy with curly blond hair, was nearly catatonic. He had been taken to the mental hospital in Saint Peter.

A sob, a moan of pain. A child's voice. Not more than twenty feet away.

The time had come for him to die.

Warren wrapped his hand around the flashlight and felt the toggle switch. He paused for a moment, clutched the light with both hands, and pointed it in the direction of the noise. He held his breath, aimed the light low, and turned it on.

The beam lit up the face of a wet, shivering child squinting back at him, blood smeared across its forehead. Warren immediately shut the light off, lost his bladder, and discovered that even in his terror he could still stand up and run.

Chapter
Seventy-Five

Will had been walking straight down the drift since he left the room with the hissing lights. His knuckles stung where he had burned them against the hot glass of a lantern when he reached out to it, trying to discern the source of the sound. He felt the heat of the lamp a fraction of a second too late to save himself from some painful blisters, thrown off as he was by the coolness of the mine itself.

He took the lantern with him, the heat of it comforting, and had worked his way from the ladder down the drift by feeling along the wall. He made his way carefully, mindful of the man rises on the right side of the drift that punched through the floor to the levels below. Man rises were escape routes, allowing miners a way out of a drift should a cave-in threaten to crush them. The miner could pull open a small, wooden trap door and drop through the chute to the level below. But time rotted wooden doors and the drift below was completely flooded. Falling through to it would be an ugly death.

Will found several rooms drilled into the sides of the drift, small, squat caves only a few feet deep. But the room with the lamps was different. It was broad, the walls smooth, and the ceiling was so high Will couldn't touch it by reaching up. It was abandoned, though he knew someone had been there moments before. He had heard a cry for help in the distance, then the patter of fleeing footsteps right in front of him, a sound that made every hair on the back of his narrow neck stand straight up. He knew that it should be impossible that he had heard anything, as the mine should be utterly abandoned. But the ladder was there, and the burns on his fingers were real enough. This mine, which should have been long dead, was alive indeed.

Will stopped, listening. Was he hearing voices? Was it imagination? He had trained his mind to listen to the cues from his ears to give him a sense of direction, but sound was different underground. There were echoes, odd, muffled splashes, and dripping. He thought he heard a moan or a gasp, but he couldn't tell where the sounds were coming from or what was making them. He began to feel truly afraid for the first time. His senses didn't work the same down here. It was like walking on an alien moonscape. He could manage without his eyes, but if his ears misled him, what did he have left?

A warm, soft pressure on the side of Will's ankle made him jump. He froze for a moment, thinking, before he bent down and reached out his hand.

"Bones?"

The dog nuzzled his palm and wiggled a happy greeting, then leaned firmly against Will's right leg. Will squatted down, petting him.

"How in the world did you get down here? How did you find me?"

There. A sound. Footsteps, maybe, or some other kind of movement. Will stood back up and realized that what he was hearing was coming from behind. His heart started to slam. Whatever it was, he would face it. Bones pushed against his leg, urging him toward the wall. Wiping his brow with one quivering hand, he turned around. Too late he realized that what he had turned his back on was coming at him at a much faster pace.

***

Butch stopped, frozen at the appearance of Will in the beam of his flashlight. He didn't have time to consider that there was another light behind Will, or the speed at which that light was moving.

What shook him out of his short petrification was the cry of terror from that other light. There was a squeal of pain as Warren Milford spilled into the circle of light, Bones tangled in his legs. The little dog freed himself with a yelp and slipped away, limping down the drift. Warren pulled himself to his

451

knees and would have crashed through all of them on his way past but for a well-aimed kick to the face by Butch that sent him sprawling backwards.

Warren sat up, mouth bloody, gibbering, his eyes rolling in their sockets. He turned and crawled back the way he had come. Butch was quicker, stepping into his path.

A childish sob echoed down the drift. Lane heard it and turned electric.

"Lowie!" she screamed, bolting forward.

Butch leaped after her. "Lane, *stop!*" He was too late—Lane disappeared into the darkness. Butch bounded after her with the flashlight, and in seconds it shone on the sweet, heartbreaking picture of Lane clutching a sobbing, bleeding Lowie to her chest.

Butch staggered forward, weak with relief. She was alive. Impossibly alive. He wrapped his arms around them both, around mother and child, pulling them to himself. He marveled at the solidness of their bodies, the wondrous warmth the three of them together could generate, heat and light. He buried his face in Lane's hair, inhaled her scent, and allowed himself to acknowledge for just a moment that she was the greater part of what he had returned for.

The grunt and rustling of a struggle behind them made Butch turn. Warren was on the ground, abject terror on his bloody face as he stared up at Will framed unblinking in lantern light. Warren slid on his backside down the drift.

"Harris…Harris…"

Will tilted his head. "Who do you think I am, boy?"

Butch moved to block Warren's retreat. "He thinks you're Clinton Harris, come to drag him off to hell. Which would be no less than he deserves."

Warren flipped his body around to all fours and started crawling as fast as he could. Butch kicked at him again, forcing him to stop.

"I didn't kill him!" Warren shouted at Will.

Will turned to follow Warren's voice. "Easy, son. I'm not qualified to take anyone to hell. I just want answers. I take it you are Reuben Milford's boy?"

"He's hardly a boy," Butch said, his blue eyes glittering in the lantern light.

"Warren Milford, then."

Will stepped toward Warren, who drew back slightly and studied Will.

"You're the blind one," he said with a flash of realization.

Will nodded. "I am. Your grandfather had something to do with that."

Warren scowled. "My grandfather was a great man!"

Will tilted his head quizzically. "You never did meet your grandfather, did you, son?"

Lane stepped toward them, pulling a clutching Lowie along as if they were one unit. "Warren, back there in that *room*, or whatever it is. That's my brother, isn't it?"

Warren ducked his head.

"How long? How long have you known he was down here?" she demanded.

Warren refused to look at her. Lane was suddenly angry. "All this time? Did you know he was here all this time, and you didn't say anything?"

"He killed Paul, Lane, that's why he didn't say anything." Butch said coldly.

"What are you talking about?" Lane demanded.

"Lane," Will said quietly. "They were boys. They were playing in the head frame. Paul fell in. That's all."

"That is *not* all," Butch said angrily. "Paul didn't fall by accident. Milford was there, and his father. They killed Paul. They threw him into the shaft."

Lane stared at Butch. "How do you know that?"

Butch opened his mouth to answer, then closed it. A rush of emotions washed across his face.

Warren turned and sat up, wiping the blood from his mouth with the back of his hand. His eyes flicked from Lane to Butch. "She still doesn't know who you are."

"It doesn't matter."

"It's going to matter to her."

"Shut your mouth!" Butch bellowed.

Lane looked at Warren. "How do you know each other?" Warren remained silent. She turned to Butch. "What is he talking about? Did you know my brother? Is that how you know so much about me, about my family?"

Will turned toward Butch. "Son, maybe it's time she knew why you came back here."

Butch opened his mouth to answer, and Lane caught him with a stinging slap. Butch rocked back, shocked. Lowie let go of Lane and threw her arms around Butch, sobbing anew.

"You tell me who you are," Lane demanded, her voice edged with hysteria. "And tell me why my brother's body is lying in that—that *cave* back there—and you tell me the truth this time!"

Butch opened his mouth to speak again, but no words would emerge. He shook his head, mute.

"Who *are* you?" Lane demanded. "If Will's right, if it was an accident, why didn't you tell me? Why didn't you tell somebody?"

Butch found his voice again. "I was with him when he died."

Lane reached out and pulled Lowie loose from Butch's waist and stepped back. Butch stepped toward her, pleading. "We were going to play a trick on the other kids. They dared Paul to go into the head frame. Remember?" Butch scanned Lane's face, looking for some hint of understanding. "I was hiding, and I was supposed to scream and yell, and make the kids think I was the ghost of Clinton Harris…we made a bridge out of a board…Milford moved it so it would fall. It did, it fell when Paul tried to cross it. He—he fell with it."

"Who moved the board?" Will asked.

Butch turned and looked at Warren. Warren rose slowly to his feet as Lane approached him.

"Warren?" She asked. The man stood his full height and still managed to look small with Lane standing before him. "Warren? Look at me. Did you kill my brother?"

Warren was silent. She slapped his chest. "Answer me! Did you kill my brother? Huh?" She slapped him again, harder. "Did you touch my brother? Did you?" Slap, slap. "Did you kill him? Did you hurt him? Didyoukillmybrotherdidyoukill—" Lane closed her fists and rained strike after strike against Warren's chest. Warren didn't resist, until in one frighteningly quick movement he caught Lane by both wrists.

"He had no right to be near the mine," he said, low and dangerous. "It's Milford property."

"Let her go!" Butch roared.

"Son, if you killed Paul—" Will said.

"No! The boy fell!"

"Or if your father did—"

"NO!" Warren bellowed.

Butch stepped closer. "LET HER GO!"

Warren looked down at Lane as if he had forgotten she was there. He released her wrists and pushed her away.

"Get out of here," he said. He suddenly looked weary, exhausted. "Get out of my mine. Get out of this cursed town. Go. Go before this place kills you all."

Butch grabbed Lane's shoulder and jerked her backward, stepping between her and Warren. "You're insane. It's just a mine. It can't *do* anything."

Warren's face hardened. "It found the little girl, didn't it?"

Butch sprung, flying into Warren with all his strength, and together they tumbled into the darkness.

Chapter
Seventy-Six

Butch's rage, long trapped in the caverns of his wounded mind, sought release in each punch as he landed blow after blow. Warren stumbled backward, arms pin wheeling, unable to throw effective counter punches as he struggled to stay on his feet. But even as Butch struck, he felt the lack of release and healing he had longed for when this moment of vindication finally came. Instead, each angry blow stirred a new level of despair. Warren and his father were the cause of Butch's long misery, but now the beating he was giving this man was not able to release Butch from the relentless sorrow that had been a curse and a plague.

So he stopped. He dropped his arms, catching his breath. Warren staggered back against the wall. They stood like that for just a moment, a tiny parenthesis of time when there seemed to be no next move, no clever countermove. Then there was a soft cushion of sound, like a sigh, and Warren disappeared into the black floor below him.

Warren caught himself with his arms, scrambling. It took a moment for it to register in Butch's mind that Warren was falling.

The rotten wooden door of a man rise fell away at an angle under Warren and he dropped through to his chest before he caught himself with his arms. He clutched desperately for a grip on the muddy floor. Butch watched Warren's struggle dispassionately, unable to find it in himself to reach his hand out to stop this man's fall. Instead, Butch he sank to his knees, exhausted.

"Why did you let your father kill him, Milford?" His fight was gone. His anger was gone. But his curiosity was still there, the hunger to know why his life had been caused to unravel but this sinking man who cut the first strings. "He was just a little kid. *You* were a kid."

Warren's eyes were wild with fear as he scrambled for a handhold. He wedged his elbows under him and stopped his fatal slide. "My father said he got what he deserved," he said through gritted teeth.

"How did an eleven-year-old boy deserve to die alone at the bottom of a mine?" Warren's body weight dragged his forearms back toward the edge of the chute. Butch didn't move to help. He watched the death struggle with detached curiosity. Warren's toe found a narrow ledge and he leaned his weight onto it, stopping his slide toward death.

"Butch."

Butch turned to see Will standing in the drift behind him. The old man stepped forward, gently probing the ground with his cane. He stepped past Butch, and his cane found the edge of the man rise. In a flash Will discerned what his eyes could not comprehend.

"Son, you need to come up out of that hole," he said quietly. Warren looked up at Will, his eyes wild and defiant. His foot slipped and his weight slid back onto his forearms, almost spilling him down the chute. Will dropped to his knees, reaching out, feeling for Warren.

"Take my hand," Will urged.

"No," Warren snapped through ragged, terrified gasps.

"Boy, you don't want to die down there. It's over. This mine has had its say. Take my hand!" Will commanded.

"*No!*"

Will responded by reaching farther forward. Warren looked at Will's outstretched hand but he didn't move. He couldn't. His grip on the edge of the chute was so tenuous any movement would mean certain death.

"Let me take yours," Will said. He reached out, gently groping, and found Warren's hand.

In that very moment, that grasping of two hands in the cold darkness of a underground tunnel a hundred feet below the warmth of the sun, Butch bore witness to a change unlike anything he had ever seen before. In a fraction of a second the vicious, bloody monster dangling on the brink of extinction dissolved, and the visage of a small and terrified boy took his place. Warren looked up into Will's face with wide and searching eyes. A sob escaped him as he surrendered what little security he had by clinging to the unyielding ground and grabbed on to Will's arm with both his hands.

The laws of gravity and physics took over, and Warren slipped down the hole, dragging Will flat to the ground and sliding him toward the brink. Butch leaped forward and sprawled over Will, pinning him to the ground to stop his forward motion, but he could feel Warren's weight pulling them both toward the chasm.

"Let him go," Butch whispered.

Will shook his head, his breath ragged. "Help me pull him up." Butch tried to gain his knees to get leverage to pull both men back, but the moment he shifted his weight all three of them lost ground and slid forward. Butch's heart was slamming in his chest. He leaned as close as he could get toward Will's ear.

"You have to let him go. I can't pull you both out."

Will turned toward Butch, his face calm. "Then let us both go."

Butch shook his head. "Will—"

"I won't let another boy die down here alone. We either get him out or I go with him."

Butch could feel the tremble in Will's narrow frame under him, but he knew the man meant what he said. If Butch was to save Will's life, he would have to save Warren's as well.

Butch climbed horizontally across Will's body, moving toward Warren while anchoring Will with his own weight. He reached down the edge of the man rise and grabbed onto

Warren's forearms. He pulled, using all his strength, and only managed to lift Warren an inch or two. Butch cursed.

"I can't pull you up," he told Warren. "You're too heavy. And I can't just let you drop, because the old man won't let me." Even with Warren's face half-hidden in darkness, Butch saw the terror in his eyes and regretted the words. Maybe Will was right. Maybe it was time to live differently.

"Try to catch your feet on something—a ledge, anything. See if you can boost yourself up while I pull."

Warren didn't answer, but Butch could feel the bigger man's weight shifting as he probed the sides of the man rise, looking for a toe hold. A few seconds later he felt Warren's weight shift again as he found a ledge and used Butch's grip on him to leverage himself up. Butch nodded. "Okay. Good. We are going to try to pull you up. Ready, Will?"

Will gave a muffled affirmative, and Butch started pulling. Warren began to rise. Butch felt him lifting, and by the shifts in his weight realized that Warren had found another toe hold and was miraculously rising from the hole. A thought flashed through Butch's mind—*this might actually work*—and a second later Warren's foot slipped, and he plunged downward with a cry of terror, his forearms sliding through Butch's hands. Will lost his grip with one hand and latched on with the other, crying out when the bulk of Warren's weight nearly dislocated his right shoulder from its socket. Butch scrambled forward. He clamped both hands around Warren's wrists. He could hear the gasps of pain from Will as the old man, stifling a scream, tried to grab Warren with this left hand to relieve the pressure on his right. Butch's grip slipped. He felt his chest sliding forward toward the hole. Will would never let go. And now, he realized, neither would he. *So, the mine wins after all,* he thought.

The appearance of another set of arms in the hole to grab Warren was like a revelation. Strong hands clamped around Warren's forearms. Butch looked to his right and saw Mike's pale, narrow face next to his.

"Pull."

The combined strength of the three was what did it. Warren came forth as the men crawled backward, drawing him from the abyss. When they stopped Butch let go his hold on Warren and, slowly, so did Mike. Will still held on.

Warren lay prone on the mine floor, panting. He gathered himself onto his hands and knees. He looked up at the Harris men. Then he bowed his head to the mine floor.

"My father moved the board they were using for a bridge. It was my fault he did it. I told him the kids were up there. But I swear, I did not push your boy down that shaft."

Mike gazed at Warren, his face unreadable. He turned and, without a word, disappeared back into the darkness. Lane turned and quietly followed him, Lowie in tow.

Warren pulled himself to his feet, then lifted Will up. Will said something to Warren and Warren responded, too quiet for Butch to understand. The two of them moved in tandem back down the drift, shoulder to shoulder, Warren awkwardly supporting Will the best way he knew how; still it was unclear who was leading and who was guiding.

Butch sat back on his heels and closed his eyes, his mind trying to stretch itself around the image of Reuben Milford pulling the plank back, balancing it on the very edge of the shaft, setting the trap that would snap closed around Paul and rob him of his life. He bent forward and a sob escaped him—just one, though there was an ocean of them pressing against his chest. Then he slowly rose to his feet and turned toward the stone room where waited both the living and the dead.

Chapter
Seventy-Seven

"Butch."

Mike was gathering the small skeleton, lifting each piece and placing it gently on his shirt spread open on the shrine's floor. Butch stood behind him and watched. He didn't know how they were going to explain what happened to Dave, but asking Mike to leave the child in the mine for even one more day was abhorrent. They would take his body out and end his exile, at long last.

He turned at the sound of his name. Lane stood in the middle of the room, Lowie clinging to her waist. She was looking at something beyond him, and he turned to follow her gaze.

Bones had climbed onto the altar and stretched himself out along the left side of John Milford's skeleton, his nose resting against the skeletal collar bone.

Butch frowned. "Bones," he called. But even before the name left his mouth, he knew it was too late.

Butch felt a pang of deep sadness. He crossed to the altar and lifted a lamp from the floor as he knelt in front of the low ledge. He placed his hand on the Bones' chest, looking for any sign of life. The little body was still. Butch stroked the dog's fur and ran his fingers over the bald spot on his left hip. He sighed and rocked back against his heels. It was an odd picture, the dog nestled against the corpse. The light from the lamp shone brightly on the flat of the skeleton's pelvis, and played across the web of silver wire that held the ruined left hip in place.

Will put a trembling hand on Butch's shoulder and gently moved him aside. The old man bent and felt the altar, his hand exploring until it discerned the edge of bone. Will let out a small moan and sank to his knees, hands exploring the two figures before him, the spare skeleton juxtaposed against the soft grey fur. The old man wept as he reached into his pocket to lift out the watch and chain. He gently traced the length of the arm and laid the watch across John Milford's bony palm.

Chapter Seventy-Eight

As the sun was setting, six weary, dirty forms emerged from a small hole in the earth hidden by a stand of red oak. They climbed out one by one and stood in a loose and awkward group for a few moments. No more than two dozen words were exchanged before a consensus was reached and the group disbanded. Four turned toward the little city of Foley Lake, one bearing a bundled shirt close to his chest. The last two looked at one another uncertainly before the bigger of the two gave the other a few brief words of instruction. Then he turned toward the west and made his way across the grassland alone. The last watched them all go. He waited until they were out of sight before he turned eastward to climb the hill alone.

He stepped into the clearing in front of the head frame and walked in through the gate, leaving it open behind him. Inside he noticed for the first time the wire running from the corner of the shaft back toward the broken vent. He followed the wire and found a small manual detonator hidden behind a pile of debris in the far corner of the head frame. He walked to the edge of the shaft and pulled the charger back, twisted it, and without hesitation plunged the rod down. The earth trembled under his feet and the black shaft channeled a sound from the depths. He felt a rush of stale air move past him, a tidal breath. In moments all grew still. The man turned away from the abyss, throwing the detonator into its maw as he left.

CHAPTER
SEVENTY-NINE

Summer drifted easily into the richness of fall. The vegetation that had been coaxed into new vitality by the return of the rains now ripened into a riot of color, and for weeks the people of Foley Lake walked about as in a dream, mouths partly opened and eyes constantly roving the bursting hillsides all around them. For the first time in long memory, herds of deer were spotted on the hills on the outskirts of the little city. Canada geese and migrating ducks graced its namesake lake, gliding each morning across the water's murky surface.

For reasons of its own, the Chinese company that owned the mine made no move toward its preparations for the open pit. Rumor had it that the company was going to try out a new technique, one that used high pressure water to bust up the ore underground and pump it to the surface as a slurry. That way the company would not require a pit at all, only a narrow well and a long, long pipe. The delay was fine with the people of Foley Lake. They had seen enough drama to last a generation and yearned for the return of their dull, small-town patterns.

The state sponsored a full-fledged investigation into the happenings at the mine, and everyone involved spent a good deal of time talking with the Bureau of Criminal Apprehension. But the suspect was long dead, and the crime scene had suddenly filled with water nearly to the surface of both shafts, while the water level at the pit had experienced a significant drop. The Bureau decided that any charges against Butch for trespassing were hardly worth their time. They left the prosecution to the local authorities. Dave and the county prosecutor from Brainerd met at the diner to discuss the case, and, over a generous helping of May's chokecherry pie, Dave convinced the assistant D.A. that the whole affair wasn't worthy of her office's attention. Warren Milford didn't harm the Harris boy. He was a child himself when Paul Harris died, and the victim of significant abuse at the hands of an insane father. Butch, too, had been a victim, the shock of Paul's death and his own narrow escape causing years of institutionalization. The assistant DA left with a Styrofoam to-go box full of pie balanced in one hand, satisfied that there wasn't anything of a legal nature to pursue in the odd little town.

Warren chose seclusion after all the facts about his father's responsibility in Paul Harris' death became known. But several weeks after the events at the mine, a taxi from Crosby pulled up in Warren's driveway and an old man with a long cane tapped his way up the walk to the front door. Will was admitted to the house, where he stayed for several hours, before making his way back out to the waiting cab. A few days later Warren was sighted in town, where he picked up a few groceries and took a long walk along the swampy banks of Foley Lake.

Mike grieved. He withdrew from public view, abruptly announcing his retirement as mayor. He met privately with Dave, and without ever admitting to anything, worked out the payment for damages for some transformers and an electrical substation that needed repair. He walked, but now his pace was slower, free of the frantic work of clinging to misplaced hope that had driven him all summer. He coasted through the cooler fall days, covering slow miles of hills and roadways.

They had a private funeral, a real one this time, with a fresh new casket and a new headstone. Mike, Lowie, and Lane were the only attendees. Mike invited Butch but he declined, saying he thought it was a private family matter. The Harris' accepted his excuse without comment, but during the graveside service Lane was sure she saw a flash of movement in the trees just beyond the cemetery boundary.

The city itself was surprisingly empathetic. No sooner had word gotten out about some of the events at the mine than casseroles and fresh-baked rolls, brownies and large pans of lasagna began to appear on the step outside the Harris household as if by magic. No one knocked or rang the bell.

The city held its collective curiosity in check; in fact, when reporters from Bemidji and St. Paul approached Eugenia for information for a story, she forgot all about professional courtesy and ran them off single-handedly. The family was left to mourn in peace, defended by their townsfolk, the casseroles and bars piling up on the counter bearing witness that their grief was not borne alone.

Lowie stayed as close as she could to Lane for weeks. She followed her about all her waking hours and asked to sleep with her at night. Lane welcomed the little girl's presence. She found herself reaching out to touch Lowie at random times, when a memory of the deep darkness of the mine emerged, or when Lowie turned her head just the way Paul used to. She didn't know whether letting the child cling to her so was healthy, and she didn't care. But when school started Lowie refused to go, saying that she wasn't ready for school, that her stomach hurt, and she didn't want to see the other kids. Lane encouraged, then cajoled, then insisted that Lowie go. Each debate would end with Lowie burying her face in her mother's waist, sobbing. School had been in session for almost two weeks before Lane rethought the situation and changed her tactics. Rather than sending the child to school, she took her. She sat on the stool at the back of Lowie's class, ignoring the glances and whispers of the other children, and she remained until lunch time. She would have lunch with Lowie, then tell her she was going to go to work but promising to be there when Lowie got out of school. At first Lowie clung as Lane tried to leave, but slowly the partings came more easily. By the time the plump, ripe orange of a harvest moon began to fill the night skies, Lowie was ready to brave school alone. Lane was glad, despite a pang of sadness at the new separation she herself didn't really want. The morning she woke to a crisp layer of frost on the ground she smiled to herself at the wonder of it. Time marched forward. They were going to be okay.

Butch left days after Paul's funeral, saying it was high time he headed south if he hoped to be in warmer climes before snowfall. Mike solemnly shook Butch's hand, then hugged him; Lowie threw herself into his arms and wept. Lane stood back, not trusting herself to physical contact, and said her goodbyes from a distance. When he walked out the door she turned away to some menial task in the kitchen, exerting sheer will to hold in check the great lump that filled her throat. She was unable to restrain her tears three weeks later when a trip to retrieve the mail yielded a thick letter addressed to her in Butch's heavy script. She carried the letter up the driveway and through the house, into the backyard, and sat on the back step facing the bare rose bushes. She examined the envelope, and slowly turned it over to open it. She pulled the thick mat of sheets free and unfolded them.

Dear Lane,

The swings up at the school's playground seem small to me now. I guess that's what happens, because we grow but those things from our memories don't. Maybe that's why as adults the world seems less. But in my memory those swings are big, and

I'm the one who is small, almost invisible. It makes me wonder if you remember me at all.

I moved to Foley Lake the summer you were eight and I turned ten. My father owned the butcher shop that used to be right across from the dime store. That whole first summer I stood in the window of the shop and watched you and your friends roll past on your bikes, racing down the pavement. Other times I would sit on the curb, and you would all come walking in a big, noisy group, headed to the diner for free ice cream from the old man who owned it then. I was a shy kid. I never even tried to talk to you. But I knew who you were. My father wanted me to go out and introduce myself to you kids, but I wouldn't go. I never went far from the butcher shop that first summer.

After school started, it seemed like I had a hard time fitting in. It just took a long time for the other kids to notice I was around, and I was too shy to make the first move. Until one day during recess. I was sitting on a swing and I saw you coming across the playground. You were small, even for eight, and had this determined little march that made your ponytail swing back and forth. You went up to the middle support bar for the swing set, that big, upside-down V, and stood there looking up. Then you wrapped your arms and legs around one pole and started to climb.

You shimmied up, your hands and feet around the pole, using your feet to boost yourself up then locking them against the pole to slide your hands up, but about four feet up you got stuck. Paul was there, and he left the monkey bars and walked over where you were dangling. I figured he would make you get down, but instead he braced his hands under your foot and pushed up. He didn't say a word, just gave you a boost, then went back and took a seat in the middle of the teeter-totter to watch. A lot of brothers would have told their sisters to get down. Paul didn't say anything. Maybe he figured you wouldn't have listened anyway, but I think he just knew you could handle yourself. He was never scared. In the short time him I knew him, he never seemed to consider that anything bad might happen.

You got to the top, to the long horizontal bar, and leaned forward to swing your legs up behind you. You got your feet under you, found your balance, and then you just stood up.

You must have been at least ten feet off the ground. From below, it was like you were floating between heaven and earth, the sun shining on your hair and making it glow, not a trace of fear on your little face. Just looking up at you made me afraid. You looked so serious, so determined, as you held your arms out and started walking.

The sides of your feet were barely visible from underneath the bar. I tried to keep the swing perfectly still and lean into the chain, but I couldn't feel the rhythm of your step when you passed over me. It was like you weren't really there even though I was watching you with my own eyes. I stopped worrying something bad would happen when you passed over me, because then I understood what Paul already knew— you would never fall.

You were so much higher than me.

On the other end of the swing set you crouched down and grabbed the bar, swung one leg over and hung by your hands. It was a long drop, but you let go and slipped back to earth. Then you just walked away.

In my mind I don't think you ever came down off that bar. For the next year I spent hours following Paul around Foley Lake, tagging behind him until he accepted my presence and made me his friend. I loved your brother, and his friendship was one of the most important things in the world to me. But it wasn't just his company I was after. It was you I adored.

The best days I ever had in Foley Lake were the days that Paul let you play with us, running down the path by the lake, climbing trees, catching snakes. I hated snakes. You liked them. I endured holding hundreds of them, just so that my skin might brush yours when I handed them over to you.

For years after Paul died, I couldn't remember exactly what happened in that head frame. My folks told me how news of the children's screams and Paul's disappearance jolted them into a search for me, and that they were scared I was with Paul at the mine and had died with him. Someone found me sitting on the bank of the lake, soaking wet, and unable to speak. I still don't know how I got there. It was years before I remembered anything about that day. No one had seen me with Paul, or suspected I knew more than the others, and at that time I didn't. I was just one more terrified kid who never spoke about what happened that day at the mine.

The mind is a funny thing, the way it seems to alternately protect, and then to destroy itself. I started sleepwalking, and having night terrors, although I rarely recalled what I was dreaming when I woke. My father remembered everything I said and did during those episodes when my conscious mind was asleep, and my subconscious took over. At some point he realized that I not only saw Paul die, but he came to believe I was the one who killed him. He questioned me over and over about where I was that day, how I ended up in the water, how it was possible I wasn't with Paul when every other day of that summer I was pinned to his side. I could never answer. He sold the shop and got us out of Foley Lake because he was afraid. He wanted to get me away where there wasn't any risk of someone hearing my night terrors and putting them together with Paul falling down into that shaft.

His suspicions about my part in Paul's death became mine. I was convinced he was right. I had killed Paul. I didn't know how, or why, but I was sure I was the cause of your brother's death.

My father died last spring. I was only there to visit him a few times before the end. He was Will's roommate for years, you know. That's how I know Will. I never made the connection between him and you, despite the last name. Will was always nice to me and encouraged me to come back more often. My father didn't. Even after twenty years, he wanted me to make a point of not coming any closer to Foley Lake than I had to. After Dad died, the home sent some of his belongings to my mother, and she left them for me to open. Most of it was just useless junk that didn't mean anything to anyone in the world but him. But there was one thing. There was a little boy's baseball cap.

The second I lifted that cap out of the box it triggered a memory. Sitting on the bank shivering wet, clutching that hat in my hands. Then there were others, memories of seeing Paul fall. For the first time in my adult life, I knew for certain I didn't kill him. I couldn't remember why we were in the head frame, or what Warren Milford had to do with it. I still only had pieces of memory, but it was more than I had ever remembered before, and I was crazy with relief that I didn't have your brother's blood on my hands. But that opened up a whole new set of questions. I came back in hopes that seeing the mine again would shake memories free the way the cap had.

I never thought about what it might do to your father, or you, if I came back and started to stir up your memories about that painful time, and I am sorry if knowing the truth about what happened is worse for you. But now, at least, there is no more guessing about Paul's fate or how he came to it. We all know the truth. Somehow, we all need to find our peace with the things we can't change.

That brings me to the reason for this letter. The years since I left Foley Lake have been a nightmare. I had my own reasons for going back there, my own questions that needed answers. But when I saw you that first time at the pit this summer, I realized that I was still doing the same thing I did as a kid. Even in death, I pursued Paul to get close to you.

I wanted you to know my story. Not just what happened to your brother that day in the mine, but how much of what I have done, then and now, is driven by how I feel about you. I have nothing to offer a woman or a child, no home, no real security. The only thing of value I had was that mirror I gave you, and you can see for yourself how little that is worth. But after all the *secrets, after all the questions and uncertainty I have lived with for twenty years, I want to make this one thing very clear to you, Lane. I've loved you for most of my life.*

I'll be at the address on this envelope for the next two weeks. After that, I head south, and I doubt I'll ever be back this way again. If you want to write me back, this is where you can reach me. But if you don't write me back, if it is all too much to handle, I will understand.

No matter what you decide, no matter where you go, what choices you make, my love won't change. To me you will always be perfect, floating high above me, with the sunlight shining on your hair.

Butch.

Lane carefully folded the letter and slipped it back into the envelope. Wiping tears from her cheeks she stood, her body stiff from the cold. She lifted her face to the silver sky and closed her eyes.

He was always there, that boy. She remembered him, but faintly. He clung like a ghost at the fringe of a hundred memories. The only thing easy to remember was his curly blond hair, and the way he looked at her sometimes. It seemed impossible that the insubstantial boy would have grown to be the man she would find impossible to forget.

Something soft brushed across her forehead. A snowflake. She opened her eyes to find them floating down all around her. She held out her hand and waited. A thick flake landed on her palm, lingered a moment, and melted. She slowly folded her fingers over the drop of moisture it left behind.

In the house, Lane pulled several sheets of lined school paper from Lowie's notebook and found a pen. She poured herself a cup of coffee and sat at the kitchen table. As the flakes grew thicker outside her window and began to swirl on the growing breeze, she leaned forward and began to write.

EPILOGUE

The truth about the February 5th, 1924 flooding of the Milford Mine is clear—it was an engineering mistake. The mine, located near the village of Crosby in central Minnesota, was simply too close to Foley Lake.

The Milford produced some of the best maganiferous iron ore in the world because its high magnesium content caused it to burn hotter and resulted in cleaner, stronger iron. It was highly prized, much in demand and by 1923, the Milford was the only mine in Minnesota producing it.

Perhaps someone got greedy; perhaps, someone was reckless. What we know for certain is that engineers at the Milford Mine said the mine was safe, and they were wrong.

Of the 48 miners in the Milford on February 5, 1924, seven survived. Those lucky few happened to be close enough to the Milford's main shaft to reach it and climb out on the emergency ladder, the same ladder that skip tender Clinton Harris lashed himself to as he pulled the emergency whistle that warned the miners something was wrong.

It's true that Clinton Harris could have gotten out. He had a clear path to salvation. Instead, he made a decision to remain at his post and to sound the alarm, tying the alarm whistle's rope to his waist so that when he died the alarm would continue to sound out its grim warning. He really did die a hero. He wasn't supposed to be at work the day of the flooding; another miner called in sick, and he responded when he was asked to cover that man's shift.

Nearly forty women we widowed when the Milford flooded. Over eighty children were left fatherless. I borrowed heavily from the real story of the flooding as a background to this fictional work, but I did so with the deepest possible respect for the men to died there and for their families. Most especially, I wish to honor Clinton Harris, a man whose decisive choice in that moment reminds us that true heroism isn't committed in front of cameras or the adulation of cheering crowds. Real heroes act alone, unwitnessed, and without concern whether the depth of their sacrifice will ever be known or remembered.

It is remembered. It is remembered here, in this small work of fiction; it is remembered at the Milford Mine Memorial Park in Crosby, Minnesota, were the scars from the shafts are still clearly visible. And now it will be remembered by you, dear reader. May you carry the story forward and find solace in it when you face your own moments alone, in the dark, deciding.

Here are the names of the men who died with Harris on that fateful winter's day in 1924. May their memories be blessed.

Earl Bedard
Oliver Burns
Emil Carlson
Evan Crellin
Minor Graves
Fred Harte
John Hlacher
Herman Holm
Frank Hrvatin
Alex Jyhla
Leo J LaBrash
Peter Magdich
John Maurich
Arthur Myhers
Nick Radich
Gasper H Revord
Jerome Ryan
Joseph Snyder
Mike Tomac
Arthur Wolford
Frank Zeitz
Mike Bizal
George Buthkovich
Valentine Cole

Roy Cunningham
Clinton A Harris
John Hendrickson
George Hachevar
Elmer Haug
William Jenson
Victor Ketola
Arvid Lehti
Henry Maki
Ronald McDonald
John Minerich
Clyde Revord
Nels Ritari
Tony Slack
Marko Toljan
Martin Valencich
John Yaklich